SKATER BOY

MARY CATHERINE GEBHARD

UNGLUED BOOKS

Line editing by Nancy Smay
Content Editing by Edits in Blue
Proof Reading by My Brother's Editor and C. Marie
Cover by Hang Le

Skater Boy (Patchwork House #1)
ISBN-13: 978-1-7338510-0-8
An Unglued Books Publication
www.MaryGebhard.com

For Rachel and Collin, because your nickname inspired this book. Both this Tweetie, and the one on the page, thank you!

PROLOGUE

THE FIRST THING YOU LEARN IS HOW TO FALL. You learn to brace for impact, so you don't break a wrist or arm or collarbone, because you'll be falling a lot—at least that's what he told me, the boy who taught me when no one else would.

Then he ruffled my hair and pushed me off my skateboard to prove his point.

It was the very first thing he taught me; it was also the last thing I remembered when we met again, because I didn't just fall for him,

I slammed.

ONE

SLAM: A HARD FALL.

TWEETIE
1989, present
Tweetie is 19

"Well, this is Patchwork House. Good luck. Don't say I didn't warn you."

"Right," I said, readjusting my duffle in one hand and my skateboard in the other. I reached for what little cash I had left to pay my cabbie, and while he got change, I took in my destination.

Patchwork House was the most notorious house in our small nowhere town of Heaven Falls. An old, three-story Victorian nestled on the corner of a forgotten street, home to all runaways, rebels, and anyone else who couldn't fit our town's very rigid definition of normal.

You knew it was Patchwork by the eponymous patchwork graffiti covering every inch of its exterior.

"Here's my card." He reached through the half-open car window. "Call me when you've had your fun. If you're hoping for a place to stay..." He eyed my bag. "Well, they'll chew up and spit out an innocent thing like you. It's a boys' club up there—*mean* boys."

Then he peeled out so fast his tires screeched.

It was just me and Patchwork, a house that infamously only opened its doors to the boys of our town—the *mean* boys.

But once upon a time, they'd allowed *one* girl to stay.

This is your life now, Tweetie.

I knew I should go up the brightly painted steps, through the door painted with even more colorful words— no one ever knocked—but for the umpteenth time, I wondered if I'd made the right choice coming back. Nervous energy buzzed through me, an ungrounded wire in my blood. I felt like a thief just about to be discovered.

In front of the house I'd lived in, been raised in.

So I walked around back, postponing the inevitable. The air was crisp and brittle like the leaves falling to the ground. When I reached the yard, I stopped short, my breath leaving me. A ramshackle wooden skateboarding ramp shone in the autumn sun, climbing above the trees.

That was new.

I dropped my duffle and grabbed my board. What a perfect distraction.

There was only one skate park left in our state, and it was two hours away. People didn't want us around, didn't want drugs and crime in their neighborhoods, and they said we brought them. That was bullshit. Either way, taking away the parks didn't stop skating.

I took a deep breath and climbed up the ramp, trying to clear my head, not think about the life I'd just willingly walked back into. Patchwork House and I had a history as beautiful and sordid as the boys who'd founded it, but as a boy who'd once changed my life told me, there was only now.

My board.

The lip of the bowl.

And the mahogany valley below.

I dove.

Speed blew my hair back, wheels grinding against the wood. This was my peace. No matter the storm, skating always calmed the rain. I always knew I was going to be a skater. It's in my blood. Just because I want it, though, doesn't mean the world will let me have it.

That was a lesson learned when I was just nine.

Back then, equipped with a too-big board and no training whatsoever, I went to my first park. I remember Dad telling me they were going to try and push me out, but to tell them I had every right to be there. Just because I was little and a girl didn't mean they could push me around.

Dad was good like that.

I kept falling over.

But I wouldn't give up, even when the older boys laughed at me.

So when one boy approached me, maybe fourteen or fifteen, hat pushing down a dark, wavy shag and shadowing darker eyes, I braced myself. Before he could even get a word out, I scrunched up my face, trying to imitate Dad when he was talking with the phone company.

"You can't make me leave," I said, folding my arms. "I have every right to be here."

He grinned and flicked a joint over my shoulder. "Yeah, you do."

He spent the rest of the day teaching me how to ride. His friends called him names they probably shouldn't have said around me, words I didn't learn the meaning of until I was much older. They whooshed past us, getting so close to him the tail of his shirt lifted up and exposed his hard, muscled skin. But he ignored them.

Then he snatched my chin and said, "Block everything else out."

So I did.

"Block it all out," I whispered to myself now, attempting a trick I'd never tried before. A reckless move that made my veins pulse. A move that felt a little like the reason I'd gotten into skating.

In the end, I became indebted to that boy in more ways than one.

I sailed down the bowl and up into the air, spinning around before coming back down.

I knew the moment I landed I was going to slam. You can tell immediately if it's going to be a good land or bad. My foot gave out, the board flying up as I flew with it. I braced myself for the inevitable crash landing with the hard wood, but it never came. Instead I landed on something hard yet malleable—*someone.*

"*Oof.*"

I blinked open my eyes, into the gaze of another.

They were dark yet warm, like fresh chocolate caramel, and there was something eerily familiar about them. My gut rang with a song I knew but couldn't remember.

I tilted my head. "Have we met?"

"I think I would remember you," he said dryly, just as my board finished its descent onto my back. My chin connected with his chest as reality came back.

I quickly scrambled off.

Pain zinged through my neck, bright and burning, but embarrassment superseded everything.

Flip. *The* Flip—that's why he was so familiar. He'd been the most famous skater in the world. I fought the urge to turn into a puddle in my sneakers.

"Uh..." I rubbed my skull. "Sorry." I tilted my head, really seeing him. He gave me an appraising look back, like someone buying a car.

But that was fine.

He was twenty-four and uber-famous. I was nineteen and people often mistook me for a boy. He had that skater boy look I went absolutely insane for, though. Thin, with muscles etching every inch of him. Tattoos climbed up one arm and disappeared into places I couldn't see. Dark, devil-may-care eyes shadowed under wavy hair and a cap. A constant, cocksure grin hooked one side of his cheek, as if a cop could put him in handcuffs and he'd say *thanks* with a wink.

I probably should have been immune to boys like him growing up in Patchwork, but everyone tried so hard to keep me out of the life, and it had the reverse effect. I was drawn to it. Drawn to any sign of a fuck authority attitude.

And Flip had it in spades.

I had no problem admitting he'd starred in many of my fantasies. Something flickered beneath his espresso brows and he dragged his index finger along his lower lip in an unnervingly slow pace. It felt like he was going to stay quiet forever, watching me.

But then he said, "Bad slam."

I shrugged, rubbing my arms, trying to ward off that odd look I'd sworn I'd seen.

Like he knew me.

"Yeah—" I started, when I was cut off by a new but very familiar voice.

"What the fuck are you doing here—*Tweetie?*" I couldn't turn to see him, though memories had perfectly preserved him in my mind. His voice changed when he said my name, going from anger to shock. I froze, forgetting everything.

Forgetting the famous boy whose poster had hung over my bed was only inches away from me.

Forgetting the words I rehearsed for this very moment.

"Tweetie, is that you?"

I turned, bracing myself.

King.

With his tatted body and just-slept-in hair. My best friend, my almost-brother, my Corrupt father figure. The only thing missing was the cigarette at his lip.

"I live here." It came out as a whisper.

King's lips parted. No words came out.

"What's with the ramp?" I asked, needing to say something to break the tension.

"You always needed a place to train." He stared at me like I was a ghost.

I chewed my lip, trying to keep the emotions from bleeding onto my face. I hadn't been here for two years, but they were still thinking of me. People like the cabbie thought Patchwork was some den of iniquity, home of the Corrupt of Heaven Falls, and if I stayed they would swallow me whole like mythical demons.

They didn't know the real Patchwork, didn't know my Rebel Gods—didn't care to.

I tugged my soft shirt. "Where'd you get the wood?"

"Donated," King said like I'd asked him the weather.

"Donated?" The skepticism in my tone was palpable.

Then Flip spoke, and I was reminded we weren't alone in a rush of noise, emotion, feeling, hitting me like a freight.

"Sure. They *donated* it. Maybe they just don't know they *donated* it yet." And just like that King's face closed off, the hurt and anguish gone.

An arm landed on my shoulder—King's—like it had thousands of times before. Years had passed, but it still fit like a glove. He shoved me behind his back. I was so startled I didn't think to react.

"Who's the am?" Flip asked. *Am,* AKA *amateur* AKA *me.* He and King shared some inscrutable look and I couldn't help but think they were having another conversation beneath the surface.

My eyes darted between them, trying to play catch-up.

Now that my nerves had settled slightly, a more pressing question bubbled to the surface: why was *Flip* at Patchwork? I'd only been gone a few years; what could have happened in that time to put the most famous skateboarder in the world in its backyard?

"Somebody talk," I said.

"Go inside," King said. At first, I thought he was talking to Flip, but then he gripped my bicep, body still facing Flip, glare still hard, and gently pushed me toward the back door.

Years passed, yet nothing had changed.

I yanked him off. "What's going on? Do you know each other?" Flip tilted his head, catching me over King's shoulder and giving me another look, this one coated in an arrogance I couldn't understand. It was almost like he *knew* things about me, things I didn't give him permission to know.

It scared me. Instinctively I grabbed King's hand like I always had.

Flip's eyes shot to the movement and whatever I'd seen

vanished. He laughed close-mouthed, as if in on some joke. I squeezed King's hand.

Flip's gaze slowly drifted from our interlocked hands to my eyes. "I was just thinking of moving back in."

Back in? "You used to live here?" I blurted.

Something passed.

Something unsaid but known.

The Rebel Gods had an unspoken language, one I'd never been able to crack, even after years, but here King was speaking it with Flip. Warning bells rang loud and vibrating.

"I think we're all full up now," King said. "Sure you're not here to pick up the last of your shit?"

The last of his shit?

I tried to remember any time King had mentioned knowing Flip.

Nothing. Nada. Blank. All the years we'd spent together, that I'd *lived* with King, and he'd forgot to mention knowing the most famous skateboarder in history.

"Pretty sure." Flip's stare hadn't relented. "Anyway, Patchwork can always fit another wayward soul, right?"

A stiff tension passed, slow and crackling, like someone accidentally stepping on uneasy ice.

King stepped to Flip, and Flip met him halfway, their noses separated by the thinnest strip of air.

"You sure you know what you're doing?" King's voice was granite.

Flip's gaze flicked to me. Maybe I should have looked away, but it wasn't my style. I met him, eye for eye.

His stare ignited. The little oxygen I had left disappeared in a rush down my lungs.

Without moving from King, without taking his eyes off me, Flip said, "I'll grab my bags."

FLIP

Present
Flip is 24

Tweetie held her board across her lap. With wild, bright yellow curls and even brighter blue eyes, it was almost like the very first day we met—but the little girl from the park wasn't so *little* anymore.

I leaned on a tree edging the sidewalk and street, the lawn the only barrier from the graffitied walls I swore I wouldn't return to. With a shuddery breath, I tangled my hands through my hair. I didn't have shit to grab, I just needed to get out of there.

She'd still gone right for King's hand, so shit hadn't changed much over the years.

But then, I wasn't surprised she didn't recognize me.

I wrote the story of our lives so I was always her shadow.

"Are you really coming back?"

I broke from Tweetie, finding a familiar denim jacket with gray hoodie, hood up. It hid his faded sides, only the dreads he kept well maintained above them falling across his forehead to eclipse striking hazel eyes.

He was someone you might overlook at first, unlike the rest of us with our tattoos and obvious bad attitudes, but anyone who was anyone knew not to look past him. Daniel was the Demon of Heaven Falls for a reason.

Daniel offered me a cigarette and I shook my hand, declining the offer. My stare locked back on Tweetie.

"Has she eaten yet?" I asked.

Daniel paused, flame flickering in his palms. "What?"

I rummaged around in my jean pocket for cash. "She needs some fucking dinner."

"King's on it," Daniel said just as King dropped a bag of burgers in her lap.

I stopped digging. She hated burgers.

"So you're back?"

"Yeah."

Another pause.

"Seriously, why are you here?" Daniel asked, blowing smoke into the night air. He followed my line of sight and exhaled.

"We agreed to leave her alone—*all* of us." Tweetie was dimly lit by the multicolored lanterns hanging loosely above the porch. She laughed at something some random kid said.

Her eyes landed on mine and her smile vanished like Daniel's smoke in the air, brows drooping with insecurity and uncertainty.

She didn't shy away though, matching my stare. Then again, she never had.

Look at that crazy blonde hair and those intense blue eyes. She's like fucking Tweetie bird.

I shook my head with a bitter smile. "I said if she left Patchwork I would leave her alone." I kicked off the tree, heading up the cobblestone path for the embellished, asymmetrical porch.

Daniel quickly dropped the cigarette and stamped it out, grabbing my elbow. "We stopped being good for her a long time ago."

I paused, and he let go of me reluctantly. Tweetie kept coming back to me, eyes flitting from her board to mine, hiding her stare beneath spirals of hair. Years ago those bright yellow curls rewrote the map of my life.

Of all our lives.

I'd been on track to be the biggest skater in the world, then a cute little girl asked me to teach her. Still, we'd tried to do good for her—as good as you can do when bad is coded into your DNA.

Tweetie looked back again to see if I was still watching, and this time the insecurity melted from her features. She tilted her head, eyes filling with curiosity.

A single raindrop fell as a grin broke my cheeks.

"I think I'm done being good for Tweetie."

TWO

FLIP: TO FLIP YOUR BOARD, AS IN A KICKFLIP.

TWEETIE

My board chipped.

Great.

Flip was outside and his eyes barely strayed from me, even as Daniel joined him. I tried to tell myself I was making it up, but every time I looked down the cobblestone path, our eyes locked.

I quickly looked away. My lap, the sky—anywhere else. Night was falling fast and bubbly gray clouds covered the stars. Another rainy autumn.

A white, crinkly, and nameless bag dropped into my lap.

"Dinner," was all King said before throwing some napkins and disappearing back into the house. My heart splintered.

That was King.

Always looking out for me.

Please don't be burgers.

Please don't be burgers.

I pulled out a plastic-wrapped burger, trying not to deflate. Setting the burger down, I reached for the fries.

"So you're Tweetie. *The* Tweetie," a kid to my left said. He stuffed orange chips into an already orange-dusted mouth and couldn't have been older than thirteen.

A scoff drifted loud and purposeful behind him. A girl leaned against the bay window, cigarette flame bright in the shadows. She rolled her eyes when I met them.

I pretended I didn't hear and laughed. "I don't know about *the*..." I trailed off as Flip kicked off the tree and headed in our direction. A few straggling raindrops fell, so few I could count them like beads of silver.

"I'm Sparky," the kid said just as Flip reached the steps. One, two. With each step closer, my heart beat louder. *Act normal. Keep talking to Sparky. You don't even know him.*

I glanced at Sparky. "I'm sure there's a reason for that." He gave me a toothy grin as I heard a crunch to my left.

Flip stepped on my burger.

I stared at the mushy mess then broke out of my shock.

"Hey asshole," I said to his back. "That was dinner."

"Oops." He shrugged, pushing the screen door open with his back. "Accident." He laughed, the sound disappearing into melody with the party music.

The girl stared at me, eyes wide, like I'd just spat in the face of the devil.

"What?" I said through a mouthful of fries.

She shook her head and went inside.

Later the party was in full swing, exactly how I remembered it: strip poker in one corner, battles over NES remotes in the other. A Patchwork party was a fingerprint, never the same for two people. If you liked games, you played games. If you needed to let loose, you broke some windows. They only had four rules here, and as long as you followed them, you were golden.

There *was* a darker side to this world, but it wasn't like what the town thought.

We weren't villains; we were outsiders.

I hung back by a row of soft curtains and tried not to stare at Flip, which meant a lot of looking at my beer or the walls. Along them imposing, shirtless figures were painted like murals of Greek gods, but with neon colors they shone even in the dark like someone broke open a glow stick.

They were the Rebel Gods of Heaven Falls, and their religion was sin, debauchery, and corruption...and they were worshipped as they should be.

I'd always loved the wild spray paint covering our house, bright and chaotic and without rules, like our life.

My smile wavered, catching another stare from Flip. I was certain it was just odd timing, but every time I looked up, he was looking back. He mouthed something. My breath caught, trying to make out the words.

"Hey, cutie."

I jumped, eyes still locked with Flip's. A guy with way too much gel in his hair leaned on the wall beside me. It actually took physical effort not to look at Flip, focusing on the guy as if he were a *Where's Waldo* book. My mind kept spinning.

Flip's watching.

Why is he watching?

Check to see if he's still looking.

"Hey," I said, shrugging my shoulders. I don't know about *cutie,* but it was nice to be called one, even if the guy was probably just drunk and looking to score. He opened his mouth but paused on the word, eyes traveling over my shoulder. I craned my neck, following.

Daniel.

Daniel used his words like he used his fists—sparingly. He said everything he needed to with his golden eyes.

"Uh." The guy's eyes darted from me to Daniel. "I gotta jet." I exhaled as he disappeared into the party. That was what it was like growing up at Patchwork, and apparently it wouldn't change now that I was back. There was a five-foot bubble around me at all times.

When the guy was truly gone, Daniel unfolded his arms, eyes softening on me. Daniel was just like the rest of the boys at Patchwork: legendary—a god. He was a street fighter, and I was told men thrice his size had been taken it out in less than five minutes.

Everyone knew Daniel was impossible to defeat.

I'd only ever seen that side of him once. Briefly. To most, he was soft and quiet. Kindness radiated from his gentle voice.

I smiled, genuinely happy to see him. "Hi."

"You're back," he said.

"Uh, yeah, I am." Another silent, questioning stare. *Why am I back?* "Where's Romeo?" I asked, needing to fill the silence with something other than my answer. I'd barely been back a few hours and figured it was just Romeo being Romeo, using clocks as a suggestion.That said, Romeo rarely missed a party.

"He left a few months after you did, little girl."

"Left? Like, *left* left?" In response, Daniel reached to a towering cassette tower, pulled one out. *The Imperialists.* A skull and crossbones made up of a cassette decorated the back and a message in white read: *Pirating is destroying record industry profits. We left this side blank so you can help.*

"You haven't heard him on the radio? They're everywhere."

"I've been...preoccupied."

Concern twisted his youthful, hot chocolate features. "What've you been up to?"

"Looking for answers."

He arched a brow. "Did you find them?" At that moment, a stack of old pizza boxes Sparky and some other kids had been using to play makeshift Jenga crashed into the TV, knocking out the NES plug, and chaos ensued. I could tell he wanted to keep talking, dig into why I'd come home, but thankfully he had to go play grown-up.

I went to refill my beer at the keg, but froze. Flip was on the other side and an insane part of my brain said he was waiting for me.

"Need a refill?" He tilted his head, lips parting to show just enough of his pearly teeth.

"Um..." *Yes. No.* I stepped backward, putting space between us, his head tilting more with each step. I spun around and ran up the stairs. At the top, I pressed my hands to the wall, peering around the corner to see if he was still there.

Yep.

He shook his head, confused, but when he took a sip of beer, his crooked grin disappeared into the red cup.

I'd dreamed of meeting Flip for years and what do I do? Run away. I had no idea what I was doing with boys. None. Especially not ones who were basically The Beatles of skateboarding. I'd had to give myself a pep talk for nearly a month just to come back to family.

I did not prepare for *Flip*.

After so many years of writing about him, dreaming about him, he was here. A legend in the flesh.

He looked up the stairs and I jumped back, flat to the wall. I couldn't go back down there, not with his slow smiles and long stares and cute, shruggy shoulders.

My eyes landed on a door a few feet down the hall.

Shit, she's crying.

We thought this would make you happy.

I am happy.

I took a breath, eyes still on the white wood, happiness swirling with sadness at the memory. Patchwork House allowed almost anyone to stay, but bedrooms were reserved for Rebel Gods only, and once upon a time, me.

Inside that door was a bedroom with frilly, feminine decor that didn't match the rest of the house. A bed I'd slept in for years, a window I'd pushed open to climb down and meet boys clandestinely. It held memories I probably should have tried to forget, but that pulled closer each day I was away.

Even though I was back, I wasn't ready to *be* back. To sleep in my bed. To explain why after two years, I'd suddenly appeared.

Next to my bedroom door, was another one. A closed one. On it was a sign that read *Fuck Off.* Off limits. It had been off limits as long as I'd lived here, and I was sure the rules hadn't changed. But I had.

I pushed the door open.

I'd only been in this room once, but those memories were warped by alcohol. It was lived-in, but more than that, it was a *skater's* room. Posters atop posters of various famous skaters. A board on the floor, the deck a patchwork of bright yellow, orange, and pink. A D.A.R.E shirt hung off the dresser, but it read *Drugs Are Really Expensive.*

I smiled to myself.

Whoever slept in this room, I liked their sense of humor.

"If you wanted a tour of my bedroom, all you had to do was ask."

My heart stuttered and stopped before starting up again at twice the speed.

Flip.

I turned around. "I...it was..." I stuttered—this was *his* room? "I was looking for the bathroom." His blush lips curved in a way that was more cruelly sensual than a smile.

The only distance between us was the rug. I circled the plush edge, fumbling with my cup, spilling beer all down my hands. He followed.

"I don't think we've met. *Properly.* I'm Flip."

"I know who you are—I mean—" I flattened my back against his dresser.

He leaned forward, grin growing, like he enjoyed my torment. "This is the part where you tell me your name."

"I..." I shimmied left, sliding out from underneath him, inching out of his room. Flip followed me into the doorway.

"Tweetie," I finished as my back slammed into something hard. I looked over my shoulder to find King and instantly relaxed. Whatever had happened between me and King, he would always be safe.

Always.

"What's going on?" King asked. Flip hadn't moved. I was sandwiched between them, the air too thin, the space too small. Flip's brows were drawn in a way that made me feel like I had when I'd snuck into my first *real* Patchwork party and the guys found me.

Bad.

Disobedient.

Flip's eyes grazed over my shoulder like a soft touch. "Just getting to know my new housemate. We share a wall, after all." Absently, King's hand landed on my elbow and Flip's stare followed, narrowing farther.

"I was talking to Tweetie," King edged.

The moment splintered into tension, seconds dragging on in an ever-tightening wire in my gut.

"Is this really Flip's bedroom?" I looked at King. With my words, the air shifted noticeably, Flip and King once again speaking without actually saying words.

"Why didn't you tell me? This room was always off limits—was it because it was his bedroom?" I could physically feel my brows pulling together. It didn't make sense.

All at once, Flip's smile returned, cocky and impassive.

"I was just about to leave anyway. Flip said it like I hadn't even spoken.

He paused just outside the door, his and King's shoulders still touching, eyes on me. We were all so close I was certain we were sharing the same breath. Flip stared at me, and as I was just about to crumble under the tension, he left.

"Knock when you need me." Flip knocked on the frame, shooting me a smile. King's grip on my elbow tightened, his chest following suit. I nodded awkwardly, but Flip had already continued on his way, leaving us alone in *his* bedroom.

I followed King out, downstairs, and all the way outside. I needed air, needed to rid myself of the feeling of Flip's eyes still on me. The rain had stopped, but it left behind a murky fog. That's what it was like in Heaven Falls, especially in the fall. Most days, it was hard to tell if it was rain or overflow from our town's titular waterfall.

I casually looked through the mist, and there Flip was, watching from inside.

"Why was that room always off limits?" I asked, needing to distract myself from Flip. "I thought you guys were keeping a monster or something inside." It was just another room.

Flip's room.

I don't know what I imagined meeting Flip would be like, but it wasn't *this*. There was an intensity blazing behind his chocolate eyes that made me uncertain and nervous and achy.

"How do you know each other?" I rubbed my hands, blowing warm air into them. "Kind of a big thing to leave out, don't you think?" Then again, I was only ever allowed a small, curtain-covered window into King's life. He never wanted me to see the ugly.

King lit a joint, raising a brow. "You still into Flip?"

I tore my eyes from the house, from Flip, feeling caught. "I was never *into* Flip."

King leaned back, taking a drag of his joint. "You had his posters on your wall and he was featured heavily in your diary."

I laughed. "Big brother King never missed anything— wait, you read my diary?"

A small smile quirked his cheeks. A King smile, I liked to call it. Not a smile by any normal human standards, but compared to his usual scowl, it might as well be a Colgate grin.

I rubbed my hands again when King brought them into his tattooed ones. He blew warm air on them like he'd done thousands of times before. "I always hated when you called me that."

"But that's what you are to me."

His eyes were hard. Heavy. "I know."

FLIP

There was definitely something between her and King. He blew onto her hands, and she stared at him like he was some knight in shining armor.

I laughed into my drink.

"Tell me you're not really staying because of her." Daniel sidled up to me, folding wiry, dark arms. "Tell me you're finally making a comeback."

Tweetie smiled broadly at King, blue eyes glittering. I nearly crushed the beer in my hand.

Is this really Flip's bedroom?

With that innocent question, reality came crashing back. I couldn't stay. It was too dangerous; she already had questions I couldn't answer. This wasn't how it was supposed to go anyway. I was supposed to stay away.

I saw Tweetie and it got messy.

Like it always did.

"Flip?" Daniel pressed as Tweetie leaned back, laughing at some joke King must have made.

Possession. Jealousy. Emotions I shouldn't be feeling— emotions I had no *right* to feel, tore through me. It was the exact same feeling as before, when she was *in my fucking bedroom*. Touching my things.

I liked it.

I more than fucking liked it. I wanted her over everything. On my desk. In my bed. Her hair, her clothes, her touch, I wanted Tweetie to permanently tattoo herself on my life. I knew that would only lead to ruin, but with her so close, I couldn't think.

Tweetie laughed and shoved King.

I worked the recesses of my memory, trying to think of any time I'd heard King make a fucking joke.

I slammed my drink on the table. "I'll be gone by morning." *Avoid her.* Avoid Tweetie for the hour it would take to grab my shit. I'd managed it for two years. It wouldn't get rid of the thoughts of her, but then, nothing would.

Daniel called after me, but I focused on the stairs. Not on the window, where Tweetie was outside with King. Not on her bright smile, or her moving closer to him. Definitely not on the way it made me want to go outside and tear them apart.

I pounded upstairs, ready to get out of here as quickly as possible, when I paused, glanced down the hallway.

Tweetie's board lay next to her bedroom door with the rest of her things—chipped. She really needed a new deck, but I could fix hers easily. I'd done it enough times myself. One last gift from her shadow.

For as much as I'd memorized the lacy curtains and the silhouette of her body behind them, I'd never been inside Tweetie's room. Always watching from the grass, a glass windowpane separating us. If I was leaving forever, one look inside wouldn't hurt.

I pushed her door open with a finger.

Then sucked in a breath.

It smelled warm and fucking infuriatingly enticing. Like sunshine, like sugar. Somehow it smelled like home; there was no other way to describe it. Like coming fucking home.

Once upon a time this room was wallpapered with posters of me, but now the walls were bare. A pile of magazines lay on the nightstand. The top one featured some random asshole, but I knew she had a small story in the back of it.

I'd purchased enough of them.

I grabbed it and fell flat on her bed, shoes still on, cozying up against pillows I'd watched her fluff and throw and hug and cry against.

I wanted to mess up her room. Get it dirty. Leave the bedspread wrinkled and pillows in disarray.

Some kind of imprint, something of *me,* even if it could never be for real.

I flipped through the magazine, finding *Raegan Fairchild.*

No one was as good as her, definitely not the jackass they put on the cover, yet they only gave her a small article next to pills for penis enhancement.

I scoffed, reading the article for the umpteenth time.

I guess it's just always been in my blood, but there was one person who helped me tremendously...

She'd come a long way from the little girl who didn't know which way to put her feet, but in a way, she hadn't. She was always going places.

If the world would let her.

So why was she back at Patchwork?

A hard lump dug into my spine. With the magazine still on my lap, I pulled it out. Red and silky, with a broken lock at the side—a *diary.* Jackpot.

I skipped to a random page and my brows flew into my forehead.

Flip.

My name. My chest pounded, eyes tearing down the page, when I heard, "I need to unpack, big brother King. We can talk more tomorrow."

Tweetie. Right outside her room.

"Well, whatever the reason," King responded, "I'm glad you're back, Tweetie."

"Shit." I fumbled with the journal, quickly shoving it back under the pillows as Tweetie walked through the door.

She stopped short when she saw me, and a smile quirked my lips.

Tweetie was unapologetically a skater with baggie pants, a baggier shirt, and a cap always covering her bright, short curls. To most, it was unsexy, but to me, it was the hottest thing in the world. I'd always wondered what she looked like beneath.

"W-What are you doing?"

I slowly stood, stretching my arms above my head. Her eyes traveled to the muscles revealed at my waistband and I grinned.

"Got lost looking for the bathroom."

THREE

DARKSIDE: YOUR BOARD IS DARKSIDE IF IT'S
UPSIDE DOWN.

FLIP

I shoved cassettes and clothes into my backpack—whatever
I could reach. There wasn't a lot to pack. It was all just stuff.
This was just the period to an already finished sentence.

The goal was to finish quickly and not think about
Tweetie, especially not the way her eyes grew when she'd
found me in her bedroom. Or the perfect shade of straw-
berry her cheeks had turned. Or the many different ways I
could make it happen again.

Fuck.

I slammed another T-shirt into my bag.

Hours later, the party was still raging, having increased
from tame to insane, and I was almost packed up, hand on
my zipper and ready to discount this night as another thing
that would ultimately fade away in Tweetie's world but
would forever stay in mine.

I glanced at my closet, the last thing to pack up, and the

first place I'd let myself get too close to her, let myself fall, let myself believe I could be anything but bad for her.

I zipped up my bag, threw it over my shoulder.

I didn't really need those clothes anyway—except my D.A.R.E. shirt, but that was already hanging over my chair. I grabbed it and headed out. Downstairs, music pounded, lights low and delirious, and some asshole with so much gel in his hair it could withstand a hurricane had one arm to the wall above Tweetie.

I paused.

Where the hell were the guys?

He handed her a joint.

Tweetie took it, the corners of her pretty lips lifting as she mouthed something. *Thanks.* Was she really going to smoke with this one-man Flock of Seagulls? She slid out from under his arm, heading toward the stairs. He followed, a shit-eating grin on his face.

The music faded out, people now a blur. My brain yelled at me to *keep going.*

I stepped into his path.

"Get lost."

His angular face dropped and he looked over my shoulder, contemplating even through my scowl. I got it. Most assholes didn't see Tweetie for what she was, so I appreciated this guy did. Didn't mean he got to have her.

Double fuck.

I needed to leave. If this guy challenged me, I might even step aside. I had no right. I never had.

He exhaled and turned away. I stayed frozen, the party coming back in a whir. The front door was only a few feet away.

I went back upstairs.

I stayed in my bedroom, backpack digging into my

shoulder, stuck between right and wrong as much as I was stuck in my doorway. Then I heard the window latch unclick, saw Tweetie crawl onto the roof, quiet and shadowed like she was sneaking out.

Shit really hadn't changed much. Like her room, my window pushed directly onto the amethyst tiles. I watched her for a good while.

I told myself I hadn't really entered Tweetie's life, not really. One slip-up was okay. Everyone had an occasional relapse, fell off the wagon every now and then. I could still leave and it would be okay.

Then I saw her pull out the joint.

His joint.

I dropped my backpack to the floor.

"Shit," she said as I came out my window. "I didn't know—I mean, I'll go."

"It's cool."

She turned her head slightly, eyeing me.

"But you gotta share."

She stared at me, blue eyes iron and glinting in the night. Then she lifted the joint to me like an offering.

I plucked it from between her fingers and tossed it off the roof before she could say a word.

"That shit is trash." I reached into my pocket and pulled out my own, giving it to her. She took it wordlessly, eyes growing wider as she latched onto my stare. *Wonder.*

Oh, fuck. Now all I want to know is all the different ways I can make those eyes grow.

Cool night air passed in our silence, and I hazarded a

glance in her direction. Blonde tendrils danced on the breeze. The joint remained unlit in her hand.

"You gonna smoke it?" I asked.

"I dropped my lighter..." She leaned over the edge, staring at the night-darkened grass. I had the urge to grab her elbow and tug her back.

Instead I pulled my trusty lighter out of my pocket.

I flicked the flame to life, its orange glow snuffing out the darkness, creating a hazy halo that engulfed us. She hesitated, looked everywhere but my face. Tweetie was fearless, so to me, her nerves were intoxicating. I drank it in. The way her middle finger dug into her thumb. The way she licked her pouty lips.

Then she leaned forward. The flame lit her face aglow. Soft skin. Soft lips. Soft cheeks. No makeup. Nothing. Just soft. A curl fell across her eye and I absently pushed it behind her ear. Her eyes widened.

I laughed, retracted my hand and released my thumb, the flame sucked back into its plastic cell.

"I'm sorry about earlier," she said on a whisper. "I didn't mean to be digging through your stuff. I didn't...I wasn't aware..." Our roof overlooked the changing leaves, and it was the perfect slant to sit and watch them disappear into the dark night. It wasn't too far to the grass, either.

"You can come into my room any time, day or night."

Her breath caught on a hiccup and I clenched my jaw to hide my smile.

Some time passed and I glanced at her out of the corner of my eye, holding the burning joint with a slight frown twisting her beautiful face.

"You gonna smoke it?" I asked again after a few minutes, the flame burning the joint down. Tweetie stared at it.

"I've never..." she stuttered. "I mean..."

"You lived with three punks and you never smoked weed?" I already knew the guys didn't give her shit, but anything could have happened in the two years she was gone. Could she tell I was fishing for information? I wanted to know everything, to hear it from her lips.

Her pouty, cold-stained lips.

She shrugged. "I was surprisingly sheltered."

I smiled to myself. No weed during those years, then. It was always part of the plan to keep her as separate from our life as possible, to give Tweetie a normal life, whatever that meant.

But she came back.

Now all bets were off.

I raised a brow, tilted my head to hers. "Want to learn?" She nodded, passed the joint to me. Our fingers stayed connected. 1...2...3...I gripped the back of her head, tangled my fingers in her hair, dragging her head to mine.

A gasp fell from her lips.

Those perfect, pink lips centimeters from mine.

Fuck.

I'd dreamed of this, of her full bitable lips so close her taste was a whisper on the wind.

"What are you doing?" Her question was breathless, eyes wide and latched on to my every move. I inhaled deeply, and as an answer blew smoke into her parted lips.

She coughed.

I kept her head tight in my grip, forcing her still, and took a snapshot of the image in my head. Her red, tear-stained eyes and pink cheeks.

Tweetie was all grown up and smoking marijuana—a big change from the little girl who'd told me cigarettes were bad.

She was unbearably sexy, and when her eyes refocused on mine, hazy from the high, I shifted uncomfortably, adjusting my pants.

"I'll teach you about the dark side," I said, tangling my hands deeper in her curls. "You have every right to be here."

My hands were still deep in her hair when the call sounded. I could stare at Tweetie for hours, getting lost in the way her lids dropped over hazy blue eyes, learning things only visible up close. Barely there freckles. A small dimple on her nose.

"God bless America!" someone called in the distance.

"God bless the great US of A!" someone answered. All around *God bless America!* was heard, the cop warning Romeo christened years ago.

Tweetie's eyes popped in fear.

"Cops," she whispered. "They'll smell the weed." She tried to pull back, and instinctively my grip tightened.

"Follow me," I said calmly. I slowly untangled my fingers, then pushed open my window, gesturing for her to join me. There was a split-second hesitation, then she came.

I hadn't hidden from cops in my closet in years.

Tweetie wouldn't realize the significance, but it was all I could think about as we nestled in opposite one another. Almost exactly two years earlier, on a snowy night, I'd found her in my closet.

Minutes passed in silence as we listened for cops. King was no doubt doing damage control. I dropped my head against the wall, still watching her. She was too fucking cute. Her head was down, the bill of her cap shadowing her eyes, tip of her nose peeking out. She'd pulled her legs up to her chest, putting as much space between us as possible, but the closet was small enough that if I stretched, our legs would touch.

So that's what I did.

My dark jeans almost rubbed against her light blue ones, when I saw it. A small, eight-legged demon. It scurried across the floor. I sprang up without thought, pressing myself against the wall. The small ones were the worst.

Tweetie's back straightened. "Did you hear something?"

"Uh, no. Thought I did." *Fucking spiders.*

I settled back down, a bit uneasily. Minutes turned into an hour, and then I heard the all-clear call so faint I almost didn't catch it. When Tweetie didn't say anything, I was pretty sure she'd missed it. I stayed quiet, not wanting to leave, wanting to soak up as much time with her as possible.

Tweetie's stomach growled and she threw her arms across her belly as if that could hide it, eyes wide.

I laughed.

Then stood, opening the door.

She eyed it. "What about the cops?"

"Your hunger is more important than jail." I threw her a grin when she hesitated.

Downstairs was quieter than usual, the cops having made everyone else scatter. I rummaged around for bread, peanut butter, and bananas. When she saw what I was making, she placed two hands on the granite counter and practically jumped.

"Peanut butter and banana is my favorite! My dad always made these for me."

I smiled to myself as I set down the plate. "So then this makes up for it." She drew her brows, not sure what I meant. "Stepping on your dinner."

Tweetie nodded, taking a bite that left peanut butter on her lip. "This is way better."

I pushed my cheek out with my tongue to keep from smiling.

"Want some?" She offered half.

I made a face. "Gross."

Her brows pinched. "So why'd you make it if you think it's gross?"

I paused, heart rate skyrocketing. *Because I know every-thing about you. Because somewhere along the line, your wants and needs became more important to me than my own breaths.*

I couldn't exactly say that.

I shrugged. "You look like someone who likes disgusting food."

She scrunched her nose. "Well, what's *your* favorite food?"

"I don't know the English word for it."

That made her tilt her head as she chewed. "Describe it?"

"It's like pork-flavored cotton candy." I went to the cupboard and pulled out the jar of *rousong* I'd brought with me, showing her.

It was Tweetie's turn to make a face. "And you dare call my food gross?" I smiled for real this time, my tongue sliding to my incisor to halt a laugh.

We settled into a comfortable silence, me with an elbow on the counter, chin on my fist. I watched her eat. Her incisor was chipped, and even though the way she'd gotten it was awful, it fit her. It was adorable.

She stopped chewing. "What?"

I can't believe this is real.

I coughed, stood up straight. "So, what brought you back to Patchwork?"

She chewed deliberately, working the sandwich in her mouth, then swallowed. "How did you know I was coming *back*?"

Shit.

Caught.

I shrugged. "Overheard some people talking."

"Everyone is such a gossip." Tweetie exhaled, pushing her cheeks out. "I was looking for someone and when I couldn't find him...I don't know. It was the right time. I missed everyone." She'd been looking for someone? I fought the urge to press her.

Who the fuck had she been looking for?

There was something I really, really wanted to know, anyway. Something I could never ask, because I'd never really been granted a good moment.

"So, uh..." I attempted my segue. "The first time you lived here, it was because..."

"King killed my dad."

I paused. I couldn't believe she'd just said it. My eyes must have been saucers because she laughed, wiping a bit of peanut butter off the corner of her mouth, nearly distracting me as I imagined doing it with my tongue.

Then she kept eating.

"I didn't think you would answer."

"Everyone knows the story. It's not like it's a secret."

It felt like one, because the truth behind what really happened could never come out.

"Do you hate him? King, I mean."

"I never hated him," she said, and for a moment I hoped. "I was mostly just so, so sad, and so *young*. I'm glad it happened then, as horrible as that sounds. If it happened now, I don't think I could forgive him, you know? I was a kid. It made it easier. When you're a kid you can move on."

She paused.

"Now I don't think I could move past it. I would be blinded by pain, and then I wouldn't have my big brother."

I fell into my seat, stared at the different graffiti pictures on the wall.

I didn't know why I ever thought it would be different. The guys had been telling me as much for years, had been warning me away from her. Over and over again they'd warned me.

Nothing but selfish desires told me the opposite.

I must have stared at the wall for minutes, sound nothing but a rush of blood in my ears. I only realized Tweetie was talking when I saw her mouth moving.

"What?"

"You used to live here too, right?" she asked. I couldn't exactly lie; she'd figured out as much when I arrived. I nodded slowly, unsure how to play it. "When?"

"A while ago."

"Why did you leave?"

Tweetie finished her sandwich, waiting with wide and open eyes for me to tell her a truth that would shatter her entire world. For the first time, I was glad King interrupted us.

"I've been searching all over the goddamn house for you." King grabbed Tweetie, pulling her from the kitchen island so she faced him. "I thought the cops snatched you."

"I was hiding," she said.

His eyes narrowed. "I checked all the hiding places."

"Not all of them," I said. King shot me a look and I couldn't help myself—I grinned. Tweetie's strong stance faltered, chin wavering.

"You shouldn't have come back," King said, almost to himself, then his grip tightened and I focused on burying my feet into the hardwood so I didn't yank him off her. "You were almost arrested, Tweetie. This life isn't for you. I think coming home was a mistake."

Her eyes shone bright like gems in water.

Then she ripped her arm out of his grip and ran up the stairs. Tweetie never wanted anyone to see her vulnerable side.

"You underestimate her," I said. King stared after Tweetie long after she'd disappeared up the steps. When he spoke, his back was still to me, arms folded.

"You were supposed to come get the last of your shit months ago. You shouldn't even be here."

I tried to stay away.

I did.

I spent two years trying to rip out the roots she'd firmly planted in my head. Then she showed up at Patchwork as I was putting the final nail in the coffin of whatever the fuck we were never supposed to become.

"Yeah," I said lamely.

"The closer you get to her, the more you hurt her— emotionally, career-wise. You're no good for her, you never were. The first time you dragged her into our life, her dad died."

I couldn't say anything, because he was right.

When I saw her, all of my self-control, what was left of my morals, go haywire.

I'd only ever done one right thing.

Years ago when the accident happened, I moved out of

Patchwork and forced King and the guys to bring Tweetie in. I stayed away. Then, one chance encounter brought me back.

I became her shadow.

It wasn't until age sixteen that I started to see her differently. I fought it; of course I fought it. Tweetie was the little girl I taught, the little girl we saved.

But when she was a few weeks from eighteen, I fell.

Hard.

King turned, jaw granite. "Are you leaving?"

"No."

"So you're staying."

I wasn't sure.

I couldn't leave, but if I stayed, I couldn't have her either. I was fucked in the head. Possessive of a girl I'd started to want when she was sixteen, a girl I'd started to need when she was seventeen, and a girl I'd fallen head over heels for when she was barely eighteen.

I shrugged, and King brushed past me, making sure to shove me hard with his shoulder.

FOUR

VERT SKATEBOARDING: SKATING ON RAMPS AND
OTHER VERTICAL STRUCTURES.

TWEETIE

"Tickets! Get your tickets!" echoed into the crisp morning air as I made my way to the back yard, excited to test the new ramp. Sparky was perched behind a crudely made lemonade-style stand with a friend I didn't know. He was bigger than Sparky in every way, taller than me—though that wasn't much of a feat.

I readjusted my board, stopping to speak with Sparky. "What for?"

"Bacon is going to eat three ghost peppers."

"Bacon?" I looked at his friend.

"He's one of them vegans," Sparky answered for him. *Of course.* Almost everyone at Patchwork came from a broken family, so the first thing they got when they arrived was a name. Even if they only stayed a night, they knew they belonged somewhere.

I bought a "ticket" then headed for the ramp. I had a qualifier coming up and I had to focus, which meant no thinking about enigmatic, famous boys who dripped sexuality from their wicked, wolfish smiles. Boys who may or may not have starred in my diary were *especially* out.

I'd been trying to win a comp since I was a kid, and I was coming up on my last chance. When you reach a certain age, going pro just isn't an option anymore.

I climbed the ladder into a lemon sun. I'd been working on a new move lately, something special and just...different. It was harder, but it was going to be worth it. A trick so amazing, so breathtaking they'd *have* to accept me, even if I came without a penis.

As I dove, I tried not to think about Flip.

I had a checklist, anyway, a foolproof list of must-nots and must-haves if I was ever to fall in love again. It protected my heart, which tended to make bad decisions.

But all I could think was, *Thank god I took down the posters of him.*

Then my skateboard flew up and I landed on my shoulder—hard.

Note to self: don't think about boys when skating. I lifted my shirt to wipe my sweaty forehead, then gasped. Said must-not stood at the top of the ramp, sunlight creating a halo, *shirtless*. His jeans hung low on his hips, boxers clinging indecently to his muscles.

Tattoos crawled up his right arm and along his right pectoral, inky and metallic in the sun. There was a new one that hadn't been on his poster, Chinese characters stretching down his ribcage to the edge of his boxers.

He was a fallen angel. A god.

His eyes traveled to my naked stomach and I quickly dropped my shirt. Deliberately, like he was memorizing my body, his stare came to my eyes, and his lips curved. "Your feet are still wrong."

What did he mean *still?*

He slid down the ramp until suddenly he was in front of me. The morning sun was warm and loving on his olive skin. Hair wavy and wild, like he'd just rolled out of bed, and milk chocolate in the sun.

"And your hair is still wild." It sounded like a compliment. He pushed a strand out of my face like he had the night before. Again, I let him. He touched me like he had the right to touch me, and it threw me off balance.

Flip looked my face up and down, settling on my cap. "I'd like to see you without your hat sometime."

Stupid. Breathless. Brain not working. A shirtless poster was one thing; Flip in person was enough to fry my neurons.

When I'd gone too long without responding, he gave me another wolfish, panty-melting grin, the kind that made my legs jelly.

His touch came to my collarbone, warm and gentle and soft. "You're bleeding." The way he spoke ignited shivers up and down my spine. Cold and hot, snow melting down my marrow.

"It's nothing." I tried to shrug him off, but Flip wouldn't move. The protective look in his eyes made my gut jackrabbit.

His eyes settled on my board. This morning when I woke, it was fixed. Magically. I assumed it was King like always, but I'd yet to find him to thank him.

"Aren't you, uh..." I swallowed, trying to think of anything except his hand on my shoulder. I had never been someone who stuttered. I actually considered myself pretty fearless, but Flip made my tongue tingle. "Aren't you cold?"

"I run hot."

Oh.

Those three words were enough to make me run hot too.

"Um...are you...you want to join me?"

Flip made it impossible to think, so I said and did stupid things, like inviting him to skateboard, when I should have been inviting him to leave.

His touch fell from my shoulder and he speared both hands into black jean pockets, face a mask. "Pass."

I blinked. "Why?"

"I don't skateboard."

A stalemate of silence passed. I knew Flip wasn't doing it professionally, but at all? How the hell had that happened? Questions flipped through my mind, but the wall in his eyes said it wasn't up for debate.

Flip had been the world's hottest skater until he just *wasn't*. Girls who wouldn't normally give skateboarding a second look lined up to see him, going nuts for his boyish, cocky charm. Boys worshipped him as a god for the way he reinvented skateboarding. He was the first Asian-American skater so he hit it *big* in Asia. Everyone was rooting for him. He was a worldwide phenomenon.

There was so much speculation around why he stopped. Some said the pressure got to his head. Others said he had a secret injury. In the end, no one really knew *why*.

The rumor about his comeback came up at least once every year, but it never happened.

"Is there a reason you don't skate?"

His gaze fell back to my shoulder. "You need to clean that up."

"I'm fine. Happens all the time."

His eyes settled back on mine with an intensity that hadn't been there before. "Maybe you need someone to catch you."

My breath caught on a hiccup. A pause followed his words. A heady, hazy pause where all I saw were his lips. Smooth and unfairly full, with a sheen over the rosy hue that made me want to lick them. I wanted to fall into it, into *him*. His arched brow said he knew, like me coming to him was predetermined.

His eyelids dropped, my heartbeat thrummed.

And a violent scream erupted in the yard.

Followed by Bacon running and ripping off his shirt, tossing it between us. Flip jumped back. Sparky ran after him, holding a pitcher of water splashing over the sides.

I used the distraction to break from Flip, running inside. Still feeling his eyes on me. Everywhere. On my skin. Inside my lungs.

When the door opened, I assumed it was King bringing me gauze—it wouldn't have been the first time. He always opened the door a slice, placed it on the dresser, and shut it without coming in.

It was our ritual.

I figured he'd seen me grab the first aid kit.

"Thanks. I could've—" *gotten it myself.* I stopped short when the door was fully open, and a boy stood there, a boy *not* King.

Flip leaned against the frame.

At least he'd put on a shirt.

I quickly scrambled, holding my shirt close. How much had he seen?

"I'm...I'm changing," I said, stating the obvious. I held my tee to my chest. This was the most exposed I'd ever been.

He raised a brow. "I can see that." He leaned against the frame like he had every right to be there, watching—no, studying me. He wasn't looking below my neck and somehow that made it worse. Heat crept up my cheeks, a blazing fire.

I swallowed. "Why are you here?"

"Is this not my room?" he asked lazily.

"Obviously not." Instead of going back out, he shut the door. I swallowed with the *snick*.

"Look, if you're..." I searched for my voice. My room was suddenly too small. "I'm not going to sleep with you." Or anyone else. I gave my heart away a long, long time ago. "I don't date skaters."

But the way my voice wavered made it sound like a lie.

The way my throat ached made me know it was.

He laughed. Hard. I tried to ignore the way it made my belly pancake. "Straight to the point." Yeah, being raised by three unapologetic rebels meant I didn't really know any other way. "I like that," he said with a wink. "It's a good thing I'm not a skater anymore."

A wash of sadness rushed through me. Flip had been my favorite skateboarder—not because he was hot, but because watching him was magnetic and inspiring. I know years had passed and the hope of a comeback was probably futile, but hearing him say it was so tragic.

He stepped closer. I immediately put my hand out.

"Stay there. Just...stay right there." As long as there were a few feet of distance between us, I was safe from the swirling, drunk emotions in my gut. From the wolfish glint in his grin.

"I like someone else," I said. "I'm just not going to go for you. Sorry."

Nate. The boy I'd spent the last two years trying to find.

The boy who met nearly all of the items on my checklist. The boy who'd showed me how to skate street style, who'd given me my first *real* kiss, then vanished without a trace.

I thought that would be the end of it, but Flip's brow arched over a sharp, confident look that made me feel unsteady on my feet. Then his eyes landed on my shoulder, where I knew blood trickled.

"You need help." It wasn't a question.

"I..." I rolled my lips. "I have King." A harsh narrow of his eyes, but in an instant they slid back into impassive amusement, and I was sure I'd imagined it.

"You and King are really fucking close." He said it like it was some kind of hilarious joke, but there was more behind his words. A darkness.

King was my savior. At one time, he was my everything. The reason for food on my table, for a house over my head. Of course we were close.

Another long minute passed, one where I was painfully aware the only thing between Flip and me was my shirt. I tugged off my hat, suddenly too hot. I exhaled, blowing a strand of blonde hair out of my face.

His gaze darkened.

And suddenly he was on me. My lower back biting into my cold dresser. He smoothed a finger along my bare shoulder, stopping before the new wound at the dip in my collarbone. I shivered at the touch and pain, breath held captive in my chest.

"I told you to stay away," I whispered. I knew I could call out for King and he would come. Kick down the door. Nothing had ever stood between King and my safety. Between King and *me*.

"Sit," he said, angling me toward my bed.

I did.

He pulled out the first aid kit I'd grabbed and sat beside me. The bed dipped with his weight in a way that made me all too aware of his presence. I'd never had a boy in my room, not beyond the three surrogate brothers who'd raised me. Now Flip had been here twice in the last two days.

His hand hovered over the painkillers and my heart jackrabbited.

"Oh, I can't—" But I broke off, as he was already reaching for something else. No matter the pain level, I couldn't use them.

"I'm not a fan of them either," he said simply.

We shared a look, and once again I got the feeling we shared something pivotal.

Then his hand was cool on my neck, my collarbone. There was a clinical interest in his gaze, something that said he was touching just to make sure I was okay.

It made me feel all the more vulnerable.

Because my heart *pounded*, fluttered so loud in my chest. Even if he was touching me like a doctor would, my skin registered his touch as a lover's. I wondered if he could hear my heartbeat because the silence surrounding us was so great.

I noticed his lips were moving, but I heard nothing.

I blinked, noise rushing in like a wave.

"Hmm?"

"I asked if you have any more wounds."

"Oh. Right." I cleared my throat. "No. Just this one."

He quickly applied the gauze.

I waited for him to go, for his hands to leave my body, but his eyes slowly traveled over me. I gripped my shirt tighter, but it was useless, like the fire in his eyes could burn up the fabric into nothing save ashes.

"You should be more careful," he said, voice in his throat, eyes still burning holes into my clothes.

"Tweetie?" King called outside my door. "I brought the gauze."

Instinctively I went to stand, but Flip's hand shot out, reflexes faster, and gripped my chin. I waited, breath pulled, eyes locked with his burning embers.

"Be more careful, Tweetie." He tilted my neck up. "I'm the only one who should be putting marks on your body." His grip tightened on my skin, voice hoarse like he'd had one too many drinks. All that, just as much as his words, dried my throat, made my legs ache and thighs clench. I found myself leaning toward him.

Then all at once he released me.

Threw the gauze away.

And left without another word.

I fell to the bed on a sigh.

FLIP

I shut the door to Tweetie's room, meeting King's stunned face. Years ago when she'd first moved in, Romeo broke the lock on her bedroom door when he kicked it in after she slammed it shut in his face.

Good thing it was still broken.

King's jaw clenched, eyes going from the door to me. "What's your goal here, Flip?"

To make Tweetie unequivocally mine.

Simple.

I was in too deep. I couldn't stop until I knew how the

flesh that had trembled against my touch reacted against my lips.

As if he could read my mind, he scoffed. "I'll tell her everything."

I released an incredulous laugh, pulling out a joint. "I don't know when I became the villain in our story, but if it means I get Tweetie, I'll gladly play the part, King."

A noise sounded and we shared a look, an unspoken agreement not to have this play out within earshot of Tweetie. We went to my room.

It was only a few seconds after King shut my door that Tweetie climbed out onto the roof. Only the glass panel separated us like it had for years.

Always watching. Always the shadow at her back.

King came to stand in front of me, blocking my view.

"You aren't the villain in our story. You're the villain in *her* story." I tore my stare from Tweetie, meeting King's. "Stay away from her," he continued. "Tweetie isn't like us. She's not from this world. We *agreed* on that."

King, the god of all other gods—at least, that was what people said about him. Going from the most powerful family in town, to here, Patchwork. The outcasts. He could take any hit thrown at him, and because of that, he never lost. His family was always trying to tear us down, and he was like Zeus against the Titans.

But he had lost once. He couldn't have his girl.

And now he was like a goddamn golem guarding *my* girl, acting all self-righteous. Did he forget? If not for me, he would have left her under the overpass. If not for me, she would be some forgotten street kid.

But I swallowed that.

Tweetie and I were destiny.

I don't know who the fuck this other guy was she

thought she liked, but it boiled down to that simple truth. We were destiny.

I couldn't control it. I'd tried damn hard to fight it, but since the day she came to me, board slipping from her small fingers, and oversized helmet falling over her too blue eyes, Tweetie cemented her place in my life.

"I gotta say, white knight doesn't look good on you man."

He laughed, disbelief lodged in his throat. "No argument here, but I'm not the one who begged for this goddamn suit, am I, Flip?" My smile dropped. His followed.

"So you gonna guard her door or some shit?"

He folded his arms. "If I have to."

I ran a thumb across my lip, looking to the girl whose room had posters of me. Whose cheeks stained crimson at my simple presence. Whose diary had *my* name.

"How about I make you a promise?" I said, stepping to him "I'll only go as far as she lets me."

FIVE

PUNK: A TROUBLEMAKER.

TWEETIE

Eye fucking.

That's what this was.

I never understood the term until now, until Flip. After he left my room, I was alone for hours. I thought maybe he'd come to his senses. Realized I wasn't worth it. But as a party roared around us, he watched me shamelessly.

I'd heard him and King arguing the night before, but could only make out one word: Tweetie. My name. What kind of argument could include me? It kept me up all night until my glow-in-the-dark stars became blurry.

Now I quickly looked from Flip. *Anywhere* else. At the shivering, crystal chandelier made uneasy by the music, the portraits spray-painted on the wall.

Four murals, three to represent my gods, a fourth sprung from my dreams, an amalgam of everything Patchwork stood for. Wild and handsome, eyes like chocolate pearls, arrogant even in the painting—and he wasn't real. That's what I'd been told.

Flip leaned against the fourth, back to the purple paint and—*oh no!*

He stood up, coming over, grin growing. I moved like a chicken without its head, left and right, as Flip arrived, smiling his ridiculous, heart-popping grin.

"Hey, beautiful."

I looked at my baggy shirt and pants, then gave Flip a look. "Right."

"Don't believe me?"

I mumbled into my beer. "I think you're a really smooth talker."

"It's not all talk."

I hiccupped, almost spilling my drink, and wiped the foam off my mouth, glaring. "What's your game? I'm not going to sleep with you."

The grin vanished. "You're not a game to me. I'm into you. I'm *way* into you." I didn't know what to say to that. I didn't think I'd ever hear those words—much less from someone like *Flip*.

So I gaped.

"You're into me, too, though," he added with a wolfish grin. I still couldn't speak, not even to refute what he'd just said. His grin widened. "I'm also straight to the point."

He kept smiling to himself like he'd just won something huge, then left. But he leaned against the same wall, getting comfortable, like he was prepared to stay there all night, watching me. I let out a ragged breath.

You don't date boys like him, my brain said.

But he wasn't just anyone. He was *Flip.* I used to write sonnets in my diary to his eight pack, form entire fantasies around his Adonis belt. I wondered what it would feel like to be touched by his calloused hands. Kissed by his thick, full lips.

And now they were here in the flesh.

Saying things like he was *into me*.

"Did I see you hanging around Flip?" I startled at the sudden voice. Then inwardly groaned.

Patchwork Girls.

In the history of Patchwork house, they'd only ever let one girl stay—me—but that didn't mean they didn't let women and girls inside, girls who clung to them like horny barnacles. I'd practically grown up with them, so you could say they were like stepsisters to me. They loved me the way Cinderella's stepsisters loved her.

The unofficial Patchwork House emblem hung from a thin bracelet almost all the Patchwork Girls wore, a cross between the anarchy symbol and an A-plus grade. It was more than a piece of jewelry too. Wearing it meant you would do anything for Patchwork, but it also meant Patchwork would be there for you.

Daniel had dealt with more drunk dads and abusive boyfriends than anyone.

Which explained why he was a Patchwork Girl favorite.

This girl was the same who'd gaped at me like a fish on the porch. I went back to my beer. Best not to interact with them. Still, she was undeterred.

"We never made a big deal about you before"—I nearly choked on my beer—"but you can't do this. You can't have Flip too."

I frowned. "Flip isn't a Rebel God." She gave me the same look she had on the porch, almost like you'd give a toddler you really, really wished you could slap. Instinctively, I moved away.

She sighed through her nostrils. "Flip is everyone's

boyfriend. Stay away."

It was my turn to scoff.

Flip was obviously fucking with me. No one like *him* would go for someone like *me*.

She walked away, climbed all over Flip, replaced his empty beer with a full one. And, as if to make a point, she shot me a smile. My stomach sank. So I refilled my own beer.

FLIP

I liked making Tweetie stutter. Her lips, when she licked them like she wasn't sure of my motives, but her body didn't care. Her eyes, when she kept flickering back to me as the party groaned into the night.

Words, eyes, *thoughts*—throughout the night, Tweetie stuttered over me.

I tapped my beer, looking down the glass neck to the lone drops as if they would spring to life just as the record player changed songs. It went from wild, upbeat punk to the melancholy, heart-wrenching sound of Romeo's true vocals. All night *The Imperialists* played, but this one was different, significant.

I met Romeo the same night I met King and Daniel, the very first night we stayed in Patchwork, when we coincidentally happened to *all* be on the run from the cops. We didn't know that night would lead to a revolution. We were just kids drunk on too much whiskey and weed, while Romeo serenaded us with what would become this song, his hit. It was King who saw what we could be.

My eyes landed on King, and by serendipity, his on me. For once the look wasn't coated in years of shit.

Then all at once, yellow curls and baby blue eyes blocked my view—Tweetie, and she was *drunk*. Her pale cheeks rosy, eyes hazy. Fuck. I'd only ever gotten into trouble when Tweetie was drunk.

I sat up from the wall.

"Have you been staring at me?" Tweetie asked.

"Yes," I said easily.

She blinked, eyelids *stuttering*. "Why are you so honest?" She tilted her head, looking at me like I was a foggy window. The black of her pupils nearly swallowed the blue in her eyes. "I don't get you."

I shrugged.

Tweetie might think I was playing a game, but my only goal was her. I'd lived the past years in a shadow of my own dishonesty. Any honesty I could offer her, I would.

"You...need a refill," she said, finishing the sentence like that wasn't how she planned to from the start. I looked at my bottle, pretending I was surprised to find it empty. I could've gotten a refill, or I could've stayed on the wall, making her stutter. She chewed the inside of her cheek and I wondered what thoughts made her pick at her pinky nail while watching me like a wolf.

"So, what happened with that girl you were with?"

"Who?" I asked, genuinely not remembering.

She rolled her eyes. "Brunette. Pretty." Ah, now I knew who she was talking about. A Patchwork Girl who came over earlier. But I only had eyes for Tweetie.

Then I saw it, the furrow in her brow, the tightness in her jaw.

She was *jealous*.

Was that why she'd come to me?

A grin broke my cheeks.

"Oh her, now I remember. I should probably go find her." Tweetie's eyelids fluttered rapidly, eyes darting back and forth, working through some kind of internal dilemma. Like a fucking snail, I moved away from her, pretending to head toward whatever-her-name-was.

All at once Tweetie grabbed my belt, yanking me close. I threw my hands up, letting her. She grabbed an unopened beer from a nearby table and put the bottle to my buckle. I was frozen with a stupid grin as her small hands rubbed against my jeans, working the cap off.

"Here." She handed it to me.

"Take this." I instantly handed the beer to the first random person passing by, then grabbed another bottle.

She blinked, mouth parting. "You just wasted that one." Tweetie was always so damn adorable when drunk.

I leaned forward. "I don't see it that way." I handed her the bottle. She shook her head with a shy smile but placed it to my buckle.

"Where'd you learn that trick?" I asked, taking the beer. Her fingers lingered at my buckle, ghosting over the denim, blurry gaze locked with mine, lips parted. Then all at once her blue depths focused, realizing she was still touching me.

She sprang off. "A—a boy."

"A boy, huh?" I asked with the glass to my lips. "A cute boy?" I took a long drag from my beer, watching as her hands went to tame unseen flyways, patting down her shirt, her hat. Anything.

I grinned.

She cleared her throat. "That's none of your business."

"I'm just trying to size up my competition, Tweetie."

"Who says you're even in competition?" My laugh was coarse and real, nearly spilling my beer. The confident way she'd stuck out her chin was so fucking cute. Once again I got lost in her, the party melting away.

Then an asshole ruined it.

"Tweetie." King's voice was low and determined behind her. "I need to talk with you."

"Of course you do," I said into my beer. He came to stand beside her. Tweetie looked between King and me, unsure.

TWEETIE

King grabbed my hand and tugged me one way.

Flip grabbed my elbow and pulled me the other.

King squeezed my hand and said tenderly, "Come on Tweetie, let's bail." To my left, Flip scoffed. King's eyes hardened. I was never graced with that look, it was something he reserved for enemies. Still, it never failed to put a shiver in my spine.

Flip leaned forward, lips so close to my ear I could feel their warmth.

It felt indecent to do it in public.

"I'd like to finish the conversation we started in your bedroom." My lips parted and I whipped my head to the side, eyes wide. He said it loud enough that I *knew* King heard.

What should I say?

It's not what it sounds like.

I was only *half* naked.

He'd only said things I'd dreamed of hearing.

King's hand clenched on mine.

"I, um..." I swallowed, staring straight ahead so I didn't have to look at either of them. "I'm going to go with King for a bit." Flip's hand clenched on my elbow. For a moment, I thought he wouldn't let go, then all at once, he was gone.

I missed him almost instantly, a thought I immediately shook off—because that was crazy. Still, I barely tilted my neck to see my elbow. His fingerprints left a red memory.

I followed King to the bathroom, needing a quiet place to talk. Except the moments it took either of us to say anything stretched on like taffy.

"Is this Romeo? The music, I mean. Daniel said something about him being on the radio." What an amazing thing. I wished I could hug Romeo. I always knew his voice was once in a lifetime, and now the world did too.

"I thought you didn't date skaters," King said.

I snapped my head up. "I don't."

It was still so awkward between us.

He never apologized.

I was never able to really hate him.

"This isn't about me, Tweetie. You can't trust him." A stare lingered between us. I loved King. I wanted to believe him, but I couldn't. Our trust was stained glass, warped and colored with intention.

"It's not fair when you call me that," I whispered, calling me by the nickname I earned when I was a kid. He smiled, but like smoke in the wind, it was gone instantly.

"Stay away from him." He stepped to me, all muscle and imposing silver eyes.

I met him, chin tilting back to match his granite stare. "Maybe I will if you tell me *why*. What's going on between you and him?"

After a minute, he exhaled, tangled his hands through his hair.

"Look, you're not a kid. Do whatever the fuck you want."

And with that, he tore open the door, doing what King *always* did when it got too hard—he left.

FLIP

Arms folded, I sank into the couch, eyes locked on the bathroom door. Tweetie had been with King for too long. It was like history repeating itself.

Watching from the sidelines.

Letting her go.

Something nudged my shoulder and I moved farther away from the two people sucking face to my left, hugging the edge. Then the door opened, slamming against the wall. King exited without Tweetie, tearing through the party, marching upstairs.

Another nudge.

"What?" My voice was harsh, eyes glued to the door. Tweetie still hadn't come out.

"I, um...um...um..." At the nearly hyperventilating voice, I tore my eyes away. It was a kid, no older than thirteen. The same who'd interrupted Tweetie and me the other day, with spirally red hair and freckles like someone had chucked them violently at his face.

I tried to relax, not look like the asshole I was. "What's up?"

"Would...would..." he stammered. "Would you sign my board?"

I breathed, rubbed an eye. "Sure, man. Hand it over."

His eyes grew wide, face frozen, like he just realized he wasn't wearing pants.

He didn't have his board. Couldn't remember where it was. I got the feeling it took a *lot* out of him to come up to me. So I helped him search.

Outside was misty and gray and it was like we were trapped in a cloud, making it harder to search, but thirty minutes later, we found it under the porch.

I paused when he handed it to me. It was a short cruiser like most beginner boards, so it wasn't odd that he had it, but it threw me back to years ago, to the first day I'd met Tweetie. The day had started out misty and gray like now. Even the bright green color of the board was similar.

I have every right to be here.

I quickly scribbled my name.

"Thanks," he said when I gave it back. "I know this is lame."

"Dude, this was the highlight of my night. You saved me from the guy going *Alien* on that girl's face." A smile broke, and with one lasting look at his newly minted deck, he dashed up the steps—where he crashed into none other than Tweetie.

They spun, Tweetie righting them both so neither fell.

"Sorry!" he called over his shoulder, already disappearing back into the party. Tweetie didn't notice me at the foot of the porch, resting my back against the wood railing. She glowed beneath jewel lanterns, hazy in the fog, staring with distant eyes into the night. Something out of a fairytale —a siren.

"Unfaithful girl," I said, after another minute of silence.

She gasped, head snapping to mine. "How long have you been there?" I climbed the steps one by one, hand sliding along the railing. She stammered through her words, cheeks stained pink. For all the confidence and iron eyes, it melted any time I got close, and that drove me wild.

I stopped a step beneath her. At this height, she only had to crane her neck slightly to see into my eyes. The mist was a silver fog shrouding us both in a private world.

She bit one side of her lip. "What are you doing out here?"

"Someone forgot something important. I'm here to remind them."

"Who—" I gripped her head between my palms, shooting one searing look into her blue eyes, then jerked her to the side, exposing her neck.

Her hands went to shove me off, but then my lips found her soft, warm skin and the fingers that would have pushed me away tangled in my shirt. Fuck, I'd wanted her skin on my lips, her taste on my tongue. Been deprived of it for two years.

Even then, I only had a taste.

"I'll give you something to make you remember who you really belong to," I said against her neck, and her body melted into mine.

She was spring. She was light. She was forbidden fruit I promised myself I would only taste, not bruise or bite. As she trembled like I knew she would, I knew I wouldn't let go. I couldn't.

Not again.

I kissed her, followed the delicate line of her muscle, from beneath her ear to her collarbone.

Then I sucked.

Harshly.

When I pulled back, her eyes were hazy. "Now everyone will know."

SIX

GROM: LITTLE KID SKATERS.

FLIP

Some time ago
Flip is 14, Tweetie is 9

She stood in the middle of whirring skateboarders, helmet too big on her yellow curls, struggling to hold up a bright green cruiser.

I came to such a sudden stop that I crashed in the bowl, causing Daniel and King and Romeo to follow suit, tumbling on top of me. Daniel dropped the video recorder and it skidded a few feet ahead.

She didn't see us, or how we'd nearly crushed her.

"What the shit?" King said, scratching his head.

"Hold up," I said, waving my hand and silencing their simultaneous *what the fucks.* "I wanna check something out."

I grabbed my board and threw it down, stopping a few inches before her. She'd pushed her helmet up, and her bright blue eyes zeroed on me. Before I could even get a word out, her face scrunched up.

"I have every right to be here."

I bit back a laugh. "Yeah, you do."

I spent the rest of the day teaching her, despite King and Romeo yelling after me. *Pussy.* Even if they were joking, they didn't get it. I knew how it felt to be on the outside, to be denied chances afforded to others.

Everyone had a right to learn.

Plus, she was talented, had incredible potential. She didn't cry when she fell. If anything, it made her *more* determined. I found myself wanting to see just how far I could push her.

Before I knew it, the sun was hanging on the mountains.

Daniel, King, and Romeo came up behind me, flipping up their boards. They weren't skaters like me. King could've gone pro in snowboarding if he'd wanted to, but like his past, we didn't talk about that. Daniel got his kicks street fighting, but the how and why of that were also a no-go zone. The only thing we could talk about, the only thing that really made sense, was Romeo, the best punk rocker I'd ever met. In that world, everyone either wanted to screw you or arrest you, which worked, because Romeo was always waltzing between the two.

"I fuckin' hate Saturdays," Romeo said. "Place is crawlin' with groms and posers."

"Today is Thursday," Daniel said, and Romeo shot him a look like it was up for debate.

"Let's bounce," King said. I glanced down at the girl, touching her bleeding elbow with clinical interest. When she heard King, she stood up so fast the helmet fell below her eyes.

"Bounce? As in, leave? Can I come?" she asked.

King laughed. "Fuck that."

"You done learning?" I asked the girl, ignoring him. She shook her head, the helmet still covering half her face. I pushed it up, revealing big, blue eyes. "Then grab your board."

Tweetie followed after Romeo and Daniel, but King hung back. I knew he was sizing me up, trying to figure out what the hell I was doing.

We hadn't been together long, but we'd built a reputation.

And a bond.

We knew enough, knew the house and life we were building came first, and we knew we had each other's backs, which was more than either of us had ever had. I knew King was worried, because he only had rule: no girls, and he knew how much I hated that rule.

Everyone deserved a home.

"Don't look at me like that," I said. "Tweetie has potential. It's not like she's coming home with us."

His brows caved. "Tweetie?"

"Look at that crazy blonde hair and those intense blue eyes," I said with a shrug. "She's like fucking Tweetie bird." Another moment, then he shrugged with reluctant trust.

"Alright, dude."

Daniel focused the recorder on me. I stuck my tongue out before flipping it off, and he got a shot of the steep, winding road I was about to carve. The day had been a normal misty autumn, but now the sky was inky black, the clouds dark gray to match.

"My dad says this hill is haunted," Tweetie's small yet decisive voice cut in.

I rolled my lips to keep from laughing. Yeah, people in Heaven Falls were afraid of the winding, poorly lit road situated a few miles from the base of our town's waterfall. Everyone called it Devil's Hill, but maybe it wasn't a hill that claimed lives—maybe it was drivers too intoxicated by their latest opioid high.

But sure, the hill was haunted.

"Are we really taking the girl along?" King asked, eyeing Tweetie, whose helmet had finally given up. It hung against her back, pulled at her neck by the strap.

I pulled her by the collar, making her trip over her heels to get to me. "She wants to learn how to skate. Who better to teach her than the greatest skater in the world?" I ruffled her bouncy curls and a collective groan followed.

Her head fell backward, wide eyes finding mine. "You're the best in the world?"

"Will be." I grinned. I'd just been signed. Just had my first magazine spread, followed by another, then another. I was winning comps left and right. My aggressive, untamed street style hadn't been seen before.

Growing up on the streets finally had some benefits.

I never really thought I'd be anything, so seeing magazines print my name next to *godlike* was a trip. The world said I'd made it. I still didn't believe it.

But there was awe in her blue pools, a heady, gold-hued awe. She looked at me like I was a god. Suddenly my tongue felt thick.

I quickly grabbed my board then lifted her onto it.

"You think you can skate this?" Her eyes grew and she shook her head. Again, I bit the inside of my cheek to keep from smiling.

I gave Daniel the nod to let him know it was time to film then we went flying down the hill, her laughter echoing with the wind in my ears.

When we landed, her hair was windblown, her cheeks red. She had that look again, the wide-eyed, I've-just-seen-fireworks-for-the-first-time, look.

"You really are the best," she breathed. "Thank you. Thank you for teaching me. Thank you." She kept stuttering over her thanks.

I glanced down at her. "You'll make it up to me." *How* was written on her small face. "Someday you'll grow up, become the best skater, and then you'll be teaching me. So you have to keep skating, you owe me, understand?"

She nodded, eyes wide and solemn.

I kicked my board up with the tip of my shoe, holding it in one hand, reaching for a joint with the other.

Drop. A single raindrop landed on my bare hand. I stopped, staring up at the sky, waiting for more. One second, two...nothing fell.

"Cigarettes are bad for you."

I glanced down at Tweetie then smiled. "I know." She frowned, a small wrinkle puckering her pink lips. I could see the question written in the furrow of her feathery, light brown brows: *Why?*

I bent low until I was eye to eye with her indomitable stare. "I like doing bad things." Her eyes grew wide as saucers, but it wasn't fear written across them.

It was curiosity.

I coughed. "Do you know the first rule of skateboarding?" She shook her head with a wide arc. "You fall." I ruffled her hair and pushed her off her skateboard to prove my point. She landed on her ass in the middle of the street.

I laughed, then laughed harder at the stunned look painting her face stone.

Drop. Drop. Drop. Drop.

Rain. Dark gray, shiny beads landing as if in slow motion. Catching the moonlight and shadowing Tweetie. The sudden sprinkle turning into an all-out pour around us. Then, all at once, Tweetie joined in my laughter.

There was something bright about this girl that shed light on an otherwise dark world. I rarely saw the day. I lived in the underground, in a place without laws or rules. I loved it, but it got heavy. She was...light.

"Flip!" King yelled for me, but I waved him off. I kicked up my board, doing another trick as the rain poured. I wanted to give this little girl a great fucking memory to take home, inspiration or some shit—

"Flip!" King shouted again, and I stumbled over my board, snapping my head at the terror in his voice. King, who never freaked out. King, who was cool even when a hoard of cops were barreling down, had terror in his voice. He pointed at the hill.

A car tore down Devil's Hill.

Moments from hitting Tweetie.

There was no time to think. With my joint still between my lips, I lunged for her. I pulled her to my chest and rolled us as far from the center of the street as I could.

One.

Two.

Drip.

Drop.

My breaths were howling wind, my heartbeat thunder.

Rain soaked into my shirt, slid down my bare arms, slick along the new tattoos I'd gotten with the guys.

I never prayed—it just wasn't my scene—but here I found myself talking to whoever would listen so this little girl would be saved.

The crash was loud and earsplitting. Tweetie flinched in my grasp.

Then someone grabbed me, tugged me up. King. Beyond him I saw the shock in Daniel and Romeo's faces. A joint was still poised in Romeo's fingers, leaking smoke into the sky. The video recorder previously in Daniel's hand fallen to the ground.

Blood.

All over Tweetie.

I reached for her but stopped. It was *my* blood. Must have scraped my arm when I dove for her. It dripped down my shoulder, into her yellow curls. Sirens wailed in the distance, but I was frozen, dripping onto Tweetie.

Drip.

Drop.

"Go." King grabbed me again, twisting me to him. "Get out of here!" He shoved me down the road. The car was twisted around the tree like a metal vine, shinier in the rain. Too shiny. An arm lay limp out the smashed front window, flat on the hood.

But the person inside was fine.

Right?

"The girl," I said. She was immobile. I didn't think I'd hurt her—I tried not to. She was so small on the road, her too-big helmet askew on the back of her neck, getting wetter and wetter.

"I'll stay," he said.

"King..." Was the most well connected, but he was also

one pissed-off cop away from serious jail time. His parents had it out for Patchwork. They couldn't accept he'd left, and they didn't do long heartfelt talks.

They did cops.

"You just got signed. You're going places. Don't fuck this up, Flip." I glanced back to where the car had slammed into the tree. Glass glittered on the road, diamond red in the moonlight. The dying engine wove a morbid melody with the sirens. I quickly looked away, nausea building.

Had I just killed someone?

The possibility was growing heavier and heavier inside my gut, a slowly sinking lead, an anchor to this moment. If I hadn't been in the street...if I hadn't done that trick...if I'd listened to King, paid more attention, this wouldn't have happened.

"This isn't right," I said. "I did this."

"King," Daniel attempted. "You've already done enough." King came from the good side of town. A girl fucked him up good, he wasn't going back, and you weren't to ask him why, but he'd splintered his family further when his grandmother bought Patchwork House and put it in his name. We all paid our way, me with skateboarding, Daniel with fighting, and Romeo with music.

We all always thought King would go back, that he only considered this a pit stop.

If he did this, how could he?

"Mate, think clearly about what you're doing," Romeo tried.

"My parents want me in jail," King said. "So I'll go to jail." I couldn't help but feel there was more to this. I knew he carried guilt on his shoulders from whatever happened to make him leave. I dragged a hand across my forehead, trying to wipe away water, only to see more red. Watery blood on my palm.

My eyes fell back to Tweetie as the siren's wail got louder. I'd never been one for doing the right thing. I lived the way I did *because* I didn't like rules. But something about this was wrong.

Cowardly.

"King—"

"Just promise me something." Tearing my eyes from Tweetie was like ripping off dried wax, but I met King's eyes; brown shag wet, falling across one iron gray eye. "Promise me you'll make it big and put Patchwork on the map. I want to see the look on my parents' faces when they see the world call our lifestyle legitimate."

He shoved me down the road and I stumbled backward numbly, eyes darting from the wreck to Tweetie. King's eyes were unyielding, forcing me to keep going until I turned around and ran, running and running until my lungs felt like they would capsize.

I didn't know the day would end like this. I didn't know I would end up a murderer, a coward, and a liar in one fell swoop. Just like I didn't know the man in the car would end up being the girl on the road's father.

I never could've imagined I would fall in love with her. One day, after so many years had passed, I was the one learning from *her*, our ending just as predestined as the beginning.

SEVEN

DROP IN: GOING FROM FLAT GROUND INTO A
STEEP TRANSITION.

TWEETIE
Some time ago
Tweetie is 10, Flip is 15

The first time I saw him, really saw him, was at the trial. It was like he couldn't care less, slouching in his chair and focusing on his nails. As if it bothered *him* to be there.

That should have pissed me off.

It made me wonder.

Kingston Ayers, or King, they called him. They said he'd saved my life but killed my father. If it wasn't for him doing tricks in the street, Dad wouldn't have swerved to avoid him. I wasn't so sure. If I hadn't stayed out past sundown, Dad wouldn't have been out looking for me.

Either way, I knew it was my fault too. I was equally to blame.

Everything was a blur after the accident. A rush of ambulances and police cars. I do remember King standing above me, eyes a unique, brilliant silver.

I could've sworn there were other boys. I could've sworn the boy who taught me was not Kingston Ayers. Kingston always frowned, and I could still remember the boy's smile if I closed my eyes.

But the woman who spoke with me after the accident said I was wrong. She said trauma has a way of reshaping memories. Kingston Ayers was the only one at the scene.

He only got ten months. *Only*. It was practically a year. That seemed like forever to be locked up.

So I waited.

I waited nearly a year for him, a year before I could say the burning words on my mind.

He lived in the big, three-story house a few blocks from mine—well, not *mine* anymore. I didn't live anywhere anymore. Technically I lived at On Angel's Wings because I had *no immediate family*, at least that was what the nice counselor who talked to me after the accident said, after asking me a *lot* of questions about grandparents I didn't have, or friends of my dad that didn't exist. Questions that seemed to mean more.

It was always me and Dad.

So they put me there.

I stayed one week before I grabbed my bag and left. Summer was quickly fading into autumn and I knew I should be worried about where I was going to sleep. The rain was already starting and soon winter would arrive. Sleeping outside would get harder.

I found myself drawn to the three-story house. It was never without a raging party. Each time I went back, a new spot of graffiti covered the front, like a patchwork quilt.

The first time I walked by, I kept going, and the second, and the third. Tonight, I leaned against the tree opposite the house, watching. Technically I wasn't on their property, but the only thing separating me from them was the cobblestone sidewalk.

They called the boys who lived here the Corrupt of Heaven Falls.

The worst, most deviant boys in our town.

"You could get in a lot of trouble being here." I jumped. It was him. King. When had he come? *Where* had he come from?

With his head bent low, a cigarette flame lit up his face.

"Go away. This isn't a place for someone like you." He didn't look at me when he spoke or even when he walked back inside.

He never came outside again.

After a month, I decided to go in.

"You can do it," I said, walking back and forth on the strip of stone. "Just do it."

So I did.

Smoke made everything blurry and secretive. Cigarettes mingled with something very distinctly sweet, like sugar and rum, a wicked Christmas. The music was live and *alive*. A man with beautiful, silky long brown hair sang shirtless and covered in tattoos, wearing leather pants.

Then everyone started jumping, and I was pushed around with them. People so tall they were redwoods to me slammed me around like a ping pong ball. I couldn't breathe. Fear crept into my gut. I was in over my head, like when I demanded my dad take away my nightlight because I didn't want to be afraid, and I'd spent months awake examining every shadow.

They were called *Corrupt* for a reason.

"Hey, what the fuck? There's a little girl in here."

Suddenly I was gripped by the elbow, dragged out, back

through the party, the kissing, the fighting. Then he threw me off the porch.

I stumbled, trying not to fall off the steps. He stood as a sentry on the top step, arms folded.

"Go away, Tweetie. This isn't a place for a kid, and I don't feel like babysitting."

I tilted my head. "Did you just call me Tweetie?" King looked stunned, like I'd caught him in a lie. I pressed. "Why?"

"Because you're annoying like a bird."

I breathed through my nose, trying to get my emotions under control. "You're...you're..." *You're the boy who saved me. You taught me when no one else would.* But I didn't say that. I couldn't—not when he looked at me like that. "You're a jerk! You killed my dad."

His eyes flared.

Something replaced the apathy.

Then all at once it was gone.

"Yeah, and you're a little girl who can't take a hint."

He turned to go inside, so I said something—anything to get him to stay. "I hate you."

He threw me a look over his shoulder and for an instant I thought he was going to say something.

He kept walking.

FLIP

Tweetie lived on the streets now. Every day she stood outside Patchwork, hoping King would appear. We had that in common. I wanted *someone* to show up for her, even if I couldn't.

And every day I watched Patchwork—watched *Tweetie* —from the shadows, hidden where trees tangled into the rest of the abandoned Victorians that made up the neighborhood.

"Jesus." King jumped, seeing Tweetie on the porch steps. "Didn't your parents ever teach you to avoid bad influences?"

"No!" she yelled. "Because I don't *have* anyone to teach me."

King paused, realizing what he'd said, then yanked her by the wrist. He threw her off the steps like he did almost every day.

Tweetie stormed past me, face scrunched in anger.

It was the closest we'd been to one another since the accident.

I waited until she turned the corner.

"Well, you look like shit."

I turned to find a tattooed, shirtless chest. Pierced nipples, pierced lip, pierced fucking *everything*—I know, the dude was hardly ever dressed. With long, slick straight hair that chicks went nuts for and a red lip perpetually curved with a wicked hook, he was like the devil, finding humor in the worst places.

Romeo.

"Maybe you should come back to Patchwork, yeah? Where are you even sleeping?" I wasn't, not really. I watched Tweetie sleep under the overpass. Then once she woke up and went to Patchwork, I might catch a few hours on a bench somewhere. How could I sleep comfortably when I'd let my brother rot in jail?

I shrugged, pushing off the subject.

"Look who finally showed up." Daniel spotted me from the porch, taking the steps two at a time to join us beneath the trees. King followed his line of sight, face immediately souring.

"I'm not giving her any more fucking burgers or fries," King said when he got to me. "So if that's why you're here, go ahead and fuck off." I had a feeling she was growing tired of the ones I'd been buying for her, anyway.

Leaves shivered in a cool breeze, our silence speaking volumes. King shouldn't have been in jail, but someone high enough put him there. At first I thought it was his parents, but they got his sentence *reduced*. I'd gone to him, told him I'd come clean. If it had been me, I'd have been out with probation.

He'd told me it wasn't about me anymore, to focus on my promise. I'd only ever seen that look the night we met. Somehow this was about his girl.

In the end, I broke my promise.

We didn't become legitimate.

We became *Corrupt*.

"How's skateboarding?" Daniel asked.

I shrugged. "Working on it."

"You've been working on it for a year," King said.

I tried skateboarding, but I couldn't.

I just...couldn't.

My body revolted. Every time I tried I remembered that day. Daniel understood, but that was Daniel—understanding to the point of sainthood.

"So if you're not here to tell us you've finally started skating again and you're not coming inside, what the hell do you want?" King asked.

I'd been thinking about that since the day I saw her leave the same orphanage they'd tried to shove me in when my parents left. Knew the answer was insane, but I had no other choice.

"You need to take in Tweetie." Stunned silence followed. Romeo pulled a cigarette from behind his pierced ear, prepping for the shitstorm.

It was a blazing copper day. The sun, the leaves, the sky —everything was golden. The rain was starting, though. Tweetie couldn't sleep in the fucking rain. She might die in the snow.

Even though both Daniel and Romeo would have to take her in as well, this was a task specifically for King. Romeo lived more on the edge than any of us, was just one windblow from falling off it.

I knew Daniel would say yes, but I couldn't put the burden on him. I had a feeling there was shit he didn't tell us and was already up to his limit. Daniel also had his own babysitting gig as well, was making sure King's sister was good. Even if King couldn't go back to Heaven's Court, he couldn't fully abandon those he'd left behind.

Since King had a sister before Patchwork, he would know what to do.

He would hate it, he would hate me, but he wouldn't say no. Because at his core, King was a protector. We all were. It was the reason four very different people could make something like Patchwork. At our core, we matched.

King let out a breath halfway between a scoff and a laugh. "Are you fucking kidding me?" He dropped a shaking head.

"I would do it myself but..." I trailed off. When King decided he was going to take the fall it meant I could never be there for Tweetie, not in the light, anyway. If Tweetie recognized me, all the months of pain King went through would be for nothing. Even if I never wanted it, I couldn't make his sacrifice worthless.

"You and her have a relationship, King," I continued.

He startled. "The fuck we do."

"You do. She likes you."

"She hates my guts. She thinks I killed her dad."

"She waits for you." I looked down the street, to where I knew Tweetie sat below the underpass, arms around her knees, staring out to where King always came with a bag of cheap burgers and fries I'd bought for her. She would perk up then quickly apply her frown and glare, like lipstick and eyeshadow.

It was cute.

"Who's going to pay for her food? The clothes she needs? It's not just bringing her in. She'll need shit—girly shit."

"Me," I said without hesitation. I had money saved up from my magazine spreads, from winning my comps. Since I'd stopped skating at the height of my popularity, I'd just become *more* popular.

More magazines printed my name. I was even on TV.

It had always been my dream to see myself on TV. Careful what you wish for, right?

The money had been going toward Patchwork; why couldn't some of it go to the little girl whose life we fucked?

King shook his head, ran a hand through his hair. "So I'm what, daddy now? Where the fuck is she going to sleep? At Patchwork with *all of us?*" He gestured behind him, where a bevy of men and boys ranging anywhere from twelve to almost-twenty lay in various angles of sleep on the porch and steps. I shrugged again because I had no good answer.

"Four rules, Flip," King said. "Four."

I exhaled, long and hard. "Really? Now?" When we founded Patchwork we decreed four rules to live by, four rules everyone would follow. We all chose our rule and it worked in creating harmony—*before*. *Before* I wrecked a girl's life and made her homeless.

"I'm not doing this," I said.

"You obviously forgot." King turned to Romeo. "Number one?"

"Number one, no rules." Romeo raised shirtless, tanned and inked arms above his head, stretching. "Still the best and only one we need, I think."

"Number two, do good," Daniel continued. "Even if they say we're the worst, we do good. We help, we fix up the neighborhood, we do good in any way we can." All eyes turned to me. King's light brown brow arched, waiting.

"Number three, we accept anyone," I bit out, glare matching King's.

"Number four, *no chicks*," King countered.

I threw up my hands. "She's not a chick—she's a help-less little girl."

King released a breath. "And Romeo can't walk naked through the house around a helpless little girl." Romeo cocked his head, plumping his red lips like *Fair point.* Silence followed. I knew what everyone was thinking: where would she fit in among the shirtless, messy boys and near-men?

I didn't have the answer, but I knew she couldn't keep sleeping in the street, and neither could she go back to that awful excuse for a group home.

I raked both hands through my hair. "I never wanted you to take the fall."

"Oh really? Because you accepted it pretty goddam quick."

King stepped to me.

I met him.

Daniel threw his arms between us. "We can't let this break us. After everything?" King and I looked at each other, then looked away.

"Friends forever or some shit, yeah?" Romeo added.

"Yeah," we mumbled, but it was weak, like the bond between us. I looked down to my black and white checkered sneakers. Beneath them, emerald moss and violets overgrew on the cobblestone.

Tweetie saw trash beneath her sneakers. Because of me, Tweetie was sleeping on the street. Because of me, Tweetie had no bed. *I* took that from her.

"We're all she has, King. We took everything else from her."

His face shifted, the hard stone cracking, and he let out a curse.

I breathed. It wasn't a win, but it wasn't another loss.

"You owe me. Big." He jabbed his pointer finger at me. "Don't think I won't collect."

I nodded. "Just take care of her."

TWEETIE

"Stand up. Get your shit. You're coming with me."

I scrambled to my feet at the sight of King. It all happened so fast, I didn't have time to react, let alone ask questions. Come with him? To *Patchwork*?

He didn't sound the least bit happy about it, but I quickly grabbed all my stuff before he changed his mind. It wasn't hard; I only had a few small mementos. Everything else could be left with the rest of the trash.

He was already walking away when I gathered everything.

My heart thumped against my ribs. Fear, of course, but really an overwhelming sense of debt. How could I ever repay him? The silhouette of him grew smaller, trash bag dangling from my hand as I tried to form words.

Thank you. Thank you for saving me again.

"I still hate you," I yelled to his back.

He paused. "And I still think you're annoying."

I followed King out of the overpass, and to my surprise, two more boys were waiting at the mouth. King kept walking, but I paused. The smaller of the two came and took my trash bag of stuff. He dressed normally, in simple, distressed light blue jeans and a faded denim jacket-hoodie combo. He told me his name in a soft, quiet voice. Daniel.

The other lit a cigarette and grinned at me. His face was lovely, almost pretty like a girl's. However, the flame lit him aglow in a sinful way, and like his wolfish smile, there was nothing lovely or pretty about it.

"You going to stare all day, luv?" He had a thick British accent with long, and luxurious brown hair and crystal blue eyes.

"No." I quickly scrambled after them.

When we reached Patchwork, nerves wrapped around my legs. The sun fell behind the steep, sloping Victorian, lighting it on fire. It was otherworldly. Demonic. Decadent. Like Hade's house incarnate. I'd only been inside once before, briefly.

Now I was going to see what Patchwork was really about.

I wasn't just entering the home I'd been thrown out of

over and over again, I was going to *live in it*. King was at the door, Daniel and the British guy walking up the steps, and I couldn't move.

Swallow. Hide my rapidly beating heart.

I have every right to be here.

Inside, not one section was untouched by something elegant and old. Everything from the ceiling molding to the purple and gold wallpaper was ornate. The mantle dripped intricate carvings like melted dark chocolate, a large mirror stood proudly over the fireplace, the pane graffitied, like most of the house. It wasn't like the walls of the underpass—sloppy and without purpose; this was art. It reminded me of an old castle, a home to some ancient vampire who'd given his life up to rebellion.

Someone dashed across my field of vision, a mummy wrapped in toilet paper, their cotton cape floating elegantly on the wind as they disappeared out the door I'd just come in. Then the whole scene unfolded.

Chaos.

That's what Patchwork House was—a quilt of chaos and debauchery like the graffiti painting the outside and inside. Like the boys who ruled over it.

I tried to look past the party like last time, but I couldn't focus on just one thing. One guy shoved another so hard he fell into a stack of records. Another jumped on a box and did a karate kick only to have the box pulled out from under him.

I stuck a finger in my ear. The music was so loud it actually hurt. Then all at once, it stopped. Their attention turned to us, specifically *me*. Some looked close to my age, while others were nearer to King's.

I stepped behind King, and instinct had me grabbing his hand. The biggest, most powerful vampire.

"What the fuck?" a guy with an indigo mohawk said, eyes on me.

"This is Tweetie," King said, authority lacing his tongue. "She's with us now."

Another long, stagnant pause. The only sound a record scratching.

"No, seriously," a shirtless guy said on a laugh. "What the fuck?"

Daniel stepped up, grabbing a pile of clothes, and threw it at the shirtless one. "Put some clothes on." The guy caught them, nonplussed. He looked from the shirt and jeans to Daniel, then to me, finally back at the shirt.

"It's a prank!" someone piped up. There was a collective *ohhh*.

"It's not a fucking prank," King growled.

Another long pause then someone said, "I didn't sign on to be a babysitter." There was a murmur of agreement.

One by one they all filed past us, sparing me a puzzled look, a shake of the head. A few stragglers remained, floating in the living room like a crowded beach just cleared after a shark warning.

In their wake, a mess was left, the likes of which I'd never seen before. I had never been clean by any standards. My dad used to call me Hurricane Rae. But this was next level. Cigarette butts. Food wrappers. Empty soda cans and even *fireworks*.

When my three guardians stepped farther inside, I didn't want to follow. I couldn't let go of King's hand either, so we created a bridge of arms and hands, of my reluctance to acknowledge just how much my life had changed.

I was already grateful to King for saving my life, now he was offering to give me a home. I didn't understand *why*. These boys had decreed they were my new guardians.

What did it mean when three boys who lived their life by a code of not giving a fuck suddenly cared about you?

I still couldn't wrap my head around it.

King looked over his shoulder, eyebrow raised. Then, as if realizing my internal struggle, he tugged me inside. I tripped and he steadied me with his other hand.

"This is your life now, Tweetie."

EIGHT

COPING: ANY MATERIAL ATTACHED TO AN
OBSTACLE FOR EASIER GRINDS AND SLIDES.

FLIP
Some time ago
Tweetie is 10, Flip is 15

"You put her in the fucking *attic*?" Tweetie's cries were
heard all the way downstairs as my eyes traveled between
King, Daniel, and Romeo. The attic was dark, uninsulated,
and filled with spiders.

A few days had passed since Tweetie had officially
moved into Patchwork House and all she did was cry. She
refused the food the remaining boys brought up to her. She
hadn't asked for help of any kind. I don't think she wanted
attention, and I was certain she didn't think we could hear
her at all.

But sounds carried in this big Victorian, and they were
at their wits' ends.

Which was why I met with them that evening in the
hazy, marigold light of the kitchen. It was my fault she was
there, after all.

"Where would you have had us put her?" King growled. "We don't have any rooms left. The guys all sleep where they can." The house was deceptively big. Though it was three stories and on a great plot of land, it was only a four-bedroom. The rooms themselves were large, with every other square foot dedicated to drawing rooms, dining rooms, a great hall, a solarium, a music room—fancy, rich people shit that was of no use to us.

"I don't know," I said. "Anywhere else would have been a good start." King looked ready to step to me and I was just tired enough, just ready enough to feel anything other than guilt and shame, to meet him.

Daniel intervened before anything could start. "Hey. We moved her."

"*Temporarily,*" King amended. "We *temporarily* moved her into my room." I settled back against the cupboards as King repositioned himself on the brick wall mural of Bill Murray some kids had painted a few months back when *Caddyshack* was big, shoulder to shoulder with Romeo and Daniel.

"And she's still crying?"

King and Daniel shared a look. "There was an issue—" Daniel started.

"She fucking slammed the door in my face," Romeo said before he could finish. "Brat."

That still didn't explain her recent bout of tears. The way they all looked at one another, I knew there was more to it. I threw my hands out, waiting.

Daniel pulled back his hoodie, exposing springy dreads with a sigh. "He kicked it in."

I turned to Romeo, exasperated. "You kicked it in?"

"I'm not going to let a seven-year-old get the best of me," he said primly, adjusting his leather jacket like he was wearing suspenders and a tuxedo, not worked leather over a bare chest.

"She's ten," Daniel said, and Romeo shrugged like *Same thing*.

"You could've put her in my room," I said, only to be met with an awkward, stiff silence. Daniel and Romeo looked anywhere else but me. King adjusted his folded arms.

I sighed.

"We moved her from the attic," Romeo said, pushing past the elephant in the room. "We gave her a bed. I fuckin' let her touch my hair, and *nobody* touches my hair." Romeo put his pointer finger to his long, bronze-hued hair, eyes wide and crazy.

We all exhaled at the same time as her cries grew louder, like the house was haunted.

"We've got to fuckin' shut her up. It's like..." Romeo fluttered his hands, searching for the right word. Finally he jammed his chest. "It's doing something here, you know? It's not good."

"You feel bad for her," I said simply.

He shook his head with a laugh. "No. No, it's not that."

"Have any of you tried talking to her?"

All three shared a look.

"We sent the kids up with food," Daniel said. "The ones closest in age."

"So no one's talked to her?"

"And say what?" King lifted his arms. "Sorry we killed your dad and ruined your entire life, wanna play Jenga?"

"Or we could..." I searched for an idea, trying to find inspiration in the kitchen, when my eyes landed above the stove. Graffiti was starlight against the dark wood pantry, a cow jumping over the moon. A smile came to my lips. "Tell her a bedtime story."

All three of them looked at me like I was crazy, but no one had any better ideas.

When we got upstairs, King put a hand to my chest. "Stay outside." *As if I wasn't planning on that already.* "She remembers you, even if she can't put it together. The clothes you were wearing, your hat, your eyes. We tell her it's us she remembers but, it's playing with fire, Flip. You're her living nightmare."

TWEETIE

"I don't need bedtime stories," I said, wiping my nose and rubbing my eyes, getting rid of the evidence. I needed them to think I was tough. Tough meant no tears, right?

I only cried when they weren't around, when nightmares of that night came back. The only thing that made the dreams bearable was *him*. I wasn't sure who he was. Everyone told me he didn't exist, but he felt so real. His checkered shoes, his snapback cap. The eyes I remember most, warm and brown. His presence made me feel guarded.

It's weird.

He keeps me safe, yet he visits me in nightmares.

"It's for me," the big one said, King. "I need 'em, can't sleep without 'em."

I squinted. "Really?"

The thought that they saw me as some little girl who needed a *bedtime story*...that was worse than the nightmares, worse than the cold, masculine room that was nothing like my old bedroom with stuffed animals and fluffy pillows and glow-in-the-dark stars.

"We all do," the smaller one with the exciting, extravagant hair said—Daniel. Disbelief grew suspicious weeds in my stomach. Someone hung in the doorway but I couldn't make him out, just his arm. Long and toned and silky, like sepia-colored moonlight.

"I'm telling it, yeah?" said the one with the funny accent, Romeo. "I'm more creative than all three—*err*, two, of you put together. Plus I have the best voice." He stretched his arms in front of his chest, cracking his knuckles.

"Once upon a time there was a land ruled by all-powerful and unyielding gods. They lived on the highest hills and preached morality, but everyone knew them as the Incorrupt of Hea—"

He paused.

"Of fairytale land. For years they lived undisturbed, doing all kinds of things like giving money to..." He blew out a breath. "Warlocks, so they could pass...dragons. They tried to say they were...beneficial dragons when really it only benefited a few—" He'd started speaking quickly, but stopped, noticing Daniel and King were staring at him hard. His blue eyes settled back on me, voice low and exciting. "Until one day they were challenged."

I leaned forward, grasping a black pillow. "By who?"

"The Corrupt."

A small breath escaped me. Was this story about *them*? "Why are they called that?"

"Because people are cruel arseholes with sticks up their bums."

My mouth dropped.

I knew they cursed, but I still hadn't gotten used to it. If I said *heck* I got spanked.

"I mean..." He let out a breath. "Because they were total opposites. Where the Incorrupt needed order and laws, even at the expense of the virtue they preached, the Corrupt reveled in the lack thereof. But really, luv"—Romeo leaned forward, arching a wicked, angular brow, like he was letting me in on a secret—"they were anything *but* Corrupt. This was a cruel word used to distract people from their true purpose."

My eyes popped. "What was their true purpose?"

"Freedom." He settled back against the wall, satisfied. "The Incorrupt wanted to shackle everyone. So even though the Corrupt weren't doing a thing wrong, they were going to pass more laws to make everything fun illegal."

"Huh?"

"I mean..." Romeo trailed off as Daniel and King stared at him, brows drawn. "They, uh, declared candy *illegal*." He wiggled his fingers, exaggerating the last word like when my dad used to say the word *Spoooooky* at Halloween.

I was a little lost.

When did this become about candy?

Still, I wanted to know how the story ended. "Okay, well, how did the Corrupt defeat the Incorrupt?

He rubbed the corner of his eye with a sniff, disinterested. "Uh...okay, so the people they freed from the Incorrupt followed them, and eventually they had enough power to become gods themselves. Um...*Rebel* Gods."

He spoke insanely fast, like he wanted to get this over with as quickly as possible. I held my breath, afraid I would miss a word.

"And their religion was sin and debauchery and corruption, but in their corruption, they found freedom, and in their debauchery, they found brotherhood, and in their sin, they found..." He trailed off, a smile forming. "Well they found more sin, but it was really fucking fantastic and—"

Daniel elbowed him so hard he fell into the wall.

Romeo righted himself, patting down his hair.

Minutes passed, I waited for him to continue. This was the most I'd spoken with them since the day they'd brought me here. I only had my first impressions. Daniel was definitely the nicest one, he even had the nicest, most normal name—not like *King* or *Romeo*. Romeo was a roller coaster about to go off the rails. King was...well, his name fit him. He was king.

The more I saw them, the more I thought the lady at the trial was wrong. I was pretty sure they were all there that night, but I would never say anything.

It was my fault, after all.

All three of them stared at me, the same look on their faces, like they were waiting for something from *me*.

"Was that the end?" I eventually asked.

Romeo made a face. "Yes?"

"But what happened? Who won?"

"They fought forever and nobody was happy and it was really just a bunch of bullshit."

My jaw dropped and tears came to my eyes again. The warmth from his fairytale almost nearly erased by the awful ending. I pressed a pillow to my face. "That's so sad," I whispered.

"It's not a fucking fairytale." Shoved again. Romeo grunted, muttered something under breath that I couldn't catch.

"They resolved their differences and lived happily ever after," Daniel finished. They stood up straighter, and I knew the story was over. They'd leave me again.

"And the gods were worshipped as they rightly well should be," Romeo added.

"Wait," I called out just as they reached the hallway. "Are they real?" *Are you real?*

The three of them paused, shared a look with some meaning I couldn't decipher.

Then, "You're living with them," a voice responded, the one hanging by the door. Awe washed through me.

Then the big one, King, shut the door.

I felt a bit safer.

Safe enough to fall asleep, hugging my pillow, dreaming of my Rebel Gods.

FLIP

"Rebel Gods?" I asked, voice tinted with humor.

"You wanted a fairytale," Romeo shrugged. "I gave her a fairytale."

"Blow more smoke up your own ass next time; I don't think the astronauts got the signal," King said. Romeo huffed into a closed fist, releasing his middle finger like he was blowing up a balloon. King shove him so hard he fell, but Romeo laughed.

"Happy late birthday," Daniel said while King and Romeo wrestled. My brows popped. I'd forgotten. As the year passed and everything happened, it wasn't important.

"Your birthday is coming up," I noted. I was barely fourteen when I met them. King was the oldest, having just turned sixteen, then Romeo at fifteen, and Daniel last at thirteen. Now we were all another year older, Daniel soon to follow.

He nodded then folded his arms. "Where are you staying?" We walked downstairs as Romeo and King continued to wrestle. It sort of felt like before everything went to shit.

I thrust my hands into my pockets. "Around."

Daniel's hazel eyes saw through me. "Dude, just come back."

"I'm her living nightmare," I said, nodding to King as we reached the ground floor and headed to the solarium. That caused King and Romeo to freeze.

There was a long, tense silence. Tree branches scratched the bay windows lining the hallway to the solarium, the leaves a brilliant emerald green even in the moonlight, the kind only seen right before they die, the finale in a firework display.

Then, with Romeo still inside a headlock, King spoke up. "I have a place for you."

"Did you buy another house we're not aware of, rich boy?" Romeo asked, face pinched in King's arm. Romeo flipped King, pulling his arms behind his back and pushed him into the solarium.

If I missed one room the most, it was this one. As bright at night as the day, the stars so vast. Tonight the starlight dripped and melted across the glass ceiling. I always thought Patchwork was too good to be true, was always waiting for the shoe to drop. Still, we'd almost had a year together before I messed it up.

That was better than anything I'd had before.

"Where is this magical place you've been hiding that can store our chap safely?" Romeo said, exaggerating his accent comically and twisting King's arm, eliciting a yelp.

"My parents' house."

Romeo dropped King like hot cookies.

Silence, while we tried to figure out if he was joking. He wanted me to stay with the people who'd been gunning for our destruction since day one?

King stood to his feet. "It's a win-win."

Romeo tapped his lip. "I don't think your definition of win matches...anyone's."

"It could be a cease-fire. A truce," he said. "I'll look after Tweetie, and you can look after Pip." He added it like it was an afterthought, but I was sure it was at the forefront of his mind. Pip, his girl. A name I'd only ever heard him use once, the night we met, and then never again. "You owe me, remember?" He pinned me with a dark, granite stare.

My mouth dropped. "You're serious?"

"Have you been, uh," Romeo made a drinking motion with his thumb and pinky.

"You know what happened," King continued. "If they think it will get to me, they'll let you." King ran away. Unlike us, he came from a relatively happy family, from parents who actually gave a shit. The tactics they used to get him back were messed up at best, but they did stem from *love*.

Not an orphan.

Not kicked out.

Not abandoned.

He had Christmas presents and happy, smiling siblings in his head.

"Daniel is already up there watching your sister." I tossed a hand in Daniel's direction, silently watching like usual. "Can't he just pop in on your girl?"

"Daniel has his hands full with my sister." A look crossed Daniel's face, almost like he'd been caught, but in an instant it was gone, and I was sure I'd misread it.

"Um. Yeah. Bizzy is..." He tugged his hood down, passing a hurried hand over his dreads that caused them to briefly lie flat before springing back into place.

King rubbed an eye. "Bizzy is a lot, but if you do this, he can stop. You'll be up there so he won't need to be."

"I don't mind! I mean..." Daniel rubbed the sole of his shoe into the floor. "I've got time. It's not a big deal."

Another moment passed, and it felt like everyone was actually considering this ridiculous proposal. "This is insane. I'm not going to stay with your parents. They're not going to let some random street kid stay in their house."

"You don't know my parents like I do."

"Rich people are all the same. They donate. They say the right things. But they're not going to let me inside their house, next to their valuables and their twelve-year-old daughter."

"Fifteen," Daniel corrected. "I mean, I think so..." He trailed off, scratching an ear.

"Whatever." Exasperation stung my tongue like hot peppers. Who cared how old she was? Obviously not the point.

"Remember how you fucking *owe me*?" King folded his arms, jaw clenched. I knew he wasn't just talking about how I'd asked him to watch Tweetie.

He'd taken the fall for me.

I hadn't come through on my end of the deal.

I exhaled, a sign of capitulation.

"Don't touch Pip. Don't even go near her. But you make sure nothing happens to her and I'll keep making sure nothing happens to Tweetie. Deal?"

I ground my jaw. "Deal."

NINE

POSER: SOMEONE WHO POSES AS A SKATER, OR
WHO TRIES TO BE SOMETHING THEY'RE NOT.

FLIP

Some time ago
Flip is 16, Tweetie is 11

I stopped short in the adjoining door between my bathroom
and bedroom—well, *King's* bedroom. My clothes were laid
out on the bed and a man futzed with them, putting the
finishing touches on what already looked perfect.

"Oh, sorry. I didn't—"

He stood straight, spinning like a dreidel to see me.
"Good *afternoon*, Mr. Li." He stressed the word, insinuating
that I slept too late. Again. "I see the bed was once again not
to your liking."

For what must have been the thousandth time since I'd
arrived, he raised a brow in the direction of the couch I'd
been crashing on in King's room. For what must have been
the thousandth time since I'd arrived, I ignored him.

"You can just call me Flip." He looked like I'd just asked
him to eat a live tarantula. "Or, Mr. Li works too..."

I thought living on the street was hard, but that was before I stepped through the gates of Heaven's Court—hulking wrought iron gates, the kind that separated people like me from people like Mr. and Mrs. Ayers.

There were so many rules I didn't know but was expected to follow. Don't sleep past a certain hour. Don't acknowledge certain people, like the maids, when they come in rooms.

It was the twilight zone. A cook. Maids. *Butlers.*

"I've washed and ironed your clothes, Mr. Li."

"Cool, man. Thanks."

His face was flat.

After putting on my *ironed* distressed jeans and the shirt I'd had since before Patchwork, I went to make myself lunch. The house was huge, and unlike Patchwork, you rarely saw anyone, save for the occasional maid who scurried away at the sight of me, whispering *Corrupt* under her breath.

The fridge slammed shut the moment I opened it, a surly, dour-faced man staring at me like I'd tried to open a bank vault. "Sir, what do you think you're doing?"

"Making a sandwich?"

"I'll make it for you. Pancetta with caramelized walnuts? Roast chicken with Waldorf salad? Jamón ibérico and Manchego cheese?"

Alright, now he's just making things up.

I blinked. "I was thinking like ham and cheese."

His jaw tightened, and when he spoke, he may as well have rolled his eyes. "I think I can manage that."

A few minutes later, sandwich in hand, I walked through the empty house. I'd seen his parents once, the night King and I interrupted their dinner. They loved King. It was obvious from the photos of him still lingering in every corner of the house, in the way they set the table for him as if he would walk in and join them any night.

And then, he did. Mrs. Ayers had dropped her glass to the floor and Mr. Ayers had run to embrace his son. They thought he'd come home, but instead he'd given them me. They accepted me like he knew they would, hoping it meant they were one step closer to a real reunion.

I learned their habits so I could avoid them: work until late, then parties every night. Weekends were spent on foolish things like donation drives for kids like me and more parties—fancier ones. I didn't think they used a tenth of their huge home, but it was always ready to be seen.

The only person besides the help I saw was Bizzy, King's sister. The first night she'd come to me, proclaiming me as her new little bro. We were the same age, but I quickly learned you don't argue with Bizzy.

"What does your real family think about you staying here? Aren't they mad?" My dad, who left before I was born? Or the mom who left her kid in the night to follow the latest douche to call her pretty? I think they're both okay with it.

"They're chill."

"Cool. My parents are the opposite of chill."

I couldn't imagine my presence made it any easier for them, a poor substitute for the real thing. I tried to make it simple by being a ghost. So when they were both in my bedroom, I paused, mouth mid-bite in the fanciest ham and cheese ever known to man.

"Nathan," Mr. Ayers said. He had gray eyes like his son, though his were a bit bluer and weathered with time. It was the middle of the day; they should be at work—or in Mrs. Ayers' case, helping kids like me get on the straight and narrow—not sitting on my *ironed* sheets. Yeah. Ironed. They did that here.

"You can call me Flip," I said, swallowing my bite of ham and cheese. At their faces I said, "Or, you know, Nate works too."

"It's been a while since you arrived, and we haven't seen you once. You don't come down for dinner. We're worried you feel unwelcome."

"Mr. Ayers—"

"Call me Tom," he interjected. "Think of me as a friend." Another bite, because I didn't know what to say. "The way we went about getting King to come home was wrong," Mr. Ayers continued.

A twitch of Mrs. Ayers' jaw, and Mr. Ayers grabbed her hand, squeezing. Mrs. Ayers had the same silky, coffee skin both her son and daughter inherited, though darker, with less milk and cream. It was her expression that reminded me the most of King. Bizzy was like her father, everything open and ready to be absorbed. Mrs. Ayers was closed.

"He'll be eighteen soon and it's out of our hands now, but we love him. We'll always love him, and there's always a place for him here—for him and *his friends*." He pinned me with a stare.

Uh huh. Sure. The people who branded us Corrupt were also completely chill with us kicking our feet up on their polished glass coffee tables?

I plastered a smile on my face. It had gotten a lot easier to smile over the years. In fact, it was almost easier to smile than it was to frown.

To let the real emotions out.

"Cool," I said. "I'll let him know."

Their shoulders fell, relieved, and they left.

I finished my sandwich, throat dry and scratchy. King didn't leave because his family was broken, so coming back wasn't that simple. And didn't that suck? There'd been a time when all I ever wanted was someplace like this, King had it, and had to leave.

Sandwich unfinished, I tossed it into the trash and went to do what put me here and put King out: watch his girl, make sure she was safe.

TWEETIE

Tweetie is 12, Flip is 17

King slammed the door shut so hard my sandwich fell from my hands. The bread split open, banana falling to the ground.

"What's the first thing you learned?" he demanded.

"I—I—" I stammered through my words. King was massive, mean, and had zero patience. I could tell not everyone was happy with me being here, but they at least tried to pretend—well, except the Patchwork Girls.

And King.

One more year had passed. One lonely, lonely year marked by irritated looks from every girl in the house and a seven o'clock bedtime. I hadn't gone to bed at seven since before I could remember, but like this room, it wasn't up for discussion.

His eyes narrowed and narrowed.

"Don't go in that room," I whispered. The bedroom beside mine was off limits. I knew that. It was the first rule they'd told me. Everyone else only had four while mine kept stacking up. But why? I was so curious. They didn't give me a reason just *off limits*.

"So are you dumb or just a brat?" His arm stretched

high above me, an iron cord keeping the door bolted shut. I couldn't cry in front of him, especially not now that a crowd had gathered. Penelope was among them and she was absolutely the worst Patchwork Girl. Despised me.

So I sprinted past them, down the stairs, before my tears could fall.

I heard Daniel say something to King in an admonishing tone, but I didn't stay to hear what. I ran until my lungs gave out, landing in the solarium.

Solarium.

It was a new word and my only safe place. Not many people came in here, so I'd sit alone and stare at the clouds, finding animals. Elephant. Unicorn. Dragon. I'd make up my own with the clouds. My favorite was the panda-roo. I stayed until the stars appeared above and my stomach growled.

I woke groggy, the stars blurry beneath the clouds. Flashing blue and red lights were blurry watercolors against the glass. I sat up straight, one side of my hair still flat from sleeping. I knew them immediately; in my short life I'd had too much interaction with police. King told me if I see the police, I hide—another rule.

I snuck outside, tiptoeing around the house.

"You've got the wrong guy. He's barely fifteen," I heard King growl. "Fifteen-year-olds don't fight for money." I craned my neck around the side, staying hidden and watching. Two cops plus King, Romeo, and Daniel.

"Don't try and play us, Ayers. He's been fighting for years. We know all about the Demon of Heaven Falls." The cops went to grab Daniel. Shy, sweet Daniel, the only one who cared to ask what my favorite food was, was a demon? I didn't believe it. "We can discuss all of it down at the station."

"Bullshit. Tell me what he's doin' wrong?" Romeo said. "It's just like boxin'."

I don't know why Daniel was about to be arrested, but it didn't matter. Something inside me said I had to help. He was family now, even if they didn't see me that way. So I did the only thing I could think of.

"Officer, please help!" I yelled, running into the front yard. The conversation came to a grinding halt, my gods not sure what I was up to, the officers wary.

Crap.

No—*shit.*

What do I say now? The officer's eyes narrowed with each moment I stayed mute.

"I..." I swallowed. "I'm lost?" *It's not a question!* "I am. I'm lost. I can't find my parents." I wobbled my lip, trying to be convincing.

The officer sized me up, then looked to Daniel, who he was just about to arrest.

"Please," I begged. "Please help me."

My gods shrugged their shoulders like *What can you do?*

The cops relented, warning Daniel that if it happened again there would be no discussion.

I led the cops on a wild goose chase before suddenly "realizing" where my parents lived, acting like I was some dumb, confused child.

They wanted to talk to my parents.

So I sprinted in the opposite direction, hoping they would let it go. I waited, hidden between two old Victorians, until they got in their car, driving away from Patchwork.

When I got back to Patchwork, everyone was waiting. It was one of the few times I could remember there being no music.

"Tweetie!" King jumped at the sight of me, and at first I was afraid. I thought I was going to be yelled at again, but then all three of them pulled me into a bear hug, King lifting me high above their heads.

Tweetie is 13, Flip is 18

I was late.

To meet a *boy*.

I had a hard time meeting boys. There was a strong reputation around Patchwork, specifically me, the only girl ever invited inside, but one boy was willing to take a chance on me.

"If he breaks your heart, I will break his face," King called out.

"Mmhmm," Romeo agreed, eyes never straying from a bottle of whiskey. Behind him, the murals he painted were bold, beautiful, and a little terrifying, but little yellow birds fluttered around them. A smile came to my lips, remembering the day they let me into their family. Officially.

"Have a great night." Daniel licked his thumb and wiped something off my face. "You should probably go because he's been outside staring at the house for thirty minutes."

See?

Reputation.

He was waiting for me on the perimeter, as if afraid to take one step inside. When he saw me, his face fell, but I thought it was just in my mind. Nerves.

But the night only got worse.

He barely paid attention to me.

It ended outside the mall with a blow to my chest. "I know we met at the park, but I didn't think you dressed like this all the time." I blinked. "I thought that was just your skating clothes, you know?"

I couldn't speak. I wished I could have. Defended myself or something, but shock had usurped my vocal cords.

I wore the clothes my Rebel Gods gave me. A lot of them were hand-me-downs or stuff they found at Goodwill. I knew I didn't dress "girly." I was *thankful* they took me in, clothed me, fed me, taught me. If it wasn't for them, I would be on the street.

I was sure if I told them I wanted different clothes, they would find them for me, but to be honest, I didn't want any. I liked these clothes. I liked the fit. It felt like *me*. I assumed, as fellow skaters, we were on the same page.

"I need someone prettier." He patted me on the shoulder.

I nodded dumbly again.

When I skated home, I was stunned—zombified. *I need someone prettier,* replaying on a loop. So I didn't notice the boy on the sidewalk. We collided, him falling flat on his ass, me flying off my board, landing opposite him.

FLIP

"Sorry," Tweetie said, reaching for her board. "I'm so sorry."

It had been almost three full years since I'd seen Tweetie. King and I didn't talk about her when we met at the gates to Heaven's Court. We didn't talk about how the reason we were standing next to the giant black metal was *because* of Tweetie. We just accepted it as our new norm.

So when she crashed into me one Saturday night in the town square, I nearly didn't recognize her.

Damn, I was happy to see she'd stuck with skating, though.

She was taller now, but not by much. A large, baby blue shirt hung to her knees, and there was sadness in her eyes.

Tears.

Why was she crying? A month had passed since the anniversary of the accident. A few leaves still clung to trees, and the ground was always wet with rain. Was it still on her mind? Maybe, like me, she never stopped thinking about it. It was her father, after all. She probably had good memories of him, and I'd ripped away any chance to form more.

"Sorry," she said again, righting her board and not giving me another look as she skated toward Patchwork, curving around the gothic, sweeping clock tower in the center of our square. I waited until she disappeared into the silver mist completely, and even longer still.

Tweetie was the only thing on my mind as I headed back to Heaven's Court. How often did she cry? How badly had I messed up her life? I couldn't get the image out of my head.

Bizzy was in her room, hunched over her desk, studying. Bizzy was wild, could give Romeo a run for his money. She was perpetually grounded—still didn't stop her from sneaking out every night. She was smart though, so smart schools didn't know what to do with her. For some reason she didn't want people to know it, either.

I tossed the bag of tampons she asked me to buy her on her desk.

She mumbled her thanks, focused on studying.

I lingered.

"So, you're kind of a kid," I said.

She sat up straight, a red indent above her eye from resting her face against a spiral notebook. "Excuse you, I'm older than you."

"We're the same age."

"I have a few months," she said with a satisfied smirk. "Also, see exhibit A—most definitely *not* kid-like." She gestured at her chest and when I grimaced, threw a studybook at me.

"Don't talk to me about *that*," I said. "You're like a sister to me."

She laughed. "My boobs are awesome. *Many* boys in my grade—"

I kicked off the door. "This was a mistake. I should've known to bring some cloves of garlic with me before I entered your lair." Cue another book, this one I ducked, before coming in to sit on the edge of her fluffy, plush ivory bed. Her room was fit for a fairytale princess with glittery pink curtains and a gauzy canopy bed. Funny, because if Bizzy was in a fairytale, she'd be the prince.

"What's bothering you, little bro?" She smiled, calling me by her affectionate nickname. I might never believe her parents loved me, but with the absence of Daniel, King, and Romeo, I needed *someone*. With King gone, she did too.

I rolled my eyes. "I'm worried about someone."

"Is that code for girl?" She waggled her eyebrows. I made a face at the thought and she threw up her hands. "Okay, Jesus. Never mind."

"It's a kid. Her parents are dead. I want..." To make everything go back to before. To give her her life back. To just fucking fix it. "She's helpless. I want to help her. I don't know what to do."

Bizzy kicked fuzzy socks up on her desk, gray eyes narrowing.

For a moment, she looked like King.

"I volunteer with kids who come from horrible situations, like, you can't even *imagine*." I bet I could. "They have nightmares, they cry—it's a mess."

"Is this supposed to be helping?"

She jutted out her sharp, mocha chin. "Though she be but little, she is fierce." At my even more confused face, Bizzy explained. "I like to think it means the smaller life tries to make you, the bigger you get. These kids are the strongest I know and they have the most beautiful souls. I think everyone in Heaven's Court could benefit from a little heartache." She stared off, like she was thinking of someone in particular.

"You come up with that?"

Her mouth dropped. "That's *Shakespeare.*"

"Ah, more useless dead guy quotes you learned at your fancy prep school."

"It's your school too," she countered. Technically. The Ayers put me in the same school as King. To save face, I think. I did horribly. Everyone had been learning shit like Latin since age three. I skipped all my classes. They donated money so I didn't flunk out.

"Nah," I said. "It requires a certain level of stupidity to go to that school." Her face scrunched in frustration, and she lunged for me. I put my hand to her forehead, keeping her at a distance as she swung.

"Bizzy—oh, I can come another time." Pip stopped short, a few feet behind me, face falling. My hand dropped and the air stilled. Three years I'd been watching, three years I was a reminder that King was there, but not speaking to her.

Pip was the easiest person to keep safe. Her parents did all the heavy lifting, keeping her sequestered like Rapunzel. She was only allowed to leave for school and to visit Bizzy. Since she didn't go past the gates of Heaven's Court, everyone knew not to come within a foot of her.

Lonely, I imagined.

Her room, at the top of the tallest turret of her home, almost made her look like Rapunzel too. Every time I watched her, she always stared back. Everyone in Heaven's Court knew me now, the delinquent friend of their runaway son. Phyllis "Pip" Westwood was no exception.

I cleared my throat. "I'll get going."

"Remember," Bizzy yelled at my back. "Just because she's small and young doesn't mean she can't handle whatever is thrown at her."

I was just to the stairs when an airy voice stopped me. "Wait!"

Pip had followed me, fingers inches from my shoulder. Instinctively I stepped back. I didn't know why I couldn't touch her, but I knew no one did. Some kind of disease. Bizzy didn't even touch her, and if you told Bizzy not to do something, she took that as a challenge.

Her face dropped, but only a little. "I know you tell Kingston about me," she whispered, quickly looking over her shoulder, then back at me.

Bizzy never called me out for watching Pip, so I had to assume Pip didn't want her to know about her relationship with King. I scratched my neck, not sure what to say.

"Just...give him this." She thrust her arm out and I scrambled against the wall. She tightened her jaw then set the paper down on the fine, plush carpet between us. She didn't wait for my response, spinning around to go join Bizzy.

A letter. A name scrawled on the ivory envelope in feminine loops.

Kingston.

The deal was to watch Pip and stay away from Patchwork. King didn't want to know any particulars about Pip, only wanted to know she was safe. He definitely didn't want to know about a letter, but...I picked up the silky envelope. Earlier today had been an accident, but now I had an excuse. I could see how badly I'd messed up Tweetie, and I could figure out how to fix it.

Later that night I opened the wrought iron gate and went to Patchwork for the first time in three years.

TWEETIE

"How was it?" Daniel yelled past the neck of a girl trying to eat his own as I headed to the stairs. There was a party going on like always. I got used to the constant sound of chaos, to the point that silence became louder. I craved the sound of glass crashing, of laughter and an overzealous guitar.

"Did he try anything funny?" King added.

"Show us the neck then," Romeo said. "Let's see those new hickeys." King threw something at Romeo and I tried not to let my face drop. I was pretty sure I was going to die before someone gave *me* a hickey.

"I had a great time," I lied, trying to keep my tears from them. They were family but they....they struggled with tears.

"What's wrong?" King asked, and all three of them

stood, the women they were with pushed aside. Patchwork Girls never warmed to me, and I could feel their irritation like poison ivy crawling up my arms.

The music stopped. I exhaled jaggedly. I didn't need the whole to-do today. Just once I wanted to be someone normal, not "the girl the music at Patchwork stopped for."

I ran up the stairs without another word.

"Get out!" I yelled, throwing a pillow at their three stunned faces moments later. I slammed the door then heard murmuring outside it, making out a few words.

Period?

No that was last week.

I groaned into my pillow.

"I can be upset without bleeding, you *cavemen*." A soft knock this time—Daniel. I sat up, prepared for him to enter. They had a routine. Daniel was the soft approach when King was coming on too strong and demanding. Romeo was the one who let me get away with stuff. Who gave me my first drink. Together they almost made a fully functioning parent

He creaked the door open. "Hey kid..."

"It didn't work out." I jumped to the chase. Silence. I knew Daniel wasn't buying it, but neither did he want to push me. I pulled my pillow to my chest, examining my room. Most definitely *not* girly.

"What happened?"

"I told you."

"It's just you and me. Anything you say stays between us."

I glared. How stupid did he think I was? I wouldn't fall for that again. After a minute of silence, King and Romeo appeared. Neither had the decency to look abashed at their lie. King pulled out my desk chair, sitting opposite me, staring holes into my soul and demanding I let him in.

I just couldn't. I was absolutely mortified, and I wasn't going to let them know I'd been rejected for being ugly.

Patchwork Girls were beautiful. Perfect lipstick and charcoal eyes. Silky hair you wanted to run your hands through. My hair was frizzy. My face round. My body, well, it was alright, because of the skateboarding. Everything else about me screamed mediocre.

"Why don't you ever fuck girls that look like me?"

King's eyes bugged as he coughed.

Romeo slapped him on the back. "Wanna rephrase that, luv?"

I sighed and threw my head back on the pillow. "Who is your ideal girl?"

"Tall. Leggy. With a penchant for blow jobs." I heard something fall into the wall, and I assumed they'd shoved Romeo. But the blow landed.

I rolled over onto my stomach, smashing my face into my pillow. "It's my fault for thinking anyone could see me as a girl."

They lingered. King inhaled, and I knew he wanted to say something, but one by one they filed out, shutting the door with a quiet *snick*.

FLIP

I stared at Tweetie's window, wondering if she was in turmoil at that very moment.

But what was I going to do? Crawl in her window? An

insane part of me thought maybe...but it wasn't like that would solve anything except maybe give her *more* nightmares.

"You need to encourage her to enter a competition," I said, sensing Daniel in the dark, still watching her window. Daniel lit a joint and handed it to me. I accepted. We were two shadows lit by an orange-red flame.

She pulled back dark curtains, staring out the window as if searching for something. Her face was losing the baby fat. I couldn't see her freckles now, but I'd seen them up close and personal when she'd collided with me.

Reckless.

I'd handed her off to King so I could stay away, but that was the problem, I couldn't. I needed to fix what I broke. She couldn't become like me, anchorless, unable to remember her last real smile.

Maybe if she entered a competition the sadness in her eyes would dissipate.

That had helped me.

"She writes about you in her diary," he said, exhaling smoke. *"Was Flip afraid when he skated?"* That wasn't so bad. *"I want Flip to be my first kiss."* Oh. *"If Flip could do it without parents, then so can I."* Shit. "And she still has night-mares, Flip. Every night."

I paused. "Why are you telling me this?"

"So you understand how dangerous your presence is." I tore my eyes from her window, finding Daniel's amber ones shadowed by a fiery cigarette. "You've become her hope. All she ever talks about is you, how you made something of yourself without parents and how cool that is."

My throat thickened.

"We want her to move past that day."

"So do I."

"Then why are you here?"

I pulled out the letter Pip gave me. Daniel lifted one inky and unimpressed brow. *Couldn't have given that to him at the gate?*

"It's important."

Still with that raised brow, he shoved it into his pocket.

The next morning I went to the park, dressed like the kidnapper from every suburban mom's nightmare. I had one mission: get Tweetie to compete. If she started competing, I could leave her alone.

She would find happiness like I did and I wouldn't have to worry I'd irrevocably damaged her life.

Tweetie was so fucking talented too. Hers was a once-in-a-generation talent.

She stared at the competition table for a few minutes, then left, resignation heavy in her shoulders.

Don't fucking do it.

Don't approach her.

Let her choose.

"You signing up?" I said. She startled at my voice, then gave my getup the once-over, before looking back at the table.

"Maybe...someday." It didn't sound very convincing. Her eyes flitted beyond the table to where a bunch of morons sat on the bowl making kissy faces at her.

I briefly wondered how wrong it would be to pummel a bunch of tweens.

No more wrong than any of the other shit I'd done.

"You look like you need someone beat up," I said.

"Are you offering?" I nodded, dead serious. She laughed, the mist and sorrow in her eyes fading. With a sigh, she got on her board, ready to head home. She was going to leave without signing up, without seriously considering how great she could be.

"Who's your favorite skater?" I called out.

"Flip," she said without hesitation. I paused, feeling the burn of the fire I was playing with.

Still... "Flip was your age when he entered a comp."

"And Flip was the greatest skater in history," she said like I was an idiot.

"You're just as good as him." *If not better.*

She stared at me blankly, but she'd paused. She wasn't going anywhere.

"Do you want to know a secret?" I asked, and she raised her shoulders. *Sure.* "Flip never thought he was any good. If you wait to do something until you're certain, or until someone tells you to do it, it'll be too late."

Tweetie folded her arms, eyes narrowing. "Who are you?"

TWEETIE

"Who are you?" I asked again when silence stretched. My bad date was only a few feet away, laughing at me with his friends, but suddenly I didn't so much care what they thought of me.

This mysterious boy was taller than me, with a hood up and a bandana around his mouth, sunglasses to block out an unseen sun. I stared at him, but his dark lenses only reflected my curious eyes.

I loved skateboarding, but enter a comp? I wasn't *that* good.

As if he sensed what I was thinking, he spoke again. "You are."

I focused on the table, a vision of myself I'd never dared to dream now implacable in my mind. When I looked back, the mysterious guy was gone.

When I got home, I was still thinking of him and competing. Could I really do it? Skating was my true love, I just never dreamed it would love me back.

When I opened my bedroom door, I dropped my board, a scream falling from my lips.

All three of my gods sprinted, at my back in an instant.

"What?"

"What?"

I turned to them, then back to my room. Romeo held a cucumber menacingly.

"What happened to my room?" It had been repainted mint green. A pink lava lamp sat on a new nightstand next to a canopy bed. On top of the nightstand were girly magazines intermixed with my skater ones. Polaroid photos hung by clothespins across my wall: me and King at the fair I made him take me to, me and Romeo at the concert where I'd participated in my first *consensual* mosh, me and Daniel getting ice cream, all of us outside Patchwork after a party. It was the perfect mix of skate and teenage girl.

And glow-in-the-dark stars dotted my ceiling.

"Shit, she's crying," Romeo said.

"We thought this would make you happy," King said, sounding distressed.

"I *am* happy." I spun to them. They wore equal looks of uncertainty mingled with concern. I laughed and punched Daniel softly. "You guys act tough, but you're a bunch of softies."

"I just broke someone's jaw this week," Romeo said, offended, but he smiled.

"You're the only one we'd ever do this shit for, Tweetie," King said, voice hard. I understood the warning: don't tell anybody.

I tried to keep my hot tears at bay, knowing how it made them feel. Everyone in this town was so afraid of Patchwork, but these boys were the only ones reapplying glue to my fractured heart.

As if sensing my trouble, Daniel wrapped his arm around my neck and rubbed my hair.

I glanced over my shoulder at my new room. "Can I make one request?" At once, all three of their eyes narrowed.

When I'd finished, I let them back into my room to show them.

"What's that?" King's voice was low, brows drawn.

Romeo laughed instantly, but it was a startled laugh. I couldn't place it, it was like he knew something I didn't. Daniel grimaced, almost like he wanted to protect me from something.

"What?" I said, though I knew exactly what he was talking about.

"*That*." King didn't wait for my response. He shoved me aside, heading straight for what I'd spent the last hour putting up: a poster of Flip. He was doing a vert trick and he looked *amazing*. I'd put it above my bed so I could stare at him every night.

"King wait!" I scrambled after him, grabbing his arms as he climbed on my bed.

"Explain this," King said as he peeled the edges I'd painstakingly cut out around Flip's flexed biceps and abs.

"What? He's the most famous skater in history." I

tugged at King, for some reason thinking of the mysterious boy at the park.

"Then why is he shirtless?" Daniel asked. I could hear the smirk in his voice.

"I don't know," I responded, maybe a little too quickly. Was my voice too high? "It came that way. Back off. King, stop!" I pleaded, and this time he listened.

Half the poster was peeled, King's entire body coiled. I waited, wondering if he would start up again. The air was so tense, and I didn't understand why.

King took a deep breath, then exhaled.

"It's *nothing*," I said, pushing him off my bed. He reluctantly let me shove him to the door, but stared beyond me, a haunted look in his eyes. I quickly shook it off when I slammed the door.

Flip would be my inspiration. My hope. My drive to do the impossible.

So what if he looked *really* good shirtless?

TEN

RIPPER: A REALLY GREAT SKATER.

TWEETIE
Present

My head pounded and screamed. I rolled over in bed, instantly regretting it when the sun streamed bright and brutal against my lids. The last thing I remembered was a party...I think? I would never get used to drinking.

And last night I drank way too much.

I struggled for bits and pieces of my memory when —*Flip*.

No, really—*Flip*. Or rather, a poster of him. It wasn't the same poster I'd spent hours cutting out as a young teenager. In this, Flip was upside down, only one wickedly flexed arm between the ramp and a valley of nothing. There was one similarity though: he was still shirtless.

Instinctively I grappled with my covers, pulling them up to my chin like his taunting paper eyes could see me.

I'll give you something to make you remember who you really belong to.

My hand flew to my neck, one still keeping the blankets tightly locked as the night came back in sunbursts.

The kiss. Oh my god. That *kiss*.

Just the memory made my throat ache. I'd never felt anything like it before. He'd practically worshipped me. The clutch on my neck faded, focusing on his dark eyes above me, tracing the spot like I could resurrect the feeling of his lips.

My door slammed open.

"Ouch..." I groaned, the brutal noise bringing me back to now.

"I made breakfast!" King sounded much too happy.

"I hate you," I mumbled.

"Get up, lazy—what's that?" His tone shifted noticeably, dropping twenty degrees in temperature. The last time it had sounded like that he'd tried ripping my poster off the ceiling.

I sat up straight and my brain flew into my skull. "What?" I tried to be nonchalant, look anywhere *but* the poster of Flip above me. I didn't put it there. It's not my fault he magically appeared sexy and shirtless above my head.

"*That.*" It took a minute for the room to stop spinning, for King to stop being two people, but then I saw. His eyes narrowed on my neck.

My hand flew to it. Had Flip really kissed me so hard he left a mark?

I would murder him.

Even if my body was warming slow and steady like a hot spring at the memory.

"I'll murder him." King spun on his heels. I stumbled out of bed, sheets tangling around my legs and dragging after me. I stopped at a mirror, needing the confirmation.

A small, reddish purple mark blazed bright and bold on my neck.

"King wait! It's not what it looks like." Or was it?

Air blew cool on my legs, and I realized I was only wearing a big shirt and underwear. I grasped the sheets, trying to cover my legs and not vomit at the same time.

"I don't know what happened."

"I know," King said firmly, rage staining his gray eyes red, darting left and right, looking for his target. I swayed, and instantly King was at my side, steadying me.

I pressed my head to his chest and his hand came to my head.

"Shocking." Flip's voice, low and silky smooth like the chocolate in his eyes, was heard behind me. My heart fluttered. I wanted to look at him. I tried to lift my head, but King's hand tightened on the back of it.

"Tweetie cries, and King comes to the rescue," Flip continued.

"Explain this," King bit out, thumb pressing into the mark on my neck.

"Easy," Flip said, voice lazy like a slow smile. "That's my work. Get used to it." My heart leapt at the same moment King dropped me.

Before I could even blink, King lunged for Flip. Flip met him in the middle, and their fists flew. King was bigger than Flip—he was bigger than almost everyone—but if Flip struggled, it didn't show.

My heart pounded painfully.

They were tearing one another apart.

Because of *me*.

This wasn't my first fistfight. Yelling wouldn't do anything; their ears were rushing with blood and adrenaline. I sprinted to the bathroom, filling up a glass with cold water.

"Stop!" I threw the water on them and it had the desired effect—sort of. They paused, a tangled mess of muscle and limbs, but their eyes gleamed like one pin drop would set them off.

Daniel came running into the hall. Shirtless and in boxer briefs, dreads mussed, I'd clearly woken him up. Two Patchwork Girls came stumbling after him, but they took one look at me, exchanged an eye roll, and wandered back into his room.

Daniel gave me a brief look then jumped between Flip and King. Daniel may have been the calmest, smallest God, but he was also the fiercest. Veins slid down his dark, lean arms and legs, evidence of his first love: street fighting. He had them split apart in no time.

"Are we really still doing this?" Daniel asked. Blood dripped from both King and Flip's noses, fists red, shirts slick with water. "What happened this time?" Daniel's eyes drifted to mine.

I pressed my hand against my neck, the kiss hot and real all over again. Suddenly it was too hot, even in the near-winter. My thighs achy, my throat dry.

I'll give you something to make you remember who you really belong to.

Flip shot me a knowing smirk.

I whipped my hand from my neck, looking anywhere but his burning, arrogant stare.

"It won't happen again," I said, trying to defuse the situation. "And nothing else happened. It was only this, King."

"You sure about that?" Flip said, drawing my eyes back.

Cue my heart stopping.

Did something else happen? Or was he talking about the poster?

Then Flip's eyes traveled me, down my body, scorching. I realized my legs were still bare and scrambled to cover as much as I could, but he still looked at me, at the thin white sheets like he could see through them.

Then his eyes met mine.

"What else did you do?"

Flip laughed. "Why are you so certain it was *me*?"

I felt myself turn beet red. King lunged and Daniel released Flip to use both hands to keep King away. My mind darted with the possibilities.

I scratched my head, thinking back to the party, to twenty-four hours ago.

What had I done?

"Did I say something embarrassing?" I asked Flip. He shook his head, smirk growing. "Did I..." I could barely imagine it, let alone get the words out. "Throw up on you?" It came out in a wince. Another shake of his head, another smirk.

I dragged a hand down my face.

It was torture, and Flip was enjoying it.

"You're an asshole," King said.

Flip redirected a bored glare to King. "I don't think an asshole would spend hours on top of her in bed." I coughed my startled breath. Flip shot me a grin before locking glares back with King. It took one heart-stopping second for me to realize what the hell he was talking about.

The poster.

How could he make something so innocuous sound so

lewd? I was frozen, my mouth parted in an explanation I couldn't give.

"Someone is going to start talking. Now." Daniel shot all three of us looks.

Flip and King stared at each other like lions about to fight over a carcass. Only Daniel's outstretched arms between them kept them from starting up again.

I didn't know where to begin explaining. It took everything I had not to press a hand to the hickey on my neck again.

"Why don't you ask sexual predator over here," King muttered.

Flip laughed. "You would know." And then King and Flip were at each other again, Daniel pressing palms to their chest.

"Everyone just shut. Up. You all were always so *awful* when it came to boys." Tears branded my lids, so I ran to my room and slammed my door before they fell. I slid down the door, wiped my eyes, and reached for a pillow off the bed to crush to my chest.

No one asked me if *I* wanted Flip to kiss me. It was just *decided* he shouldn't.

The past came spiraling back, full speed.

Sun shone bright, warming my knees and painting my walls in white gold. Flip's *new* poster was aglow. Part of me thought he was just trying to get under King's skin. I hadn't done anything last night. I hoped not, at least, because if I had done something, it was somehow worse than throwing up on him.

Through the wood, I heard muffled voices, and then someone tried to push in through the door. Reluctantly I stood up, allowing him entry. I sat on my bed as King pulled out my desk chair, sitting opposite me. It was almost like years ago, but King had never come to me with bloody hands over his dark jeans.

"You okay?"

"Peachy," I snapped. He raised a brow. "Sorry." Another minute passed.

"Is there something going between you and Flip?"

I don't know.

Maybe.

"No." It wasn't a lie, but it *felt* like one. It really felt like he knew me. When he watched me, it was like there were years of history between us I was forgetting.

"What's going on between *you* and Flip?" I countered.

"Long story." King scratched his nail. The morning leaked in through the cracks in the door. I could picture kids with their hands in cereal boxes, fighting over who got the toy at the bottom, while older kids slept off hangovers. I sighed, leaning against the wall.

We were two old friends having spotted each other at the train station. Everyone whirred around us, but we paused, unsure if we should get on our trains and go, or take the first step closer. We were never really good at talking out our feelings, but somehow we needed to have this conversation.

Why I left.

Why I came back.

"You said you would never come back," King said softly, so quietly I almost didn't hear it over the sound of a cereal fight starting up.

That hurt.

Maybe I said I wouldn't come back, but I always thought there would be a place for me.

I rubbed my heather bedspread. "We said a lot of things we didn't mean."

FLIP

Daniel stared holes through my skull.

I pressed a raw steak to my eye. "What?"

"You jacked up?" he asked. I narrowed my free eye. Daniel threw up his hands. "Why else would you act like a complete lunatic?"

"No one did an intervention when Romeo went off the deep end."

"He's touring with a pop star."

"Exactly."

Silence passed. Me on the floor, Daniel sitting backward on my desk chair, arms over the back.

"It was your idea in the first place, Flip."

It was *King's* idea, but I stood by and let it happen, which was just as bad, if not worse.

"Flip—"

"You had eight years with her! It's my turn." I was just as surprised by the escalation in my voice as he was. Didn't even realize I'd stood up. That I was breathing so hard my lungs hurt. That I gripped the steak until the red juices ran down my wrist.

Daniel's eyes widened. I never raised my voice. Didn't see the point in it.

But something about Tweetie had always turned me upside down.

I took a deep breath, sat back on the floor, against my bed.

I waved a hand, signaling I was fine for him to continue.

"Have you forgotten *why* you asked us to watch her? Have you forgotten what led to that?" No, I could never forget. It was scarred into every bone, every organ, every memory of my being.

Out my window, autumn was almost over, the conflagration atop the trees fading. It would soon be that ugly time just before winter when all the trees were naked and shivering and waiting to be covered in a blanket of snow.

"What are you going to tell her?" Daniel asked. "How does it figure into your happily ever after?" I picked at my nail.

Maybe I didn't have a happily ever after planned.

Maybe all I'd ever have was *now*.

I kept staring out my window until after he left. Until the sun set across the mahogany ramp. Even until Tweetie appeared, ready to shred.

Holy shit.

I scrambled to my feet, moved closer to my window to get a better look.

What did she call that move? I'd followed her career, seen the few underground VHS tapes she'd released, but it was nothing to the real thing.

She was magnetic.

She lifted up her shirt, exposing a tight stomach. Sweat beaded her abdomen, dripped between the valley of her muscles, down where I couldn't see. Then her eyes locked with mine and she dropped her shirt, startled. But she didn't look away.

I stifled my laugh. Years later and Tweetie still didn't

back down. If that wasn't hot as hell, I didn't know what was.

I leaned back against the bed, listening to her wheels grind like meditation.

Hours later, I'd pulled the blanket off the bed, fallen into a limbo of almost-sleep. When there was a knock on the door, I figured it was Daniel again, coming to try and convince me what I was doing was insane.

"Go away asshole."

The door pushed open slightly, and Tweetie stood in the frame. Tangerine softly flamed her dewy skin and she ducked to avoid the sun's glare. Her eyes narrowed, probably wanting to know why I was asleep on a makeshift bed on the floor when a perfectly good one was just above my head.

I sat up. Coughed. Scratched my neck. "I thought you were someone else."

She worked her jaw, hiding her eyes beneath the bill of her cap like she wasn't sure of her decision. "King told me to stay away."

Of course he did. "You should have listened."

I had a black eye from earlier and I assumed more bruises had formed since I'd last checked. She studied me without anger, and instead looking confused. Sitting in the dark of my room, the setting sun lighting a poster of *me* from the early eighties ablaze, it was like a time capsule.

I looked caught in the past.

I felt it.

She rubbed her neck. "Will you tell me what I did? Last night."

After I'd removed my lips from her neck, Tweetie had run, but later in the night, when the music was loud and the lights were low, she'd found me. Drunk.

Drunk Tweetie was always adorable, always handsy.

"Flip," she'd said, enunciating the P with too much air. "I used to have a crush on you. Why couldn't you be all cocky and broody in my life back then?" Then she fell forward so I had to catch her. "I had a poster of you...I miss it."

That's when I realized I liked honest Tweetie a hell of a lot more than handsy Tweetie.

Never thought that would happen.

I stood, ignoring the twinge at my ribs, and went to her.

"I was just fucking with you," I said. "You didn't do anything."

She eyed me like she wanted to press but changed the subject, gesturing to my black eye. "You knew that would happen."

I nodded.

"Why?" she whispered. "Why give me *this*"—she gestured to the mark on her neck—"when you know that it's just going to end up in a fistfight?" I didn't expect the question to make me pause and stumble over my words, but it was so innocent and so perfectly highlighted the knowledge disparity between us.

I'd fight to the death for her.

I'd give up everything—I *did* give up everything —for her.

A fistfight was nothing.

I thumbed the tears at her lids, ones I knew she would never let fall publicly. She swatted away my hand, so I slammed it on the wall by the side of her head. She inhaled sharply.

"You still don't understand the situation you're in." She found me through light, feathery lashes. "You belong to me. You've always belonged to me."

Her eyes widened. "But I don't even know you."

"This..." I grazed the small, reddish purple mark on her neck and her flesh rose to mine. "Is just the beginning." I let my thumb linger until the goose bumps dissipated, then walked to my bed, situating myself with one arm on my knee.

Eyes locked.

ELEVEN

STREET SKATEBOARDING: SKATING ON THE
STREETS.

FLIP

Tweetie was in the kitchen, face in my jar of *rousong,* when
I came down the next morning. I stopped on the stairs, still
obscured by the wall. She looked left and right like she was
doing something wrong, then pulled out some dried pork on
the tip of her finger. She sniffed, small nose twitching, then
with a cautious tongue, tasted it. Immediately her face
scrunched, and she shoved the jar back into the pantry.

I couldn't help my smile.

I was about to make myself known when another beat
me to the punch.

"Oh, Tweetie—" King stopped short in the kitchen. I
paused, stepping back up to where I'd been.

"King." Tweetie slammed the pantry shut. "Hi."

"Hey."

Tweetie pressed herself against the pantry. King stayed
frozen in the doorway, his eye eggplant in the morning sun.
Probably hurt like hell. I know mine did.

An awkward silence bloomed.

"Do you...?" Tweetie scratched the back of her neck. "Do you have time to talk?" Her voice had changed so much from the little girl I'd known. She'd been bright and happy and cute, like her eyes. Now every word was measured and even, steady and calming and smooth.

King looked over his shoulder. "It sounds like the kids are waking up." The kitchen was silent save for them.

"We can't just keep acting like nothing happened," Tweetie said. My jaw clenched. I knew something went down between them the night she left.

King ignored that, turning round the way he'd come.

Tweetie lifted off the pantry, arm reaching. "King—"

He left.

I stayed hidden by the shadows, watching her. She gripped the counter, breathing heavily. No tears though. I waited another minute, watching heavy breaths push her body up and down, then I cleared my throat loudly.

Her head sprang up, eyes bright and wide, shooting in my direction.

I walked to her and grabbed her hand wordlessly, tugged her toward the back door. We were almost there when she came to her senses and tried to yank it out of my grasp, but that only made me pull harder.

"Where are you taking me?" she asked, planting her heels into the hardwood. Tweetie was maybe a hundred pounds soaking wet, barely five foot four. It was futile.

"Where are we going?" she tried again.

"Outside."

"That. Doesn't. Answer. My. Question." She tugged on my grip, enunciating each word with a breath.

Outside the air was chilly, the sky white. Winter was

almost upon us. We were nearly to the front when Tweetie yanked herself away with a final, hard pull.

"Flip!" She almost fell over with the inertia. After a few hard breaths, she looked at me. I could tell when she'd focused on my bruises, because the anger in her eyes melted away.

I put a hand to my forehead, pretending to block out the sun so I could cover it. I'd wanted to distract her from whatever made her grip the sink so hard, not this. The way her eyes pinched and her brows creased ripped away layers.

Soft. Light.

I jolted at the sensation. Tweetie touched just beneath my eye, exploring the bruises. They were sorer from the night, from healing. My heart pounded with uncertainty, locked on her.

She focused hard on my cheek.

"Last night..." She lightly danced along the bruise.

"What about it?" I tried to be easy. I thought she would ask me a question I couldn't answer. Why am I so certain when I barely know her? What did I know that she didn't? Last night I'd once again let too much slip.

Her fingers paused. "Are you okay?"

"What?"

"I was worried about you," she said, hand falling to her side.

She was *worried* about me? She wanted to know if I was okay? I didn't know how to process that.

So of course I shrugged it off with a smile. "Never been better." Her brows furrowed; I could see the new questions forming.

I gripped her hand again, dragging her toward the front yard while changing the subject. "You need some fun. It's still a week before the comp, you shouldn't be so stressed."

I think she knew *I* knew that wasn't why she was so wound up, but she didn't call me out.

"There's only one thing that cures any ailment," I continued over my shoulder. "Skating." That had her perking up. Her entire face lit up.

"You're going to skate?" she asked, breathless.

"No," I clarified. "You are."

Her face fell. "Why won't you skate?"

I shrugged. "Not in the mood." She gave me a look, one I was beginning to understand meant she knew I was lying.

"Well, the ramp is the other way," she said.

"We're not going on the ramp, Tweetie." I coaxed her like a scared foal. "We're going to the streets."

Her eyes grew in excitement as I grabbed a bike lying in the front yard. She picked up her board. Together, we headed out.

It was like the first night I'd skated street with her, when she was just sixteen and I was much too old for her but fate had once again thrust us together. I'd been behind her then too as she skated down the median, sandwiched by angry cars. Her reckless laughter and brilliant skill, all I could focus on.

It was the first time I really felt the intensity of my affection.

It was no different now.

We stopped at an abandoned railroad, so old the tracks had been filled with pebbles to make a walkway. Tweetie kicked up her board, holding it beneath her arm. My touch came to her board without thought. The grainy, galactic black. For a brief, fleeting second the idea of skating didn't fill me with dread.

I wondered if Tweetie could sense it—my yearning—because she asked, "Wanna turn?"

I dropped my hand. "Let's take a break." I didn't wait to see how my response sat with her, settling against a bright turquoise and fuchsia steel beam. A moment or two later, she followed.

For a few minutes the only sound was our breathing, the chilly breeze. In the summer, the trees would bloom with bright blossoms. Now they were raw.

"Flip..." She took a breath. "When did you live at Patchwork? Why did you leave?" Here it was. I knew this was coming. I'd been preparing for this, rehearsing my answer over and over in my head.

"I never actually lived at Patchwork."

Her forehead wrinkled. "Then why do you have a bedroom?"

"The media was always hounding me, making up shit. Every house I ever had they found. I met King by coincidence. I paid him to let me store stuff there, things I didn't want anyone to find. I told him to keep it under wraps and not let anyone inside." I waited, staring into the distance, trying to be nonchalant.

Tweetie nodded, seeming to accept the answer, and I breathed.

"I'm sorry," she said. She's *sorry?* "It must have really sucked not having any privacy."

I'm such an asshole.

"You have so many tattoos," Tweetie said, shifting topics. I lifted my arm a fraction. Not compared to King or Romeo, but compared to someone like Daniel, yeah.

"What do they mean?" she asked.

"Gonna have to be more specific."

"This one." She touched the Chinese script inking my

forearm, the end visible past the sleeve of my hoodie. "What does it say?" Her finger traced the lines. While she studied the black ink, I studied her. The sun was setting on her face and, if it was possible, she was growing more beautiful.

My voice was rough. "It's Eastern philosophy you wouldn't understand, too difficult to translate into English."

Her eyes shot to mine, wide.

My mouth lifted slightly. "Penis." She slapped me and I laughed. Damn, it felt good to laugh for real. So many of my laughs were hollow.

"Is the one on your ribcage a dick joke too?" The one on my rib was for her. I'd gotten it the two years we were apart.

I settled back against a beam, watching the sun set through branches and beams. "Yeah."

A pause. "So technically you're covered in dicks."

I bit my lip on a laugh. "Yeah, okay." When I smiled with Tweetie, it wasn't hollow or plastered. It was real. And it was so goddamn refreshing.

We settled into another comfortable silence. That's what Tweetie was: comfort.

"Why don't you sleep in a bed?" she asked quietly. I caught her sunny image in my peripheral. How long had she been watching me?

I tensed, jaw tight. "Just don't."

"Does it have anything to do with your fear of spiders?" My brow furrowed. When had she seen that? "I noticed when we were in the closet."

I rubbed my lip, focusing on the pebbles ablaze in the sunset. Tweetie looked forward. She wasn't going to press. She wasn't going to force it out of me, but did she honestly want to get to know me?

"It's dumb," I said. Her head tilted slightly, not making

eye contact but giving me her full attention. "When my mom left, she told me to wait up and not to go to bed until she came back. She never came back. I dunno, it just stuck with me. As I got older, I stopped thinking about it."

Tweetie's eyes met mine, giving me her full attention.

"I was by myself for awhile and the house was filled with spiders. It was probably worse in my head, but it felt like they were everywhere. It didn't get any better when I went to the group home."

"On Angel's Wings?" she asked. I nodded. "Don't blame you," she whispered. "That place is hell. One of the caretakers rapped my hands with a ruler and stole my only picture of my dad when I kept my elbows on the table at dinner, telling me I could have it back when I learned manners." Half the people at Patchwork had been at that group home at one time or another.

No one stayed long.

"I didn't know you also stayed there," she said. She shifted, and our thighs barely touched, our shins and shoes still apart. Tweetie kept her legs straight like she was nervous to touch me completely.

I watched her sneakers, waiting for her to fall into me.

"I have one good childhood memory," I said. "My grandma. She lived in Taiwan but came to visit when I was a kid before she died." On my mother's side. I don't know shit about my father's family.

Her head swiveled to mine, but I couldn't decipher what was in those blue eyes. I quickly looked away. I'd shared too much.

Way too much.

"Your competition is coming up," I said. "You excited?"

She paused, then said, "Yeah."

Our legs in the sunset made a painting, the white, rubbery tip of her sneaker inching closer to me.

I had the urge to drop my shoes the rest of the way.

Instead I said, "Tell me about your first one."

Her face dropped. "It was like all of them. I did everything right. I was better than all of them. And I still lost."

"The good parts," I clarified. The sun dropped, the sky lingering in a dusky afterglow, the heat gradually disappearing with it. Her legs finally fell to mine, jeans warm in the dark. Tweetie looked away and hummed to herself like nothing happened.

Inside I triumphed.

"I remember someone from that day," she said. "He was dressed in all black. He was the same guy who told me to sign up. It felt like he was a guardian angel."

She *saw* me?

I coughed. "Anything else?"

"A boy called the house. That was also the last time a boy ever called the house. I vividly remember King's growl, asking my *honors math* buddy who the fuck gave him our number. I jumped for the phone, but King was too tall."

I smiled.

"Once the guys figured out it was for me, they all had so much fun keeping the phone from me and grilling him at the same time, sounding mean and scary, trying to live up to the Patchwork name—" She stopped speaking when I shrugged out of my hoodie and put it on her legs. Tweetie looked at the dark gray fabric, mouth frozen.

"What happened?" I prompted.

"He—he hung up."

She moved some of the jacket over to my legs, patting it into place. The simple action had my chest thumping.

"So...boys at school," I said in an awkward segue, trying

to lead into what I really wanted to know. She scrunched her face at me. "Did you have a lot of friends before Patchwork?"

Tweetie laughed. "I never fit in with anyone in school, even before the accident. The boys didn't want to play with me, the girls didn't want to play with me. There was only one boy who ever did."

One boy.

Me.

My breath seized. This was why getting to know Tweetie was so damn dangerous. I should have recognized the warning signs and quit while I still had oxygen, but I just wanted to dive deeper.

"What about you?" she asked

"Me?"

"What was school like for you?"

"I went to a fancy-ass boarding school. It was shit."

"You went to a fancy boarding school?" Her brows caved. "How?"

Shit. *Shit shit shit.*

"I...had another family. For a brief period of time."

"Oh." I could see her trying to work the puzzle out. "Who—"

I stood up quickly, cutting her off. "It's getting cold." I gave her my hand and a smile. "Let's warm each other up."

———

We skated for hours, until we wound up a few houses from Patchwork, between the abandoned Victorians that made up the ironically named Patchwork Court, cloaked in shadows.

"Play a game with me," Tweetie said.

"A game?"

"See who does it better." She rode into the street and did a trick. *My* trick, the one I'd invented years ago that put me on the map. When she finished, she rode back, stopping a few inches from me, a smile on her face.

"Your turn."

I shrugged. "Pass." But Tweetie captured my arm, dragged and pulled me to the board.

"Come on, Flip," she said, laughing. I couldn't blame her, it was exactly what I'd done earlier.

She had no idea the pain.

I missed it. I missed skating so much it was like a knife that never left my side.

"Think you'll lose to a girl?" She laughed. "Afraid I did it better?" In any other situation, I'd be fucking ecstatic to have Tweetie on me like this. Hands all over me, pushing with all her body to get me on the board.

The past crawled inside my head like venom and hot peppers.

"Let it fucking go!" My yell bounced off the empty Victorians. Tweetie froze, then jumped off me.

A loaded, stiff silence followed, only the distant sound of Patchwork's party leaking into the darkness.

The look on her face was scalding.

"Shit." I tore off my hat, rubbed a hand through my dark brown waves. "I'm sorry, Tweetie."

"It's my fault." She wouldn't look at me. "I pushed." More silence. More Tweetie not looking at me.

I needed to fix this.

"You're right," I said with a smile. "Didn't want to lose to a girl."

We walked back to Patchwork in silence.

When we reached the house, neither of us made a move

to go up the steps, but we didn't talk, either. We stood by the tree in the street. Her with one foot on her board, balancing. Me with the bike.

"So I lied before," Tweetie said. I raised a brow. "I'm not excited about my competition. I'm afraid. No, I'm terrified."

I didn't say anything.

"Afraid of not achieving my dreams. Afraid it has nothing to do with being a girl and everything to do with my talent."

More silence.

"Were you ever afraid?" she asked. It was loaded with so much more. In the way she looked at me, once again tearing apart my layers. She wanted to know what happened before.

"At your competitions, that is," she added.

I'm terrified.

Worried I'll never skate again.

The shaky wall I'd just reconstructed was breaking.

I laughed. "Me? I'm the best in the fucking world."

She rolled her eyes. "I don't know why I bother." She hopped on her board, ready to leave. I should've taken the out I'd made for myself, but I grabbed her by the elbow, pulled us beneath the tree. Tweetie fell off the skateboard and it skidded into the street. Her hoodie capsized beneath my fingers to reveal her small arm. Her breath pulled, eyes grew, waiting for my next move.

"I was mad."

I pressed her against the trunk, an arm above her head, keeping her pinned.

"Mad I was on the streets. Mad that people looked at me and made opinions and judgments before they knew me. Mad I had to work for what other people were given.

"And then I became the first. Suddenly that was a huge

fucking deal. The same people who'd told me I couldn't have anything because there'd never been anyone like me were now eager to give me everything because I was the *first*.

"Suddenly everyone was rooting for me. People who didn't give a shit about me when I was nothing were telling me I couldn't fail." I paused. "It will happen to you too."

Her eyes popped. "That didn't scare you?"

It should have.

I shook my head slowly.

"I have fears now, Tweetie, but back then I was too naive—too lucky—to be anything but angry." Her forehead creased, slowly trying to process what that meant. I pushed her farther against the tree, bodies pressed, and flipped my hat around so there was nothing keeping me from her.

Our lips so close to touching.

TWEETIE

I was certain Flip was going to kiss me.

What scared me most was I thought I would let him. Break my rules. All my life I'd been stuck in the middle, wanting to be wanted, but not sure how I could be when boys had always made it clear I wasn't pretty enough.

Flip made me feel like I could have both.

I could be myself *and* be wanted.

"Don't do this with other guys," he said again. His breath was on my lips, my heartbeat hazy—and he wasn't even touching me.

"Hmm?" He was blurry, the only clear thing the intensity in his eyes.

He smiled, crooked and lazy. Flip was the hottest man I'd ever laid eyes on, and each time I did, I was stunned anew. His posters didn't do him justice. In print he was dulled, but in person he was *fire*, with a heat that made my thighs ache. Tall but not too tall, with tousled, just-slept-in hair. Slight black eyes that said he didn't give a fuck about anything, but a smile that said he'd fuck you blind.

Still, the smile was a broken one.

Like after he'd tried to play off what happened when I'd pushed him to skate.

He acted so happy all the time, but happy people don't get black eyes. They don't brood in their room for hours beneath posters of their past. They don't sleep on the floor next to a perfectly good bed.

They don't give up something that makes their heart beat.

There was so much in his eyes that I wanted to understand, bruised like the skin beneath them, but not green and healing. Just bruised. Black. Lonely.

He leaned closer, elbow above me bent, forcing me to press my back even harder against the bark. So close the breeze made our clothes kiss.

"This..." His knuckles grazed my cheeks, and a flurry of goose bumps rose all across my body. "Is only for me."

My lips parted, still not understanding.

"Your fears," he said. "You're so damn fearless, Tweetie. So when you're afraid, only tell me. Hide behind me, let me fight what you can't. Give in to me. I promise I'll do a good job of it."

My breath rushed out of me. Flip studied me for a long, scorching second. Then he stepped back.

I saw everything through throbbing heartbeats. Flip grabbing his bike. *Beat.* Riding back to Patchwork. *Beat.* Never looking back at me. *Beat.*

I slid down the tree, legs weak.

TWELVE

SPEED WOBBLE: WHEN THE SKATEBOARD BECOMES UNSTABLE, LEADING TO LOSS OF CONTROL.

TWEETIE

I paused when I heard Flip's voice. The solarium door was open and cold autumn air drifted inside. Light leaked through the windows, and so did Flip's voice, as well as another's: Bacon.

"I still don't think I'm good enough," Bacon said.

I inched closer to get a better view. Bacon was on a skateboard in the center of the ramp. Helmet too tight on his round face, skateboard dipping in the middle.

My comp was only a few days away, but I couldn't stop thinking about Flip. His lips on my skin or how he'd looked at me last night. Not burning like the night he kissed me, but unyielding. Nothing would get in the way of what he wanted, and I felt what he wanted was...me.

I was still hot and itchy with thoughts of him, so I was going to do what I always did—skate.

So of course he was out there.

Flip held Bacon by the shoulders. "Everyone deserves a chance to learn. I had people try and keep me out of the park when I was a kid. Thought only a specific type of person should be a skater." He adjusted Bacon's helmet. "They were idiots. Weren't real skaters. That's not what skating is about."

My heart grew as I listened to Flip. I knew it was wrong and I should make myself known, but I desperately wanted to know more of Flip.

Last night wasn't enough. It was like being given a crumb of delicious cake.

He'd lived in the same orphanage, he'd felt the same anger, but Flip didn't meet my checklist, wasn't the boy I'd spent two years trying to find. I was finding the more I got to know him, though, the less I cared.

Flip held his hand out to Bacon, and then it was back to teaching. Bacon kept falling off the board, making silly, stupid mistakes, but Flip was patient. *So* patient. So kind. The greatest skater in the world, many magazines had said, helping someone who didn't know his left foot from his right.

They took a break.

"Why did you stop skating?" Bacon asked.

My heart thumped. I *really* wanted to know this.

"Tweetie?"

I spun on a gasp. Daniel. Flip and Bacon's heads lifted in unison, following Daniel's voice. Flip's inky brow arched, and his grin grew slow and satisfied.

Caught.

"Oh, hey..." I slapped my thigh, coming out from behind the iron and glass door. "Hey. I was just, um..." *Was what? Why was I hiding? Screw it, I'm going to gloss over it, hope no one notices.*

"Competition coming up," I said. "Gonna...you know... do the thing. With the board. And the ramp. And the, uh..." I dropped my board, buckling my helmet. "Yep, uh huh."

Daniel gave me a look like *are you alright?*

Flip's grin grew until his dimples popped, eyes glittering.

Please god, let him go inside.

Stop looking at me with that self-satisfied smirk.

I stared holes into the starry gray grip of my board.

"I think we oughta head inside, let Tweetie practice in peace, Bacon. She must be dying to get on the ramp. She just got here, after all." It was like he'd swallowed a thousand canaries. I ground my jaw, staring at the ground until he, Daniel, and Bacon went inside.

I skated until my thighs screamed and lungs burned, trying to punish the thoughts of him away with intense practice. When I was finished, I was sweaty and in desperate need of a shower. But still I thought about him.

I should have heard the water running or registered how steamy the bathroom was. Growing up, we had a rule: always lock the bathroom. It was obvious, but after one traumatic interaction between me and Romeo, it became iron-clad. So when the bathroom was unlocked, I didn't think twice.

And that's when I saw Flip.

Naked.

I stared.

I stared much longer than I should have. His perfectly toned, almond colored butt with dimples digging into the muscles. His thighs. Oh my god, his thighs. Slim, yet muscular and defined and—

He turned around.

Instead of running like I should have, my eyes dropped, and I stared harder.

He toweled his hair like this was no big deal. "Hey Tweetie, sleep well?"

I blinked. "You're naked." He wasn't like I imagined him—he was *better*. So much better.

"I've been meaning to ask, I saw you a few days ago doing a trick. I've never seen it before." My eyes flashed up to his, then back down, then up again. "What do you call it?"

"You're naked and asking me about my skateboarding." He slowly wrapped a towel around his waist, and that's when I realized I'd been absolutely violating him.

"And you haven't answered any of my questions. Guess this makes us even for your bedroom though." My eyes shot to his. One arched brow, a slight smirk hooking the right side of his mouth.

"I...uh..." I looked around the bathroom for an excuse.

"Where the fuck are your clothes?" I jumped at Daniel's voice.

"Ask Tweetie." He grinned, the dimple on his cheek feathering.

My mouth dropped.

"It's not what it looks like." I immediately backtracked, shooting Flip a look. Why was he always starting shit? At least it wasn't King.

"Daniel—" I tried to explain again.

"Tweetie, *out*."

His voice was hard—he *never* talked to me like that. I opened my mouth to fight back, but he gripped my elbow, shoving me behind his back, and slamming the door in my face.

My shoulders fell, the bathroom door mocking me with

its various poop puns scrawled across it in anything from brilliant, neon calligraphy to terrible handwritten sharpie.

Mary Poopins.

The Log Father.

Fartacus.

A part of me wanted to tear it open; instead I released my frustration in a long sigh. Then I tiptoed down the hall, past my room, to the one that read *Fuck Off.* I pushed it open and headed straight for his closet.

I was so sick of Flip getting the best of me.

Making me blush and lose control.

Almost, maybe kissing me, then leaving me weak-kneed and wanting.

I rummaged through his clothes, searching for the shirt I'd guessed was his favorite by how often he wore it, the one I'd seen the very first night I'd come back: his D.A.R.E. tee. It fit him way too well and—there I went again, blushing.

I had a reputation of being shy. The one magazine that interviewed me called me *sweet* which, honestly, still bugs me. You wouldn't call a guy skater sweet, but it wasn't a hill I wanted to die on, I had bigger fish to fry.

I'm non-confrontational, not *sweet*. If I can avoid a fight, I will. I don't think that's a bad thing.

Unfortunately, being a girl in this industry, you have to fight. For a place in the competitions. For equal pay. Every day I learned of a new fight, something the guys just *had* and I *had to fight* for.

I didn't know why Flip kept pressing my buttons and starting fights. Since I'd arrived at Patchwork, we were constantly colliding. I couldn't help but think there was something in his burnt toffee eyes searching for *something*.

Occasionally, like the previous night, I got glimpses of him without all the smirks. Maybe there was something deeper, or maybe he just thought what that interviewer at the magazine thought. *She's sweet. It'll be easy to get in her pants.* It was the only reason that douche even interviewed me.

But my life had been one battle after the next.

"Aha!" I said aloud, finding the shirt. I quickly grabbed it and exited. No one would suspect it wasn't mine. I dressed like the guys.

But Flip—he would notice.

And that's all that mattered.

FLIP

Daniel. "What are you doing?"

I tugged on a pair of jeans. "Trying to put on pants."

"What are you doing *here*? With her?" It was a happy fucking accident. Remind me never to lock the door again. Pants still undone, I rubbed my temple. I couldn't lie to Daniel, couldn't fuck around with him.

"It was an accident, dude."

Daniel released a breath, dropped his arms. The steam from my shower was evaporating, leaving the room cold and wet.

"I'm worried about her, Flip," he said. "What are you going to do if she finds out?"

"She forgave King." It fell out uselessly like all the other hopes I had in life. Hope my dad would come back. Hope my mom would get clean, not leave me. Hope I'd skate again. Hope I'd have somewhere to belong, forever.

"Is that all that matters? Forgiveness?" *What about what*

it will do to her? Went unsaid but was nevertheless apparent in his concerned, soulful eyes. "King wasn't the dream that kept her going during her nightmares. What's going to happen when she learns her orphan idol is the one who *orphaned her?*"

Then Daniel left. Left me to make a decision we both knew I already should have made. It attached to my already pretty heavy shame and doubt.

Yesterday had been fucking amazing. I could count on my hand the number of times I'd gotten to experience Tweetie real and raw.

But the reality was in Daniel's words, in the lies I had to apply to the truths she'd given freely. Why I couldn't skate, why I'd been at Patchwork.

I went downstairs, hoping to lose myself in the solarium. When we'd first moved in it was my safe haven. I'd grown up just a few blocks from Patchwork, but the difference a few blocks could make was stark. I never had a solarium, I had broken cupboards and bad carpet.

I used to love making up new animals in the clouds.

Silly, but fun.

But, when I came downstairs, *TWEETIE* was everywhere. On handwritten posters, name bold in glitter. On the ground, springy blond curls veiling her heart-shaped face, encircled by the four boys helping her make signs for her competition.

I froze, slowly backing up.

"Flip!" Bacon called for me. *Shit. Spotted.* He waved for me to come help just as Tweetie looked up from the floor, catching my stare. She was in another baggy shirt, a halo of curls under a damn baseball cap. Did she know how adorable it was when she tugged on the bill while biting her lip?

Wait—that's *my* shirt.

"He's probably busy," Tweetie said, blue eyes flickering from me to her poster. *Very busy.* Too busy to wonder why she was in my shirt. Too busy to *like* that she was in my shirt. Too busy with the reality Daniel had reminded me of.

I smiled. "Not at all."

Eyes still on Tweetie, I sat beside her and grabbed a pen. Clouds blasted through the glass above us, graffiti like stained glass on the windows.

"Nice shirt," I said. She swallowed, hard, and chewed her bottom lip. I forgot everything then, watching her white front teeth prick her rosy bottom lip.

Eyes never straying from her poster, she said, "I actually think it's kind of hideous." She smiled, and I couldn't help but return it, especially when her blue eyes shyly met mine.

"Asshole!" Both our heads jerked up at Sparky yelling at Pants.

"We're not going to let you play if you keep insisting." Sparky, Bacon, and Pants had stopped drawing, now in an arguing match over something that wasn't immediately clear.

"But you owe me!" Pants shot back.

Remember how you fucking owe me?

The present dissolved and swirled away like I was caught in a watercolor blizzard. Then it was me and King, Daniel, Romeo in this room, years ago.

The pen fell.

I was on my feet.

Saying things I should have said then. "Don't be fucking stupid! You only have each other. Who are you going to turn to? Who's going to have your back? You think it'll be easy going back to before because you've always been alone —" I stopped, closed my mouth as if I'd swallowed a fly.

You could hear a pin drop.

"I mean..." Sparky broke the silence. "I guess we can let Pants be Dungeon Master, but he's just so bad at it."

The tall, gangly kid's mouth dropped in indignation, his hand to his heart. "It's called being realistic."

"We always end up dead! In all of your campaigns..." Their conversation trailed off, as I realized what I'd done. Tweetie watched me intently.

"Right, yeah." I slowly sat back down. "You should do that." I went back to drawing, focusing on some terrible, lopsided skateboard.

"Are you okay?" Tweetie whispered.

I grinned. "Great." I could feel her watching me, blue eyes headlights in the fog. Bright, searching, coming right at me.

I dropped the pen. I should never have sat down.

"Flip." She touched my elbow from the floor, fingers light like even she wasn't sure what she was doing. "Will you just be real with me for a minute?"

I laughed. "This is me. I'm real. All the time." The way her big eyes narrowed, I knew she saw through me, through my hollow laugh.

I stepped back. Stupidly, foolishly, I missed the touch.

"Flip—" She reached out for me again, but I made sure to quicken my pace, leaving the solarium as she called after me. I headed outside, but first, I made sure to grab a bottle of tequila from the kitchen.

TWEETIE

I woke to the sound of grinding wheels. It was three forty-five in the morning, and someone was skateboarding. I climbed over my desk, unlatching my window to see who was using the ramp at this hour.

Flip.

I paused, arm outstretched. He'd told me over and over that he was done skating. Yet it was clearly him. In a short-sleeved shirt despite the cold, milk chocolate hair inky in the night. He ground the edge of the ramp and I got a flash of his board's deck—bright pink. My grip slipped.

Was that my board?

I didn't know anyone else who had a bright pink deck at Patchwork. Flip, who apparently didn't skate anymore, was skating with *my* board.

Anger hit me first. Who gave him permission? But as I leaned on my sill, it dissipated. I once got to see a video of him skating back in his heyday. Aggressive. Untamed. Wild and unafraid. He did moves no one had ever seen or tried since, cracking through the air and imprinting on my memory.

Watching him now, the sadness was so stark, like picking up glass with my bare hands.

I don't know how long I stayed at the window, seconds blurring into minutes. The love he had was glaring. So palpable it hurt. Yearning dripped from his shoulders.

There was a melancholy beauty to him, like I'd stumbled upon a lumbering beast.

Pearly moonlight was chiffon on his olive skin. In low-riding tight gray jeans and checkered shoes that had seen many days, I could've watched him for hours. *I'm always real*, he'd said, but that was such a lie. Earlier in the day something had messed him up, bad. I saw it in his eyes then and I saw it now. But *what*?

Seeing him skate, it felt like I was getting closer to the real him.

He glanced my way, then did a double take when he saw me. Tripped over my board, slamming hard into the wood. Slowly he stood, our eyes locked.

We stared. Him up from the ramp's valley, me down at him from my window. My gauzy curtains fell on my head, but I didn't move. Stuck on him.

Why?

Why give up something you love so much?

Suddenly, he kicked up the skateboard, put it under his arm, and walked inside.

I breathed, needing to let out the steam building inside my lungs.

I'd just shut my window and gotten my heart under control when there was a knock at my door. I jumped, smacking things askew on my desk like a scared cat.

"It's not..." It couldn't be him, right? I was rigid, staring at my door. Heartbeat racing, hands gripping the desk.

I was still in *his* shirt. I meant to take it off but then I'd lain down. Let the feel of it lull me to sleep.

A moment passed, and I was sure I'd imagined it. There *was* a party going on, after all. I could hear the reckless music, the occasional crash of something shattering to the floor.

I righted everything on my desk, putting pens and pencils back, stacking magazines in their place.

There was another knock. My hand froze on my Walkman, looking over my shoulder as if a bogeyman was going to get me.

I opened my door a crack. Flip was outside, board under his arm. An indecently hot sheen of sweat on his neck that only highlighted the cording muscle.

If anyone else had taken my board I'd be pissed, but somehow he was so sexy holding it, the line in his forearm flexing. Like he *should* be holding it. I bit my lip and opened the door all the way. He looked me up and down, practically licking his gaze over me. There were no sheets to hide my bare legs this time. I tugged at the hem of his shirt, then paused, hoping he didn't notice.

Of *course* he noticed.

His cheek feathered slightly. "Sleep well?" It was said with the same cocksure attitude I'd become accustomed to, like he already knew the answer, but it was missing the lightness.

Some kind of heaviness weighed on his eyes, held his shoulders down. It was the same I'd seen while he'd skated. I wondered what happened between now and a few hours before to make him so different than the Flip I'd come to know. His smile was hollow. A jack-o-lantern not even bothering to put in a candle.

He always acted like everything and everyone was a game, life just another trick to master and tame.

But I was beginning to think that was an act.

I wanted to ask if he was okay. I'd wanted to ask earlier but chickened out.

"What are you doing?" I asked instead.

"Returning your board."

"Keep it," I said instantly. *Anything, so long as you keep skating.* "You're the best skater in the world. I don't know why you aren't skating, but..." I trailed off, feeling silly. "But I know when I feel broken, this is the only thing that fixes me." I *know* he felt that way too, why else would he have suggested it the other day?

Flip handed it to me, so I took it.

But then he held on to it, so we both grasped it. My brows drew as I waited for him to let go. The longer he waited, the more I wondered if this was the moment.

I had no right to ask.

None at all.

Yet...

"Why don't you skate anymore?" It was barely above a whisper. If he was bothered by my question, I couldn't tell. I couldn't tell anything by his face, actually. His always smiling, always in on some kind of joke face was completely blank, like the smooth surface of untouched vanilla coffee.

"If you answer my question," he said. "I know you struggle with that." My cheeks flamed, remembering earlier in the morning, well, yesterday morning now.

"Sure," I squeaked.

"It's not an interesting story. Guy gets big. Guy can't handle the pressure. Guy flames out. The end." I didn't believe that. But he didn't give me a chance to counter, immediately saying: "Now answer my question."

"Anything."

He tugged me an inch closer. "Why did you *start* skating, Tweetie?"

I thought it was going to be something hard. It caught me off guard. I could recite the answer in my sleep.

"You," I said, but instantly clarified, hopefully to ward off sounding weird. "I mean, I didn't know it was you at first. My dad had your first magazine and read it to me. You said skateboarding was an escape. You can go faster than cars. You can *fly.* If you go hard enough, nothing can get you. I wanted that. Someplace to go where no one could get to me. My parents couldn't find me. The world couldn't find me. It sounded magical when I was a kid. I love my dad but he...had his issues."

I wished he would give me anything. Full, pink lips straight, almond eyes black and stoic.

"Does that, um, answer your question?"

There was a split second where his face cracked, his brows caved.

Then he yanked the board, drawing me so close that the only separation between us was the wood, the grainy grip. I could feel the heat of his breath. See the veins throb beneath his forearm, snaking down to his strong hands.

"Take it off."

"E-Excuse me?" My hard exterior vanished into a puddle. He dragged that unfeeling lower lip down with his teeth, filling it with sensual purpose. All the color drained into my cheeks.

The only thing between us was my board. Not enough space from his smoldering eyes, looking down at me from his nose like he couldn't decide if he wanted to eat me or save me for later.

"That shirt doesn't belong to you." He tightened his grip. "Take it off." I tried to step back, but he held my fingers over the skateboard like a vise. I scoffed. Anything to try and regain composure.

My plan was epically backfiring.

The whole idea when I took his shirt was to take back power, but here he was, siphoning it.

So I dropped the board and he released me. Grabbed the hem of his shirt and tore it over my head. While inside I was shaking, shivering. My heart pounding louder than the punk outside.

I acted like it was nothing.

Like I was always in a sports bra and tiny sleep shorts, even though he was the first to ever see me this way.

I thrust it out to him with one hand, eyes on the ground haughtily.

"Happy?"

One second...two...he stared, his amusement at my

discomfort growing. But more than that, something reckless and untamed grew in his silence. If I didn't know better...*pain*. He was out of control himself.

Dust floated in the air like star shavings. I heard murmurs just outside my room and sweat grew on my chest. Anyone could walk by any moment. King going to bed upstairs. Daniel to his room across the hall. One of the boys to the bathroom.

My false confidence broke, the crack spreading like a spider web as I looked at him.

I wished I hadn't.

Wished I hadn't seen the way he was watching me. His hand hadn't strayed from its position, frozen mid-grab after I'd handed the shirt to him. His entire being was frozen— but his eyes were hot, fiery, blazing. A conflagration of action, intent, demanding I know what his body refused to act on.

In his eyes I saw the war. A battle to the death between what he showed the world and what lay beneath the flames.

My lips parted.

My breath caught.

He dropped the shirt at my feet. "I always wondered what you looked like under all those clothes."

THIRTEEN

THRASH: AN AGGRESSIVE STYLE OF
SKATEBOARDING.

FLIP

"You're skating again?"

I came to a crashing halt at Daniel's voice. He and King were at the valley of the ramp. When had the sun come up?

Excitement revved Daniel's usually silky voice. Even King's brows lifted in anticipation.

Tweetie was a few feet behind them.

Her eyes narrowed on *her* board.

Silence passed, her brows drooping as she came to stand next to Daniel and King. I kicked it over to her. The levity before fractured as the weight of my actions broke through. Daniel and King's brows furrowed as Tweetie took her board.

I rubbed the back of my ear. "No. I'm not."

Daniel's face dropped.

King released a bitter, closed mouth laugh. Without a word he turned back and went inside.

Pity. Concern. Daniel and Tweetie may as well have the same face.

Screw this.

I walked past them, rubbing my neck furiously, refusing to look back. I didn't know why I had this goddamn handicap. I actually preferred when I couldn't touch a damn board. To *this*. Having to steal hers.

I didn't know. I didn't know why Tweetie was the only one who could bring it out of me. I didn't know why I couldn't skateboard without her.

I didn't know.

The night before, when I'd brought her board inside, my blood buzzed. I'd tested it beneath my foot, and suddenly I was breathing again.

I'd been trapped in a sarcophagus for ages, but now I saw sunlight, my blood was pumping. Tweetie ignited something dead and buried.

So after that, I thought maybe I was cured. For the first time in years, skating didn't fill me with dread. In the morning, I tried skating on a random board. And another. And then another.

I couldn't.

I could only skate on Tweetie's. While she was still sleeping and the rest of the house was silent, I grabbed her board again. I told myself I was just going to skate for a few minutes. I needed that rush. It had been *so fucking long* since I'd felt it.

"Flip wait!" Tweetie called after me. I kept walking, but she must have run because moments later she clung to my bicep. "Just stop." Reluctantly, I turned. Beyond her, Daniel watched, brows pinched.

"You can be a really broody jerk sometimes," she said, almost under breath. I raised my brows, but she was already plowing through to the reason she'd caught up to me. "Look about last night—"

"What about it?" I plastered a smile on my face.

She eyed me the way she had the night before. A way that said she wouldn't let me pretend anymore. But then, Tweetie had always been like that.

Small. Fierce. Precocious.

I closed the distance between us, filled with an urge to break every rule.

Daniel's out-of-focus figure came into view.

I exhaled and took her hand off my arm.

"I can handle it," she called to my back. "Whatever it is you think I can't, I can."

TWEETIE

Oh, share your fears. Oh, you belong to me. Oh, I want you. Oh, I'm so. Full. Of. Shit.

I slammed my knife hard into my bagel.

"Little girl—"

"What?" I snapped, looking up. Daniel's eyes popped, and the kitchen came into focus. Everyone—King, Daniel, Bacon, Sparky, and Pants—stared at me. How long had I been in my head?

"We think maybe you should apologize to that bagel," King said gently. I looked down. The inside was completely hollowed out. Crumbs lay like shrapnel on the dark granite. It was a disaster. I'd completely forgotten to even put schmear on it. Just ramming my knife at it over and over.

I sighed.

Dropped my knife.

"Nervous about your competition tomorrow?" Daniel asked.

No. "Yeah."

King settled his hand between my shoulders. "This time will be different."

I glanced up the stairs.

I knew my problem, and it wasn't nerves.

"Maybe," I said.

After some video games, some more stewing, some watching Sparky accidentally light his lunch on fire and learning how he got the nickname Sparky, and some more glaring at the stairs, I climbed them, determined to solve my problem.

I kicked open Flip's door. He sat up, the magazine he'd been reading falling to his lap. It was the one magazine I'd been featured in. I almost forgot why I was there, so startled to see him reading it. It was months old. Why did every part of me want to get to know him when I should be pushing him away?

I grabbed the nearest soft item and threw it at him—a towel.

"Hey, you!"

He caught the towel, raising a brow. I hated that brow. That stupid, hot, perfectly shaped and cute and cocky like him brow, and—I loved it. Dammit.

"Me?" He gently set the towel beside him.

"Yeah, you. Stay away from me."

He looked left. Then back at me. "You're in my room."

"Don't try and twist my words around and—" I fumbled. "Stay away from me. Just don't come near me anymore. Flip, Tweetie, ten feet of space at all times." I stretched my arms out, showing him.

So of course he did the opposite. He stood up. Set his magazine purposefully on his desk. Eyes narrowing on me. I kept my arms spread wide because I didn't know what else to do.

Until he was right in front of me and I had to tilt my chin, to see past his sharp one.

My arms still wide like I was starting a group hug.

"When was the last time you broke the law?" he asked, perfectly pink lips hooked right, making his right eye pinch slightly, glittering with mischief.

He always had me on my toes.

Not asking: why are you here, throwing towels in my face? Instead he's poking at parts of me I very much want to know. I'd lived at Patchwork, caged by rules they placed on me as they broke them themselves.

"Um…" I should put my arms down.

"You've never broken the law." His grin grew wider, exposing a few wickedly white teeth.

"Yes, I have," I responded, maybe too quickly. He tilted his head, a soft understanding lighting his eyes. "Well…I jaywalk all the time. I guess that doesn't count."

He gave me his hand. "Do you want to?"

FLIP

"This is the richest neighborhood in town," she said, a hint of fear tingeing her lips as we passed through the wrought iron gate to Heaven's Court. The excitement was evident on her face, though. The last time I was here with Tweetie I was dragging her back through gates, not opening them to lead her inside.

"Wanna turn back?"

"Hell no." She beamed, lips bright, cherry red. Fuck, Tweetie in the winter was something to drive a man insane.

We stopped in front of a three-story Victorian. Unlike Patchwork, this home spread down the street, demanding attention, each level stacked in perfect symmetry, with sky blue shingles and early winter snow that settled on the slate roof as if it were powdered sugar poured perfectly from the heavens.

"Whose house is this?"

The family behind the strings. The one I never should've had, but was thrust upon me, and I foolishly believed could be real.

"The people closing the parks down," I said, then gripped her chin, bringing her lips close. "I bet you taste like snow."

She sputtered.

Then shoved me off. "Ten feet Flip! I bet you're used to girls falling into bed with you, being the *famous* Flip. But that's not going to happen."

"They don't fall, exactly." I rubbed my neck. "I'm curious why you keep pushing me away."

She raised a brow. "Because there has to be some great reason why a girl doesn't want you?"

No, but I want to know why *this* girl doesn't. Her blue eyes softened like the sky at sunset as if she knew my thoughts.

She cleared her throat, raised the bag of spray paint. "So, uh, are we going to be delinquents?"

I pushed open the gate.

The lights were on but it was Friday night, if the

windows weren't swarming with people then they were at a party somewhere farther down the street.

"This place is massive," she said. "I thought Patchwork was big."

"It's even bigger inside."

"You've been inside?" Tweetie did a double take as I set the bag down, reaching for a can and handing her one. I wasn't sure how to get out of what I'd just slipped, so I shrugged, acting like it was no big deal. I started to show her how to use it when she cut me off.

"I may not break a lot of laws, but I do live at *Patchwork*. This isn't my first rodeo." I hid my grin as she uncapped the lid and drew a long, bright pink line. "Did you know that I was the one who put those murals on the wall? Well...I was there. It was my idea. Romeo painted my vision—except for the birds, that was their present to me after I almost left Patchwork when I was a kid."

"You almost left Patchwork?" If I sounded shocked, she must not have noticed. I was only aware of her leaving once.

She shrugged. "I felt like a burden. So I packed my shit and left. They found me. They always find me. They said if they were Rebel Gods, then I was their goddess. It was stupid, but it made me feel better."

I didn't know that. How could I not know that?

"It also meant Romeo called me the goddess of morning breath forever. Not that I have bad breath—" she added quickly, shooting me wide eyes. "I have amazing breath in the morning..." She trailed off, shoulders sloped. I still couldn't believe she'd left once before.

When I'd gone too long without speaking, she eyed me.

I quickly spoke. "Why four if there are only three gods?"

She paused with the spray paint. "It will sound weird."

"Even better."

"I dreamed him up. The guys told me he wasn't real, but he felt so real. There was one night I was certain he *was* real...anyway, I made them paint him." She eyed me. "Kinda looks like you now that I think about it. Probably because I was such a huge fan. Maybe *you* should be a god."

She laughed, and after a second of being frozen, I coughed a laugh into my fist.

I leaned with my back to the wall, arms folded. Watching her. She was laser-focused on her task but kept sneaking looks at me, and then when she found me watching her, would focus even harder on spray painting. Almost like she was nervous.

"You've got secrets, Flip." She shook the can, drawing another line. "Like I know the reason you stopped skateboarding isn't because you felt pressured." My brows lifted. "Maybe if you tell me one, I might share."

I shifted closer. "Do you have a secret in mind, Tweetie?"

"Well, you know why I skate..." She trailed off like there was more to it. I'd always wondered why that little girl showed up at the skate park. It was one of those *what could have been different* answers. What if she'd gone a different day? What if I hadn't been there?

And it was *me*. I was the reason she was there.

Fuck.

If that isn't the worst best answer to ever hear.

"And if your story is true, you know why I skate too," I said, hoping that would be the end of it.

She stopped spraying, turning to me, meeting eyes. "But what were you escaping?"

Well, shit.

Tweetie turned back with a sigh when I took too long to answer. "Fine, but I'm keeping my secrets too."

"Family," I said. Or rather, that I had none. "The first time I picked up a board I was seven, the day my grandma died. I never knew my dad and my mom always had a revolving door of losers. She eventually followed one out the door. After that, the streets were more than an escape. They were home."

She paused, and I could tell she was trying to think of the best thing to say.

I didn't want to hear it.

"This is fading," I mused, touching the mark on her neck. Goose bumps pricked my finger as I feathered my touch along her neck. "I'll have to fix that."

She jumped back, hands high. "Ten feet Flip."

I stepped back on a laugh.

"Do you miss them?" she asked after a minute. "The people you called family, the ones after On Angel Wings."

"They don't miss me."

"I didn't ask that."

I looked at the enormous powder blue house, at the window I'd slept behind for years. "Yeah. I miss them." She worked her jaw like she wanted to say more, but I was done digging into my past.

"So goddess of morning breath, huh?" I said on a grin. Her face reddened and she spray-painted harder. "You owe me a secret, goddess."

"I'm painting you my answer." She drew an arch high above her lines, emphasizing her point.

"I didn't ask you anything."

"It's what really you want to know, though." She waggled her brows and I couldn't help my laugh. I liked being with Tweetie this way, seeing her out of the shadows.

"But I should still get to ask. It's only fair." She waved her aluminum can like, *go ahead*. "So...you must hate that you had to live at Patchwork."

"That's what you want to know? Easy. I loved it."

"Don't you wish you could have had a normal childhood?"

It looked like she was about to laugh. It took a minute or two for her to collect her face.

"My dad was an addict," she said. "So was my mom. Not really Sesame Street."

I think I stared too long because she paused, insecurity growing on her features. "What?"

"I didn't know that." I couldn't stop myself from sounding blown away. How did I miss something so huge? I thought I knew everything about her, at least, all the big things. I always thought Tweetie had a normal life. A happy life. And I'd ripped it away from her.

She narrowed her eyes. "How could you?"

I cleared my throat and quickly picked up a can, finally taking to the wall.

TWEETIE

"That's a dick," I said, examining the wall.

"I'm a real Michelangelo, huh?" He smiled, and god, my face must have gone stupid because I know my brain did. It was unfair for someone to be so hot.

"Yours is...a heart?" He arched a brow. "Are you saying you're going to give me the secret to your heart? I'm all ears, Tweetie."

I shoved him and he smiled.

"I'm saying, the reason I'm not falling into your bed is true love. I'm waiting for it." He bit his smile off. "I also don't want to be called a pro ho and I want to focus on skateboarding, but really, true love."

He folded his arms, leaning back against the wall, eyes probing. "How do you know I'm not it?"

"I have a checklist."

"A checklist?"

I nodded. "It's foolproof. There's only been one boy who ever met it." Well, almost met it. The older I get, the more insane I think I am, especially now that there's a living, breathing, *beautiful* boy threatening everything I've ever felt.

"Let's hear it."

"You already know one. No skaters."

His eyes narrowed. "And the other two?"

"No one from Patchwork."

"So I've already met two of the requirements. What's the last one?"

"Before I, um, do anything, it has to be true love." When I wrote it, I said no kissing, but I was sixteen. I've since amended it.

He rolled on his shoulder, getting his hoodie covered in spray paint until he was inches from my face. My jaw tightened with nerves. How was it that just a simple change in proximity had the ability to steal my breath, scramble my heart rate?

Flip grasped my chin between his thumb and forefinger.

The world slowed until there was nothing but his touch and his burning eyes. My mouth parted and his eyes dropped to my lips. His grip tightened a fraction of an inch, such a small movement, but so purposeful, like thin wire being pulled to its snapping point.

"You don't know this yet," he said, "but you're in love with me."

Laughter. The gate creaking. Someone stumbling and more laughter.

Both our heads shot in the direction of the noise. Whoever owned this home had returned.

"Do you know the first rule of skateboarding?" Flip asked. I think my heart stopped—I hadn't heard anyone ask me that in *years*—but if Flip noticed, he didn't let on. He didn't answer his question with words but pushed me off the porch. I landed with a thud, then Flip joined me. He made a *shh* motion with his finger, and we crawled underneath the porch, barely fitting, forced to lie flat, his chest pressed against my back.

Then they were above us.

Oh, what in god's name?

Call the police.

One walked away, but the other was still there.

"You're going to get me arrested," I said, but joy and excitement coursed like Christmas lights through my veins.

"Well you always had awful taste in boys," he whispered against my hair. My eyes grew. How could he even know that?

"Are you counting yourself among them?" I meant it sarcastically, and it epically backfired.

"Yes."

I couldn't breathe.

It wasn't the police, it was Flip. We were close, *much* too close. When we were separated by a room or even a few feet, it was easier to pretend. Now everything was up close, intertwined. I could feel his heartbeat at my back, his lips at the shell of my ear. If I moved, our shirts rubbed against our flesh.

In the distance two police cars pulled to the curb, quickly finding the owner of the house.

This was real, very, very real.

"So who was the boy?" Flip whispered against my ear. Now? When the police could find us in minutes? He nudged me when I didn't respond. "The great love of your life?"

"I never got his name," I lied. Nate. His name was Nate. Nate had only been in my life for two nights over the course of two years. Could I really say that equaled love?

I don't know.

But it was enough time for him to burrow himself into my heart.

Flip tsked. "How am I supposed to fight him for you if I don't even have his name?"

I blushed, biting my lip, and he threw his head back, groaning; a sound that went straight to my gut and was much too loud.

Did you hear that?

I elbowed his stomach. *Mistake!* Abs—Rock. Solid. Abs.

"Not playing fair, Tweetie," he said, voice lower, softer, and much too close to my skin. With Flip, I couldn't think straight. I wanted to throw everything to the wind.

I asked quietly as if that would discount the question. "Why did you groan?"

"When you blush like that it makes me wonder where else you're blushing." *Oh.* I swallowed. He laughed quietly. His laugh was liquor, dripping down my throat and settling uncomfortably warm in my stomach and thighs.

His lips twitched. "You look flushed, you okay?"

"Fine," I squeaked. I was not okay. I throbbed. I ached.

If he moved an inch, I was certain I would explode. His smile grew wide until he was grinning, full bright, white. It was unbearably sexy. The dimple at his cheek popped, his jaw got squarer.

"How would you like it if I just stood up right now," I hissed my threat. "Let everyone know where we are?" Police were yards away, their flashlights beams of moonlight on the snow, but I refused to let him win again.

I think I see something—down the street!

And just like that everyone was running in the opposite direction.

Now was our time to go.

"Tease." His words ghosted the shell of my ear, then he *bit it.*

He *bit* my *ear.*

So hard I was sure it left a mark. My breath left me in a wispy, steamy gasp that curled into the night sky like a ballerina. I clamped my thighs hard, and I didn't care if we lived and died beneath the porch.

"I'm not like the rest, Tweetie," he said, licking the bite. "You're mine, I'm yours. Everyone else was just a distraction."

FOURTEEN

PRO HO: A GIRL WHO LIKES HANGING AROUND
PRO SKATERS.

TWEETIE

I tore apart every room in the house looking for my board. The solarium, the foyer, the great hall, even the pantry. Nowhere. Gone. My comp was in an hour and it took fifteen minutes to get there. Panic and desperation crept up my spine as I searched my bedroom again. I'd showered but still hadn't dried my hair, curls dripping into my T-shirt.

Where was it?

"You probably need this," Flip said, and I spun. He held a skateboard by the wheels—*my* board. Somehow this was becoming our new normal.

I dragged a hand through my wet curls with relief. "Uh, yeah." I accepted my board and then stayed stuck in some kind of awkward limbo as all my panic disappeared. Something had happened again. I could see it in his eyes.

After we came home last night we were filled with giggles and smiles. I had to force my head down on the pillow, repeating over and over again I had a competition. Flip was all smiles too.

Now his eyes were heavy, mouth a melancholy twist. I tugged at the end of my curls, thinking of something to say, when his hand covered mine. Grasped the end of my wet curl, a thought obvious on his mind but not readily available to read.

"Still so fucking curly." He dropped his hand.

He was going to leave. Just like that.

I struggled for something to say. "Do you think you'll ever compete again?"

Wrong thing to say.

Worst thing.

Dammit.

His eyes broke, and briefly I saw something. Shame? Yearning? Quickly he mopped it away with a shrug. "Nah. Not my scene anymore." When he skates, the love is so apparent. You don't just *stop* loving something.

"But, haven't you ever loved something so much you'd give up anything for it?" The air changed with my question, suddenly thick and heavy with an intention I hadn't foreseen. Flip's eyes were darker than I'd ever seen and my chest pounded with the rumblings of an avalanche about to fall and bury me.

"I'm starting to think you like getting hit."

I startled at King's voice, once again lost in the separate world Flip's presence created. My eyes flitted behind Flip to where King was. He was upset. He rarely spoke his emotions aloud, but they bled across his face.

He wanted to punch something—someone.

I could take a wild guess who.

Flip blinked, and suddenly his face was all smiles. "Good morning, Kingston. You seem chipper." I let out a breath. I'd imagined it. I'd imagined the want in Flip's eyes and the swelter in the room.

King grabbed Flip's shoulder, forcing his attention. "Is everything a joke to you?"

"Just the funny shit," Flip said. They were going to start another fistfight. With a deep sigh, I shoved them apart.

"Really? You're doing this *today*?"

King's eyes softened with shame, while Flip's sparkled.

He was infuriatingly hot and cold.

My ear was still sore from how he'd bit it. It was a *good* sore, though. A throbbing, aching sore that matched the one between my thighs. As if he knew, a wicked grin melted across his face.

"My bad," Flip said, raising his hands in surrender. The playful, cocksure lilt of his smile belied his contrition. He stepped backward, spun on his heel, and disappeared down the hall.

"Big brother King," I said when Flip was out of earshot, grabbing his hand. "Why are you so mad? Flip wasn't doing anything. Are you going to tell me he can't walk by my bedroom?"

He stilled. "Where were you last night?"

"Here," I responded quickly. "In bed." I yanked my hands back, worried he'd see the spray paint I couldn't wash off.

His eyes narrowed, then he exhaled. "You should be downstairs, Tweetie. It's time to go. Let's win and have something really fucking great to celebrate on your birthday." Oh, right. My birthday. Another year gone and another year closer to never accomplishing my dreams.

I plastered on a smile. "I'll be right there."

FLIP

I arrived just as Tweetie was warming up, glad I didn't miss it. The way she skated was almost as sexy as when she bit her lip. The competition was fierce, but no one was better than her, that was fucking plain as day. She was going to own it.

No doubt about it.

Finally, she would win and get what was owed her.

The smell of fresh kettle corn and hot dogs lingered in the air. Extreme sports vendors and clothing stalls were set up around the converted parking lot, like a punk circus. Skateboards, graphic tees, decks, loud music, all being shoved in my face.

I wandered to a black and white striped tent with decks mounted inside and outside for perusing. Tweetie's board was getting old and worn, and the new ones had better grip. I was examining one with a pink deck, when I was shoved against the stack of mounted boards. They rattled and the vendor leaned forward, startled. I stood up, meeting the person who'd shoved me in the eyes as much as I could.

King.

I wasn't small, but King was a fucking beast.

"I heard people are doing fist bumps now, you might want to try that sometime, caveman."

The vendor leaned farther across her table, out into the parking lot, watching her boards more than us. "Uh, excuse me—"

"I told you this morning to stay away and where do I find you? In her bedroom." It took King all of a few minutes to figure out I'd spray painted his parents' house. Mr. Ayers thought it was King, and naturally, knowing he didn't do it, there were only a few paths to follow.

King grabbed me by the collar. "You're corrupting her."

"Maybe you can take this outside?" the vendor suggested. "Or—a different outside..."

"Isn't that what we do?" I knew it was a low blow, and maybe that's why I said it. All at once he dropped me, wiped his hands on his jeans, happy to get rid of me.

The vendor stepped in, pushing us away from the skateboards. We mumbled apologies as we shuffled away from the stall and closer to the center of the action. People walked in either direction, occasionally bumping into us, cotton candy or foam fingers in their hands.

Daniel broke through the crowd. "So I just had to convince that woman not to call the cops. At least we're consistent." We both shot Daniel apologetic looks. I hadn't even realized he was around, and I think King was in the same boat. Daniel always had the hardest time watching us fight.

"I don't know what happened with us..." Daniel shook his head, dreads falling over his eyes.

King speared me. "Flip only thinks about Flip, that's what happened."

Then he left to go join Tweetie. He tapped her on the shoulder, and she smiled when she saw him. A genuine smile, no hesitation or caution.

"What happened all those years ago wasn't your fault," Daniel said.

Daniel, good Daniel. He was always the best of us.

Eyes locked on Tweetie as she laughed with King, I said. "Then whose was it? Hers?" I met Daniel's golden stare, and he couldn't answer. Obviously it wasn't the little girl whose only mistake was being innocent among the *Corrupt*.

"He's right." I dragged a hand down my face. Tweetie didn't deserve this, she didn't deserve me coming into her life. I'd messed her up with one selfish decision after the other.

I took her to Devil's Hill—selfish.

King took the fall—selfish.

I love her, I'll do anything to have her—selfish.

Daniel frowned at me. "King has his own shit to work through." Wherever his words were coming from, didn't stop them from being true.

With an exhale, Daniel went to find his seat.

Legs kicked out at a metal picnic table, I watched Tweetie finish her warm up from the food court. Every few minutes she would glance at me from beneath the veil of her curls. They were shoved under a beanie, her nose red in the winter cold, lips even redder.

I needed to leave, give her space, but I'd followed her career from the start. I wanted to see her win, to take what she deserved.

But that was *selfish*.

So I thrust my uneaten hotdog off the rubbery, metal green table into the trash in one motion.

"So they're just letting any random bitch in here now?" someone said just as I was about to throw my beer away and leave.

"As long as your gag reflex is under control." Two chuckfuckles had settled by the garbage can, knocking their cigarette ashes on the rim. Stray ashes floated to the ground like snow.

Oily gazes fixed on Tweetie.

I fingered the slick outline of my beer's neck. Listening.

"She's got a nice rack though," the one still dressed like all the teenagers said. Mr. Glory Days.

"Eh," the other said, a man who really needed a shower. Mr. Rabies. "Too small for me. I like 'em thick." He made an s motion with his hands, describing the poor chick who'd end up with him.

"Shut the fuck up," I ground out without looking up. They paused. I could feel the weight of their question and indignation. Had I spoken to them? I kept my eyes down.

"Who the fuck are you?" Mr. Rabies eventually piped up, all testosterone.

"That's *Flip*," Mr. Glory Days whispered. After the appropriate awe, impassivity washed over them.

Mr. Rabies laughed. "I thought you died."

I leaned back, breathing in cool, winter air. Not dead yet, unfortunately for them.

"Why do you care?" Mr. Glory Days asked.

"He must be fucking her," Mr. Rabies concluded.

"She could skate circles around you, which is probably why you're overcompensating with your dick," I calmly told them. As Tweetie tore off her beanie and finished warming up, I broke my beer inches from their faces. Bottle green shrapnel shattered and cut their skin.

Lucky.

If I'd been Romeo or King, it would have been on their heads.

"What the *fuck*?" they yelled. I wiped my hands on my pants, walking away as they dropped their cigarettes, swiping beer from their faces.

I should just leave.

That was the plan, anyway.

My eyes zeroed on Tweetie.

TWEETIE

They were calling my name when Flip came to me. A five-minute warning for me to find my position. I should've told him to get lost. He leaned against the ramp, eyeing me.

"I wanted to wish you good luck before you went on," he said. "You're going to do that move today, right?"

"Maybe..." It was still so raw. I hadn't perfected it.

"Do it. That move is wild and stunning and unforgettable, like you."

I looked away, not wanting him to see the way just his voice made my flesh flush like a warm summer's day in the middle of winter.

"Thanks," I said. When I looked back, he was already walking away—and not toward the stands. Toward the exit.

Don't do it, my brain argued. *Don't be stupid. Don't even think about—*

I ran after him. "Flip, wait." He stopped instantly, spinning to me. "You're leaving?" I had no right to care. "You're not leaving, right?"

Something flitted across his eyes. "I'll be here."

Lie.

Take your place, Raegan Fairchild. Three minutes.

The competition dissolved, faded away. I was lost in time, in a hope. Tender, feverish piano our soundtrack and direction. It was just Flip and me on a ballroom floor as I waited for him to give me his gloved hand.

"Do you know how sexy you look when you're in the zone?" There was nothing wolfish or predatory about him. By the soft backlight of his eyes, the warm glint in his voice, and the way he tilted his head, I knew it was a genuine compliment. Somehow, that was scarier.

I turned into my shoulder, hiding my involuntary Flip blush.

"Not fair, Tweetie. You know what that blush does to me." Again, his voice was soft and smiling.

"I don't understand you, Flip," I said. "One minute you're—" I broke off, almost about to say *sweet and charming* like a fool. "I just don't understand the game you're playing."

His face dropped, serious. "I'm not playing."

I made a noise in my throat.

Right.

What happened between last night and this morning, or even just *now*? He was all over the place.

"Ask me again." He took a step closer, eyes metal, tugging at a magnet in my gut I didn't remember existing.

I tripped over my heel, putting space between us. "What?"

"Ask me again. Ask me if I've ever loved something so much I'd give up everything."

Why did I suddenly feel like we weren't talking about skateboarding? There was an edge in his eyes, the same as there'd been last night. It made my skin tingle.

I paused, looking over my shoulder at the ramp I needed to climb. They called my name again, but I had to know.

"Have you?"

"Yes."

I met his eyes, dark and flinty even in the bright winter sun.

My mouth went dry.

I licked my lips to wet them.

His eyes darted to that, then back to mine. "I really want to fucking kiss you." The brazen honesty shocked me.

I couldn't get used to it—to *him*.

It felt like a game, like the minute I gave in the floor would be pulled from beneath me.

Everything in my head said not to kiss him. He was unpredictable. Hot then cold. But all I saw were his lips. Full. Soft. Kissable. I wanted them on me like I'd never wanted anything before. I felt it in my gut, a raw, aching need.

"So do it. Kiss me."

FLIP

"Kiss me," she said again, and fuck, that was all I wanted to hear. What I'd been waiting to hear. She took a shy step closer, just barely grasping my shirt.

I was stuck between right and wrong.

I never cared about what was right until I met Tweetie.

And I never wanted to do wrong more than when I was with her.

"I don't think I heard you," I lied, pressing my forehead to hers, focused on her lips. She smiled, tongue darting out to lick her lower one. Her silky rose petal lips.

I'd love to bite them, wound them, mark them.

Drag it out with her groan.

"Kiss me, Flip." All it would take was a wind blow, a feather's touch, and her kiss would be mine. I wanted to fuck the rules, kiss her like I'd wanted to for years, since the first and last time her lips had found mine.

Final call for Raegan Fairchild.

"Final call," I said, and lifted my forehead from hers. Her eyes were misty with lust, but when they finally adjusted, they were not what I wanted to see.

Despair.

Shame.

Anger.

They flashed like a slideshow of hurt.

And then I saw why—we'd been blown up on the monitor. The camera found Tweetie, ready to film her for the comp. Instead they found *us*. It was too grainy and fuzzy to be sure, but just enough picture to confirm everything people like the assholes at the food court thought.

"Pro ho," someone uttered under breath, walking by her.

Her face caved, and she shoved me off.

"Tweetie, wait—" I started, but she grabbed her board, running to take her position.

FIFTEEN

SWITCH STANCE: RIDING THE BOARD WITH
OPPOSITE FOOTING THAN USUAL.

FLIP

Some time ago
Tweetie is almost 16, Flip is almost 21

Tweetie had awful taste in boys. Her first date broke her heart, and now this guy? He called that a kiss?

There was no way she was enjoying that slug tongue or the way he grabbed her hand and placed it on his dick after thirty seconds of foreplay. I counted—because it literally took that much time before he said, "Just the tip..."

I rolled my eyes so hard they must have hit the back of my head, then wondered if this would be the time I made myself known. I'd managed years of being a shadow, even through the certified-blind dick that told her she wasn't pretty enough.

But no way was she losing her virginity to some guy who thought the G-spot was some kind of rapper.

He was way too old for her too. Nineteen. If Tweetie

was going to date a loser, she should at least date a loser her age.

It was getting harder to stay in the shadows.

As Tweetie went on these failed dates, I told myself if she found someone who was kind and who took care of her like she deserved, I could finally stop checking up on her.

My blood didn't boil because they were kissing, my jaw wasn't tight because her hands were on him, it was just that they weren't *good enough*.

At least, that's what I told myself.

I stepped forward, when suddenly he was pulled from the car.

King, Daniel, and Romeo stood above him like stone golems. The kid looked like he was going to wet himself. I bit back a laugh.

It had been a light winter. Snow fell as sugar, and tonight was no different. There was only a dusting on the ground, enough to glitter in the moonlight. The kid scrambled back, melting the snow beneath him.

"What the fuck?" Tweetie yelled, climbing out of the car. "Why are you here?"

Romeo looked like he'd rather be anywhere else. Daniel had a look of sympathy. King had murder in his eyes.

"You know who we are?" King asked. The kid nodded frantically. "So get lost."

He kicked up and ran, not bothering to zip up his fly, and sprinted away from *his* car.

"Wait!" she stumbled after him. "Come back..." But the boy was long gone. He knew the reputation around Patchwork. I had to give him props for even attempting it.

She made a white fist, staring after the boy.

Then spun on them. "I'm never going to have sex!"

Good, I thought.

"Good," King parroted.

She shoved him hard in the chest. He was unswayed.

"This isn't fair. You guys drink and have sex and break laws. Why can't I do the same?"

"Have you ever seen any of that?"

"No, but I hear rumors—"

King stepped to her, arms folded, jaw tight. "Have you ever *seen* any of that?"

"No," she conceded with an adorable push of her bottom lip.

"As far as you're concerned our life is the regular fucking *Andy Griffith Show*."

Her nostrils flared as she glared at King, taking deep breaths. "I'm not a kid anymore! I'm basically sixteen. You can't keep me in the Patchwork bubble forever, King."

He laughed, or made as close a sound as King could get. "The hell I can't."

She let out a noise halfway between a scream and a groan and stormed away, leaving small angry footprints in the snow. I thought they would for sure follow her, but they stayed.

"Flip," King said aloud.

Shit.

I stretched my arms, coming out from my spot in the shadows.

"Oh, hey." I rubbed the back of my head, tangling my chocolate waves. "Fancy meeting you assholes here." Daniel spared me a smile, Romeo arched a brow the way he did, like he knew more about me than I did. King...King was pissed.

"It's time to stop," King said. Right to the point, as always. "Her birthday is next week. She's smart. She actually *likes* doing homework. She could be better than this life, than us. Hanging around like this..." He trailed off, jaw twerking.

I didn't need him to finish. I knew what he was going to say before he'd thought the words, because I felt them myself.

"It's just not good for her, mate," Romeo finished. What had begun as me hoping to help her, transformed as she grew up. I kept waiting for that moment I was certain she would be okay, but instead I got to know her from the sidelines. She was funny, smart, determined. Her favorite food was peanut butter and bananas and she could raise as much as hell as the Patchwork crew gave her.

Like Bizzy said, she was little, but she was fierce.

"Or you," Daniel added. I knew he was right. I wasn't sure what I was doing anymore. I couldn't be in her life, but I couldn't leave it either.

So I pushed.

"Who are you to decide what she needs?"

"We're the closest thing she has to family." That hit me like a punch to the chest. I'd watched her grow up. Helped her silently, secretly. But what was I to her in the end?

Nothing.

What's worse, I knew that was how it *should* be.

King arched a brow. "Agreed?"

I didn't nod, but they didn't wait for me to. With an almost pitiful pat on my shoulder, Daniel said goodbye, and they took off toward Patchwork.

TWEETIE

The room beside mine was off limits. When I was younger, I accepted that fact. Today I woke up new and determined. Officially sixteen. Old enough to drive. Old enough to have sex according to the state. Old *enough*. Finally.

I was *so* curious what was inside.

As I cracked it open, I heard behind me: "Happy Birthday—" King cut off mid-sentence and I turned to see all three of them. Romeo held a lopsided cake with frosting dripping down the sides like melted candlewax. *Happy Birthday* was scrawled in messy black handwriting atop the white frosting.

King slammed the door shut so fast the air singed my nose.

"Shit." Romeo exhaled. "Here we go."

"That room is *off* limits," King said, hand flat on the door like I might try and open it again. "

I glared. "You have a lot of fucking rules for a group of people who supposedly live *outside them*." King's eyes softened, but I wouldn't be swayed. Not after what happened last week.

I *knew* there was more to Patchwork than Warheads and cereal boxes and Jenga. I heard so many rumors about Patchwork, especially living in it. My Rebel Gods may have taken me in, but they never let me out. They locked me up and refused to let me play in their Corrupt paradise.

I turned, ready to go to my room, when King grabbed my elbow. "Come on, Tweetie. It's your birthday. We got you a present." His brows dropped, as close to pleading as King would ever get. I caved.

They took me downstairs and Daniel sat me gingerly on the orange couch, hands floating on my shoulders like he wasn't sure he wanted me there. Then he disappeared.

I kept my arms folded, trying and failing to stay mad.

I heard arguing, King and Romeo.

No. Not that. We discussed not *that.*
What's she gonna do if he asks if she takes it up the—
Oh, fuck off.
You *fuck off, prude.*

Then silence. I tapped my knee. Every day at Patchwork was a new experience.

They came out, Daniel carried an easel under one arm. Romeo carried a large slice of paper, big enough to tape to it.

"Oh my god," I groaned when they set it up and I saw what was written.

"If you're going to be sexually active, you're doing it smart," Daniel said.

"No pregnancies," King said.

"We don't want you gettin' one of them coat hanger abortions." Romeo lit a cigarette without looking at me, like he'd just asked me what I wanted to eat for dinner.

My eyes must have eaten my face.

"Jesus," Daniel said under breath. Romeo exhaled cigarette smoke and shot Daniel a look like *What?*

"What is happening..." I said it more to myself, but Daniel answered anyway.

"As much as King would like to lock you in your room until you're sixty, we all agree, that's not exactly fair." I made a noise like *Right.* "So, Happy Birthday—you're getting the sex talk."

After thirty minutes of my personal hell had passed, the white paper was scribbled with everything from the word *penis* to *UTI* to an amateur drawing of a uterus courtesy of Romeo. It looked like a wilting tulip. Daniel had attempted to draw something inside of it, but now it looked like a Shel Silverstein drawing gone awry.

"Understand?" Daniel said, wiping sweat off his brow.

"I..." I looked at the page. "Yes?"

"She should know about the male G-spot. Write that down." Romeo gestured with his third cigarette. "We haven't even begun to cover fetishes."

King and Daniel shot him daggers.

"Nope. No. We're done." I stood up, waving both hands. "You have nothing to worry about, okay? I'm not having sex until I'm in love. *True* love. I thought..." I thought the last boy was the one. I was an idiot. I won't make that mistake again. I'll wait until I'm one hundred percent sure.

"No offense, luv, but you thought that popped collar-wearing choad was the one a few days ago." Romeo squinted, scrunching up his red lips in a way that read, *You know I'm right.*

"I have a checklist now," I said, keeping my voice steady. "It's foolproof."

Number one: he can't be a skater.

Every skateboarder except King, who'd taught me, had been a massive, colossal *douche*. They either treated me like dirt or were nice to me because they expected me to be a pro ho.

Number two: he can't be involved in this life.

I could never tell them that. I loved King and Daniel and Romeo with all my heart, but every boy I'd met broke my heart and they'd done it because of where I'd lived, who they *thought* I was.

The next item was the most important.

Number three: no kissing until I'm absolutely certain they love me.

Pretty self-explanatory.

King folded his arms. "Let's hear it."

I shook my head. "That's mine to know."

"Maybe it needs to be spell-checked," Romeo added, raising his brows suggestively. I glared, so he threw his hands up in surrender. "Well then, let's eat some fucking cake."

After too much birthday cake and more presents, we sat around as Romeo's newly cut vinyl played a powerfully melancholic song.

"Someday you're going to be famous," I said to him, as his voice filled the room. When he stopped thrashing to sing, *really* sing, it was no wonder he was called a god.

He laughed. "If I ever sell out, you lot have permission to put me down because I've obviously gone rabid." The record ended, and all at once they stood, heading toward the door.

"Where are you going?"

"To give you your last birthday present," Romeo said, and Daniel elbowed him while King shot him a glare.

"You've already given me so much." *Too* much.

A magazine I'd been eyeing from King.

A bracelet from Daniel.

A joint from Romeo, which King promptly confiscated, much to my dismay.

And a new set of wheels for my board from all of them, my favorite present.

"Well, what is it?" I asked when the silence pressed.

"It's a surprise." King placed his hand on my shoulder. "You have a comp to sign up for this week, focus on that." My shoulders fell and I wiggled myself out of his hold. They'd been forcing me to go to those signups for a year now, and for a year, I'd lost and been laughed at.

"I think I'm going to take a break from them." I kept thinking about what the stranger had said to me, even as I continually failed.

You're the best one here.

He'd been so certain, and that made me certain too.

But that didn't match up with what the world thought. I was officially past Flip's age when he'd first entered a competition and I was watching my opportunities pass me by simply because of my damn gender.

"They won't laugh this time," King said.

"That's not why I don't want to do them," I lied, unable to look them in the eyes. "Wait, why won't they laugh?"

Another pause, then Daniel said, "We're going to have a polite conversation."

"How?" All competition officiants told me no, but one in particular had made it his mission to make sure I knew I didn't belong.

Do you need help, little girl?

This is a male competition.

Maybe the mall would suit you better.

Can't have you crying and ruining it for the rest.

He lived in Heaven's Court. You couldn't get past the gate unless someone let you in. So of course he was the most important, without his say-so I'd never enter a competition anywhere.

When no one responded, I pressed. "Does it have something to do with your reputation? Are you going to do something?" I looked between all three of my gods, trying to find an answer.

King looked away.

They all did.

I chewed on the inside of my mouth. The rest of the town may call them Corrupt, but there was a reason the underground revered them as Rebel Gods. They always offered shelter to anyone who needed it. They were only a few years older than me, had been only teenagers themselves when they took me in, but they *raised* me.

So why was everyone so afraid of them?

Finally, King looked back.

"Those are rumors, Tweetie," King said.

The air from the open door drifted in. Cold. Tickling.

"Let me come, please. I'm sixteen. I'm not a kid anymore. I can handle it." They gave me soft, patronizing smiles. I wanted to scream.

I wanted to demand they tell me.

But then they would *never* see me as anything but a child.

King's face hardened. "Just go tomorrow. Sign up."

"Sure," I said through gritted teeth. I waited until they left. The moment the door shut, I ran to my room and pushed my window open.

I was done being shackled to Mount Olympus.

SIXTEEN

CATCH: STOP THE BOARD FROM ROTATING WHILE
IN THE AIR.

TWEETIE

I followed them until they reached Heaven's Court, the fanciest neighborhood in all of Heaven Falls. Somehow they'd opened the gate without effort and I'd sprinted after before it closed.

Then I got lost.

One minute they were in my sights, the next it was just breathtaking Victorian mansions, sprawling like they were entitled to the land. I forgot I was here to follow them. I knew about this place—everyone knew about Heaven's Court—but seeing it was another thing entirely.

Some people jokingly called the neighborhood I lived in Patchwork Court, and now I understood. The differences almost as stark and important as the similarities, like yin and yang. Both our sidewalks were cobblestoned, but unlike ours, where moss and flowers grew without care, here stones were carefully and purposefully placed. Maybe the designs were meant to be beautiful and breathtaking, but to me they were sad.

From free, to caged.

Movement to my left caught my eye—the three of them heading toward a particularly decadent home. I made my way.

It was massive, with pearly gray shingles and an eerie beauty like the ghosts of kings and queens. In fact, the whole neighborhood had that lost-in-time eerie, regal beauty. Like discovering a perfectly preserved abandoned palace, whose only residents were long dead.

It was so quiet I thought maybe I'd mistaken what I saw, when I heard voices, what sounded like a scream.

Fear raced up my spine.

I should go home. This wasn't for me. This haunting and beautiful place where screams drifted on the wind. My Corrupt, my Rebel Gods, hadn't opened the gate for me. I'd snuck in.

But I ran up the porch, tried to quiet my breathing, hid behind a column. Through a great paned window, a crystal chandelier hung in the gray dark, glinting in the moonlight.

"And you'll tell her *yes*." I froze. That was definitely King's voice—no, his growl. So I *had* seen them but, it couldn't be coming from inside the house?

How did they get inside?

"Kingston Ayers—we can work something out. I know your father—" he broke off in a cry. I didn't know that voice and it sounded distressed. I'd never heard a grown man cry before.

Kingston Ayers?

I had the strangest feeling that I was being followed myself, but every time I turned there was nothing—no one.

I spun around again.

Trees, swaying ghostly gray in the night. Fancy street-lights dotting empty lawns before each mega house, before an emptier street. Like an oil slick.

I gently pushed open the door. It creaked.

The entryway would have taken my breath away if not for the cries coming from deep inside the house. I felt like I was at a haunted house at the fair with King again.

"You'll say you're happy to have her in your competition." That was Daniel. I'd never heard him speak like that before. He was always so nice and sweet, but now it was low, steady, and...*dominating*.

I paused just before the kitchen, afraid of what I would find in the iron blue dark.

"Yes," the man cried again.

Sucking in my breath, I looked around the corner. King, Daniel, and Romeo surrounded a man. I covered my mouth with two hands, stifling my gasp.

It was the man from my competition! The one who kept telling me no. A face which I only knew to be twisted in amused contempt was now broken with tears.

Can't have you crying and ruining it for the rest.

"Glad we're on the same page, mate." Romeo took his lit joint and leaned back, giving space for Daniel to grip the man by the chin. King wound his arm, fist heading right for —I covered my eyes, but the man cried out.

The breath I'd been holding left me. *Too loud*, I instantly thought.

Silence, save for the man's whimpers.

I peeked through gaps in my fingers.

And all three of their heads had twisted to mine.

"What the fuck are you doing here." It wasn't a question. I opened my mouth to come up with an excuse—any excuse—yet King wasn't looking at me. His eyes were above my shoulder. "Never mind. I don't want to know. Get her out."

Who was he talking to?

"Way ahead of you," a new voice said, and then I was yanked back by my shoulder, dragged out of the kitchen, out of the decadent entryway, back into the night.

———

It was too dark and he was wearing too much black. A hoodie shrouded his head, a bandana covered his mouth. He'd dragged me out of Heaven's Court and silently brought me back home, his grip on my wrist tight.

I trusted him only because my gods did.

But why did I feel like I knew him?

Now we were just yards from the house, weaving between the abandoned Victorians that made up Patchwork Court. Overgrown vines sprinkled with snow twisted through broken glass windows, shadows a thick velvet curtain.

"Who are you?" I asked to his back. The house glowed in the distance, the night eerily quiet. No cars on the street, no party at Patchwork to be our soundtrack—nothing. It was strange. Whereas Heaven's Court was apparently calm and spooky, Patchwork was usually lively. Loud, filled with life and music and lovely debauchery.

"Who are you—" All at once he spun, dragged me to him, just as a motorcycle whizzed down the sidewalk. He pulled me against his chest and away from danger.

He uttered some kind of curse as the bike's buzzing faded into the night.

Then it was quiet again.

Just us, the sound of his breathing and my own.

All that was clear in the night were his eyes. Like shiny, chocolate pearls. Eyelids that were lazy in the way they fell almost to his thick lash line, low and entitled.

Beautiful.

And like everything else about him, familiar.

He didn't let me go at once, fingers curled into the fabric at my shoulder. Staring at the road.

Then slowly, he met my eyes, and they stole my breath. I'd never had anyone look at me the way he did. Like he wasn't sure if he wanted to push me away or pull me closer. Like he was holding back a bay of torment and the only thing that could cure it was me.

That scared me. It wasn't not knowing who he was, or his grip tightening on my arm, or being dragged miles by a near stranger—but the look beneath his heavy lids.

I licked my lips and his lids dropped.

Then all at once he leapt off me, putting feet between us. Like he was terrified and startled by *me*.

He dragged hands down his hoodie, let out a ragged breath, and our eyes locked once more.

"Happy Birthday."

SEVENTEEN

CARVE: MAKING A SHARP TURN WITHOUT LIFTING
YOUR WHEELS.

FLIP

What the fuck?

What the fuck was that?

That was too close. The sun was rising a bright, bubblegum pink in the sky and I paced back and forth in the shadowy trees of Patchwork's backyard, brain still trying to process just how close I'd come to kissing Tweetie.

When I brought her back from Heaven's Court, I was a second away from it. She'd licked her lips and I thought she wanted it too—but she was only *sixteen*.

And I'd known her since she was a fucking child.

I opened my palm, looking at Tweetie's bracelet. It fell when I'd pulled her from the street.

I kept pacing, the embers of my joint falling like fairies to the frosty ground. I knew I shouldn't keep coming back here. She was old enough now to deal with her own night-mares. A sixteen-year-old didn't need someone like me.

Instead I bought her a birthday present and made

Romeo lie to the others because his moral compass was the most warped.

I liked seeing her face light up when she unwrapped the wheels.

I went nuts for the way she screamed when she realized how good the brand was.

It was so. Fucking. Wrong.

After they'd opened presents, I'd waited for her to go to bed, but like an unfinished charcoal drawing in the night, she pushed open her window. Climbed onto the roof, hoisted herself down, then fell. I shouldn't have followed her, but I did. Hidden in the shadows as she followed her gods into Heaven's Court. That's what I was now, her shadow.

You can't tell a shadow to leave.

Even if the shadow is bad, even if the shadow ties you to a past best forgotten.

It just...is. Always.

Now there was movement in her bedroom and I shifted, eyes locking on her. Tweetie finally going to bed, probably. She tore off her shirt, exposing a flat stomach, the top of her underwear riding on her hips, peeking past perpetually baggie pants.

I hissed and quickly looked away, heart thudding.

I'd have to tell them Tweetie needed to shut her fucking curtains.

"Flip." King's voice cut into the cool, dark air. The three of them were back.

"Don't say it." I held my hand up. "I'm done." I stopped pacing. "I'll stay away. For good."

I was losing myself.

In her.

A feeling of want growing inside me.

When they didn't talk, I looked up. All of them wore matching frowns.

My shoulders tightened. "What?"

Was it possible they knew already? Somehow they'd figured it out before me.

King stared at me, hard. "We need you to stay the night."

I couldn't believe I was stuck as a glorified babysitter for the girl I couldn't get off my mind. If that didn't sum up how twisted this was, I don't know what would.

The guys weren't finished handling all the biased comp officiants and were afraid she'd follow them again, which meant I was here.

At least Tweetie had a bedtime.

And, as if God heard me that very moment, Tweetie appeared on the stairs.

I dragged two hands down my face. "God fucking dammit."

I sank deeper into the couch. Of course she had to break the rules the one night I was stuck here in my demented purgatory.

It was brutal, but for a different reason than I'd thought. No one talked to Tweetie—and she tried. She tried to talk to so many people. Patchwork Girls made a point to glare at her, one in particular said something that made her face cave. The boys at the party avoided her. The dazzling look of excitement Tweetie'd come down the stairs with slowly dulled.

She headed to the keg. Two people talked on the opposite side and again she tried to start a conversation. They looked at one another, then left.

The party droned on, and Tweetie drank. She drank more, and more, and more. Clung to the wall, eyes on the floor, and was always quick to move out of the way to let people pass. My muscles tightened, watching her go from tipsy to outright drunk.

I wished I could give her all my attention.

Let her know how special she was.

Songs changed, Tweetie making herself permanent wallpaper. I started to relax. She was the most well-behaved rule breaker in existence.

Then some asshole approached her. I immediately sat up straight. Almost everyone had been ignoring her while simultaneously giving her all of their attention. Tweetie was at a party. Tweetie was never at the parties. The gods weren't there.

They knew what that meant.

This guy apparently either didn't know or didn't care. I was betting on the latter by the shit-eating grin on his face. I leaned forward, watching their exchange. I had no reason to do anything. I was only here to make sure she didn't leave.

The dude said something and Tweetie shook her head slightly, taking a step away from him. He slammed his hands on either side of her head, caging her.

I stood up.

Fuck this guy.

I was almost at her back when Tweetie slapped his arms out of the way and poured her beer on his pants.

"The fuck?" He jumped back. It looked like he peed himself.

"Oops," she said, and the guy ran off to go clean off his

pants. I paused. Tweetie definitely didn't need a man saving her. If anything, the man needed someone to save *him*.

I inched back, about to melt into the party again, when she moved to let someone pass. We collided, so close our sneakers kissed. The music whirled and waltzed, our eyes locked. I wore the same get-up as when I dragged her from Heaven's Court, and I saw her working it out.

Time to bounce.

I was on my heel when someone knocked into her. She fell tipsy into me. My hand came to her lower back, steadying her, and her palms landed on my chest.

"Hi," she said.

"Uh..." I knew I should move. "Hey," I finished.

"I met someone tonight," she said, voice quiet. "He wore the same mask. Had the same eyes too."

My hand tightened a fraction of an inch on her back.

Then I sprang off her like fire.

"Wait—" she called, as I wove through the crowd, disappearing.

This was a goddamn nightmare.

I lost Tweetie somewhere around the kitchen. After lying low for thirty, I grabbed a beer, then climbed upstairs to hide like a coward. I slammed the door to my room and slid down the wood, rubbing my temples. I just needed a few minutes to collect myself.

Now I understood what Daniel meant.

The danger.

There were so many things I wanted to say to her. Do to her.

The sounds of vomiting interrupted my thoughts, coming from my closet.

I stood up, knocked on the door. "Hey asshole this isn't a bathroom."

A muffled sorry followed, then Tweetie stumbled out, grasping the doorframe. She was so fucking shitfaced, barely standing. I grimaced at what she'd left in my closet. She tried to walk again and tripped.

"Woah, there, drunko." I gently caught her elbow and set her down on the floor. She placed her head in her hands, then opened one eye to study me.

I should've let her go now that she was on the floor, but this was the first time we'd really looked at one another. Even still, there was a layer of fabric between us. Her eyes were deep, blue pools of diamond. I could count the cuts in the irises.

Her lips parted. "Hey...*you*. Were you running from me?"

I dropped her. Coughed. Stared forward.

"Were you chasing me?" I countered. There was a breath.

"Maybe," she whispered. "Why did you run?"

The way you make me feel is terrifying.

I never did respond.

Minutes dragged in a silence I shouldn't have found so comfortable, all too aware that the only thing separating her body from mine was a thin slice of air.

Then her head fell on my shoulder. My entire body tensed.

"Is this okay?" she mumbled.

It's perfect.

I opened my beer on my belt like I'd been doing since

the first day I had a drink. She lifted her eyes and they were filled with awe like the very first day we met.

I drank, hoping a buzz could numb the effect of her.

"Thasss so cool," she slurred.

My lips twitched. "You sound a little drunk."

She made a face. "You sound a little sober." A smile came to my lips, but I quickly wiped it away.

Another pause. I eyed my beer, wondering if being tipsy was really the best idea, but being sober wasn't working either.

"You should go back to the party," I said after a minute.

"It's funny, all I've ever wanted was to be let inside that party—the *real* party—and now I just want to be upstairs. Here."

A jagged breath. "You should really go back downstairs."

"They don't want me—*really* don't want me." She sighed. "Do you ever feel like you don't belong?"

Yes. Every day.

"I don't know what I'm doing here. I live here, but I'm always on the outside. No one will touch me because they think I'm on the inside. At least, that's what I tell myself. Guys don't date girls who also wear their pants, you know?"

My voice was frozen. Is that what she thought? Objectively, I could see it, but to me, she was *stunning*.

"Sorry." She wiped her nose. "You don't even know me and I'm unloading all my shit." I stared at the top of her blonde head, her small nose just barely peeking out. That was all I wanted, to know her beyond the years of separation. She sat up from my shoulder and I had the insane urge to tell her to go back.

She looked at me like she could see me through my mask, blue eyes slimming just a bit. "Who are you?"

EIGHTEEN

CHIP: WHEN A PIECE BREAKS OFF THE DECK.

TWEETIE

"Who are you?" I repeated when he didn't respond. My gods hadn't told me a single thing about the mysterious stranger who'd dragged me back home. They simply acted like nothing happened. Like I hadn't followed them to the richest neighborhood. Like they hadn't beat someone to a pulp in his own home.

"We'll know if you leave," was all King had said, before shutting the door, leaving me feeling less like a rebel and more like a little girl.

I was speechless. Actually speechless. After everything I'd seen, I was supposed to go back to the dark? To a *bedtime?* Another party I'm not invited to, another party I have to just listen to. Like the mysterious stranger, I'm not allowed to know the truth of it.

But sitting next to this boy, an insane seed of an idea took root inside me. I waited for his response, to water it and see if it could grow.

"Tweetie—" he started, just as the door burst open.

"Whoops." Penelope drunkenly stumbled in. "Didn't know the room was occupied. *Oh.*" Her eyes settled on me. "Hey, Yoko."

Look, it's the Yoko of Patchwork House. Finally out for a real party.

Penelope had said the same thing when I'd come down the stairs, staring at me like I was a piece of art, memorizing my different contours, objectifying the parts she didn't agree with. I didn't understand what it meant, but it hurt all the same.

The boy sprang up, pushing past Penelope in a flash.

"What is wrong with you?" I snapped. I ran after him, catching him at the bottom of the stairs. I held on to his elbow. "Why do you keep running?"

He'd called me Tweetie.

It was entirely possible he knew *of* me. A lot of people knew of me. Or maybe he was exactly who I thought he was.

"Do you know me?" I asked, just as whispers started up I instinctively thought were about me.

"That's a Rebel God," they whispered.

I dropped the boy, filled with a new worry. Were my gods back? Suddenly he grabbed my hand.

"Want to hear a story?"

Uh, *no.* I want to know who you are. I want to know if you're the boy I think you are. His eyes were earnest, fervent. More whispers surrounded us, rustling leaves on the wind. I lifted my head, trying to see who they were talking about.

His grip tightened. "Come on." Suddenly I wanted nothing more than to say yes.

I nodded.

He wove us through the party while my heart beat too loud. King held my hand—*all* of my gods had held my hand. This was nothing.

At least, that's what I told myself.

We stopped inside the kitchen. It was busy with people drinking and laughing and flirting. All I saw was him.

He grabbed a paper from a drawer, I *hoped* to write down his number, but then he slid next to me. Our shoulders touched again, the party and its noise faded away.

"My grandmother was Taiwanese, but she only spoke Japanese because of the Japanese occupation," he said, folding the paper. "I speak Mandarin, but could never talk to her, as I don't know Japanese. So this is how we talked."

He handed me a beautifully folded paper crane.

"A bird for my bird."

He laughed.

He had a nice laugh. Like everything else about him, his skin, the color of his eyes, his voice...it was silky. I didn't quite understand why he was laughing or what he meant by *a bird for my bird* but the paper crane was beautiful and I liked the way the small bird looked in his big, veiny hands. So I took it.

"I don't think I've ever seen you here." I twirled the bird. Most everyone at Patchwork was a regular in one way or another. Though occasionally you got a wanderer. "But you look so familiar."

"You haven't seen me here," he said firmly. "This isn't my world."

"I'm starting to think this isn't my world either," I said quietly. "But if this isn't my world, then what is?" I wondered where he came from, where he belonged. I'd only ever known the Patchwork life. Our eyes locked, and it looked like he had something he really needed to say.

"That's a Rebel God," someone said, awe washing their voice. The same thing they'd said out in the living room.

"That's the *lost* Rebel God," another said. My brows dipped as nerves tangled my chest. *Where* were the guys everyone was talking about?

All at once the boy's back straightened and he gave me his hand. "Let's go."

I stared at his outstretched hand. "Now where are we going?" He ever so slightly crooked his finger, motioning for me to come. He wasn't going to tell me. I either went with him or stayed. At a party where no one wanted me, or in my bedroom, locked away once again.

The whole room had that blurry, headlamps-on-a-highway feel. I was still very tipsy.

It probably wasn't the best idea to go somewhere alone with a stranger.

"Lead the way," I said.

We went outside and he tossed me a board. I don't know how he knew I skated; maybe he guessed it by the way I dressed.

"Are you a skater?" He shrugged. A gush of warmth I had no right to feel drenched my stomach. Rule number one, after all. "Are you going to ride with all that on?" I gestured to his getup. Another shrug, like *Yeah*.

"Well, grab a board."

"I don't feel like skating. Tonight I'll...bike." He grabbed one of the many littered across the grass.

I dropped the board, testing it beneath my feet. "Do you have a park in mind?"

"We're not going to a park." At my face, he clarified, "Street."

I'd never skated street before.

The idea thrilled me.

"I've never done that." Flip was my favorite skater, and he skated street. He introduced the style into competitive skating.

It was dangerous.

It was illegal.

All reasons the guys wouldn't let me do it.

"Well," he said, "let's change that."

We carved through the median, cars on either side of us, their headlights bright in the night. I lead the way, but when I looked over my shoulder, he was always there. Following.

We stopped a few blocks from Patchwork, and I threw my head back on a sigh. I felt weightless. Every single care gone, disappearing into the cloudy, starry sky.

"So what does the bird mean?" I reached into my pocket, edges pricking my fingers.

Something flitted across his face, but it was gone in an instant. "If I fold a thousand your wish will come true." Another pause passed between us. I twirled the crane in my fingers.

"Did you have a wish in mind when you made this?"

"Yeah." His eyes were so intense I almost looked away. Like meteors falling from the sky. "I wish someday me and my girl can be together."

"Oh." I deflated. "I bet she's pretty."

"Beautiful." He was talking about his girlfriend, so why was he looking at me like that? Filled with some desire I couldn't place.

I cleared my throat, hopped back on my board, and we rode out.

It was so *thrilling.* Rules went out the window. Cars

were so close they blew back my hair. Their angry honks only made me laugh.

We stopped at the top of Devil's Hill. I'd avoided this hill my entire life. Street style didn't kill my father, but the way the guys kept it from me, I often wondered if they thought it did.

In my memories, it was so big, so winding and scary. But now, it was just like any other hill.

I'd carved bigger ramps.

"Let's go back," he said, some kind of fear tearing apart the serenity in his voice. I threw a look over my shoulder, then back at the hill. The wintery night air was bewitching; tranquil and just the right temperature. The stars behind the clouds fuzzy and blending into endless black.

Maybe the boy at my side was the one who'd dragged me back to Patchwork.

Or maybe he was just someone who knew exactly what I needed.

"You think I can't skate this?" I asked, then I flashed him a smile, and dove.

FLIP

With a cheeky smile, Tweetie tore down Devil's Hill, the past colliding with the present. Her laughter then swirling with her laughter now, the image of her curls floating on the wind cracking to reveal her windblown ones right before I pushed her into the street.

Tweetie reached the bottom, tossing her head to the side and giving me a look. Why hadn't I joined her?

I took a breath and dove.

"See, not so scary," she teased when I reached the bottom. One foot on her board, the other steadying herself on the street. She was beautiful, so damn beautiful, and that was the problem.

"Yeah..."

Then it happened, so fast I didn't have time to think. I heard it behind us, gravel crunching and slicing through the air. I grabbed Tweetie, pulled her to me, spun us in an embrace.

It was nothing. Not even a car, just someone on a bike. But in my head, I heard the earsplitting crash.

Go. Get out of here!

"Hey." Tweetie's soft, gentle voice pulled me out of the memory. Her blue eyes were pinched in concern, but she didn't press. My heartbeats were painful against my chest.

"Thank you," she whispered. "How did you know this would help?"

Another slam against my ribcage.

Another breath too loud in my ears.

"You didn't need a party," I said, voice rocky and uneven. "You needed this. You can be dealing with the worst shit in the world and a good ride will fix it." I couldn't let her go, even though I knew I should. I held her tighter, like any moment she could be ripped from my hands and tossed back into the road.

Snowflakes started to fall, landing heavy and soft on her cheeks and eyelashes.

Distracting.

Too pretty.

"Is that what you do when you're dealing with something heavy?" she asked. "Skate?"

That's what I used to do.

Now I just let it pile on and on.

The bandana was muggy and humid, but the air outside was cold. Snow landing icy on the fingers holding her tighter.

"I'm going to take the bandana off now," she whispered, grasping the edge. *Danger,* a voice in my head warned. But the few stars above were a glittery, secret shelter. Maybe if it happened here, it didn't count.

I caught her hands just as she revealed my nose.

"Why?" Her lips were just a thread's width from mine. "Why can't I see who you are?"

How ironic that Tweetie asked this question when the answer was the very hill we were on.

She blinked, wet lashes settling on round cheeks before coming back to mine.

Hazy.

I swallowed, jaw tight. "Let's head back." I stepped back, tugging the bandana up.

We didn't talk the entire way back. Once outside Patch-work Tweetie tossed the random board I'd handed her into the pile on the grass. I did the same with the bike.

She didn't go inside, and I didn't leave. I knew I wanted to prolong this moment, but I wasn't sure what Tweetie was thinking.

"I wanted to kiss you," she said. "I'm not normally like this but, I don't know, I really wanted to kiss you." She laughed, nervous and a little self-deprecating, like she couldn't believe what she'd said.

Her eyes were on the ground. Snow landed, but it was too warm to stick, melting into the grass.

My throat stopped working.

Her bracelet was in my pocket, a reminder of how messed up it was to feel anything other than fraternal care for her. But *man*, did I want to hear her say that again. It was all I could think about now. *I really wanted to kiss you.*

Her eyes flashed to mine like she knew, then she stepped closer. This time I wasn't sure I could resist. Her hands settled on my chest, light.

"You should go inside." My voice was raw. She stood on her tiptoes, sliding her hands up my chest. Icy fingers came back to the bandana, but her breath was steamy and warm.

I focused on her perfect pink lips. All I wanted to know was what she tasted like. God help me.

Then Tweetie was yanked from me. Dragged far, far back by the collar. Dragged up the steps with such force she stumbled.

King.

"What?" she yelled, elbowing him and forcing him to drop her. "What is the big deal?" Daniel and Romeo stood on the perimeter of the porch, watching.

"What part of stay in your fucking room went over your head?" King asked, voice low and unamused. "You don't fucking think. You really don't fucking think."

That cut her to the core, I saw it in the pain that flashed through her blue eyes.

"Well you *hurt* people," she shot back, jaw clenched. I wondered if she was holding back tears.

"He knew the rules," King said, and Daniel and Romeo nodded in agreement. "Everyone knows the rules."

"Which are?"

"We'll fuck up anybody who even makes you think about crying and everyone in this town knows it. Deal with it."

Her mouth dropped, and then King dragged her toward the door again, clearly done with debating.

"Why is it such a problem that I'm down here?" Silence

followed her question. I knew it had nothing to do with the party and everything to do with me. "I didn't even *do* anything," she continued. "I just vomited in a closet and went for a ride."

"Some days I forget you're a teenager, then you pull this shit." Her jaw dropped farther, but before King could drag her again, she shook him off and stormed inside. At the door, she threw me one last look.

Curiosity.

Disappointment.

Then her eyes landed on her gods.

"Well happy fucking birthday." She slammed the door.

King descended the stairs and pulled me by the back of my shirt. "I said watch her not kiss her. Are you so fucking corrupt that you can't see how wrong this is?"

I had nothing, no excuse. Even as King threatened to break my nose, I stared at the door. Stared at where she'd been moments before, her bracelet cutting into the skin of my palm.

Knowing that no matter how wrong it was, I could never let Tweetie go.

NINETEEN

TIC-TAC: REPEATEDLY TURNING THE BODY AND SKATEBOARD FROM ONE SIDE TO THE OTHER.

TWEETIE
Present

"Happy Birthday!" King opened my door with a chipper voice—as much as he *could* be chipper.

Another happy fucking birthday...

"I don't feel like celebrating my birthday today," I said without sitting up, eyes wandering to my window, catching glances of Flip outside skateboarding.

Still using my board, sort of like the way he used me.

The way I let him.

Up and down the bowl, like a pendulum swinging. His dark curls blew in the breeze. His shirt lifted as he descended, revealing a cruelly toned Adonis belt. Skater boys always had the *best* Adonis belt from all the twists and turns they did. One of the reasons I was such a sucker for them growing up.

I sighed, fell back on my bed with a bounce. We hadn't

so much as looked at each other since my comp, let alone talked.

Of course I didn't win.

I could still feel their stares. The ramp had felt miles long.

Pro ho.

I knew that's what they were whispering. I'd just been caught with Flip, *the* Flip. I'd had a snowball's chance in hell of winning *before* I was the chick screwing Flip.

"What are you looking at?" King craned his neck, trying to see. I pushed his face away, changing the subject and sitting up.

"I'm fine. Everything's fine." The lie bled through my body in visions of Flip. "It's nothing we haven't dealt with before." Except it's totally different. I believed Flip might like me. The words, the touches, the almost-kiss might mean something more than strings to yank at my heart.

There was one moment after I finished my set when I thought he might talk to me, come tell me it wasn't all in my head, and I could apologize for the way I'd reacted after we'd been blown up on screen. Instead he just left. Now it's been silence.

I broke my rules.

And here I was, hurt.

King gave me his patented *I know what you're really thinking*, narrow-eyed glare. "And we can fix it, just like we did before."

I sighed.

I knew how they fixed it.

You hurt people.

I don't know why I was thinking about that now. The night I'd nearly kissed the mysterious boy who would become my everything, when I learned just how far they would go for me.

The boy who called me ugly came to school with a serious black eye, but I'd always considered that a fluke. When King and my gods stormed in after me, I pieced it together.

We'll fuck up anybody who even makes you think about crying and everyone in this town knows it.

It wasn't just the dicks at my competitions; it was everyone and anyone who hurt me.

After that, I didn't talk to my gods for a week.

Part of me wanted to fight back. When everyone played dirty, it was tempting to play dirty too. But then it didn't *feel* like a win.

King grabbed my hand and yanked me out of bed. I stumbled.

"No more moping. We're going snowboarding. Happy Birthday, Tweetie."

"I don't want to," I grumbled petulantly, feeling even more childish. Inside I perked up. I loved snowboarding and we rarely got to go, it was too expensive. King folded his arms, staring holes through me like when I was a kid.

"There are other competitions. This isn't the end."

"It's my fault," I whispered. Everything. All of it. I didn't know how I let myself get into this. My competitions were *all* I should be focusing on, but instead of boards, I'm ruminating on boys.

I could feel the questions King wanted to ask like gravity pressing heavy on my neck.

"First one down the mountain owes the other fries?"

A smile cracked my lips. "I'll hold you to it."

I rubbed my shoulders. It was a lot colder than I'd expected. Even as we all crowded around a fire. It lit our group up and made the night around us tight and dark, a shadow trying to embrace us. I put my hands against the bonfire, warming them from red to pink.

"Um, blah blah, avalanche warning in backcountry, no going out at night alone, blah blah—let's shred!" Sparky tossed the warning paper in the air and Daniel snatched it before it landed in the fire, proceeding to list the *no-go* zones.

The way Sparky had read it reminded me of Romeo, a sudden pang of sadness hitting my gut. The most I heard him now was on recorded music, and no one had said how or why he left.

"I told you to bring a thicker jacket," King said, sitting on a log next to me. "Here, I grabbed yours anyway." He reached into his duffle and placed it on my shoulders.

"Thanks." I tightened it, staring through the flames to where Flip sat, Penelope and Sparky on either side of him.

He hadn't looked at me once.

Not *once*.

I exhaled jaggedly into my drink.

"Why aren't all of you together anymore?" Penelope whined. She sat next to Flip, knees angled to his, eyes locked on his every movement.

"Because when they come together, the world ends," Flip joked. *Joked*. While I wondered what our kiss meant, while I hoped he would look at me, he was fine. Nothing ever mattered to him, anyway. Why had I thought I would be different?

Inside I crumbled.

"Too much power in one place," Daniel agreed.

"I miss Romeo," another said.

Me too.

"But we have King, and Daniel, and *Flip*," she crooned, hearts practically falling out of her eyes. But she kept looking at Daniel as if to make sure he was watching.

"Flip's not part of Patchwork," I sputtered.

"He's the *lost* Rebel God, you idiot," Penelope said. Sunken, drunk memories floated to the surface.

The lost Rebel God.

Where had I heard that?

Everyone shot her daggers, but she was drunk and had something to prove. "He's a founding member of Patchwork House and before you came along—" Suddenly she clammed up. "I mean, I misspoke. It was only three." I had a feeling she'd been wanting to say that to me for a long, long time by the way it fell out of her like candy from a broken vending machine.

"That's not even a convincing lie. If you want to make me look dumb, try harder." I laughed into my beer, but when it grew quiet, night air cool and pressing, I looked up. King's face was a stone mask while he stared at her. Daniel watched her as well, lips a hard line. By their faces, I'd be surprised if she was let back at Patchwork, which for a girl like her may as well be a death sentence. By the way her face broke as she stared at the snow, she knew.

She couldn't be serious, could she? Flip insisted he never lived at Patchwork, not really. If so, when did he leave? And why? And how had I not heard of it? Our town was tiny. The underground community? Even tinier.

"What?" I broke the silence. "What is she talking about?" Everyone was quiet. It was like they were in on some giant secret. "Is what she said true?" My voice wavered. There was no way they could keep such a giant secret from me, but my heart thudded, my fingers grew numb. Why wouldn't someone just *say something*?

I'd *lived* here. As far as I knew, there were only *three* founding members of Patchwork. My eyes traveled back between King and Daniel, who seemed determined not to look at me. What reason was there to keep that from me? I thought to the wall. The larger-than-life mural of a god they insisted existed only in my dreams.

Then I looked to Flip.

Who for the first time in twenty-four hours *finally* looked back.

He stood up so quickly the log shook, and Penelope and Sparky fell off in his wake.

I stood seconds after.

King grabbed my arm.

"What?" I snapped. He tilted his head, telling me not to leave. His jaw could break stone it was so tight. "I need to pee. Are you going to tell me I can't pee, King?"

He breathed fire through his nostrils, but let me go.

FLIP

"Flip, wait!" Tweetie called for me, crunching footfalls growing closer as she tried to catch up. "Flip, stop!"

I kept going. I had imagined this day over and over again. The thing was, I never got to the end. It was a movie without enough film. How did I tell her who I really was without hurting her?

All I'd wanted to do was rent a damn cabin and give her a nice birthday.

One drunk girl fucked everything up.

"Flip!" Her voice gave out like she was falling and I spun just in time, catching her before she crashed to the snow. She was breathless, hat fallen and landing in the powder, revealing a wild, curly yellow halo.

She was so fucking beautiful.

She glanced up at me, blue eyes wide. "Was anything you told me that day true?"

With that, reality came crashing.

I dropped her like hot coals and kept walking. I had no destination in mind. The truth dangled on a precipice. One side of me desperately wanted to fall and let her know, the other paled at the thought.

"Was it all a lie?" she yelled at my back. "On Angel's Wings. Your parents. Your fears. Is this who you really are? A liar, a player, and *apparently* Corrupt. After yesterday, I was starting to think I misjudged you, now I realize that was a trick too."

I stopped but didn't turn around. "Is that what you think? That I...I—"

"Tried to kiss me," she gritted.

"Right. Yeah." I took a breath, voice low, eyes on the ground. "You think I did that to throw you off?"

"Honestly, I don't know," she said on a sigh. I could picture it, picture the way her frustrated breath would blow her curls up. "I don't know what your intentions are with me, Flip. None of this makes any sense. You've ignored me all day. You haven't even made eye contact with me. Now I'm hearing you not only lived here but founded the place."

If I was a good person I would leave forever. Let King make up some bullshit about how I was once one of the stray kids who wander into Patchwork from time to time, needing a temporary family until they're ready for their permanent one. It was all a misunderstanding. We could let this be a nearly harmless blip.

But I wanted to kiss her because *I loved her*, because I couldn't stop loving her even though it was the worst thing for both of us.

"I know I ran away," she said, voice small. "I was startled and my competition was starting..."

In a flash, I spun and pulled her until her chest was pressed to mine. Her gasp was hot musical steam. I lessened my grip on her biceps, rubbing my thumb along her coat. I loved her eyes, loved how even when she had every reason to push me away, she looked at me like she just wanted to heal me. I didn't deserve it.

I wanted it anyway.

She tilted her chin, lips parted, giving me the signal.

My last chance to be decent.

I slid one hand to the nape of her neck, pulling her closer.

"Flip." King's voice was sharpened steel slashing through the night.

"God *fucking* dammit," I said on a frustrated breath, eyes going to the sky, before settling back on her. Enthralling pools of blue filled with uncertainty.

"Don't," she whispered, so quietly King couldn't hear. "Don't let go."

I tightened my grip a fraction, then released her because I knew I never should have pulled her to me in the first place. Her shoulders fell with her face, with the small release of her lips when my hands dropped.

Don't let go.

A deep, hard bob of her throat, a swallow I knew was tears. It landed hard in my gut. Tweetie and tears wrecked me beyond anything else. I would do *anything* to make sure they never fell. Yet here I was, causing them.

Then she spun. Running back to the bonfire. She sat on the log, head turned from me. I was still watching her when I spoke to King, anger on my tongue.

"Is your new job professional cock blocker?" I bit out. He folded his arms and I tore off my hat, ran a ragged hand through my dark waves. "What do you want?"

"Should I spell it out for you? Hire a skywriter? Get you a damn hearing aid? Leave Tweetie alone like we agreed."

"So you and her can live happily ever after? She isn't even the one you want, dude. And you know it. Stop fucking around with my girl and go after yours." I knew it was a low blow the minute it passed my lips.

King blinked. I rarely saw him stunned. He was the kind of man who saw the punch coming, actually reveled in the pain. A guy like that wasn't caught off guard easily.

But here he was, stunned.

And I felt like shit.

He unfolded his arms, speared his hands into his jeans. Both of our eyes traveled to Tweetie, talking with Daniel, who was giving her some advice on how to make s'mores. A distraction technique from her sadness.

When King spoke again, his voice was softer.

I kept my eyes on her.

"I'm not saying this to be a dick."

"I have a feeling you're going to sound like one anyway."

"I'm saying this *because* I can't have the girl. I know what you're feeling more than anyone."

This was the first real conversation King and I had had in years. It was almost like before everything got fucked.

When we could be real with one another. When we called each other on our shit but knew we had the other's back.

I met his eyes.

"What's your end goal here? Are you going to lie to her forever? Get married, have babies, and keep quiet forever the reason you know everything about her is because you're the boy who killed her father?"

I knew he wasn't saying that to be an asshole, which honestly, made it worse. I wish I could've punched something, started a fight so I didn't have to think about my answer. King's hard, granite stare was unrelenting, but there was no animosity there. I loosed an openmouthed exhale and stared at the darkening sky.

I didn't know.

So I pushed those thoughts away. "Who do you think you are?"

He reeled. "I'm the person you entrusted to protect her. From everyone. Even you." And just like that, my anger dissipated.

Replaced with the true emotion.

Shame.

I dragged two hands through my hair, tangling it.

"I thought you finally saw the light," he said.

"She followed me." After staring me down all night, hurt in her eyes like a hot lance to my side. "She came to me."

He wasn't convinced. "That's all it takes, she shows up and you give in?"

"Yes," I said without hesitation.

Silence. A heavy, loaded breath.

"Just leave, Flip," King said without anger. Without anything. "It was a mistake coming back."

Once upon a time, we'd been best friends. Brothers.

A part of me was holding on to the hope I'd fix that too, but now I finally saw how foolish I'd been.

"Yeah," I agreed. "It was."

———

TWEETIE

It was four-thirty in the morning. I could still hear the faint sounds of partying, of those clinging to the last shreds of debauchery like night clung to the sky. I hadn't slept. Daniel and King ushered me to bed, probably hoping I wouldn't think any more about what Penelope let slip.

I'd asked tons of questions about Flip. How long did he live here? Why did he leave? Most importantly: why didn't you tell me?

We'll talk about it later.

Later meant never.

I just didn't understand why they lied, and that question got reworked over and over in my head as I stared at the ceiling. Until the house was quiet, until a new day broke. Flip wasn't a bad person, but maybe he believed he was. He was just like everyone else here, like me, a patchwork. Tragedy had sewn itself into the bright colors of his life. I saw it in him. I just wished he would stop pushing me away and open up to me.

Trust I wouldn't judge him.

I threw off my covers, snuck into the hall growing light by dawn. Down to where I knew he was sleeping. I gently pushed open the door.

Flip was on the floor again, sitting up. Shirtless. The moonlight reflected off his muscled, olive chest. One arm draped over his leg, dark eyes staring straight at me. It was like he was waiting for me.

"You should go."

"Probably," I agreed, but stayed put. Slowly he stood, and with each step he took, my heart pounded louder than a drum.

He stopped a few inches from me. Far enough away that I'd have to stretch to reach him. Close enough that I could hear his breathing, smell his clean, intoxicating scent. It wasn't cologne, or shampoo, or gum, or even laundry. It was just...*him.*

He smelled like a never-ending weekend. Wild nights and cozy memories. Warm, sweet, flirtatious, and a little savage.

Silence passed, my heart rate dripping to an ache between my thighs. I chewed my bottom lip and his stare dropped to the motion, before gliding slow and leisurely back to my eyes, memorizing every contour on my face.

My thighs clenched.

His jaw tightened.

"I want to know something." My whisper was so loud in the deep quiet.

Why didn't you tell me the truth?

What happened to you to make your eyes so sad?

Do you like me as much as I like you?

When I didn't speak, Flip canted his head.

"Do—"

"Tweetie?" Somewhere in the hallway, King called out for me. "Where are you?" As old as I got, King was always checking on me. Which meant he would find me sooner or later, like every other time I snuck out.

In one swift motion, Flip grabbed me above the elbow,

pulling me close and shutting the door behind me. One arm bracketed me, my back pressed against the cool wood.

My heart quickened, his head bent, stare close and urgent.

"I should go," I whispered without conviction. In response, he dragged his thumb across my lower lip, from corner to center, exposing my teeth. I let out a ragged breath that matched his own. Then his knee separated my thighs.

I felt him.

His need.

He caught my wrist, guided my hand down his chest. Along every groove. Every intricately defined muscle like it was chiseled by god. Hot under my hand, worked iron in the cold night. Until he stopped just at his waistband.

I was the one who went farther, slipping my hand beneath the elastic. I curled my fingers, grazing the top of him, coarse and silky and so damn tempting. A rough, quiet groan fell from his lips.

"I'm so bad for you. If I was a good guy, I'd stop. I'd let you be happy."

I didn't understand any of what he was saying, but the pain I felt. Deep. In his rocky, strangled voice and his desperate, cracking eyes.

"Whatever it is I'll understand. If you did something...if something happened...I'll understand."

Tell me. Please.

Let me in.

His stare dug into me, and again I was certain he was searching for something. I desperately wanted him to find it.

He exhaled, resigned.

"I'm not a good guy. I'm the fucking worst." He captured my face in his palms, grip sure and almost painful in its desperation. The way he looked at me, I was sure he would kiss me. The way I felt, I was certain I would let him.

But then, with slow and almost agonizing determination, his lips came to my forehead.

I was frozen. Mute. Struck dumb. Everything stopped working all I knew was his lips on my skin. Soft and so tender, a complete contrast to his grip digging into my skull.

He pulled back, pressed his forehead to mine, and looked at me from beneath hooded lids.

"I'm going to put the awe back in your eyes," he said, and my breath caught. "You looked at me like I was a god once, and you'll do it again."

"Tweetie?" King's voice was closer, urgent. Flip closed his eyes, burrowed his forehead deeper into mine then with another ragged exhale, stepped off.

He gently cupped my shoulders and opened the door, putting me back in the hallway.

I was winded.

It was only a minute before King saw me and rushed to my side.

"What are you doing out here? Are you okay?" He pressed his palm to my forehead. "You look feverish." My fingers buzzed with adrenaline, thighs jelly.

"Just getting air. Got a little hot."

He nodded, face pressed in concern, and walked me back to my room.

TWENTY

DROPPING: SKATERS YELL THIS TO PREVENT A
COLLISION.

FLIP

"I. Am. An. Idiot." I said each word with a thrust to the pillow. I'd spent the better part of the night thinking about what King said. I should stay away from Tweetie. I wasn't good for her. None of us were.

Then she came to me last night and I nearly caved.

That's all it takes, she shows up and you give in?

How true was that? I was weak for her. Anytime I was alone with her all of my stony right crumbled into wrong.

The shower started up and "Blitzkrieg Bop" dying cat version echoed through the cabin walls as Tweetie sang. Fuck. Everything she did was adorable, even when criminally off tune.

I groaned, banging my head against the pillow harder.

Then, like some sign from God, Penelope stumbled into my room. Still drunk, and looking for love. She shut my door behind her, mid-morning sun shining on her tanned face.

"Flip..." She chewed her lip, then pulled her shirt over

her head. Tweetie's singing ceased as seconds dragged into minutes. Penelope waited, eyes wide, and I wondered if she was the perfect antidote to forget about Tweetie.

Meaningless. Mindless.

But even I wasn't that messed up. "Penelope, babe, what are you doing? I am wrecked for Tweetie. She's the only one I think about."

After that night two years earlier, every interaction with a girl always ended the same way: in a goodbye.

Not a moment later, another light knock came on the door, followed by a creak when it opened. Wet hair. *Soaking* wet hair. Does Tweetie not know how to use a towel? And why the *fuck* did I find it so hot? I stifled my groan, digging my fingers into my blanket, creating rosettes in the plaid fabric.

"Oh, sorry—I—wrong room..." Tweetie trailed off, stumbling upon Penelope shirtless next to the dresser. The door shut quietly.

I could run after Tweetie, let her know what she'd seen wasn't what it looked like.

Pull her into my arms.

Kiss her, *finally*.

And then what? I still hadn't written the final feet of film. I still didn't know how to do this without hurting her.

"I don't care," Penelope said quickly, drawing my attention back. "I don't even like you. I like someone else. We can help each other. I can help you make Tweetie jealous and you can help me...or...whatever." She pulled her lip between her teeth and my brows dropped, briefly wondering who Penelope liked.

I dragged a hand down my face. "You deserve better."

"Let me decide that."

It could work. Penelope might be what I needed to push Tweetie away for good.

———————

TWEETIE

Penelope. In his bedroom. The same one who looked at him all googly-eyed. I leaned against his door, wondering what was wrong with me. My fingers zinged, remembering how he'd felt in the dark. My flesh still on fire from his kiss.

You looked at me like I was a god once, and you'll do it again.

"I. Am. An. Idiot." I groaned, hitting my head against the door with each word. It hadn't even been hours since I'd left him, and Penelope was there?

The door opened, smacking my forehead.

"Sorry." Penelope shrugged, obviously unapologetic, and continued down the hall.

"Why do you hate me so much?" I yelled at her back. "I've never done anything to you!"

"I'm jealous!" She spun, red hair a billowing curtain.

My mouth dropped. What the hell could someone like *her* be jealous of me for? She was objectively gorgeous. An uncertain, wavering moment followed, then she spoke, but her voice was quiet.

"It just sucks, okay? My dad is a drunk. I've never met my mom. Patchwork is my home too, but they don't see us like they see you. Every one of us wishes we could be you."

Her words hit me like a kick to the chest.

I'd spent most of my life resenting her and all the Patchwork Girls, considering them mean girls who didn't like me because I wasn't pretty.

"I never..." I never thought about it that way. I thought their looks made them shallow and exclusionary, but this entire time I was the one who couldn't see beyond their beauty.

"And now because I said—I spilled—I might...they might...I could never get to go back—" She choked up, but seconds later she was stone. "You don't even realize how lucky you are." Jaw tight and eyes firm, she exhaled and left.

As she was about to round the corner, I grabbed her elbow. "Wait! What aren't they telling me?" Her dusty brows pinched then she yanked herself free, first sparing me an exasperated breath.

She rounded the corner, and I stayed, staring at the empty hallway.

I couldn't decide whether to be ashamed or angry.

So I snowboarded.

"Want company?" Daniel asked on my way out.

"Are you going to tell me what the fuck is going on?" I countered. He shared a look with King. "Yeah." I snapped my goggles on. "I think I'll go alone."

I tried to work out all my frustration, anger, and insecurity on the powder. When I got back the night had long fallen, and another fire was up. I was still frustrated. Still angry. Still insecure. But now with sore limbs.

And Flip was still with Penelope.

I wanted to hate her, but now I wasn't sure how.

"So the powder was fucking weak today," I spat, landing on the log as Flip threw his arm around Penelope. I ground my jaw, trying to ignore how that made my chest crack. The stitches in my life were coming undone and when I tried to rethread one, it pulled apart another.

"I thought it was pretty good," Daniel added.

Flip and I locked eyes.

His lips tilted.

My stomach pancaked.

"What happened to your coat?" King asked.

"Wet." I put my hands to the fire and focused on that, not on the boy opposite me. S'mores were brought out. Sparky lit a marshmallow on fire and freaked out, dropped it on Pants, who fell into the snow to ward off the burn from *still not wearing pants*.

I actually cracked a smile, just as a coat landed on my shoulders. I looked up in time to find Flip walking back to Penelope. Leaving me with the awkwardness of everyone staring at me. I looked back at the snow, but sneakily tried to smell the hoodie. It smelled like Flip. Warm and oceany, somehow unassuming yet heady. When I looked up, King was glaring.

Then my stomach dropped.

Across the fire, Flip kissed Penelope. Lips that had so recently been on me, hot and firm and possessive. The mere thought sent a slice of heat through my gut.

Suddenly the coat felt less like an act of love, and more like an act of dominance. It shouldn't bother me. It shouldn't. Why should I care what an asshole who didn't meet a single item on my checklist, who abandoned me without reason, is doing with a girl?

I was about to rip his coat off, when Flip's eyes opened.

Locked with mine.

As he continued to kiss her.

The muscle in his cheek throbbed and pulsed like his stare. I could practically feel the power of his kiss. I dropped my cup into the snow, spilled rivers of dark beer into the white powder.

"I...have to get some air."

I knew by the footfalls that King had followed. Before he had a chance to say anything, I turned, rounding on him.

"You can't kick out Penelope."

His beachy brown brows drew like he was thinking. "Who?"

"Are you serious?" My mouth dropped and contrition twisted his sharp features. I rolled my eyes on an exhale, finding the blanket of glitter in the sky.

"You guys can be jerks sometimes, you know that?" I said.

He gave me a soft shrug of apology. I knew what he was thinking. You can't be nice all the time and keep something like Patchwork alive.

"Nice jacket," he said, brow arched.

"Oh, uh, I didn't realize I was still wearing it." What a damn lie. Flip's smell wrapped around me like a warm blanket, and I let myself believe it was him.

King shrugged out of his sweatshirt, and I had no choice but to take Flip's off. It fell to the ground, curled in the powder. King rubbed my shoulders, warming me up like he used to. Silvery night eyes locked on mine.

"Are you going to tell me what's going on?" I asked. "The truth."

"He used to live here, now he doesn't. You know everything."

I nodded, jaw tight. I didn't know why I bothered asking.

"Just like I know everything about what happened that night?" I pressed.

"Tweetie..." His hands froze on my shoulders, but his eyes were hard, his mouth stayed sealed.

"Please tell me." *Tell me something that's not a lie.*

King dropped his hands. "Why do you keep bringing that up?"

"Why do you keep avoiding it?" I could feel my face growing hot even in the icy air.

"The only thing you need to know is that night I gave up any hope of being with the one I loved." My gut dropped. King had a *love*?

"King—"

"This is over, Tweetie. Stop bringing it up. Forget that night. Forget Flip. You came back, the past stays in the past. Got it?"

"You know what," I said, jaw tight. "I feel like snow-boarding."

FLIP

Tweetie glowed through the flames, orange and soft. They crackled and popped a fiery halo around her. A snowboard stood next to her, almost as tall as her—and she was wearing *King's* sweatshirt.

"Going snowboarding?" Daniel asked. "Be safe and stay away from the no-go zones."

She nodded. Still not looking at me.

"Shit," she said aloud.

"What?" I asked at the same time as King. We shot each other glares.

"Uh..." She looked between us. "It's no biggie. I lost my beanie. It was fine during the day but now..." I remembered her running after me the night before, the beanie falling to the snow.

"I have an extr—" Before King could finish his thought, I took mine off and stood up, Penelope falling off my lap into the snow. I slammed it on Tweetie's head. Dammit. She looked adorable in my hat. It slipped a little past the ears, drooping a bit over her big eyes.

"Hey!" Penelope yelled, rubbing her head. Daniel, good Daniel, was at her side, helping her up.

I don't think I've ever seen anything cuter.

Maybe if Tweetie wasn't wearing anything else.

"It doesn't look like it fits very well," King ground out.

"It fits fine," I bit back. A silence settled, various people around the bonfire shooting each other looks.

"I can get you one that fits," King offered.

"Um..." She chewed her bottom lip and my eyes darted to the plump thing. Remembering the way it tasted. How perfectly it fit between my teeth years ago.

As if she knew, she looked up. Locked eyes.

"I'm okay," she said, voice low.

I grinned.

King sighed through his nostrils but said nothing. He walked back to the cabin, and Tweetie worked her mouth, looking after him like she wanted to follow, but at last her eyes settled on me.

"Last night..." She said so quietly I almost didn't catch it, and reality came back.

"Penelope is waiting." Though she looked pretty happy now that Daniel was checking on her.

"Flip!" she called to my back. "Why do you keep running from me?"

I stopped short. "I'm not running." I threw her a grin, but her eyes narrowed.

"You know, at first I thought you were the most brazenly honest boy in existence," she said. "But you smile through your pain so much I think you might be the biggest liar I've ever met."

My smiled dropped.

The bonfire had grown quiet. Everyone watched us. I saw the worry etched in Daniel's youthful face. I never should have started this a month ago—*years ago*.

It was time to end it.

I grabbed her wrist, pulled her far away, until we were shrouded by snow-covered trees, the moonlight bouncing off them like diamonds. There was no light, save for the little glow coming from the cabin and fire, but it was bright and silvery gray.

I could see everything.

Like the insecurity on her face, and the way she came to a stop just at my chest.

She fit me. Perfectly.

"About last night...and this morning..." she stuttered. Fuck. It was cute. And that was the problem. I leaned against a tree. Looked at the stars. The snow. Down the mountain. Anywhere besides her unrelenting stare.

"Flip, about last night...the kiss..." She took a breath like she didn't want to say what was on her mind. The insecurity on her face grew. She dragged her sleeve down with one hand, over her cherry red hands.

End it. Now.

I stepped closer, covering her cold hands with mine. Her eyes popped open.

"Didn't it mean something to you?" she whispered. "Or is this really a game?"

Of course not.

"We need to stop, Tweetie." My voice held no conviction.

She rose on her tiptoes, angling for me, eyes wide with anticipation, lips wet with hope.

"Don't." Was that my voice? Warbled and rough and raw, like sandpaper. It even grated my throat coming out. "Please. Don't." Yet I tightened my grip on her hands.

"Why?" Her brows drooped.

I ground my jaw, so tight I was certain to feel it in the morning.

Because the truth of us would devastate you.

"I'm barely holding it together, Tweetie." My eyes darted to her lips. Wet and shiny and red with cold. I bet they tasted like icy cherries.

"Then don't," she whispered. "Kiss me." My eyes flashed lower to breasts that pushed against her sweater with heated breaths. *King's* sweater. An insane caveman part of me wanted to rip it off. As if she knew what I was thinking, her lids drooped.

And fuck if that look didn't push me to the edge.

One more look. One more sigh. One more *anything*, and I would fall off it.

"Tweetie, I'm leaving Patchwork." Her eyes narrowed, reading me, ripping apart my layers like she had for years. "Sorry," I finished.

"You've been in control of this from day one. Well." She swallowed. "Now I'm in control. There's nothing you can say that will stop my feelings. I like you. I might even..."

My eyes popped. She couldn't be about to say what I thought she was.

Summoning every ounce of willpower, I shoved her off me. She stumbled back, surprise and shock and pain slashing across her face. Her eyes shone, tears building inside them.

Fuck.

I wanted to pull her back into my embrace. Apologize. Tell her the truth. All I wanted was her. That was all I *ever* wanted.

She clenched her jaw, wiped the pain away, and came to me. With each crunch of the snow, my heart pounded louder and louder.

"Nothing you can say will change my mind about you. I know you want me too. I know it. I felt it last night." She placed her palm on my cheek. My heart was fire. Rapid. Beating. "I don't know what you're afraid of, but it's making you push me away. I *told you*, you can't."

Maybe I couldn't by being nice.

Maybe the only way to avoid hurting her a lot was to hurt her a little.

I placed my hand over hers and her shoulders sagged.

"What about last night?" My voice was low. "I'm not sure what you thought happened, Tweetie, but I don't go for easy girls who come searching for sex in the middle of the night."

Her mouth dropped.

She tried to yank her hand back and I tightened my grip over it, holding it tight against my cheek. I wanted to make sure she never came looking for me again, because if she *did* come looking for me, I knew I wouldn't be able to control myself. I'd take her, hold her and kiss her and love her like I'd been dreaming of, like I didn't deserve. I never deserved her.

So I buried the knife deeper.

"Last night was pity. It's all been pity. You're not my type, Tweetie," I said, voice hard. "I like pretty girls. Take the hint." I let her go and she stumbled back, nearly falling to the diamond frosted powder. I reached out, then dropped my hand before she looked up.

"Don't call me that name." Her voice was soft, but her eyes were hard on mine. "Don't ever call me that name again. King calls me that, my family calls me that. It's not for people like you."

Rage bubbled up inside me, but I tamped it down. Tweetie was *my* name for her.

I was certain she would curse me. Tell me to fuck off.

When she spoke again, I wished that's what she'd done, because the broken way she whispered wrecked me.

"I used to write about you in my diary." She couldn't look me in the eyes. My Tweetie, who never backed down from a stare off, couldn't meet my eyes. "I guess what they say about not meeting your heroes is true."

Then she grabbed her board and disappeared into the trees.

TWENTY-ONE

PUMP: FLEXING YOUR LEGS AT THE RIGHT SPOT
ON A TRANSITION TO BUILD UP SPEED.

FLIP

I crooked my neck, sore from waiting for Tweetie to come back, and scanned the room. The winter sun was blinding and bright, illumining the passed-out bodies littering the cabin.

Sparky spooning Bacon spooning Pants, next to the embers of a fire.

Two Patchwork Girls asleep under a table.

Food everywhere. Warheads. Squeeze-its. Cans of beer.

But no Tweetie.

I went to her room. Empty. Clothes on the floor, a towel draped over a chair. One long, uneven breath. I was always irrational when it came to her. It was nothing. She probably passed out somewhere else.

So I scoured the cabin.

I went to Daniel's room to see if he knew where she was but stopped short in the doorway.

Naked.

Thrice the amount of naked limbs I should've been seeing.

Daniel lifted his head between two girls as I shut the door. I went back out, kicking legs and arms until everyone woke, grumpy and groggy.

"What the fuck?" Pants groaned. "The sun is still out." He rolled over, curling into his box of cereal.

"Has anyone seen Tweetie?" A chorus of *no* followed, and my heart sped up. At that moment Daniel came out, perfectly dressed for the day among a group of heathens.

"What's going on?"

"Have you seen Tweetie?"

He closed his mouth, thinking hard. "The last time I saw her was at the bonfire." *I'd* seen Tweetie later than that. I couldn't have been the last one to see her. That was over five hours ago.

"She's probably with King," he added, clapping my shoulder.

I sighed through my nostrils, sitting back uneasily on a wingback. Nails gripping the fabric, I waited. I waited while the cabin came alive. Too-loud music reverberated against the wall. Bloody Mary breakfast was served at five PM. Drunk snowboarding races started up.

Still Tweetie didn't return.

TWEETIE

You don't think.

Why did my dad die? Because I didn't think he would come looking for me.

Why did King go to jail? Because I didn't think about what would happen if I asked to come along.

Why did my gods hurt people? Me. All because of me.

As the second night fell and the air got icy once more, fear crept up my spine. *Maybe I won't get out of this.* My fingers grew numb beneath their gloves, snow started to fall, settling on my already red and bitter nose. I got lucky the first night. It was warmer and dry.

Luck didn't happen twice.

In my embarrassment, in my haste, I tore down the mountain into a *no-go* zone, into loose powder, and dropped into a crevasse, leg pinned in branches and too high to hoist myself back out.

I didn't think about leaving and telling no one where I was going, didn't think about how fast I was going or *where*. I didn't think.

Now I was stuck with only my memories to keep me company.

Nothing you can say will change my mind about you.

"Aargh." My scream was loud at first, before spiraling quietly into the trees.

I had rules to prevent this. A checklist to follow so it never happened. Don't put my heart out there unless I'm absolutely, one hundred percent certain the guy at the other end is going to pick up the phone. Instead I gave Flip my beating heart and he stepped on it. Crunched it beneath the snow boots he wears untied at the top...

I smacked my head against the dirt and snow wall at my back.

I should have hated him.

I should not have found the way he wore his boots alluring.

The moon was bright. I could see the tops of the brushy

gray-green pine trees. I wondered what he was doing. I wondered what happened to make him so closed off and afraid. I wondered if he'd ever had anyone to confide in. What a lonely life, if not.

I should have hated him, but instead I was worried about him.

While this tree is trying to get frisky, I'm worried about *him*.

That was going to be my legacy as I died out here. Not Raegan Fairchild, first female skater to win an international competition, first female signed to a major sponsor.

But Tweetie, hopelessly in love with a man who wanted nothing to do with her.

FLIP

She still hadn't returned.

Even as the sun set and another round of beer pong started, Tweetie hadn't returned.

I tore my beanie off. Ran my hands through my hair. It was black outside now and no one had seen her.

It was almost seven when King returned. I jumped off my wingback guard duty, going right for him.

"Where's Tweetie?"

"Fuck off, Flip," he said without looking up, setting his board against the wall.

"You haven't seen her?" I could tell when my tone registered in his silvery blue eyes. The muscles in his neck corded and he stared too long at the waxy sheen of his board.

Finally, he looked at me.

We were speaking the silent language we'd used years ago. The one developed when running from cops. One I thought I'd never share again.

"What's up?" Daniel asked,

"Tweetie is missing," we said at the same time.

"Did something happen?"

I thought of the cruel words I'd spoken to her. King had a similar look of guilt plastered on his face. He looked up, we locked eyes, and once again we spoke that language. We quickly looked away.

"Not sure," I lied.

Daniel looked between us, not buying it. "We can call the ranger, but it could take some time—"

"Fuck that," we said. I grabbed my board, determined to find her.

King lifted his own off the wall. "I'm coming with you."

"Fine," I said, too filled with worry to give a shit if King helped. The more, the merrier, anyway. I'd do whatever it took to help Tweetie.

Daniel opened and closed his fists. "Someone has to be here for the ranger."

"I know," we said at the same time. I zipped up my jacket. King put on his gloves.

"I want to come—"

"I know," we repeated, snapping on our goggles.

There was an insane fear inside me, an unmanageable terror. I'd flown into the air without a helmet, dove down roads faster than cars. This...this was a weed. It grew untamed inside me and I knew the only thing that would kill it was finding her.

I felt it leaking from King as we tore down the mountain.

We reached the bottom easily, no sign of Tweetie.

So we climbed back up, looking over every inch of snow, when we stopped at a fork. Trees and rock and cliffs—the backcountry on the *no-go* list.

We gave each other a look, speaking that silent language, sliding into dangerous terrain.

We wove through trees, jumping over rocks, still with no sign of Tweetie. When we stopped, our boards created simultaneous waves of snow. The night air was a cold quiet that pressed on our ears.

King lifted his goggles.

"She's not out here." *Then where was she?* went unsaid. "She could've gone home," King continued. All her shit was still at the cabin.

I narrowed my eyes even though he couldn't see. "Did you do something that would make her want to leave suddenly?"

"Did you?" King countered. I tore off my goggles, ready to dig into our bullshit. Sick of years of beating around the bush.

"Look man I did what you wanted. Whatever was going on between me and Tweetie is history. You know what, now that we're on it, I've *always* done what you asked." From taking the fall to living with a family that only ever wanted him, I never said no.

His brows shot into his head. "The hell you have—"

"I never fucking think."

One brief, loaded stare, then our heads both snapped in the direction of Tweetie's voice. Suddenly nothing else mattered.

"Tweetie?" King called out after a minute more of silence.

"King?" Tweetie rang back. "I'm down here!"

We followed the sound of her voice through dense ever-greens and firs. King called her name, Tweetie answered. We went hastily, without thought for our own safety, until I stopped short. The snow blended into the rest of the mountain like white waves but was actually a steep drop off.

I grabbed King just as he was about to fall, pulling him back from the edge. Two heart-pounding seconds passed, then I quickly dropped him. Wiped my hands on my pants.

"Uh, thanks," he said.

"It's nothing."

Tweetie was at the bottom of the cliff, wedged between a tree and its root.

"I knew you would find me," she yelled upon seeing King. I ground my jaw, trying not to let it bother me.

We undid our boards, studying the cliff's edge, coming up with the best way to get her.

"I'll hoist her to you then climb out," he said. I let out a noise like *yeah right.* "I'm taller," he explained.

Not knowing where Tweetie was and if she was okay had been absolute chaos in my soul. I wasn't leaving until *I* saw her to safety.

Before King could say anything else, I jumped down, landing with a thud at her side.

Her eyes grew bigger and bigger.

"Flip, what are you...?" She trailed off as I ran my hands lightly along her leg, from her knee to her ankle, where it was wedged at the root. "Why are you here?" she asked, breath tickling my neck. I shot her a look, filled with every word I couldn't say.

I would *always, always* find her.

I would *always, always* be there.

I would *always, always* save her.

Even if it could only be as her shadow.

She sucked in a breath just as I dislodged her ankle.

I lifted her up to King, who pulled her the rest of the way. Then I followed, climbing up the snowy wet cliff. King was holding Tweetie at his side and I fought the insane urge to pull her to mine.

"Someone has to go back," King said. "Let them know we found her."

I eyed Tweetie. "She's in no condition to make that trek."

"We passed a ranger station on the way. Looked abandoned. We can hole up there until help comes."

Someone has to go back, I said to him silently.

Someone *does,* King shot back with his eyes. I raked my gaze up and down her. Wet. Shivering. And in someone else's arms. I dug my nail into my palm.

"Should probably be the someone who was going to go pro in snowboarding," I said aloud. "Considering the dangerous terrain." King's grip tightened on Tweetie's waist. My jaw clenched.

"Or maybe it makes more sense that someone stays."

I laughed. "How?" The wind howled, King's stare and mine hardening like the icy snow.

"If you're worried someone has to go back, I could go," Tweetie offered, reading our stares. "I'm the reason we're here after all—"

"No," we said at the same time, stares still locked.

The station was old and small—not even the size of a bedroom—but it would do for a night. Boarded up windows allowed only slivers of a silvery, snowy night to escape. There was a barren fireplace in the center so maybe I could find some wood.

King gave me another tight-jawed stare, tried to say I needed to go, but on this I wasn't budging. As far as I was concerned, we could both stay until the day broke. I wasn't leaving Tweetie. Not now.

With a sound in his throat he grabbed me, tugged me to the side, and asked low enough so Tweetie couldn't hear. "You said you did what I wanted, that still true?"

Tweetie watched us near a boarded-up window, light brows pinched.

Could I still let her go after everything? After almost losing her?

King read the doubt in my eyes. "All you're going to do is hurt her."

I met his stony glare. "I know." With a breath through his nostrils, he dropped me and went to Tweetie.

"I'll be *right back*." He gripped her shoulders. "Go into a separate room and lock the door."

I laughed. "I'm not Jeffrey fucking Dahmer." King glanced at me, then at Tweetie, then back at me. "I'm going to be back. Soon. Real fucking soon." He said something under his breath, then left.

The *click* of the door was loud in our heavy silence.

I knew I would hurt her, but I couldn't leave her. So we just stayed in our respective spots, hers against the window, mine near the door. The night was silent, with no wind, only the soft, invisible quiet of snowflakes landing on the ground.

"Sorry," she said, voice like the fluffy flakes outside. "I was stupid. Going out like that was stupid."

I glanced up, a truly stupid, fatal mistake.

Her curls were wet, *dripping* wet.

"Tweetie..." Her name was my prayer. A simultaneous prayer for will power and against it. I'd been keeping myself on a leash for years, but the thing was frayed and one thread from snapping.

"I told you not to call me that." She was breathless, but everything in the way her eyes dropped and locked with mine like iron links told me she wanted to hear it from my lips.

Another long second, then, "Why did you stay?"

"I needed to see you're okay with my own eyes. You have no idea what it did to me last night when you didn't come back."

Sandy eyelashes fluttered. "What did it do to you?"

"Drove me insane. I kept wondering where you were. I stayed up all night until I couldn't. Watching the door. Waiting for you."

She lifted off the window, inching to me. *Go into the room,* my last shred of dignity said, but the rest of me only cared about how she'd stopped within grabbing distance.

"Why?" she asked.

I love you. I'm so fucking in love with you. It's ripped me apart since you were a teenager. It will continue to rip me apart. I just don't want it to rip you apart too.

I leaned closer, so close her hot spring breath warmed my lips. "Do you really not know?"

"Don't. Don't push me away with questions. Let me in. *Please.*"

Conversations in masks and behind trees. Drunk in my bedroom or sober in hers. In the past and in the present, Tweetie knew me.

So I answered honestly, even though I knew it was reckless. "Tweetie I have let you in. That's the problem." Her eyes grew, and I pressed on. "I can't think of any reason why we should be together, but I can think of a hundred why we shouldn't. And yet..." I trailed off.

She looked at me with her big blue eyes, in the darkness they were like a lake at night. "Yet?"

I gripped her face between my hands. "All I can think about is kissing you again."

TWENTY-TWO

RAD: GOOD OR GREAT.

TWEETIE

"I was never any good at playing by the rules," he growled, dipping his head toward mine. *Finally*, I thought. I would get to taste him, those soft, pink lips that had been on my mind since I'd taped his poster to my ceiling.

But then I shivered, body still frozen by the cold.

And ruined the moment.

His eyes contorted, taking me in. My wet beanie, my frozen curls, my red nose and redder lips. His fingers fell from my cheeks, jaw clenched like he was holding something back. He let out a jagged, grieved, breath, and stepped back.

"Let's see if we can find a blanket or some shit."

"Wait," I whispered, limply lifting my arm. I was freezing and I couldn't feel my fingers, but I'd rather kiss him than get warm. He raked his eyes over me again. It was a look that ignited me, one that could burn the very clothes off my body.

I wondered if he knew how much I wanted this. Could he tell by the flush on my skin? Could he hear the way my heart ran toward him like a startled deer?

He went to scrounge for supplies.

One blanket. Two pieces of firewood. A box of matches.

"I'll get the fire started. You take off your clothes."

I blinked, mouth a puffer fish.

He grinned wolfishly and was on me in a second flat. "To dry and get warm. What were you thinking?"

Getting naked in front of Flip? No boy, let alone man, had ever seen me naked. My Rebel Gods had made sure of that. I didn't want Flip to know that. I wanted him to keep thinking of me as a badass. One woman against an institution.

I chewed on my lip. "I think I'll just freeze."

His grin evaporated. "I'll strip you before I let you freeze." I hiccupped at the idea. After another long look, he started the fire.

He faced the door as I peeled off my wet and frozen clothes. My eyes were glued to him, expecting him to turn around at any moment, heart thudding. But he watched the door like it was a blockbuster movie.

I slid under the blanket, still staring at him. Pulled it up to my chin.

The only thing left was the beanie. But I was scared to take it off. Scared to be completely naked.

"Okay...you can turn around."

He waited another moment, then turned. His smile dropped, the look on his face and tightness in his jaw making my heart flip.

"That's a good look on you," he finally said with a smile, but gone was the wolfishness in his eyes.

Replaced was something softer, like the firelight.

I gripped the blanket harder.

He came to me and gently slid the beanie off, placing it with the rest of the clothes to be warmed. Then he gave me generous space, sitting against the door. I wondered if he was cold. His jeans were wet. He hadn't even worn proper snowboarding gear. He'd only removed his shirt to warm by the fire.

We'd been so close to kissing but now, with room to breathe, I couldn't help but think about how only a day before he'd shoved me away with cruel, cruel words.

"I thought you only dated pretty girls." I tried to say it nonchalantly, and I'm sure I failed.

"Tweetie, you're the most beautiful girl in the world."

I choked on a breath.

Flip smiled.

I rubbed my chest, trying to soothe my breathing and heart rate at the same time. It was difficult with Flip watching me so intensely.

After steadying my breathing, I asked quietly, "Then why would you say something so hurtful?" Silence stretched. He looked away.

"Nothing I say will be good enough," he said.

"No more secrets. *Please*."

Three heartbeats, a stare that throbbed with each count. The fire burst like pop rocks and I jumped just as he spoke.

"I was afraid."

My brow creased. "Of what?" More silence. Flip's jaw locked tight. I sighed. Would he ever let me in?

He took a breath, muscles rippling cruelly.

"You."

I swallowed, suddenly unable to speak. Flip continued.

"Everything I told you was the truth, Tweetie. My mom

was an addict. She left me. I never met my dad." My heart crumbled. His truth had me inching closer to him, it was instinct to offer him comfort. "That wasn't a lie." The earnestness in his eyes, in his voice, made me believe him.

"Then why did you lie about Patchwork?"

He paused. Flip's stare found the fire, flickering and gold.

"I didn't know how to tell you the truth. About who I was. Where I came from. I had something great at Patchwork and I broke it. I didn't want that to happen with you." All at once he looked right at me.

I paused, his stare glowed brighter than the flames. I didn't look away even though I couldn't breathe

"Tweetie I want you. I want you more than anything. I can't lose you, but I can't hurt you either. Both possibilities have me frozen. Fuck." He looked away. "I'm such a fucking coward."

All the things about Flip that hadn't added up—the broken smiles, the hollow confidence—suddenly made sense. He was like me, afraid. Afraid of being vulnerable, of not having somewhere to belong. He wouldn't say it, but I knew it intimately. As much as I wanted to be fearless, that's all I felt: *fear*.

"You have me." It fell out of my mouth before I could think to hold it back.

Flip's chocolate eyes flashed to mine. The only sound was the crackle and pop of the fireplace. Suddenly I was aware of how naked I was. Our conversation had dulled it, but now the knowledge was back with painful clarity.

I looked for something to lighten the mood. His tattoo glowed and flickered inky in the firelight.

"So, how many other dicks do you have on your body?"

I tried to laugh but it came out in halting, nervous breaths. Flip's hand settled absently on his ribcage, his stare burned.

"I only have the one on my arm."

"Then what does your rib mean?" I asked. He tilted his head, watching me until goose bumps slid up and down my body.

"I guess you could say it's a love note." Serious Flip was the most dangerous. More dangerous than cocky Flip, even more dangerous than flirty Flip. I suddenly wished I had a paper bag to breathe into.

"Oh." The word was barely audible. Flip didn't offer any more explanation, but I didn't press. His eyes were dark, my throat thick. Goose bumps pricked my flesh, but out of nerves, not cold. It was the way he stared at me unrelentingly. No amount of space could cure that.

I tightened the blanket to my chest.

"Tell me more about this checklist," he said, voice lighter.

My lips parted. What a random question. "What about it?"

"There's a boy who met it, right?"

"Almost." One boy. Nate. As ridiculous as it was, I felt guilty, like I was cheating on Flip with Nate—someone I never expected to meet again, but whose lips nevertheless cemented themselves in my heart, and whose late night lesson in freedom and courage irrevocably shaped my future.

Nate met all of my rules...except one.

Flip broke all of my rules...except one.

No kissing until I'm absolutely certain they love me.

My heart yearned for Flip.

I wanted him on me.

In me.

All at once Flip stood, bent down before me, dragged his thumb across my lip.

My mouth froze mid-word.

"You had something on your lip," he said, licking it. "Tastes like...*you*." He tilted his head, lips curving with wicked humor. I nodded, unable to speak past the heat scorching my belly. I stared at his mouth, wanting to know what he tasted like too. An unbridled need now sewed itself along my veins.

Flip sat back against the door like nothing had happened. Firelight glowed against his well-defined upper body. My fingers tingled, vividly remembering the way the muscles felt against them.

Nerves hummed under my skin.

"Want to hear a story?" he asked after a minute. We stared at one another in warm, saturated silence. I began to wonder if he was asking me so many questions to help rid me of my nerves.

I nodded, throat too thick to form words.

"My grandmother was Taiwanese, but she only knows Japanese because of the Japanese occupation. I know Mandarin..."

My heart stopped.

Just stopped working.

I suddenly couldn't hear him, couldn't think above the roaring in my ears.

It *couldn't* be.

I'd heard this story. The night Nate gave me one one-thousandth of a wish and disappeared for two years. Only to return to set off a domino chain of events leading to my first and last kiss with him, and me leaving Patchwork.

It had to have been just a coincidence.

But...

What if it wasn't?

Flip must have mistaken my silence for more nerves because he kept talking. I stared at him trying to reconstruct drunk memories. Was it possible?

"What's your name?" I blurted. "Your real name."

Flip blinked. "Nate."

TWENTY-THREE

EARLY GRAB: GRABBING YOUR BOARD BEFORE
THE TRANSITION.

TWEETIE
Some time ago
Tweetie is 18, Flip is 23

I thought about the mysterious boy I nearly kissed every day
for two years. The boy who dragged me through the gates of
Heaven's Court, but opened another and taught me street
style. I kept his crane on my nightstand, falling asleep every
night to the pretty pink pattern.

I asked my gods, but they still gave me nothing.

Drop it, King said a few days ago. *Stop asking me this
fucking question.*

Another rule. Another locked Patchwork door.

One morning I slammed my hand on the nightstand,
looking for the crane. It wasn't there, but I wasn't immediately alarmed.

Maybe it had fallen off in the night.

I searched high and low in my room but couldn't find it.

"Have you seen a crane?" I asked my gods. "It's like..."

this big." I made a claw with my pointer and thumb. Romeo raised his head from the couch an inch, clearly hung over, and shook his head.

Daniel gave me an apologetic no.

King glanced up then his eyes widened. "Put some goddamn clothes on." I looked down at my outfit. I was in a shirt and pajama pants. I *always* wore this around the house. The only difference between this and my normal clothes was the lack of sports bra.

I looked at Daniel and Romeo for help. They shrugged.

"Have you seen it?" I asked King again.

"I'm not talking until you put some fucking clothes on."

"These are my pajamas. I always wear this. I've worn these clothes for years." I was so nonplussed. Why was he acting this way?

"You're not a kid anymore, Tweetie. Cover up." He gestured to my chest. Instinctively, I folded my arms, feeling exposed even though this was what I wore every day.

"You're not wearing a shirt," I pointed out. "Romeo is in his underwear." And that was a lot of clothes for Romeo.

"We're men."

My mouth dropped. Betrayal and indignation froze my veins. I wanted to argue, but that wasn't why I came down here. "Have you seen it?" I repeated, tone icy.

"Saw it. Tossed it."

It took me a minute to realize what he meant. "You *tossed it*? Why?"

He shrugged without looking at me. "Thought it was garbage."

Anger, sadness, shock—it all swirled in my gut.

I ran to the kitchen and knocked over the trash, searching through the refuse.

The lines were always blurred with King: brother, best friend, father figure.

I often wondered how blurry the lines got for him. As I grew up, I saw him with women, but they never lasted long. I was always his priority.

I never asked to be, but I never had to. We were an unconventional family. He couldn't teach me how to wear makeup or how to do my hair, but he was there for me when I started my period and bought my first bra. He was the only one I wanted to tell about my first kiss. He saved up money to buy me new skateboards.

He was my family.

Which is why this broke my heart.

If the crane had been tossed in the kitchen, it was long gone now. I gave up, pissed and disappointed. King leaned against the frame.

"You don't get to control my love life," I said.

He ground his teeth. "That's not what I'm doing."

"Then *why*? Why would you take it? What other reason is there?"

"I'm trying to protect you!" He rubbed between his eyes with one finger.

"From a paper bird?" I knew I shouldn't have responded with sarcasm, but I was so fed up. King's face became a mask. His mouth sealed shut.

With a frustrated scream, I stormed out of the house.

FLIP

For two years I kept the gates at Heaven's Court closed. I

stayed away. Heaven Falls was small but divided. Other towns of our size were so close it was impossible to hide, but not ours. We gossiped in myth. Before coming here, I didn't know a thing about the other side. I was Corrupt, they were Incorrupt, and that's as far as it went. There was still so much I didn't know, even now. Parties, sweeping ballrooms, old buildings with mysterious names.

The only things the Corrupt and Incorrupt shared were Devil's Hill and Heaven Falls, the waterfall.

So hiding from Tweetie was easy.

I immersed myself in watching Pip. I tried to distract myself with girls. They always had interest in me, considered me a bad boy from beyond the gates. I even kept King's family happy.

We took a picture together.

A fucking picture. It sat on the mantle like we were some kind of family.

Still, all I thought about was Tweetie.

I fell back on the bed with a sigh. Why couldn't I stop thinking about her?

Bizzy leaned in the doorway. "Are you upset because we took a photo together? I tried to tell them you wouldn't want to. They don't really listen to me. Or anyone."

"I..." I trailed off. *No.* I was a little wary, maybe. Years later and I kept waiting for the shoe to drop. I'm pretty sure they only did it to make King jealous.

They wouldn't actually want me on the mantle.

"Just thinking," I said.

"Is that code for kid?"

I grimaced. It *should* be code for kid. What the fuck is wrong with me? "Girl," I said. "It's code for girl I absolutely shouldn't be thinking about." A long silence. They'd put the photo of us up on the dusty, iron blue wall in King's room, next to the old family photo featuring King. I closed my eyes.

"You can't help who you love," Bizzy said. "If you could, everyone would be so much happier. But also not, you know? Because the struggle is what's worth it—I hope," she added softly.

I opened one eye, looking at her. "Is there something you're trying to tell me, Bizzy?"

Her eyes grew, caught.

"No," she said quickly. "I'm just saying it's pointless to fight what your heart wants. You should follow it, even it leads you to the edge of the earth."

If Bizzy knew the whole story, she wouldn't have given me this advice.

I knew that, and yet, I let her words lead me to the edge.

I arrived at Patchwork just as Tweetie stormed out of the house in nothing but a loose top and pajama pants. Fury was written across her face. King followed to the brink of the porch, yelling after her. She flipped him the bird over her shoulder and he stopped, defeat in the weight of his shoulders.

Why was I here? I couldn't understand why I had such trouble staying away from her. I'd always had problems following rules, call it a character flaw. It was one of the reasons us Patchwork crew got along so well. But this was different.

This was *my* rule. I knew I needed to fuck off and let Tweetie live her life.

I followed her.

Tweetie had aged well. It was fucked up to think that about

the once-little-girl I'd saved, but then, I'd traded my soul to Devil's Hill a long time ago.

Every time I came to Tweetie, I told myself it would be the last time, but my draw to her kept growing. We were connected through a tragedy that should have destroyed any seedling of a relationship. Instead we bloomed. She was the only one who saw me. Even as a shadow, even in the dark, she saw *me*.

The real me.

"Who's there?" Her head turned sharply at the sound of wet grass sliding beneath my shoes. "King?"

I scratched my neck, staying hidden. "Not quite."

"You sound like the boy from the bedroom..." She trailed off, uncertain.

"You sound like the girl from the bedroom."

She laughed. "I should be worried. This is stalker behavior."

It was my turn to laugh. *Yeah.*

"Well, are you going to come out?"

"Do you not remember what I look like?" I hedged.

"You were all bundled up," she said. "And I might have been a little drunk..."

"Understatement," I said dryly, and she laughed again. God, I loved her laugh.

"How are you here right now? It's like you knew I was thinking about you." She'd been thinking about me? Fuck. I wanted to ask her how often. Was it possible it was as much as I did her? Daily. Hourly.

"You were the one who dragged me back from Heaven's Court, right?" I didn't say anything. "How do you know the Rebel Gods? Who *are* you? No one will tell me anything."

"I can answer your questions, or I can stay, but not both. Not tonight." One untouched, perfectly preserved memory. That's what I told myself, at least. Before I left her for good.

She mulled it over. "Okay, no questions." A breeze blew. She fiddled with her thumbs. "I...I lost your crane."

"Lost?"

"It was...confiscated." Immediately I knew who took it. She dove into what happened and it was a breath of fucking fresh air. These rare moments when she opened up were like fucking crack to me.

I never wanted her to stop.

"I just...I don't understand. Why would he take my crane, and why would he get upset with how I'm dressing?"

"Sounds like he likes you." I looked at the house. I had a suspicion that King was developing feelings for Tweetie. He wasn't like me, twisted in the head because the little girl we'd brought in was no longer little. King was ignoring his real feelings.

Pip had sent a letter.

Pip was waiting.

King, for some reason, wouldn't go to her.

She laughed. "No. No way. That would never happen."

I bit my tongue.

Silence passed, a wet breeze rustled the leaves on the trees. It had been an unusually warm winter, with many wintry showers instead of snowstorms. Now as we headed into spring the stars were a shimmering blur beneath puffy clouds. They were getting ready to open up, a final warning to leave.

"Well, should we show ourselves?" My heart palpated. I considered myself her shadow. Shadows shouldn't show themselves. They stayed hidden.

The slick sound of wet grass, Tweetie moving.

"Wait!" I don't know why, I'd never considered myself a

romantic, but suddenly my heart was pounding. "Close your eyes." Her mouth parted like she would say something, instead she sucked in a breath. Did as she was told.

I took a moment to look at her.

Really look at her.

The soft of her round cheeks. The red of her button nose. The dip just before her lips.

And, of course, the wild tangles and brambles of her curls.

"Goddamn," I hissed. "You're beautiful." I could stay like this for hours, learning things only possible up close: she had two small moles just beneath her left eye, spider bites; an almost unnoticeable divot in her chin.

But her eyelids fluttered like she was going to open them, and panic mobilized in my blood along with the first wet kiss on my cheek. Rain. Or snow.

This could be the last time.

The *only* time.

So I took her, held her, and kissed her like my world was ending.

She was surprised at first, lips unmoving. It was wrong in every way. She was too young, I was too corrupt. But when she melted into me, her sigh dripping down my throat, any thoughts beyond *her* disappeared.

I angled one hand on the back of her neck, the other on her lower back. Her lip bent by her moan against mine. Soft. Supple. Intoxicating.

She was addicting.

An elixir.

Her fingers made rosettes on my shirt, pulling me close. "Who are you?" she asked on a hot breath. "Please tell me."

Crack, slam, shatter—the sound of reality breaking from the moment and falling to the floor.

I stepped back. Her eyes remained closed, still lost in our kiss. Slow, intermittent drops of rain and snow veiled her in blurry harmony.

So. Goddamn. Beautiful.

A goddess.

An uneven breath, then I spun and left before she could answer her own question.

"Wait," she called after me. "At least tell me your name."

I stopped. "Nate."

TWENTY-FOUR

BAIL: TO FALL.

FLIP
Present

Tweetie went silent after I told her my name. Staring at me with a face I couldn't figure out. The snow behind her fell thicker and faster, and for some reason, I was thinking of the night she'd first asked my name. It was slow then, wet and rainy.

I wanted to kiss her.

I wanted to do more than kiss her.

"I'd pay a thousand dollars to know what you're thinking right now." My voice was sandpaper.

She smiled, biting her lower lip to keep it from growing, looking down at her warming fingers.

"Alright, two thousand." She laughed, throwing her head back, and I knocked my head against the wall, focusing on the pain and not her laugh or the way it matched the stars in the sky.

Quiet grew after her laugh faded. She watched me with

the same inscrutable thought swirling over and over again on her face.

Uncomfortable?

Probably.

She was naked beneath her blanket and I may as well have been a leering, unwanted stranger.

I stood quickly. "Fuck, I..." I rubbed the back of my neck. "I'll sleep in the other room."

"Flip," she called after me.

I stopped short, shoulders tight. "Call me Nate."

"What?" Breathless, a blush in her voice. I stared at the door, focusing on the knots in the wood and not the bubblegum I knew was leaking into her cheeks.

"Nate. My name."

"Oh, um...Nate." The quiet in her voice let me know the blush was spreading. "Do you still want to know what I'm thinking?" I looked over my shoulder, just enough to see her let the blanket drop, exposing the slope of her shoulder.

I sucked in a breath, eyes back on the door.

"Nate—"

"Do you know what you're asking?" Was that my voice? Low, warbled—speakers with the bass turned up too high. Quiet continued, and against everything in my brain saying not to, I looked back over my shoulder. Tweetie bit her lower lip, looking down like she was embarrassed by the smile, and nodded slowly. The blanket dropped more, exposing the delicate line of her collarbone, the tops of her breasts.

And then I was done for.

"Tell me not to do this." Even as I cautioned her, I went to her. "Tell me to go into that room and shut the door." I lowered myself on top of her, weight on my arms, searching her lakewater eyes.

"I want this." Her throat bobbed with the breath. I zeroed on it.

"You wouldn't if you knew everything." I dipped my head to her neck, sucking the peachy soft bone through my warnings.

She groaned. *Fuck.* I'd do anything to hear that again.

"But I do." She arched into my lips. "It was you. You were the boy I was waiting for. The boy who kissed me and left me with a mark on my heart. The boy who met my checklist. It was *always* you."

I paused, lips at the base of her neck. She'd waited for me like I'd waited for her? My heart rammed against my ribcage.

But all I could think about was that there was still so much she *didn't* know.

"I know everything," she said as if sensing my hesitation. "I've put the pieces together." I lifted my head, her eyes pierced mine. "I know everything. It was you the whole time. You were there the night my life changed."

―――――

I paused. My simultaneous hope and fear had fallen from her lips and I stared blankly, not certain I'd heard her correctly.

Unsure if this was a dream or a nightmare.

She *knew* I'd killed her dad. She knew.

You were there the night my life changed.

I had to sit up, get space, but stayed on the chunky flannel, plaid blanket.

My throat was thick, my heartbeat fast and tense. "What did you say?"

"I know about us." She cupped my cheek. "Our past.

Our history. Our connection. You've been in my life so much longer than this year, Nate. I don't know why you kept it from me."

The wrinkles in my brow deepened. "Did King tell you?" She shook her head. "How?" Before she could answer, I asked what I really wanted to know: "You're not mad? Not...hurt?" Tweetie moved closer. So close our foreheads nearly touched, shadowing the blanket between us with our bodies.

"Why would I be?" she whispered. "*You* were my lost god. I searched for you for two years—" she cut off, looked away, embarrassed. Another jolt, my heart kick-started like someone pressed electric paddles directly to the skin.

I grasped her chin, pulling her eyes back to mine. "You did?" A split second pause, like she was embarrassed to admit the truth, then she tried to nod. I reluctantly let her go.

"I gave you my heart years ago, but I gave up hope you'd come back to get it."

I couldn't believe what I was hearing. My heart pounded, the blood rushed in my ears, a roaring river. She'd been searching for me. She wanted me as much as I wanted her.

Tweetie shifted and the blanket fell. She quickly scrambled to cover herself, cheeks red. I tried to keep my brain focused—*How do you know? How much do you know? How long?*

All I could see was her, forever tattooed in my memory. A body I'd been imagining in forbidden bursts for years. One I knew I needed the day she'd handed me *my* shirt.

The pads of my fingers slid along the fabric, thumbs dipping beneath the flannel edge, feeling her soft skin along a razor-sharp line like the one I rode. Her heartbeat thumped against my fingers, breath gusting my chin.

Suddenly there was only one question I cared about.

"If I asked, would you let go?"

"Yes," she said it as she sucked in. Our eyes connected in the shadows our foreheads made.

And that's the moment I decided to figure out how Tweetie learned about me later.

"Let go."

She did.

The blanket dropped to her lap and my mind went blank. Memorizing every forbidden inch. A silhouette I'd learned through her window, now in the flesh. I decided then and there I would relearn it with my tongue. Kissing, sucking, swallowing fingers that had settled on her sill.

"Flip..."

"What's my name?" I said, tearing my eyes from her body. God, her blush was adorable. It stained her cream cheeks red like paint drops in water. And just like I'd predicted, it spread *everywhere*.

I thumbed her lip, memorizing her reaction.

"Nate."

I swallowed a groan and pressed a hand between her breasts, pushing her down gently.

"Do you want this?"

She nodded, lips pouty and perfect.

"Words," I ordered leisurely as I continued to drag my thumb across her silky lip, twisting, massaging, eliciting jagged moans that made my own breath rocky.

"I want this," she breathed, eyes locked on me, breath ghosting over my thumb. "You."

She couldn't know what those four simple words did to me.

I'd wanted this moment for years. Dreamed of it. It had driven me insane. Driven a wedge between my closest friends—my brothers.

And here she was, offering it.

"I'm going to take my time with you, Tweetie."

TWEETIE

Flip was so caring.

So gentle.

So sweet.

And *so agonizingly slow*.

How could I not have seen it? The boy who couldn't meet a single item on my checklist was somehow also the only one who had. Flip was Nate. Nate was Flip. He was there the night my life changed, the day I left Patchwork.

"I can't wait to see the faces you make," Flip said, biting the skin at my collarbone softly. "I've memorized almost everything about you. Like how you always sleep in an oversized Ramones shirt, or your inability to talk without a full mouth. Or the way you realize halfway through and freeze, covering your face with both hands."

"Please," I breathed, dragging my hands down his back, then up, feeling a body that had once been pasted above my bed. *Hard*. Muscles flexed and worked beneath my fingers.

He lifted, catching my stare. His eyes were fire. Absolute fire.

"But those are for the world, Tweetie, and I want the secret sighs. To swallow them. To see the moment your blue, blue eyes change after I've just given you everything."

His voice dipped low in the way that drove me nuts, making my gut clench with how his tongue licked over *everything*.

Just when I couldn't get any hotter, he said something like that, and my blood became lava.

He grinned, tracing a knuckle along my jaw, down my neck. "Like that one."

Then he kissed me.

If only we'd kissed sooner.

I would have remembered *this*. His voice, his eyes— everything that I instinctively felt, but had written off as coincidence, this was not one of them. His lips were forever inside me. Soft yet unyielding. Hot. Promising. I was catapulted back to that night, the tattoo he'd put on my heart suddenly white-hot and searing.

"You idiot," I said against his lips. He paused, eyes opening as his brows rose. "Why did you take so long?" Flip grinned and kissed me more.

He ruled me. Bit my lip, dragged it out. His tongue found mine again, harder and deeper. Fervently making up for all our wasted time. All of our almosts.

I parted for him, begging him silently. He slid between my thighs, jeans scratchy and torturous against my skin. I just wanted to feel *him*. He broke the kiss, palms grasping my face.

Then everything stopped.

There was an emotion in his eyes, pain and hurt and sorrow swirling like a violent storm. His grip was so tight, but it was nothing like his jaw. Granite—no, even that wasn't hard enough. He didn't look at me, at least not my eyes. My lips. My nose. My neck and farther down, keeping my head locked between his palms as if I was going to disappear at any moment.

Studying me.

Memorizing me.

"What?" My insecurity leaked through. I thought Flip liked me, the real me, but maybe I was wrong.

Then his eyes shot to mine.

"You have no idea how long I've waited for this." And then he kissed me ferociously, the intent behind his rocky words in the feverish way his lips met mine. Every slow minute before sped up as I tangled my hands in his hair and he tangled his in mine. He bit me, sucked on my lip, dragging it out with my groan.

With a jagged breath, eyes still closed, he pulled back.

"Are you ready?" he asked, voice low and steady and enthralling.

"Yes," I whispered.

TWENTY-FIVE

FACEPLANT: LANDING DIRECTLY ON YOUR FACE.

TWEETIE

"I've wanted your orgasm for years." My eyes grew at his confession, then slacked as Flip pressed a kiss between the dip in my hip bones. The muscles of his back flexed and rolled like waves in the ocean.

"How many have you had with others?" he asked.

"None," I whispered. Small. Shy. Afraid he'd judge me. His groan filled the small room, touch bruising my skin.

"It belongs to me. Do you know that? It always has." I nodded as he came up to me, chest to chest, and dragged his pointer finger along my lower lip, back and forth, knuckle to tip. A slow, delirious meditation. "Say it."

"It's yours," I said. He was at my thigh, hard. Wanting. Growing with my words. So tauntingly close and yet far.

"Again."

"It's yours, Nate."

"I'd give you the world if I could." He pressed his lips to mine, talking through breaks in his kisses. My cheek. My jawline. Beneath my ear. "It still wouldn't be enough." His lips found mine again. Searching.

"Just give me now," I said against his mouth. Another groan I swallowed, and then he was *there*. Only the fabric of his boxer briefs between us. He reached down to tug them off, lips never leaving mine, tongue in my mouth hot and deep and—

"Perfect," he said. "You're perfect. I'm going to make this perfect for you."

Knock, knock.

Our kiss stilled.

The cabin had been our own personal castle, alone on the mountain, just us. Now pale, powdery blue light leaked through wood slats. The night had already come and gone?

The same realization passed through our eyes: *King was back.*

I quickly scrambled off him and he me. I'd barely managed to put on a shirt just as the door opened. Daniel and King stood like shadowed knights in the wintry light.

"Uh, hey," I said, rubbing the back of my neck. "You're back." Heat drenched my skin. Seconds ago Flip's tongue had been in my mouth, his everything between my thighs. More red bled to my cheeks and I looked anywhere else.

Oh my god.

My bra.

A beacon of my promiscuity on the plaid. In my haste, I forgot to put it on. Flip took a subtle step to the left, concealing it beneath his foot. My knight in shining skater shoes.

"We would've been here earlier, but someone insisted he come..." King trailed off annoyed, and out from behind Daniel stepped a third. I think my heart dropped to the floor, or maybe I did, because Flip grabbed my elbow to steady me.

"Romeo," I gasped. I hadn't seen him since I left Patchwork, and he was changed. The boy who used to think leather was the only viable clothing option was wearing jeans and a shirt—and his *hair*. What had he done with it?

"Hey, luv," Romeo said, an amused tilt to the corner of his lips.

"You're...you're in a shirt! And you *cut your hair*." Romeo had always been fists and fucking, leather and piercings. I could count on one hand the times I'd seen him with a shirt. His hair was his pride and joy. I couldn't for the life of me begin to imagine what would make someone like *him* go legit.

He shot me a grin. "Is that really what you want to talk about right now?" *Yes. No. But really, yes.*

I stared at all four of them. I couldn't remember the last time I'd seen all three of them together, much less with Flip, who apparently *should* have been with them all along.

The Rebel Gods of Patchwork House.

Finally together again.

I ran and wrapped my arms around Romeo's waist. He always hated hugs, but he tolerated mine. "Oh fuck, she's crying." I stepped back, wiping my eyes and pretending it was nothing. It had been *so* long.

"Why are you up here?" I said after I'd gotten my eyes under control. A silence followed.

"Someone put up the bat signal," he replied simply, wiping the tears under my eyes. Then with a faux-stern brogue said, "Have you been getting yourself into trouble again, luv?"

"So much trouble she can't find her own shirt," King said wryly. My mind went blank as I met King's eyes. I didn't understand, then I looked down. In our rush, I'd put on *his* shirt. Heat bled into my cheeks.

I heard Flip's soft, satisfied laugh behind me.

"Are you back?" I said quickly, voice high. "Are we all back together?"

Romeo gave me a sad smile and threw his arm around me, shepherding me outside. "I hear there's a party being thrown in honor of you not being dead."

———

When we got back to Patchwork, the party was already raging. Porch lanterns jiggled with music just as someone fell through the open door, somehow covered in glitter and feathers. The Rebel Gods stepped over him like it was nothing.

I lifted my foot to the step, but was yanked back before it could land.

Into the arms of Flip.

"I was going insane being apart from you, even just for the ride." His hand slid up my shirt—*his* shirt—stopping just at my stomach. My breath caught. We were barely hidden by the porch. People moved above us, streaming past the open door like fish in an aquarium for the debauched.

"Never take off my shirt." His teeth came to my neck, a gentle scrape along the flesh. "Unless *I* tell you to."

Then he went inside, leaving my mouth aching, my gut empty, my legs weak.

Inside I plopped between Romeo and Daniel on the couch, overheated and woozy. Romeo wasn't drinking, his jeans were acid washed and perfectly tailored.

He tugged at the hem like it was itchy or something, but it looked *amazing*. He raised a brow at my gaping.

I shrugged. "You're different."

"Same insides, different packaging." I made a face, but even if Romeo was different, he was back. I scrunched myself against the couch happily.

Finally we were all together.

Over and over again, girls *and* boys came up to Romeo, asking for autographs. I could barely contain my joy for him, though he didn't look happy. He smiled, gave them a Romeo grin, but it was like when I first met Flip. Hollow.

"You, on the other hand," Romeo said, after giving his one-thousandth autograph. "Same packaging, a bit different insides." I tilted my head, not sure what he meant. He grinned wickedly and said, "You're sharing those insides with someone special now, yeah?" His gaze shot to Flip, and my mouth dropped, fell to the floor.

Daniel reached behind my back and smacked Romeo, uttered some names, which of course had no effect.

Romeo lit a joint. At least that hadn't changed. "Maybe it's time to stop battling the wind." He exhaled smoke up to the ceiling.

My eyes locked with Flip's.

How long had he been watching me? He stared with purpose, even as he took a drink from a red cup, his eyes were locked with mine.

It belongs to me. Do you know that? It always has.

That's what I felt when he looked at me. That was the inscrutable glint in his eyes, the thing that's been bugging me since day one. Like he always knew we were meant to be, and even if I tried to fight, it would be useless.

We were inevitable.

My lips parted and his eyes darted to that. I could see the dirty thoughts in his head and as if he could see the ones heating up my own body, he tossed me a complete, bone-melting grin.

"You alright, little girl?" Daniel asked after I shifted in my seat again. They followed my line of sight and shared a look, lips a tight line, something flickering between them. Worry maybe? But that couldn't be right.

"I...uh..." I couldn't tear my gaze from Flip, his grin stretching cruelly. I swallowed. "So you're a pop star now," I said, turning to Romeo. "What's that like?"

Romeo's face dropped—*heartache*—but he was saved by another autograph. I studied him a moment, his jeans, his short hair. The only thing still Romeo were the tattoos and piercings.

I turned to Daniel on a whisper. "What made Romeo change so much?" He eyed me, then turned forward. I should've known better than to expect Daniel of all people to spill the beans.

In my peripheral, I caught King's unmistakable tattoos disappearing upstairs. King hadn't said a word to me since the cabin.

I caught him right before he disappeared. "King!" He paused on the second to last step. I gripped the railing, leaning forward. He shifted like he wanted to keep walking. "Big brother..."

Finally he turned around.

Leaned against the wall, half hidden in shadows. Folded his arms, biceps bulging. He was always big, and over the years he just got bigger. Where Flip had a lean, swimmer's body, those thin skater muscles that drove me mad, King was built to do damage.

"What is it, Rae?"

Rae.

I nearly bowled over.

He'd never called me by my real name, ever.

"Was..." I trailed off, staring into his gray eyes for longer than I should have. Finally I shook my head, getting back to why I came. "Was Flip the reason you kissed me the night I left?" Everything else had fallen into place but this. Still my missing puzzle piece. The night I left. The night of my first kiss with Nate. The night King had come in bloody, angry, and kissed me after.

King was silent, staring down at me with no emotion in his eyes.

Nothing I could read.

A long silence passed; music, laughter, glass shattering. I closed the distance until there was only one step between us. He was still so much taller, I had to crane my neck back.

"I know Flip is the one who gave me the crane. I know he's the one who was there that night I followed you to Heaven's Court. I know Flip is Nate. I know everything."

His eyes narrowed a fraction, but he didn't say anything.

I sighed. "Are we ever going to talk about what happened?"

King unfolded his arms, the mask he'd worn crumbling. Yet he looked above my head. "Do you remember when you watched *The Shining* for the first time?" I looked over my shoulder to where he was looking. Flip watched us, the look on his face not easily readable.

I turned back to King. "What does that have to do with anything?" He shot me a raised brow, mouth a hard line. So reminiscent of my childhood. It was my turn to fold my arms. "I tried to crawl in your bed."

"I told you to sleep on the floor."

"Which was scarier because *monsters under the bed*," I enunciated.

"I woke up to you asleep at the foot of my bed like a fucking dog."

"You shouldn't have shown that to a twelve-year-old."

He shrugged. "You were a pussy."

I shoved him. "What's the point of this trip down memory lane, big brother King?" It was the first time he didn't make a face at my nickname. I had a feeling this story was more than random reminiscing. He was trying to tell me something.

It took awhile for him to respond. "You'll always be safe with me."

I tried to lighten the mood. "At the foot of your bed?"

He nodded to himself, lost somewhere I couldn't see. "At the foot of my bed." King walked away, disappeared up the stairs to his room in the attic.

I knew he would always be my older brother, always be my King, so why did it feel like he was letting me go?

All at once I was grabbed, ripped away, mouth covered so I wouldn't scream. Fear crawled up my throat but was just as quickly replaced with heat.

"Unfaithful." Lips at my neck. "Wandering." Teeth on my skin. "So easily swayed." I melted when Flip spun me, immediately kissing me.

Hollowed out my mouth.

The world was hazy and rose-colored when he finished. He pushed back my hair. "You owe me a lesson."

TWEETIE

I furrowed my brow. "A lesson?"

"Time to teach me that move, Tweetie. You've got a debt to pay. Skating lessons aren't free, remember?" I wasn't sure what he meant by that, but then he flashed me a smile and my stomach flipped. When he took my hand in his, leading me outside, I couldn't think of anything else but his skin on mine.

"So you really want to skateboard?" I eyed the ramp suspiciously. There was something leonine in his eyes that completely belied his nod. Still, I got to work.

He was unbearably attractive when he skated, but it was intolerable when I taught him. He was patient. Kind. Never once making fun of me when I messed up.

"Tell me the name of this trick," he said. When I didn't say anything, his mouth dropped. "You still haven't thought of a name?"

"Your feet are all wrong," I said, pushing past the subject. I brought my hands to his waist, showing him how to move, and I had to remind my brain to *focus* because I needed to teach.

His fingers slid between my thighs.

My brain stuttered, then I slapped them away.

He laughed, a self-satisfied full-bodied sound that did not help my brain get back to normal.

"Just trying to steady myself." He shrugged as if to apologize, but the wicked way he smiled said if I got close, he'd do it again.

So I shoved him.

He fell to his ass, and I chewed my cheek to hide my smile.

"First rule of skateboarding," I said as I laughed. When I stopped, his eyes took my breath away. The intensity. The raw emotion. It did something to my gut. Made it squeeze and tighten, hot and fiery, then loosen like the first time I drank whiskey.

He blinked.

Then grinned.

"Uh, you did good," I said after we finished, looking at my thighs, worried he'd see the heat in my cheeks. He was one of the best skaters in the world. He definitely didn't need *me*.

"I had a good teacher," he said. "But you've always been easy to teach. I'm not surprised you're a good coach." He winked at me and I tripped over my tongue. What did he mean I'd always been easy to teach? There was more behind his eyes, there was definitely more behind his words.

Suddenly he changed the subject. "Tell me why you left Patchwork."

"You." He didn't blink for a good thirty seconds, and I knew I had to add more context. "The night we kissed it opened up something inside me. I realized how sheltered I was. I'd never known anything but Patchwork, and then King kissed me—"

"King kissed you?" He growled so low it almost didn't sound human.

"Yes," I said evenly, worried he'd run in and grab King by the collar and start another caveman fight. "But I only thought about you. For those two years, all I ever thought about was you." I finished quietly, embarrassed. More silence, and this time I wondered if I'd shared *too* much, but then he leaned forward and all thoughts vanished.

"All you thought about, huh?" he whispered on the lobe of my ear, before biting it. I released a shuddery breath, and then his hand slid up my jean-covered thigh, before curling inside. "What kinds of thoughts?"

"Well, sometimes I thought about skating..." I was too

hot, burning from the inside out, changing the subject so I could cool down.

"You still need to name your trick, Tweetie," he said, licking the new wound on my ear. How could he make such an innocuous thing sound so dirty?

My breath was unsteady. "Maybe I'll just never name it."

He laughed, the sound vibrating against my skin, down in my gut. "Tricks need names."

"Yeah, but..." I'd invented tricks before. I never named them.

As if he knew what I was thinking, he gripped my face. The games ended. The double entendres shattered. And the intensity in his eyes stopped my breath.

"Name it," he said. "Own it. Let people know *you* did this."

FLIP

Her eyes grew at my words, and I crushed my lips to hers. Losing my hands in her hair, her cheeks, up her shirt.

I groaned. "You're not wearing a bra?"

Her gasp breezed my lips. "I didn't have time to grab it this morning, remember?"

I cursed in the same breath I said her name, diving for her neck. "I'm not complaining. No more bras. Ever." Perfect soft skin, hot against my touch. The pads of my fingers ghosting her stomach, up the center between her breasts and around, teasing. She arched up as if giving herself to me in an offering, one I would gladly take.

"Flip?" King's voice.

Are you fucking kidding me? What the hell did he want?

Professional. Cock. Blocker.

Tweetie froze, I kept my hand up her shirt.

"We have to go," she whispered, trying to push me off. I stayed firm. I didn't care. I wanted everyone to know what I'd known forever: Tweetie was mine.

She would always be mine.

Just like I was hers.

"Show me a new face, Tweetie," I said low, soft, and coaxing. "Show me what was stolen from me this morning." King's voice was getting closer, but we were hidden by the ramp, and I knew it wouldn't take me long. I pushed her to the ramp, unbuttoned her jeans, and her lips parted, shock and desire melding into one.

"I can't not with...not with..." She trailed off into a sigh as my hand slid further down. I groaned into her neck.

Fucking. Perfect.

I dragged a finger down the center of her, kissing her in rhythm with her sighs, listening to her heartbeats.

Blue eyes wide, then low and dusky.

Her back rose and rose like the crescent moon above us.

Her small, quiet cries fevered to match her nails scratching the wood. Then her breath caught, eyes stuck on me, shining with something so very close to awe. All at once she slackened.

"There it is," I said, and pressed my lips to her jaw.

"Flip?" King called again, but all I saw was Tweetie. Her eyes were so beautifully misted. Aglow like an early morning sky. I bit her collarbone, leaving a tiny, visible mark, then buttoned her jeans and pulled down her shirt.

King called again, and she blinked back into reality.

She scrambled up. "I..." she breathed, running a hand down a still flushed face. I dragged my thumb across her lower lip, back and forth, pulling the panic off it with each stroke.

"I'll meet you inside," I said quietly.

Tweetie's eyes creased with gratitude. I kept my thumb locked on her lower lip, then dropped it. She licked the place it had been absently before getting to her feet and going inside. King spared her a glance like he always spared her a glance.

Just like that, the rosy filter Tweetie applied to my life vanished.

King kissed me.

I grabbed his shirt, blinded. "I fucking knew it. I fucking knew something went down that night. I think it's time we settle this."

"Her favorite food is a peanut butter and banana sandwich," King said.

I blinked, taken off guard by the calm, almost defeated tone. King and I were always two bulls going head to head.

I loosened my grip. "What?"

"When she's sick she likes tomato soup. She'll lie and say she's not hungry, but she wants food—and she will *always* lie and say she doesn't want extra, but if you come back with anything less than extra she'll look at you like you've betrayed her entire family." King shook his head as if recalling the memory.

I knew that already. I knew everything about Tweetie.

I dropped him completely. We stood another minute. The thing that had simultaneously connected and divided us slowly dissipating. King exhaled and turned to go, but not back inside.

"Wait." I grabbed him "What's going on?"

"Just take care of her, Flip."

TWEETIE

I was still scorching when Flip came back from his talk with King. He didn't come to me but settled by the doors, eyes up close and personal. I think I'd been talking to Bacon, but whatever I'd been about to say vanished with Flip's next move.

Across the room, Flip licked his finger, slid his tongue over the knuckle that had just pressed into me.

I sucked in a breath, suddenly desperate for air.

Just then Pants suggested putting in a VHS, an old skate video from back before Flip was discovered.

I hopped on that idea, Flip's intensity scorching me from the inside out. "Let's do that!" Romeo and Daniel looked less than enthused, and Flip mirrored them.

"Come on," I begged, so lost in the glittery, champagne bubbly feeling of nostalgia. I was desperate to see more of Patchwork House before me. I knew Flip and I needed to have a serious conversation, but every time he was near me I got lost in him.

Romeo groaned, Daniel sighed. I knew that meant I'd won.

The movie was about to start, so it was only *mildly* loud. I could actually hear myself think. It was warm, but the air outside had been so frigid my hands were red. I blew on them, wishing for King to keep them warm like always.

In an instant Flip was there. He tugged them to his lips and blew, eyes never straying from mine.

"Thanks...Nate." I tested the name on my tongue, outside the bubble of firelight and flesh. His lips curled warmly, eyelids growing hooded.

"Do you think you and King will ever be friends?" I asked. "I can't imagine a life where my brother and boyfriend don't get along."

"Boyfriend?" A smile grew slow and content.

I rolled my eyes to push past the way that smile made my gut squirrel. "He raised me. Even if he's responsible, the accident is something that connects us, you know?"

His lazy smile dropped. "What do you mean?"

I hesitated. "You know what I mean."

"Say it."

"King killed my dad..." I felt really awkward. Why was he forcing me to repeat this? My focus drifted to Bacon asking for help while fiddling with the VHS. Flip's grip tightened ever so slightly.

"Why are you saying King killed your father?"

I looked back at Flip. "You're being really weird." He didn't press any more, but some thought made his eyes dark, jaw tight. The video started, so thankfully I had a distraction.

Suddenly Flip's grip tightened on my hands until it felt like he was squeezing the blood out.

"Ow," I said, trying to pull them back.

"Let's go." The urgency in his voice had my brows caving.

"I want to watch."

I followed everyone's eyes to the small, black box TV. I didn't register it at first. I couldn't. It didn't make sense.

"What the fuck is this?" Daniel said.

"I thought we destroyed it," Flip gritted. He was close,

but his voice was so, so far away. I was in a bubble, floating into space.

It was me on the screen. As a little girl.

"What wanker chose this?" Romeo asked. I tried to tear my hands from Flip to walk closer to the screen, but his grip was a vise. I recognized the hill, it was tattooed on my blood.

Devil's Hill.

Was this the night King caused my father to crash? Then why was Flip the one with me?

First rule of skateboarding: you fall.

My heart thrummed uncontrollably as I watched Flip push me into the street. The camera panned shakily to me as whoever held it laughed.

Flip!

A car came tearing down the road—the old woodie wagon that I could still smell if I tried hard enough. Always a little bit like musty fabric and my dad's too-pungent cologne.

"Someone turn the fucking thing off," Flip growled. Sparky joined Pants, frantically pressing buttons.

"It's stuck in the recorder!"

I couldn't take my eyes off the screen. The camera fell to the ground, landing sideways on the asphalt just as Flip lunged for me. Blood snaked its way toward the sidelong recorder as Flip lifted himself up, checking my younger self for injury.

Romeo and Daniel pushed them both out of the way, calling them dumbasses, and pressed power. Silence. Silence on the screen. Silence in the room.

I looked back at Flip.

Images of him merged and flashed with King like a broken projector.

My *real* savior.

I pulled at my hands, but he wouldn't let go, grip tight. For a minute I stopped struggling. Then I said, my voice barely a breath, "We said no more secrets."

Flip dropped my hands like he'd been burned, and I sprinted out of the room.

TWENTY-SIX

SKETCHY: UNTRUSTWORTHY.

TWEETIE

So this was my real answer.

Why Flip doesn't skate.

Why he's the lost Rebel God.

Why he left Patchwork.

Why he and King hate each other.

Me.

Guilt slammed into me so hard I gripped my sheets, looking at anything in my room to anchor me. So of course at that moment, my door opened.

"I don't want to see any of your fucking faces," I said without looking up from my bedspread.

My world was collapsing.

Everything I knew was a goddamn lie.

I couldn't breathe.

"Too bad."

I whipped my head up. It was Romeo, Daniel, and *Flip*.

"Where's King?"

Flip's face darkened. "Why the fuck do you want King?" He practically growled it.

Because I can't look at you.

Because guilt is eating my throat alive.

"Because *he's* been there for me for my entire life. I don't care what that video says. I never knew you—not really—until this year."

"He's gone," Flip said, icy.

"What do you mean *he's gone.*"

"*I mean*, you're stuck with me."

"Flip—" Daniel started, but I couldn't stay to hear the rest. My heart was spiraling out of control with my thoughts, breathing rapid and uneven. I scrambled off my bed, onto my desk, and pushed open my window. They called after me, but I was already falling flat on my ass like usual, landing on the grass with a thud.

My breath was rocky and shallow, the air quiet save for the music still blaring from the party. Cold caressed my skin. I stared at the grass, fingers digging into the ground, anything to avoid looking up. My pulse raced with the fears I wanted to escape.

"Still sneaking out the window."

That voice, that familiar, familial, voice. "King..." I whispered, and the tears I'd been keeping at bay fell.

King groaned. "Waterworks? Really?" He leaned against the back door, thick arms folded and one eyebrow raised as if he'd been waiting for me.

"Tell me this is a joke. Tell me this isn't happening. Flip is just someone who used to live at Patchwork, right? Just another kid without a home like Bacon or Sparky." I stood to my knees, closing a bit of the distance between us. "Right?"

He worked his jaw, eyes shifting to the floor.

I fell back on the grass. His silence spoke volumes.

I'd ruined two people's lives.

The boy who took the fall.

The boy who couldn't forget.

A hand was suddenly on my back, rubbing slow and concentric circles. My heart rate steadily evened out. For a minute it felt normal, like my world hadn't been turned upside down again. I was Tweetie, he was King, and it was back to old times.

"How did you know where I'd be?" I asked after a moment.

King made a noise, an almost laugh, the closest he ever got. "You can't escape us, Tweetie." Maybe it was supposed to make me feel better, but I just felt worse. I couldn't escape them? They couldn't escape *me*.

I'd ruined everything for them.

What could they have been without me?

In the short time I'd seen Flip and King together it had been heated, hated tension. Glares and fistfights. But they were all so happy on that video. Best friends.

King's hand on my back slowed to a halt, and he stood, eyes taking me in. I waited for him to say something, give me advice.

He shrugged, let out a breath. "I'll be seeing you."

What?

My brain sputtered, shooting out bits and pieces of emotion like a broken blender. All the while King was walking away.

He'd be *seeing me?*

I scrambled up, chasing him to the front. He was already at his Chevelle.

"Where are you going?" I furiously swiped tears from my face. "Come back inside. This is where you live. This has *always* been where you live. The four of us. You, me,

Romeo, and Daniel. Just us four."

Flip is still a famous skateboarder I dream about, but know I'll never have.

Nate is still the ordinary boy who changed my life, but I know I'll never meet again.

And I'm not responsible for either.

King came back to me, and I hoped. He cupped my cheek, thumb grazing back and forth, wiping the tears away. "He was the one who named you Tweetie."

I sputtered. "What—why?"

"I think that's something you should ask him." I didn't want to ask him. I wanted everything to go back to normal. King dropped his hand, and with a last look, went to his car.

"Come in. Come back. Come inside." I was on the verge of hysteria. Tears running without care down my face. King looked at Patchwork, hands gripping the door of his car. "Please, big brother."

Something passed across his face, then he shook his head. "Nah, you'll be okay." He said it more to himself than me, the distant tone wracking fear through my body. He opened the door, shooting me a sad smile. "And I've got someone to see."

Anger.

I latched onto it.

It replaced the searing pain knifing its way through every organ.

"Well, glad I could be the glue keeping everyone together," I said, sarcasm acid on my tongue. I didn't wait to see King drive away. It hurt less that way.

The front door slammed at my back. All three of them, Daniel, Romeo, and Flip, were waiting. They stood up immediately on entry.

I walked past them and grabbed a bottle of tequila.

FLIP

"This is your fault," Daniel said.

"I know."

Tweetie danced on a table, a bottle of tequila in one hand and two beers in another. Romeo tried to coax her down, but she completely ignored him.

"This is why we agreed to stay away," Daniel continued.

"I *know*."

"Why you shouldn't have put your goddamn hands on —" I shot him a glare, and Daniel threw up a hand, eyes still hard, jaw still tight, letting me know he hadn't conceded the point. Romeo joined us after his fifth failed attempt at getting her off the table.

"Where is King?" he asked after a quick scan of the room. "Isn't this his specialty?" That burned my gut. *His* specialty? Tweetie was my girl, and I could take care of her. I pushed through the crowd gathered at her feet.

"Good luck, mate," Romeo called to my back.

Tweetie danced, hips swayed, flinging her curly hair. In any other situation this would have been hot as hell, but I saw the damage in her hazy blue eyes. A drink was always at her lips, trying to get the thoughts in her head blurry.

I folded my arms. "Get down."

She kept dancing.

"Get down, Tweetie."

In response, she bent down until we were eye to eye. A blue-eyed, fire-coated stare. A look that said *Make me*. She gave me a saccharine smile, took a deep swig of her beer, eyes still locked. Then she stood back up and danced harder.

Alright.

Fuck playing nice.

I slammed my foot into the stereo, smashing through the speakers until the wailing punk rocker warbled off into nothing. There was a collective groan of disappointment. With one arm, I gripped Tweetie's shins and pulled her off the table. She yelped as I threw her over my shoulder. Her fists pounded against my back while I carried her up the stairs.

I kicked open her door.

Threw her on the bed.

Hair covered her bright, furious eyes. Cheeks red. She was wild and angry and still so goddamn beautiful.

"I know you hate me right now." I bent down, pressed her into the mattress. "You should hate me. But I'm not leaving until you stop." Until I *make you* love me. "Even if we're old and fucking gray."

She blinked, her mouth parted.

And then she said the one thing I never expected. "I don't hate you."

TWEETIE

He paused, confusion flittering across his features, then slowly stood up. The weight where he'd pressed into the mattress stark and empty like the holes in my heart. He arched his neck, studying me from a shadowed brow. Uncertain.

"You don't?"

I shook my head.

That launched us into another interminable silence. The house was unnaturally quiet after Flip broke the speakers and I couldn't help thinking I was still the girl the music stopped for.

"Why?"

I shrugged.

It would be so much easier if I hated him. If I was mad.

I kept reaching inside myself trying to redirect my anger but the more I reached inside, the more self-loathing I found.

The way his jaw tightened and his brow creased said he didn't believe me.

"It wasn't a total lie, Tweetie." Desperation was talons in his throat. Scratching, bleeding, clawing their way out. It matched the ones in my heart. "I *was* only a part of Patchwork for less than a year. King's rule was no chicks allowed, and mine was we accept anyone. We always clashed. But yeah, I was a founder. And yeah, I left because of you."

My hair had fallen across my face, but I was too broken to push it out of the way. Through blurry yellow I saw his hand lift. To move it out of the way maybe?

His hand dropped.

I wished he would push it behind my ears like before.

"I went to King's house," he continued softly. "Stayed with his family. Watched King's girl, tried to live, tried to move on, tried to skate and forget what happened."

That had me perking up. King had another house? A family other than Patchwork? And a love—the one he couldn't have—Flip had been watching?

A trillion thoughts fought for front seat, but a single one speared me: the family Flip had been missing was King's.

Flip who wanted nothing else but a home, had been missing someone else's.

My god that must suck for him.

I think Flip mistook my inability to look at him as brutal coldness, because he came to my knees. Grabbed my hands.

I still couldn't look at him.

"I'll tell you everything, Tweetie. I was the one who taught you. I still vividly remember the way that helmet fell over your curly hair. How you weren't intimidated by any of us." He was warped in my head, mixed with King. With what everyone *told me* happened. The only reason it was changing now was because Flip added new memories—but it wasn't a teenage Flip, it was adult him.

"I don't remember," I rasped. Tears at not being able to remember him the way he did me broke the surface.

He squeezed my hand as one tear fell. Too tight. For a brief second the pain of it distracted me.

"It's all my fault," he said. Tears were in his eyes now, like glistening black pebbles. "If I hadn't brought you along. All of it's my fault…"

All of Flip's anguish bled into his grip, stronger than he'd ever held me, bruising and painful. Then he dragged me to his chest, hand sliding to my neck to hold me there, throat bobbing against my forehead. I thought his tears landed in my hair, but I didn't look to see. For a minute, I let this moment be unbroken.

How would our lives have been different if he hadn't brought me to that hill? Flip would be a legend, not a myth. Maybe I never would have discovered skating, but my dad would be alive.

A sick, sick thought tore through me: maybe I didn't want that.

How could I ever choose between my dad and the love of my life? My love of skating?

Maybe I couldn't choose, but Flip had. He'd chosen me. All those years ago. When my dad's erratic, intoxicated driving had cemented the course of our lives, Flip chose me when he should have had the world.

"You'll really tell me everything?" I said, voice muffled by his chest. He pulled back and nodded. His eyes were shiny, jaw tight like he didn't want his throat to bob. It tore open my stomach. My everything. I didn't want him to hurt. I wanted him to be fine and free.

I swallowed the courage to find my question.

"Why don't you skateboard?" Now it was his turn to look away, to build silence like a wall, but I wouldn't back down. "Have you skateboarded at all since the accident? Entered any competitions?"

Silence pressed and I knew he wasn't going to answer, but I already knew it anyway.

Remembered it starkly in the melancholy way he skateboarded.

"Get out," I said, voice barely a whisper.

I woke up with the sky still dark and damp. It was snowing, shadowy flakes falling past my window. It didn't immediately hit me. I felt before I remembered. The ache in my chest an unmatched puzzle piece.

Then my eyes settled on the shadowy shirtless poster above my bed, and it all came rushing back.

Flip. King. The truth.

I was the reason. The reason Flip didn't skateboard.

The reason for the pain in his eyes. The reason for the melancholy way he skated.

Me.

I sat up, groaning, and rubbed my head. In two days, I had the most important competition of my life and I felt like I'd been hit by a truck. I wanted to curl up in a ball and never see the world again.

"I keep thinking I should never have made myself known."

I didn't startle at the voice. Flip was leaning against the wall, watching me. His eyes weren't red or shiny, but he looked tired. Used up. Voice low and hoarse, like he'd been screaming. I wanted to pull him to me and make him full again.

I wondered how long he'd been in the room. Waiting for me to wake up. Like that was where he belonged.

"None of this is your fault," I said. He made a sound in his throat that said he didn't believe a word. "It isn't," I insisted.

While everyone tried to warn me to consequences, I remained deaf. In my head I thought, I can handle it. So long as I was fearless, I could handle anything the world throws at me.

I didn't think about what the world would throw at others.

I never did.

Because I was selfish.

"You are my greatest regret," Flip said, and my stomach dropped. "Why do you think I don't skate? I can't. The thought of it used to make me vomit."

I tried not to let the pain of hearing *greatest regret* or the fact that he'd confirmed my greatest fear show.

Me. I did it to him.

I swallowed, steadied my voice. "So what changed?"

He lifted his head, eyes locking with mine. *"You."*

He came to me, palms cupping my cheeks, gently raising me off the bed. I never realized how *big* his hands were until he was cradling my face. From my jaw to my eyes, he held me like I was a doll. Eyes searching mine, brows caved in emotion.

"Without that day, I never would have found you. And I don't regret that."

I stopped fighting, eyes meeting his.

"I was there, Tweetie. I was always there. Your first date. Your first heartbreak. Your first competition and first loss." The second revelation shook through me in a rush of air from my lungs. Little bits and pieces of memories that had never quite made sense but I'd written off as oddities that couldn't be explained suddenly had an explanation.

You're just as good as him.

My eyes narrowed. "You said you were at King's. You were trying to skate again. Move on." What I didn't say was *Tell me I didn't steal your entire life.*

"I was. Then one day you crashed into me with your skateboard, and I had to know you were moving on. I said it would only be the one time, but I couldn't stay away." He placed his thumb beneath my chin, tilting my head, forcing me to look into his eyes. "I was the shadow below your window, one step behind you at all times."

I pulled my head from his grasp, focused on the bedspread. "You don't meet my checklist. You don't meet any of the criteria." I could barely get the words out.

I was certain if I looked at him, I would crumble. But where did that leave us? I'd taken a vital part of him. I couldn't imagine what my life would be like without skateboarding. It was a part of my soul. I knew the same was true for Flip, because his love and fire had ignited my own.

"Fuck your checklist," he growled. "You didn't think I would come back for your heart, and I didn't. It was always with me. Don't tell me to leave now."

Tears fell as silent traitors. The image of him blurry in my periphery.

The pain in his voice was stark. I wanted to turn and slide into that perfect spot against his chest. Wrap my hands around his warm skin, have him hold me tight. I focused harder on the bed.

"You asked me what this tattoo meant. It's for you. It's only ever been for you." He grabbed my hand, dragged it beneath his shirt against the hot skin. His muscles were hard and cruel beneath my fingers. I still couldn't look at him, even as my hand connected with his flesh.

"It says *Always your shadow*, Tweetie. Always. Even when I knew I shouldn't be there for you, I was. Because you saw me, Tweetie. The real me."

The room lost focus, his confession blasting through me. I couldn't feel my legs.

He'd tattooed himself for me?

I couldn't meet his eyes, but the black characters forever marking the side of his body popped into my head. Darker, bolder.

"Even when you didn't know who I was, even when I was hidden in the dark, you *saw* me. I know I saw you too. Look inside yourself and tell me I'm not the one for you."

He was, from beginning to end, forever and always.

Flip was my *everything,* but he should have had everything—been everything.

I took that from him.

All these years I'd been worried about my heart. I took

all of these precautions and steps to make sure I'd never get hurt, but never once prepared for the eventuality that *I* might hurt the one I love.

I'd already hurt Flip so much. I'd taken away his skateboarding. I'd taken his family, taken his *life*. To avoid hurting him further, maybe I would have to hurt him just a little more.

In this moment I was a coward, but I wouldn't be selfish.

I swallowed and lifted my head, meeting his eyes. "You're not the one."

TWENTY-SEVEN

TAILSLIDE: SLIDING WITH THE TAIL END OF A
BOARD.

FLIP

Sometime ago
Flip is 23, Tweetie is 18

"I love her."

Silence.

Couldn't say I didn't expect that. It was only minutes after I'd kissed Tweetie. Given into temptation. Finally acknowledged the want, the need, the *feeling* lurking in my gut. I couldn't go back to before, to being her shadow.

She was the one.

"I'm coming clean," I continued. "I never wanted you to take the fall anyway." King scoffed, which ripped a new thread of fire in my gut. I swallowed it down. I had one goal in telling them this: avoid a goddamn fistfight.

It had stopped raining and snowing, but the sky was uneasy, the clouds dark and hesitating.

"What?" I asked, keeping my voice level. "You don't believe me?"

King folded his arms. "It's just convenient."

More silence, this time from me.

I looked beyond him, where light glowed in Tweetie's bedroom. In a few minutes her shadow would pass by. She liked to stare out the window, at what I wasn't sure. I didn't really give a damn. It let me see her face.

"She doesn't need you."

"Maybe it's the opposite," I said, turning to King. "And maybe that's why you're looking at me like I pissed in your beer." What I said must have struck a nerve, because he looked about to swing at me. Daniel and Romeo shot me looks, telling me not to push it.

So of course I did.

I narrowed my eyes on King. "Are you into her?"

He dropped his arms. "She's barely eighteen. And I've basically been her father."

"So you know how wrong it is." A pause passed. "Coward."

"The fuck did you say?" King growled.

"I said you're a fucking coward. You won't tell the one you want you love her, so you're going after my girl." There was a tense, barely there moment. Long enough for Romeo to whistle. Just long enough for me to know what I'd done was reckless and stupid—my motto.

King cracked his neck and swung at me.

Daniel and Romeo ripped us from one another, the only thing keeping us from tearing each other's heads off.

My hand was broken, but I didn't care. I'd done a good number on his face.

"King?" Tweetie came out. "What's going on?" She peered into the darkness. For once I didn't want to scurry back into the shadows. I wanted to stay. Let her see me.

"Let it go," Daniel said as if sensing my thoughts. "None

of us is good for her. Not you. Not King. This wasn't how it was supposed to play out!" His voice rose, and he took a breath. "No one was supposed to start fucking her," he hissed low, the vein in his neck pulsing.

"Daniel?" Tweetie's voice lilted in caution, hearing his raised voice.

I fell back.

So did King.

"Everything's fine, little girl," Daniel called back before going after her. He shepherded her inside. She looked over her shoulder, into the shadows where we lay, unconvinced. King gave me one final, scorching look, then went to join them.

"That was a low blow," Romeo said, taking the joint from behind his ear. Lit it. Offered it to me. I watched Tweetie through the glass doors. With King.

I exhaled.

Yeah, it was.

"He went to see her tonight," Romeo said, exhaling smoke. "Went to see the girl you say he's too much of a coward to love."

I stared at Romeo, processing the information.

King had gone back to Heaven's Court? To Pip? How the fuck did I not know that? I silently asked Romeo how it went, and he shook his head, indicating the answer was not well.

Well, now I felt like even more shit.

Both of us stared at the three-story Victorian.

"She's happy. Coming forward isn't going to do anything but tear open old wounds. Don't be selfish." He stared at me, blue eyes glowing in the night. Selfish. Coward. All things I'd branded myself with over the years for letting my friend take the fall.

Now if I were to finally take ownership, I'd be the same.

And if fucking *Romeo* was telling me this... I dragged a hand down my face.

I offered him his joint back and he made a motion as if to say no. "Go get your hand looked at—but, mate, I think you know it's time you stop coming by. Until you get yourself under control."

TWEETIE

King tore open the backdoor minutes after Daniel, leaving it open and bleeding light into a black night. Briefly I looked over his shoulder, wondering what happened. Less than an hour ago I'd had my first real kiss, but butterflies in my stomach now battled with the fear in my chest.

King's sharp cheekbone was split, his full lips cut, and he walked by me like he wasn't going to explain. Why was King *always* bloody?

I grabbed his arm, my earlier fight with him fading. I had an impossible time staying mad at King anyway. I imagined this is what it was like having a sibling. You fought tooth and nail, and then just as quickly you loved again.

"What happened to your face?" I asked. He didn't answer, but he didn't move. I stood on my tiptoes, ran my palm from his forehead to his chin, inspecting the blood. I was just about to take my hand away, when his own rose, locking it in place.

I paused.

"King?" I hesitated, heart stuck in my throat, as his stony gray eyes ignited. He never looked at me like that. I was always an impassive annoyance. King was often covered in blood and hot tempered, but never at me. Now his eyes settled on me like hot coals.

"Big brother—" Then his lips were on mine.

I kept my eyes open, bright and wide in shock. I couldn't even register the way his lips felt, my brain too loud in *What is happening?*

King was a good kisser. Demanding and possessive, but gentle and devoted. But King didn't make my belly flip. My lips were still hot from Nate, my thighs still ached from him. Who'd kissed me like he was meant to kiss me. Whose touch seared me, branded me, tattooed me with intent.

I shoved King off. I stared at the floor, breathing heavily, trying to unscramble my thoughts. Instinct told me to wipe the kiss off.

Finally I said the only thing I could say. "What the fuck?"

There was a wildness in his eyes I didn't recognize. A demand I couldn't understand much less answer. Pain had warped him, tightened his jaw. King was gone somewhere I couldn't follow.

I saw the way Patchwork Girls looked at him. How people on the street looked at him. Objectively he was attractive. No, more than that. He was downright gorgeous.

Lips red like the devil. Jaw sharper than his stony gray eyes. Tall, with tattoos spiraling across his golden skin. Somehow both massive and lean, with muscles that could cut glass. He had a lethally sexy look.

But he was *King. Big brother King.*

Tears welled in my eyes.

"Forget it," he said. "Let's forget it happened." And then he left, headed into the kitchen. I glanced up the stairs. Imagining my cut-out posters of Flip. The stars glowing on my ceiling. Maybe I should forget it. Dive under my covers. Read a book.

Just another day.

I bounded after King. Romeo and Daniel were already in the kitchen, sitting at the bar. Absently I noted the kitchen door was open, and they looked like they were having some kind of serious conversation themselves.

"I can't forget," I said.

More tears undulated against my lids.

Tears at King.

Tears at betrayal. At the roots of our love being twisted and tangled.

"Forget what?" Romeo piped up from his seat at the bar.

King stared at me. "Let's watch TV."

"You can't distract me, King. Not this time." Both Daniel and Romeo sat forward, gauging this was something serious. Not a fight over who ate the last of the cereal, or why there was always so much hair in the drain.

"I'll make your favorite." He went to the pantry. "Peanut butter and bananas." He rummaged through the cupboards.

I'd never had sex. I tried not to count that guy in the car, because he really only dragged his tongue across my neck and shoved my hand against his pants.

I thought that was King being overprotective because he loved me like a father—now I wasn't sure. Something was terribly off with him tonight, but did that make it okay?

Maybe I should have blamed him.

I was forever indebted to him, but we'd come to the end of our road.

"I don't think I should live here anymore." Tears dripped down my face, hot and steamy.

King paused. Romeo and Daniel leapt from their seats,

synchronous *What the fuck is going on* falling from their lips. But it was King I was watching.

The stillness.

Like the final leaf frozen in autumn, waiting for wind to tell him to fall, or stay. His grip on the sink white. Bright white. Looking at it like it was the freaking Sistine Chapel. The silence was killing me. King was never one to talk about his emotions. I only knew something was bothering him by the length of silence. The longest we went was four minutes when I told him about the boy who broke my heart.

The next day the boy had a black eye.

A minute passed.

Two.

Five minutes and my heart was going to suffocate me.

"King...talk to me." He let go of the sink. Turned to me. Nothing. No emotion. Not like I expected it, but seeing it was another thing.

"Is someone going to tell us what the fuck is going on?" For a bona fide rebel, Daniel rarely cursed. If I looked at them, I'd fall apart. Maybe I was overreacting. I owed them my life. But neither did I want to be The Only Girl at Patchwork forever.

A glorified nun in a house of sin.

King nodded to himself, like he'd just come to some agreement in his mind.

"Tweetie's ready to leave the nest."

He reached into his pocket.

Shoved the crane at me.

FLIP

It was dark and raining outside, but I saw her. Sitting

beneath the underpass like the very beginning. I kept thinking if I left her alone life would have been better. For both of us.

Never agreed to teach her.

Never made King take her in.

Never followed her like a shadow.

And yet.

I shrugged out of my coat, ignoring the twinge in my wrist, placing it over her shoulders. She straightened her back, startled, and looked up. The rain was a thick, heavy curtain of glass beads, blurring both of our faces.

Maybe this would be the moment I acknowledged her, and she me.

We'd been stumbling drunk on one timeline for years, always a few steps behind or ahead one another. I wanted to sit next to her, finally in the same place. I eyed the duffle at her feet. Curiosity raged in my gut.

I didn't know why every time I tried to talk to Tweetie I clammed up like some fucking school kid. I was famous. I'd had girls offer their virginity to me on poster board.

"Weather..." I said. *Weather?*

She shot me a look, stared out at the rain.

Minutes passed, the rain a soft hum. I dove my good hand into my jeans, watching her instead of the rain.

"I met someone," she said. For a moment I thought maybe I imagined it, but then she continued. "I blew up my entire world for him."

She held out a paper crane.

My paper crane.

What did *that* mean? She tilted her neck, locking eyes with me. They were a soft, dusty blue in the dark night. Then she took my jacket off and dropped it to the ground, looking to the street.

"You shouldn't help people you don't know." She looked back at the rain.

I didn't pick it up.

I went straight to Patchwork.

Kicked open the door.

They all stood up then deflated when they saw me.

"Expecting someone else?" I asked.

Daniel rubbed the back of his neck. "So you heard?"

"Saw," I said, eyes locked on King. His jaw twitched. "I wonder what the hell could've prompted her to leave."

"It's over now. It's done." King said. "She's not coming back." I stared at King, ready to rip his throat out. Something happened between them. He stared back, unwilling to cede any ground.

"Not really an explanation."

"This has been coming for a while," Daniel said, trying to mediate.

"She's not going to make you forget about Pip," I pressed. "Someday you're going to have to confront her." Whatever the hell happened tonight, it was like everything else with King: motivated by Pip. And like everything else with King, he'd pretend otherwise.

"You think I don't fucking know that?" King yelled.

Silence followed his explosion. I ground my jaw, folded my arms.

"This was never gonna be permanent anyway, yeah?" Romeo said. "Perhaps it's for the best. She can move on. For good."

"As long as she's not at Patchwork, we're out of her life," Daniel proposed. "Agreed?"

I knew it was for the best. The look on Tweetie's face still echoed in my gut and anyway, was I really going to pursue her? How could we have a future with such a bloody beginning?

King and I stared at one another a long time, both thinking the same thing.

Can I trust this motherfucker to stay away?

"Agreed?" Romeo prompted.

"Agreed," we gritted.

TWENTY-EIGHT

BACKSIDE: A TRICK WITH THE SKATER'S BACK TO
THE OBSTACLE.

TWEETIE
Tweetie is 18, Flip is 23

A name, a kiss, and a mutual love for skateboarding. That was all I had to go on as I searched for Nate. My search kept me occupied. If I thought about Nate, I didn't think about the three god-sized holes in my heart.

"Have you seen anyone named Nate around?" A line of skaters sat on a concrete wall smoking, boards propped against their feet. One of them threw flannel-clad arms behind his head, eyes pinning me.

"Shit, baby, I'll be Nate."

"Yeah, fuck, I'll be whoever you want me to be," his friend said. The entire wall of skaters laughed. I rolled my eyes and kept walking as they whistled to my back. That's usually how it went.

I didn't know why I kept trying.

There weren't a lot of parks left in my state to search, for some reason they were all closing down. So I went where all the skaters went. Where I was pretty sure he would be, anyway.

The street.

As I bounced from one terrible couch to the next, I missed Patchwork even more. I didn't have a lot of money, only whatever was left from Dad's insurance, but I had to do this for myself. I'd never been on my own, not really, and the more I was, the more I learned. The worse the couch, the more my memories unraveled.

There were a lot of addicts in Heaven Falls, and like most of my new roommates, my parents were among them. It took me some time to realize because my memories of them were hazy and sugarcoated with childhood.

But that's what they were.

After realizing it, anger really took root—not at my parents, but at Heaven Falls. Instead of dealing with the problem and calling a spade a spade, saying addiction exists, we have stupid lore like Devil's Hill is *haunted*. Now both my parents are dead, and my big brother lives with a guilt that he caused it.

King never should've gone to jail in the first place. I was certain my father was driving high. The more I learn, though, the more I'm certain King and the Rebel Gods are keeping an entire world of explanations from me.

"Have you seen a guy named Nate?" I asked the next wall of skaters, thumbing the origami crane in my pocket.

"Bitch," one said. "You sound desperate, let me help." He leaned forward and pushed hair out of my face. I took one look at his unscuffed shoes and the way he held a similarly unmarred board.

I smacked his hand away. "*Bitch*, you're a poser. I wish I could help." His friends let out a collective *ooooh* and he scoffed and walked away.

Note: did not get on his board.

A guy behind them with long blond dreads jumped up on the rail, grinding all the way down, landing just at my feet. "Why you lookin' so hard for this guy?"

I shrugged. "My business."

He blinked, then nodded. "I'll keep an eye out."

"Thanks." Feeling slightly better, I took in our town square. Grinding on hand rails, hopping over flower-filled medians, jumping cars. The spired clock tower in the center of it all.

"So, we can skate here?" I asked. I'd never really skated outside of parks, only the one time with Nate. It was a totally different vibe than the parks. Reckless and wild.

"Yeah."

"And it's legal?"

He laughed like what I said was the funniest thing in the world. "Sure sweetheart. It's legal." He took a puff of weed. "We're on the straight and fuckin' narrow around here—"

"Five-oh, five-oh," someone yelled out, and everyone scattered.

FLIP

"What's the charge this time, officer?" I teased as a gruff, no-nonsense woman slapped cuffs on me.

Second time I was arrested in one week.

And for the second time, Bizzy was waiting outside when they released me on bail I didn't post. I attempted to walk by like I didn't see her, which of course failed.

"Come back," she said. I stopped, rubbing a hand down my face before turning to face her.

"Bizzy..."

She held the family photo we'd taken, fingers white.

"You left. You just *left*." I never should've been there in the first place. They never wanted me. With Tweetie gone, there was no reason to stay. I massaged my neck, hating this.

"I know what you're thinking," she said. "You push people away because you're scared of being abandoned." I sucked in a breath. Bizzy never sugarcoated anything. "You'll feel their love, though, Flip. You'll feel it like King felt it." I looked behind Bizzy, at the police station.

Yeah, I was feeling it all right.

So was the rest of our state.

All the parks were closing down and at the rate the new laws were being passed, there wasn't going to be a safe place left for any skater.

I gave Bizzy a soft smile and headed to leave.

"They're not going to let this go," she yelled to my back. "First King and now you. Their hearts are broken and they're out for blood."

I doubted they could make me hurt anymore than I already did. My days consisted of getting arrested on behalf of the Ayers, bouncing from couch to couch, and trying to get Tweetie out of my head.

I kept her bracelet with me at all times, saying I was moving on while simultaneously feeling the rough chain in my pocket as the months faded into one another.

She was the only thing on my mind.

I paused outside a shop a few blocks from our town square. Inside the glass window was a brilliant deck made up of a patchwork of pinks. It screamed Tweetie.

I kept walking.

"Yo, do you know a guy named Nick?" A guy with blond dreads grabbed my shoulder as I crossed through the square, stopping me at the clock tower. "Supposed to hang around here."

"Sorry, no."

"I don't think that's his name, dude," his friend said.

"It was," dreads insisted. "It started with an N."

"I think it had a T in it," the other guy said. "Matt? Ryan? Or maybe, fuck, Joe?"

"Yo, what the fuck? How do you get Joe out of Nick?"

"I don't know anyone around here," I interrupted. "Sorry."

Flip is 24, Tweetie is 19

Two years had passed since we agreed to leave Tweetie alone. I sat at the bottom of Devil's Hill, back against the tree Tweetie's dad crashed into, staring into the street I'd pulled her from all those years ago.

The street that started and ended everything.

The sun was setting in cotton candies and creamsicles. My new tattoo stung, fresh on my ribcage, the pain all at once fitting and not enough. The words I'd inked into my skin simply putting words to a fate already sealed.

A single flower bloomed on a lonely branch above me. Pink. Tweetie's favorite color. An early spring bloom—too early. It would probably die in a late winter snowstorm.

I hadn't lived at Patchwork in years, but I always thought I would go back. In the back of my mind, it was an inevitability. King's parents had been going hard on both of us, trying to force Patchwork down and us back. Until one day it was just eerily silent. No more arrests. Nothing.

"This isn't over," I said. "They're going to go all out on us when we least expect it."

"All out on us," King clarified, pointing at him and the house. "Not you."

Now I saw the real inevitability was our divide.

I let Tweetie's bracelet fall like water between my fingers, focusing on the glinting gold, the street fading away.

I tried to date and get her off my mind. Move on. Each one ended in failure. So I figured as long as I stayed away, that's all that mattered. I'd grab my shit from Patchwork, maybe even move out of Heaven Falls, and keep living like this. Forever stuck loving her.

So long as I didn't see Tweetie, everything would be fine. Like the words I'd inked into my flesh, I would stay in the dark. Always her shadow. I curled my fist around the bracelet, pressed a hand to my rib.

Always your shadow.

I couldn't destroy something I didn't have.

TWEETIE

With my legs on either side of my board, I stared down the windy road of Devil's Hill, twirling the crane in my fingers. The sun was setting in a wicked array of vibrant neons. Nearly two years had come and gone since I left Patchwork. I kept holding out hope I would find that mysterious boy who put me on this journey. I would get the answers, a conclusion.

All I'd found were more questions.

I was almost out of money. Almost out of will.

I was surrounded by trees still mostly barren from winter, but one branch bloomed. One lonely pale orange bloom that would no doubt die. It reminded me of Patchwork. Of the blossoms outside my window.

I missed Patchwork. I missed King, Daniel, and Romeo. Living on my own was exhausting and depressing. I'd had a family, and now I had a collage of couches and anonymity.

How did I go back to Patchwork? Knowing the truth of my dad, knowing that the boys around me carried a guilt I was certain didn't belong to them.

But I had nowhere else to go.

I balanced the crane on my pointer finger, holding it up to the sky so it looked larger than life against the sunset. Maybe if I went back, I'd find Nate.

A gust of chilly spring wind blew, knocking the crane from its precarious perch.

I snatched the paper bird before it could float away on the breeze, and paused, watching the sky darken.

Maybe. Maybe I'd find my love.

More likely I'd find more heartache.

TWENTY-NINE

POP: STRIKING THE TAIL OF THE BOARD AGAINST
THE GROUND TO PROPEL UPWARDS.

TWEETIE
Present

"As if things couldn't get worse," King said.

I sat up straight, listening. The house had been quiet until now, like they were afraid to disturb me in any way. I wasn't even aware King had come home.

I hadn't left my room since Flip had sandblasted me to the spot hours ago. My competition was in a day, but I couldn't eat, couldn't drink. I just played with my crane and stared at the wall that separated us.

Knock when you need me.

How many times had I lifted my fist to knock on the wall only drop it back to my lap? Too many times to count.

I lifted my fist...and dropped it again.

Outside my window, a pale orange blossom bloomed on a branch still covered in snow. My heart cracked, remembering the two years I'd been gone.

Searching for Nate.

When all I'd had to do was look at my shadow.

Always your shadow.

"What's the saying? If it pours it rains?" Romeo's voice carried to the second floor. I left my room, needing the distraction. I tiptoed to the lip of the stairs. A pang of nostalgia wrestled with the hurt in my heart. All three of them stood in the foyer, early memories tumbling in my mind. But Flip wasn't there, and now I knew he should be.

"That's...not it." Daniel shook his head. "And anyway, this is a flood. This is biblical."

"We knew this was going to happen someday."

"What's going on?" Everyone whipped their heads to me, like children caught with their hands in the cookie jar. I wanted to groan. Still? After everything, they're keeping things from me?

"How are you doing, little girl?" Daniel asked like my question never passed my lips. "Need breakfast?"

I feel like I've been donkey punched in the gut.

I shrugged at Daniel. "Peachy."

"One more day until—" King started.

"My last competition," I finished for him. My last shot for the year, my last shot ever, really. I really needed to get my head on right.

If I *ever* wanted to go pro.

If I *ever* wanted my dreams to come true.

But all I could think about was Flip.

"What's going on?" I pressed. "Really?"

Another silent communication, eyes saying words they wouldn't allow me to know.

Please don't lie to me. Please.

"I'll take care of it," King said as if that answered everything.

"You'll take care of it," I repeated numbly. I didn't think

I slept more than an hour the night before. I should have been filled with emotion and worry and fear, but it felt like I was watching this through a snow globe.

Then everyone looked at each other, the same question written across their faces.

"Don't do that," I groaned. "Don't talk in that secret language." I threw up my hands. "You know what? Whatever. I don't care anymore. This is me not caring." I turned, ready to climb back up and dive under the covers, when the unthinkable happened.

"I think it's time we answered your questions," King said.

They leaned against my mint green wall, murals come to life. Out of this world, a twisted Greek myth. I felt like I was ten years old again, not twenty.

"You must have a lot of questions," King said.

A billion. "No." They gave me a look like they knew I was full of shit. "Fine. What made Romeo cut his hair?"

Romeo laughed.

"Really?" King asked. "That's what you want to know?"

"It's weird and it goes against all laws of nature," I mumbled petulantly.

"She's got us there." So much silence passed I thought they would never answer my question. Then Romeo spoke again, this time quietly. Hurt. "Not what, luv. *Who.*"

My eyes grew, my lips parted. Romeo was always such a playboy. I could barely fathom a reality where he actually cared about someone, let alone enough to cut his hair.

"A leggy blonde?" I joked, trying to lighten the mood.

Romeo's jaw clenched, eyes stark with more emotion than I'd ever seen from him, and I wished I could take it back.

Another long minute stretched where I was forced to feel my own hurt. Flip had only been in my life for a short time—at least...only made himself known for a short time, but his absence was stark and obvious.

A chalk outline inside my soul.

"We're being condemned," King said, answering his own question, the real question. He exhaled, rubbed a hand along the back of his neck.

I couldn't believe they'd told me the truth.

The shock of that almost usurped the shock of his answer.

Almost.

"Condemned?" I sat forward on my bed gingerly. "But you own this house and it's not even remotely bad enough to be condemned."

"Patchwork isn't just a house, it's a way of life. People want to take away this life. But when you love something, you fight for it."

That hit me in my gut.

Should I be fighting for Flip?

I thought when you loved something, you let it go, and all that cliché bullshit.

When I spoke again, my voice was low. Soft. "You said you were going to stop it. How?"

King rubbed the muscles in his neck, looking like he really didn't want to answer my question. "I'm related to those assholes."

That did me in. I fell back on my mattress with a bounce, staring at my empty ceiling, drunk and dizzy.

He was related to them?

And people wanted to destroy us.

"I knew I heard the name Kingston Ayers when I followed you that night," I mumbled. There was an entire *world* they'd kept from me. I knew they sheltered me, but I didn't realize the extent. I was naive enough to think I'd peeled back any newspaper they'd taped to my window.

"So what does that mean?"

"I used to live beyond the gates. When I left, I started Patchwork with the rest of the guys, and they've been trying to get me back ever since. Whether that's arresting me, or trying to shut the house down."

"Why did you leave?'

There was a pause so palpable I wondered if King would ever answer.

"I almost killed the girl I love."

Love. He said it present tense. I watched King a moment, though he wasn't looking back, lost somewhere I couldn't follow.

Romeo cleared his throat, and Daniel spoke, quickly changing the subject back to the house. "It's okay to be afraid, little girl."

"I'm not afraid," I said quickly, sitting back up. The only home I'd ever known was on the brink of being torn down. The only love I'd ever had was living a half-life because of me.

I wasn't afraid, I was terrified.

I could tell they didn't believe me, but on this they didn't call me out.

"We'll be fine," King said. "This isn't the first time Patchwork House has been close to extinction."

I raised my eyes. "It's not?"

"You weren't the only one who had adventures while you were away." King smiled when he spoke, so I knew whatever had happened couldn't be so serious.

"Please stop keeping things from me." I pulled my pillow into my arms, hugging it tight, wondering what else they kept from me.

Romeo put his hand to his heart. "I told you everythin' the first week you got here." I frowned, not understanding. "Once upon a time, there was a land ruled by all-powerful and unyielding gods..." My grip slipped a little, silky pillow falling.

I'd always known there was truth to that story—it was about the Corrupt after all—but all of it? He'd spoken in so many convoluted metaphors I assumed most of it was fake.

My Rebel Gods were fighting the Incorrupt.

Silently, they came and sat down on my bed. King next to me, Daniel at the corner of my bed, even Romeo, who I knew hated this kind of thing, sat on the very edge of the foot.

"He paid for the burgers and fries I gave you," King started, voice low, and I knew we were getting to the meat of things. "He ordered me to take you home. He was always inserting himself where he didn't belong."

My heart thudded, all at once wanting to know everything and nothing.

"At the time it made sense for me to take the fall," King continued. "Now, well, now I don't know." I drank in all the information, breath pulled. "I think from the day you showed up at the skate park, he was doomed to love you." My face must have betrayed me because Daniel immediately shoved King.

"Shite choice of words, mate," Romeo added.

"I mean," King rubbed his eyes, looking like he hadn't slept much either. I wondered where he'd gone last night, what kept him up all night, but I didn't have the bandwidth to ask. "I was trying to protect you, we all were, but you and him, there's no point fighting it. And I don't think we should."

"He's probably outside right now, watching your window," Daniel finished, in a low voice.

Without consent, Flip popped into my mind again.

Slightly crooked, full smile that made his crescent eyes crinkle. Teeth bright with a little gap between the front two that drove me nuts when he ran his tongue over it. I squeezed my thighs and fell back, throwing my elbow over my eyes, as if that would vanish him.

There was a poke at my ribs, and I lifted my elbow, peeking out. Romeo held a joint in his outstretched arm. I lifted a brow when King didn't immediately take it away.

"We agreed it's time," Romeo said. "What with the ass fucking your life is receiving."

I took it, sitting back up. "Thanks...but this isn't my first time."

"You're not supposed to tell us that, little girl," Daniel said.

"You keep that stuff from parents," King said.

That filled me with warmth.

I twirled the joint in my hand, unable to help my smile. It was the first time they'd ever really acknowledged us as a *family*. We always just *existed*. But that's what we were, a family.

And then King ruined it. "Even if they're terrible and give you an awful childhood."

I couldn't take it. I couldn't.

"You didn't rip me away from some great, beautiful childhood! It was ugly. My dad was an addict. My mom had already overdosed and died. You—*you* were my beautiful childhood."

They paused, faces frozen in *What do we say to that?*

Then finally King spoke. "Are we who you really want to be telling that?"

No...I fell back against the mattress again with a sigh.

No, they weren't.

FLIP

I was back outside of Patchwork, in the shadows, watching them through the window. Maybe this was where I always belonged, should never have come into the light.

I watched until the guys left, and Tweetie came to the window. Opened it and stared out into the night like years ago. Her eyes searched, and it was almost like they were looking for me.

Twigs snapped, and I knew I wasn't alone.

King pulled out a joint, the flame offering meager light.

"I destroyed her life all over again," I said on an exhale.

It was a moment before he responded. "A few hours ago I might have agreed. I would have said you should have stayed in the dark, stayed away."

"What changed?" Some minutes passed, and I began to wonder if King was ever going to answer. I tore my eyes from Tweetie.

When he spoke, it didn't exactly clear up my question. "It's happening," he said. "My parents. The shit you warned me about. I went up there yesterday. Thought maybe if I just talked to them we could put it behind us. Finally."

A pause.

"But I pissed them off and they're coming for us."

"We'll figure it out, man," I said. "This shit is nothing new."

"I handled it. Did something remarkably stupid." King rubbed his temple. "I saw her again." Pip, his girl, the reason he left home for Patchwork. I didn't need to ask him how it went, it was clear on his face. "If you can have your girl, take her and don't let her go."

King had been wrecked over this girl for as long as I could remember. Longer than I'd been over Tweetie. Longer than I knew him, even. Somehow, whatever happened, broke him further.

So I did something reckless and stupid. I grabbed him by the shoulder and pulled him into a half-hug. He tightened. King would never ask for affection. He wasn't accustomed to it.

None of us were.

Then slowly, years of filth, of anger, of bullshit, faded away. His arm landed on my back. For a second, it was us just two teenagers from a broken past.

We broke apart just as quickly, clearing our throats at the same time.

King took a slow drag from his joint, and our eyes traveled back to Tweetie. She leaned on the sill, blue eyes stained with melancholy.

"You're both so blind. She's head over heels for you. She's been head over heels for you since she put your fucking poster up in her bedroom. She fell for the real you the night you gave her that damn crane. It became impossible to fight the night she left."

"And I fucked it up." I fucked it up irrevocably the very first day.

King handed me the joint with a frustrated grunt. "She

thinks she fucked up *your* life." My hand froze midair between us.

What?

Our eyes connected, finally. All at once she slammed the window shut.

"Just go to her, dumbass."

TWEETIE

A joint flickered to life below my window and I saw Flip, or rather, his outline shadowed by King's flame. His eyes were aglow like black glass being blown. Our eyes locked, and I slammed the window shut, heart racing.

So many nights I'd stared out that window searching for something but not sure what. When Flip's eyes met mine, I knew instantly.

Seconds turned into minutes turned into an hour. I sat on the bed, wondering if I should try and go to bed. I even turned off the light, like that would help. Yet I traced the cool, textured surface of my wall, wondering if Flip had come inside. My lids were heavy, shoulders weighed, but they were propped up by possibility.

I knocked, a light rap at first. So softly I knew he couldn't hear me.

Then harder.

I missed him so terribly, but I couldn't form words. I missed him, and I didn't know how to fix what was broken between us. So I let my fists talk against the wall between us.

Knock. I'm sorry. *Knock.* Come back. *Knock.* Please.

I knocked and knocked and knocked, getting bolder as lack of sleep deprived me of inhibition.

Yet each knock went without a response, and eventually I fell asleep with my forehead pressed to the wall.

Missing him.

I woke up groggy, neck aching from the position, but somehow asleep and under the covers. It took a minute to get my bearings. I'd had nightmares. So many nightmares, the past colliding with the hurt and pain of the present, making them starker. I even dreamed Flip crawled into bed and held me through them, but that was insane because Flip didn't sleep in beds.

Everything was slow and sluggish, and I was blinking like I could fall asleep at any moment after such a restless night.

But then I saw, and I was wide, wide awake.

My board was propped against my desk like always, but it had a brand new, bright pink deck. It was like the patchwork decorating our house but in my favorite color. Resting over the deck was my origami crane, but it had been made into a bracelet.

I picked it up, examining the thin gold chain. I *knew* this bracelet. I thought I'd lost it years ago, the night I first met Nate. Was it with Flip this entire time? Had Flip held on to it?

I fell back against my wall.

Punched in the gut.

I was certain Flip left it for me, but without a note, I didn't know what it meant.

Was he returning my knock, or was he saying goodbye?

THIRTY

AIR: RIDING WITH ALL FOUR WHEELS IN THE AIR.

TWEETIE

All I could think about was Flip. Not the looming threat of
Patchwork disappearing, or the fact that I had to be at my
comp in an hour. This was my very last chance, and all I
wanted to do was twirl the bracelet on my wrist over and
over again.

Daniel, Romeo, and I were in the kitchen. Romeo held
my board, Daniel my helmet while King went to get his
keys.

"Helmet?" *Check.* "Board." *Check.* "Devilishly good-
looking Brit?" I rolled my eyes, but smiled, appreciating his
levity, appreciating that no matter how dire the situation, I
could always count on Romeo to light a cigarette on the
flames of the house fire.

Bacon, Sparky, and Pants made signs for me again and
even Penelope tossed out an olive branch, offering to braid
my crazy curls to keep them out of my face.

"You'll do fine, little girl," Daniel said, but I think he

knew the crease around my eyes had nothing to do with fear.

Daniel and Romeo's attentions were redirected to the other side of the kitchen as Sparky once again earned his nickname. I settled against the wall twisting the bracelet on my wrist.

"You're being too hard on him," King said softly. I lifted my head to find him next to me, leaning on the Bill Murray mural.

"Coming from you that's...a surprise." King shrugged, bending forward to ruffle my beanie, messing it up until the fuzzy gray and orange fell across my eyes.

I pushed it up with one hand.

After a moment passed, he said, "Maybe it's time to forgive him, even if you're still mad."

"I'm not *mad*! I'm ashamed." I jumped off the wall in my vehemence. "I ruined his life. How can I look him in the eyes? I can barely look you in the eyes." I paused. "If it wasn't for me he would be this great skateboarder. Instead he wasted his life on me. Wasted his life beneath my window."

I had no idea what was happening these past years. How much he gave up. How do I even *begin* to fix that?

"I don't blame him for my dad's death. Dad was driving intoxicated. It was sad and tragic but if anything, *Flip's* the victim."

"If he wasn't there—" King started, but I refused to let him go down that path.

"Then Dad might have killed someone."

"You're really not mad? Not disgusted?"

I gasped, spinning at the voice. Flip. The kitchen door was open, streaming morning light. He held a board under one flexed arm, forearm straining.

How long had he been there? What had he heard?

"Um...no," I said after a minute. "I'm not."

"Wow, uh, look at that really cool thing in the other room," Romeo said, and then I remembered it wasn't just Flip and me. Every time we were together, I got sucked into his vortex. "We should all go see how...cool it is."

"I don't see anything," Pants said, and King shoved him by the head so he stumbled forward into the living room. Everyone followed and then Flip and I were alone.

His eyes landed on my wrist with a soft smile. "Nice bracelet."

I touched the crane, my heart fracturing into a billion pieces.

I don't deserve this, I thought, just as I noticed the board under *his* arm. Sweat shone on his muscled forearms and some beaded his neck. Had he been skating? But I'd had mine all morning.

"Were you skating?"

He looked down, eyebrows lifting like he forgot he'd had it. "Yeah." Now I wished all the junk that piled between us was gone, simply so I could hug him, be happy for him.

Flip skated without my board.

Another silence splintered between us. There was so much I wanted to ask him but I didn't even know where to start.

"I—"

"Did I—"

We started at the same time.

"You go," he said, and suddenly my mouth was dry. *Did*

I ruin your life? Would everything have been different—would you be happier—without me?

But the questions I'd been dying to ask shriveled up at the earnest, open way he looked at me.

I chewed my lip. "What have you been doing this whole time? I mean, besides keeping tabs on me?" Beating around the bush, that's what my dad used to say. I'll ask one question hoping you answer with what I really want to know.

"After I lived with King's family, I spent a couple years getting to know myself...tried to get you out of my head."

Oh.

I looked to the floor.

Suddenly his touch was at my chin, lifting my eyes with his free hand. "You were the little girl we saved. Do you know how fucked it is that I fell in love with you?"

My breath rushed out of me, my heart stopped.

Did he say love?

"I love you," he repeated like he knew my thoughts. "I've always loved you. I loved you even when it was wrong. I can't stop loving you. And I've tried. Relentlessly." He said the last bit more to himself.

My brows caved. "But I ruined your life."

Flip smiled. Actually *smiled*.

I tried to shove him off, but his grip tightened, thumb digging into my chin.

"Ruin me. Ruin me over and over again, Tweetie. Because, goddamn, it feels good." I tried to ignore the leap in my heart at his words and smooth, heady voice. How could he be smiling at a time like this?

"You lost skateboarding," I said. "You lost Patchwork. You lost *everything*."

An even bigger smile—real, too.

Flip asked me if I was mad before, well, now I was

starting to get angry. Cocky, arrogant Flip was back. The glow of knowledge I didn't possess behind his grin.

I ground my jaw, trying not to yank my face from between his fingers.

"I didn't lose *everything*." Then he dropped his board with crash to the floor and kissed me. Kissed my gasping open mouth, not waiting for an invitation. Cradled my face, holding me hostage, using me as a vessel for his hunger and desperation and anguish.

Cauterized my crumbling heart.

He broke for a breath on a groan, lips still pressed to mine. "Tweetie, you *are* everything."

Melting, absolutely melting into him, when—
BANG.

The front door kicked open. Both Flip and I turned just in time to see King, Daniel, and Romeo run into the kitchen.

"We've got—" King started.

"Police!" echoed into the kitchen.

"Yeah, that," Romeo said.

FLIP

I rubbed my thumbs softly on Tweetie's shoulder, needing some kind of connection as I turned to King.

"Thought you took care of it," I said. There was no bitterness or animosity in my voice. It had been ages since we'd had a run-in with the cops. It was how we'd met, the birth of Patchwork, and in a weird way, it felt like a rebirth.

King grinned. "Consider it a swan song." Daniel and Romeo shared the same look as King and I, excitement like fireflies in their eyes. We told the younger kids to get lost quick, as soon as the back door slammed shut after them, problem solved.

"You thinking what I'm thinking?" I asked. I twisted the fabric at Tweetie's shoulder, smooth beneath my thumb. There was still shit we needed to address, and she hadn't said a thing after I told her I loved her, but seconds ago her lips had been on mine, her sighs hot on the roof of my mouth. Progress.

A good guy would let Tweetie go. She didn't say it. After the kiss, after everything, she didn't say it.

But Tweetie was a miracle. You don't let miracles go.

I'd slept in a bed for the first time in over a decade. Holding her through her nightmares, I didn't think about mine.

"Bait and switch?" Daniel suggested, and then we all looked to Romeo.

"It's really a bit on the nose how you always force the immigrant to be the bait." But he flexed his knuckles and went to find the cops. The sound of broken glass, cops cursing, and Romeo laughing soon followed.

Just another day at Patchwork.

"Does bait and switch get you all out?" Tweetie piped up.

"Uh..." Everyone exchanged looks. "Sure." It gets *one* of us out, two if we're lucky. King and I exchanged a look. We needed to get Tweetie ready, Romeo would only distract them for so long, and then it was time for the switch. He'd lead them to us, and once the cops saw the opportunity to nab *three* of us instead of one, they wouldn't think to follow.

Reading my mind, Daniel tossed her helmet to me. I slammed it on her head, King shoved the board under her arm, complete with the new deck. I'd been lucky, the shop didn't carry that design anymore, but they'd had one left, in the very back.

"But you're all coming to my competition, right?" Tweetie asked, looking adorable with her eyes hidden under the helmet. We all paused. I removed my hands from the helmet. She shoved it up, looking at all of us. "Right?"

Another crash, another curse, this time closer. She picked at the galaxy grip on her board, sparkly in the sun.

Then it was like she was only looking at me, something weighing her blue eyes.

"Nice board," I said.

Tweetie's mouth parted on a breath, just as there was another loud crash, a curse, then Romeo appeared. A small piece of wood protruded from his arm, blood staining his shirt. He smiled as if everything was fine.

He bowed to Tweetie, throwing his arm out lavishly. "Your chauffeur, my dear."

"There's wood in your arm," she said flatly.

"I assure you I'm still a much better driver than at least two percent of the population," he replied, still bent ninety degrees.

"That wasn't why—and that's not a very high—" Romeo picked her up before she could finish, throwing her over his shoulder, shoving her board under his arm, heading for the back door.

"Wait!" she yelled, and Romeo froze. Her eyes locked with mine again. A deep swallow of her throat, like something was stuck, something she really needed to say.

Hope sprang thin and spindly, like the first spring blossom in my chest. I wondered if maybe she would say the thing I needed to hear from her. Three words that would clear all my doubts.

Another crash and Romeo took off running.

"Later, luv."

We sat shoulder to shoulder on our porch, arms behind our backs, in handcuffs. They didn't have shit on us, but it wouldn't stop them from keeping us in a forty-eight hour hold.

"Brings back memories," King said. He paused, then turned to me. "You're staying for good now, right?"

"Yeah, but," I said, and King held still, waiting. "Everyone deserves a home. We're revisiting the rules. This isn't over." I smiled, and he returned it.

"Maybe when we aren't in handcuffs?"

"I think they've upgraded the hardware." Daniel wriggled his wrists in the cuffs, which earned us a searing glare. We grinned.

The cops were busy in their car, barely paying attention to us. I exhaled. I really didn't want to miss Tweetie's big day, and I'd been working on a surprise for her myself.

"Think we can get out of here in time to beat Romeo?" I asked, and King and Daniel exchanged looks.

Legally? No.

"Sparky, Pants, and Bacon," I whisper-yelled. They'd been spying on us from behind the porch. One by one, they lined up, soldiers reporting for duty.

"Yes?" they asked.

I pinned Sparky. "Time to put your nickname to use." They shared a look, then dashed off. Sparky threw some leaves in the cop car and lit a fire. While the cops were distracted, Pants and Bacon snatched keys from the car, releasing us from our handcuffs.

Daniel rubbed his wrists. King watched me, picking up I had a plan brewing.

"What are you going to do?" he asked. I looked across Patchwork's sprawling lawn, down the neighborhood, our story replaying as an old film.

When King brought her burgers. When she stormed past me. When I dragged her back through Heaven's Court. When we went street skating. Our first kiss.

I'd kept waiting for the green light, but why? When the fuck had I ever done that? I was Corrupt. I was a Rebel God. So I was going to give one last all or nothing. One more mountain to move.

I turned, meeting their eyes. "What I always do—the wrong thing."

THIRTY-ONE

BANGER: AN EXTREMELY DIFFICULT TRICK.

TWEETIE

I pressed my fingers to my lips, reliving my kiss with Flip for the thousandth time. Wrung my hands, nervous, but not because of the competition. We were in line to check in, but once again, all I could think about was him. The grounds were huge, bleachers packed with more people than I'd ever seen. This was the big time.

"Is everyone going to be okay?" I asked Romeo. Is *Flip* going to be okay?

"Just focus on your competition," he said. The ramps were bigger than anything I'd ever skated on in my life. A patchwork of smooth, slick wood.

Flip popped into my head.

When you blush like that, it makes me wonder where else you're blushing.

So do it. Kiss me.

I shook my head, clearing the image.

I eyed Romeo in my periphery. "Should we get you a

doctor?" He looked at the wood sticking from his arm absently like it was a bug that landed on his shoulder. Without a second's thought, he ripped it out. Threw it on the ground.

My mouth dropped.

I don't think I would ever get used to this.

"Doctors are charlatans," he said by way of explanation.

The sun was wistful, a few early blooms clung to empty branches. Why couldn't I just tell him? *I love you.* How hard is that to say?

On a TV a few booths away a music video played. I nearly gasped when I saw who it was. *The Imperialists.* Romeo! But there was another guy singing as well. He was tall and blonde, and movie star hot.

I eyed Romeo.

"When do you have to get back to your famous world tour?" I asked lightly. He'd been back for a while. Wasn't he supposed to be making girls' panties drop? Something dark flickered in Romeo's eyes, then he nudged me. There was a foot of space between me and the registration booth, the man waiting for me to sign in. I quickly shuffled to the front.

"Name?"

"Oh, uh, Raegan."

"We don't have a Raegan." He didn't even look at his papers.

"Uh...Tweetie?" I tried my nickname, though officially I went as Raegan Fairchild. The look on his face answered for me and my heart thudded nervously.

"What if they don't let me compete?" I whispered to Romeo.

"Check again, mate," he said, humor gone, voice like freshly hewn steel. First Patchwork being condemned, then the cops, now this? But if Romeo was worried, he didn't show it. Smile pearly and leonine, eyes sharp like knives.

"Oh, here it is." The man pulled out a number from beneath a stack, handing it to me like I was asking for his firstborn child.

"Aces." Romeo snatched it. "Don't quit your day job." Romeo gently cupped my elbow, leading me from the table, but I froze. There was a name scribbled at the top of the list, above the ones neatly printed in ink. It didn't make any sense.

"Why does it say Flip?" I pointed at the name.

The registrant eyed me coolly. "Because he's competing."

"At *this* event? Today?" I think the man thought I was scared to compete with him, and who wouldn't be? He'd been the best in the world.

Romeo tugged me out of line as I was frozen, still trying to comprehend what it meant.

Was he really competing?

"How—" I broke off, eyes traveling across the asphalt.

Flip. Flip, King, and Daniel leaned against King's shiny black and red Chevelle. Arms folded, one leg crossed over the other or propped against the body, smiles lazy and humor glowing in their eyes. My heart soared at the sight of them, even with bloody lips and gashes beneath their eyes I knew would become black and bruised.

A billion questions spiraled in my head.

How did they get away?

When did they get here?

Soon the questions were background noise, and I was running and running. Jumping into Flip's arms as he caught me, my legs wrapped around his waist. His hand anchored my lower back, arms around his neck. *Pro ho*, they might whisper, but at that moment I didn't care.

They would always whisper.

"They let you go?" I asked.

A grin broke his cut cheek, dimples feathering. "Define 'let.'" My jaw dropped. He'd ditched the cops? They would be looking for him and they would be angry. As if reading my mind he added, voice lower, hand on my spine tightening, "We weren't going to miss your big competition, Tweetie."

Beside us, King coughed, and I remembered we weren't alone. I jumped off Flip, rubbed my beanie furiously to get some sense into my brain. When I was around him, I lost all self-control.

Flip rubbed his thumb along my wrist, tracing my bracelet, pulling my eyes back to his. In my periphery I saw my gods scatter, leaving just me and him. Alone.

My mouth dried. This was the time to tell him everything, but I didn't even know where to start. Skateboarding? Easy. From the minute I grabbed my first board it had been instinct. You know instantly if it's going to be a good land or bad.

Love was messy. Love was complicated. You took a leap and you hoped you didn't slam.

I love you.

I'm so in love with you.

"I saw your name," I whispered. "Are you really competing?"

FLIP

I nodded and her eyes popped adorably. They closed

registration months ago, but the prospect that *the* Flip could do his comeback at their regional competition had them practically scrambling all over themselves to make accommodations.

"I'll stop if you want," I said, thumb still on her bracelet, connecting us as a loosely, fraying wire.

"Don't you dare," she said. "I'm not afraid of you, Flip. I know all of your moves."

I couldn't help my smile. "Yeah. You do."

Her eyes glowed with the knowledge of my hidden meaning. I still felt her legs around my waist, her arms on my neck, her chest pressed to mine.

Seconds pressurized, a balloon ready to pop. I wouldn't let go of the bracelet. Allowing myself the simple touch. Enough to graze the bone at her wrist. Knowing if I pulled her any closer, I'd kiss her and tangle my hands in her hair, my tongue in her mouth. But that would scare her off, so I held the chain at her wrist tenuously like my control.

"You're not doing this just to make me happy, right?" she asked softly.

"Oh, I'm going all out, Tweetie. Get ready to lose." I grinned, and she scrunched her lips, trying to hide a smile and failing.

Our smiles faded like spring wind, leaving nothing but a bereft silence.

"You never told me why you named me Tweetie," she said quietly after a moment. I thought it was fitting she would ask me now, because we met at a park like this one. We were heading into winter, though, not out of it. Like now, she stood in the middle of the chaos, ready to tackle it.

"You had big blue eyes and wild blonde hair," I said. "Most importantly, you wouldn't shut up." I zeroed on her mouth. "Fuck, I want to bite those lips." Her eyes grew and

I laughed. "I didn't realize just how well the nickname would age, though."

"What does that mean?" Her eyes darted to mine.

"You're still too fucking cute." She looked away, hiding a blush and smile in her graphic tee.

People swarmed us, going from concessions to the stands. The announcers gravelly voices echoed over the speakers. *We've been told Flip is gonna make an appearance, so we've got bets going if we'll even recognize his old ass.*

Still, it felt like we were the only two people in the word.

"So we're really doing this?" she whispered. "If I win, you lose. If you win, I lose."

"That's how competitions work, Tweetie."

She ground her jaw adorably as they called my name and a murmur grew in the crowd, a buzz, a hum, a slowly approaching stampede. Heads looking left and right. My grip tightened on the bracelet, then I let her go.

"You better do your trick," I warned. "It's a once-in-a-lifetime trick, one to change skateboarding."

"And if I don't?" she goaded, arching a brow. I dropped my smile, brows caving in faux-disapproval, and was rewarded with a cheeky smile.

Fuck, her *smile.*

I'd missed that. I looked over her shoulder at the crowd waiting, then once more at Tweetie. Eyes sparkling. Cheeks red. With another call of my name, I headed to the ramp.

I paused mid-step.

"One last thing." I tugged at the elastics in her hair, loosing the curls from her braids. "Better." I tousled my hand in her hair, getting the curls wild and tangled, loving the way her lips parted in shock. I put her hat back in place then I was off to make the comeback everyone had been waiting for.

"Why do you love me?" Tweetie called out when I was several steps away. I stopped and turned, a smile breaking my cheeks. They called my name once more, but I ignored it, walking back to Tweetie.

"Do you have a year?" I asked.

She shoved me.

Progress.

She chewed the inside of her cheek. "I'm serious."

I arched a brow. "So am I." Where did I even start? "I tried to fight it. Every day I tried to fight it. The night you threw up in my closet I gave up. The moment I kissed you I knew there was no going back. Because you are light, Tweetie. Even the darkest moments of my life were brighter with you in them."

"But I *ruined* your life."

"You changed my life." I gripped her face between my palms. "With purpose and *joy*, you changed my life." Because this was it, the now or never, I opened up and bled everything left of my heart, into her blue, blue eyes.

"You're fearless. You're loyal. You're dazzling. But most importantly, you give me somewhere to belong. A home, Tweetie. With you, I finally have a bed to sleep on."

Her lips parted.

I dropped her face, heading toward the growing cheers of the crowd.

THIRTY-TWO

FLAT GROUND: SKATING WITHOUT ANY
OBSTACLES.

TWEETIE

Flip was on fire, absolutely on fire. It was a dream come true to watch him. I worried he was going to go easy, let me win, but he was tearing it apart. He spun through the air like a missile. Aggressive. Scary. Dominating. *Magical.*

I swore I saw his deck painted with bright blue eyes and yellow fur. Yet he was so fast, I couldn't be sure.

When he went up in the air for another trick, he grabbed the board and our eyes connected. My heart throbbed like a magnet, pulling it closer. Then he landed, tore off his shirt to wipe the sweat off his brow, giving me one last searing look.

The crowd went wild.

He exited to let the next competitor get ready while the judges deliberated.

As if they needed any time—he'd killed it.

"He was amazing, right?" I stood next to Daniel on the edges of the bleachers and a frenetic crowd. Romeo had gone to help Flip. I wasn't sure where King had gone. "Daniel?" I turned when he didn't reply.

Daniel stared across the ramp, over the tops of mingling fans and skaters giving autographs, at two girls who looked like they belonged more at an upscale party. They spoke with King near the concessions.

One had really beautiful gray eyes, sort of like King's, and intense, voluminous brown hair. The other had gorgeous porcelain ivory skin, silky straight cappuccino hair that fell down her back, and eyes hidden behind thin, round glasses.

"Who is that?"

"The tall one is King's sister." They were *both* tall, but that wasn't what I latched onto.

"King's *sister*? King has a sister?"

"He has an entire family, little one."

I mean, I already sort of knew that, but still, I balked, trying to process it. Growing up, I always assumed King was an orphan like me, like Daniel. Or at least abandoned, like Flip. All of us *without* the normal family life most had. I *assumed* Romeo was as well...

I wondered what she was doing here, and who the pretty girl next to her was.

"Do you know them?" I asked.

It was a moment before Daniel responded, then he cleared his throat. "No." Daniel's eyes were glued at King's apparent *sibling,* and it wasn't the stare of a stranger. I'd never seen Daniel look at anyone like that.

There was a storm of emotion swirling in his amber eyes.

As if he knew I was looking, he snapped out of it.

"I'll go find Flip and Romeo." Daniel went off, leaving me alone as I worked my mouth, an idea brewing in my head that I knew would get me into trouble. If King wanted me to meet his *sister* he would have introduced us, yet...

I walked over to them, stopping just shy of the girls. King's sister had tan skin like him, but unlike King, her face lit up from the inside, like her entire soul was smiling with mischief. She was too far away to introduce myself, though, so I went for her friend. The thick lash line reminded me of Flip's, but hers weren't lazy and entitled. She was stately, reminding me of a queen, but somehow also shy in the way she fiddled with her fingers.

King glared at me, silently telling me to leave.

I wouldn't be swayed.

"Hi, I'm—" King stepped between us, blocking my hand. "Tweetie," I finished, trying to see around his massive body.

"Go," he growled, but I wasn't sure if he was talking to me or the other person.

I got my answer when her head dropped, and she left, King's *sister* following.

"What the hell?"

"You don't touch her. Ever. Understand?" I could count on my hand the number of times King had spoken to me roughly, and it was *never* like this. Like a lion guarding its cub, as if he would rip me apart if I disobeyed.

His face softened, he rubbed the back of his neck. "Ah... shit...sorry, Tweetie."

"Was that her? The one you love?" The girl everyone kept referring to, the one he wanted but couldn't have for whatever reason. The one he'd said he'd nearly *killed*. I still couldn't wrap my head around it, protective King almost killing someone.

She was really beautiful.

It took King so long to speak I was certain it was going to

be another unanswered question. Then he said, "Yeah." We stood side by side in silence. Late winter air was glistening ice in an early spring sun.

Then King said, "Dammit Tweetie, I'm so sorry."

This was it. We were going to hash it out.

"I could never really be mad at you," I whispered. "I tried, but I couldn't."

"You should be, Tweetie. You should hate me."

"I can't. You're my big brother."

"Exactly. It was fucked up. It was wrong." I shrugged. Maybe I should have been mad, but all this time I didn't really want an apology, I wanted an *explanation*.

Now I had one.

King kissed me in a moment of pain.

Before that he'd sacrificed everything for his brother.

Everything for me.

Was I really going to crucify him forever over *one* mistake?

"You're calling me Tweetie again," I said with a small smile. Some time passed, then he smiled too.

Romeo joined us with a bottle of open whiskey in his hand, just as Flip came into view. The only thing separating us the ramp. He ran both hands through his wavy hair, getting it out of his face. His biceps quivered, pulsed. The left side of his cheek tilted when he caught me staring.

"So when are you going to get over yourself and jump his bones, luv?" Romeo asked, taking a swig. I swallowed my groan. Romeo might dress like a regular Joe now, but he was still the same Romeo—wildly inappropriate.

"Don't you think you've both given up enough already?" King asked, but he was staring at the girl again, and she was staring back with wide, black eyes.

My own wandered back to Flip.

No. I don't know. Flip has, but there's a debt I need to pay. How could I tell him I loved him before I showed him what that meant? Before he knew I would do anything for him and I was sorry for everything I'd taken? Words weren't enough.

"You mean well, luv, but if you keep this up, you're only going to hurt him more," Romeo added.

I knew that—I did—I just didn't know how to even start going back to him.

Flip waggled his eyebrows and I ducked my head with a smile, eyes catching the bracelet. An idea popped into my head. It definitely wasn't enough to fix everything, but it was a start.

"Where can I get nine hundred and ninety-nine origami cranes in less than an hour?"

King's brows rose.

Romeo took another sip of whiskey. "I want to say the mall?"

It came down to me and Flip in the finals. I'd just completed my run and felt nervous, but good. I'd nailed every trick. Did everything I possibly could. It was out of my hands.

I tore off my beanie, rubbing my curls as I studied the judges, hoping to decipher anything from their matching masks.

"Do you know how sexy you are when you're in the zone?" Flip was propped against the back of the ramp, iron crisscrosses his background, board at his feet, and a self-satisfied smile on his face. The ramp was so tall it created shade against a blue sky and bright sun, almost like we were a secret. "You killed it."

"You're up next," I said, voice way too shaky. "You should be getting ready." He ignored me, kicking off the ramp, until we were so close I had to look past the wicked edge of his jaw to find his sparkling eyes.

"I'm not saying this because I love you and hope you'll finally admit you find me irresistible." *Remember to breathe.* I would never get used to his brazen honesty. "This is purely objective," he continued. "They saw it too."

Then he gripped my hips, spinning and pulling me against his chest, pointing over my shoulder. I tried to focus on his finger and not the way his muscles flexed against my back.

"Look at that little girl in the third row." Lips hot at my neck, a voice that throbbed from its point at my flesh, down my spine, deep into my thighs.

Focus.

Follow the finger.

She had a crude hand-drawn sign that said I LOVE REGAN. I loved it, even though she'd spelled my name wrong. My face heated, and when Flip spoke next, it completely set on fire.

"You're once in a lifetime, Tweetie. I see it. They see it." I turned my face into my shoulder, hiding my blush. He groaned. "That blush, Tweetie. You know what the blush does to me."

I spun so I could meet him face to face. "I don't think I remember. Remind me?"

His eyes darkened, hands on my hips harsh and bruising. "Don't tease."

I bit my lip, his eyes dropped to them. I wanted that—him—and I was so ready to tell him.

Just as I was to open my mouth and pour out everything I'd been keeping locked tight, sirens sounded and three cop cars pulled into the parking lot.

Worst. Timing. Ever.

Police piled out, fanning in all directions. King and Daniel didn't bother running, throwing up their hands in annoyed surrender. Romeo, however, ran backward from them, finishing his bottle of whiskey as he went and flipping them the bird.

"Flip..." Fear leaked from me, because they would be here soon, and because we knew what this meant. Flip wouldn't be able to compete, and he'd be disqualified. Yet his smile was easy, thumb at my at my hip rubbing a lazy circle.

"Why are you smiling?"

He was about to be arrested and disqualified. Yet his smile grew, stretching his smooth cheeks tauntingly, once again acting like he knew something I didn't.

Romeo tripped over a fan's legs, and police launched themselves at the opportunity, wrangling him. Now having subdued Romeo, they set their sights on Flip. He was full-on grinning, his perfectly crooked smile glinting in the sun, simultaneously making my belly flip while frustration climbed hot up my neck.

I shoved him and he stumbled back, tripping over his heels with a musically scaled laugh that kick started my heart. The fans were a blurry oil painting between us when he tilted his head, a smile soft on his face like the hue in his eyes.

How he could smile as cops zeroed on him? It was like the greatest thing ever just happened, but cops were about to take him down before he could make his comeback.

"Tweetie," he said. "You *won*." My throat thickened.

What was he talking about? "I'd like to see them justify not giving you the win when you're the only one left."

Hot and cold, something I'd wanted my entire life finally manifest. I won. I *won*.

But—was this his plan? To compete only to fail and hand me the win?

"This was a happy accident," Flip said like he knew what I was thinking. I searched his eyes, trying to find the truth. "There will be other competitions. Really. And I'll win them." His smile was gone now. He went back to the ramp, kicking up his board to certify a truth I'd thought I'd seen earlier. "Now I'll have you with me. My good-luck charm. The only reason I'm even skating again."

I traced my finger along his wooden deck. "This feels wrong. I want to win the right way."

"When the world is stacked against you, when you're competing on an unfair playing field, when everyone wants you fail, it isn't wrong to accept help. You *should* win Tweetie. You should've won years ago. Stop being so goddamn stubborn."

I loosed a breath, kept my fingers light on his deck. I still wasn't sure. In my dreams, I won because they finally admitted I *should* win. I wouldn't have to crash through the glass ceiling; they would open it up for me.

"You can step down, and the guy in third place can win..." Flip suggested. "The one who doesn't know his ass from his board."

My eyes shot from the board back to Flip. "No!"

He was horrible.

I couldn't lose to someone like that *again*. As police barreled toward Flip, he gripped my hands, pulling me close with his board, like the night I'd found him skating on mine.

"You'll have other competitions, and you'll win them, because now they can't say you don't deserve it."

A smile I couldn't stop spread across my face. "I won?"

"You won."

The glint in his toffee eyes and the relieved, ecstatic stretch of his lips mirrored my own. It was like he'd been waiting for this moment just as long as I had.

Flip stroked his thumbs across the back of my hand. It was just us, our eyes, and the feel of him.

Then he was torn from me, ripped away as two police officers slammed him to the ground. Flip grinned the entire time, and I couldn't help but return his smile.

They announced my win as they marched the Rebel Gods to the car. All four of my gods cheered for me as they were carted away. Whistling as their heads were pushed into the car. The crowd went wild, actually went wild—for *me*. The little girl waved her sign so intensely I couldn't even read the words.

But something was still missing.

I hopped off the stage before they could hand me a trophy, tearing through the crowd.

I stopped between Flip and the black and white.

"Ma'am get back," a stout, walrus-looking officer said.

"Tweetie?" Flip stared at me, confusion writ across his smooth features.

"Get back ma'am, or we'll have to arrest you too," another, younger officer said, barely looking out of his teenage years.

Flip was inches away from being arrested, and who knows how long he could be in jail? If I missed this chance, he might not give me another. There was no time for a pep talk. No time to think about how this could backfire.

But maybe *not thinking* was a good thing. Maybe checklists and fail-safes weren't the answer. Maybe this has always been about trust. Trusting the other person will catch me. Trusting even if we slam, it won't break them. Or us.

"Tweetie," Flip started again. "What are you—"

I kissed him.

Hard.

Needing him to feel everything I'd been holding back.

I love you. I need you. I'm sorry. With his hands handcuffed, and the police officers shouting at me, we kissed. Their warnings faded into nothing. The world around us melted away.

Only us.

My heartbeat and his smooth, sure lips.

Even handcuffed, Flip took control, furious and ruthless, giving me no space to breathe or think. As if he wanted to punish me for making him wait. Warn me never to do it again. His growl vibrated against my lips. My sigh floated along his.

Until a police officer tore me from him, hand at my collar, and slammed me against the side of the car.

"Do you have a fucking death wish?" Flip glared at the officer, ready to kill. "I'll gladly grant it."

"Flip," I said, bringing him back to me with a smile. He wasn't convinced, eyes darting to the man at my back. "I love you," I said softly.

This probably wasn't the best time to make my grand gesture. In the movies there were boom boxes and rose petals, but if I kept waiting for the *right* time, maybe it would never come.

Flip froze, mid-threat to the officer.

Then his eyes popped, slowly finding mine. "What?"

"I love you."

"Say it again," he said instantly, eyes still wide, face taut and stony, like he hadn't heard me properly.

"I love you," I laughed. An eyebrow twitched, a dimple quirked—a smile so close to breaking the surface. Still, Flip wasn't sure if he could be certain.

"One more time." His voice was low, slipping inside me warm and heady like whiskey.

"I love you," I whispered. "I loved you in the past, I love you in the present. I loved you when I didn't know it was you. I loved you when you were competing against yourself. I love you and I can't stop loving you. Flip or Nate, Nate or Flip—it doesn't matter. It's *always* been you."

Flip grinned, a smile of pure satisfaction, and I knew I'd reached him. It stretched his cheeks and pushed his dimple out and nearly made my legs buckle.

"You love me, huh?" he said, still sporting that smile. "I am pretty irresistible." I rolled my eyes, but inside I was all butterflies, especially as Flip continued to watch me, eyes soft and heated, tongue pushing out his cheek. It was insane how he had this ability to make me feel like we were utterly alone, even surrounded by police officers.

But King, Romeo, and Daniel whistled and whooped from inside the police car, and it brought me back to the present. Then the officer slammed handcuffs on my wrists.

Oh, ouch.

Flip and I were shoved into a second car, about to be carted off to jail. He never once took his eyes off me and all I could think was, *totally worth it.*

THIRTY-THREE

LAND: TO PERFORM A TRICK SUCCESSFULLY.

TWEETIE

Flip murmured sweet and dirty things against my neck, trailing his middle and pointer finger up and down my arm. His words stoked the fire inside me from hot to blazing and it didn't feel like we were in jail. Plus it was oddly nice, like I was finally one of them.

He wrapped his arms around my waist, pulling me tighter against his chest.

"You're a jailbird now." He laughed against my hair, the smooth, confident sound so heady and so intoxicating. "Dirty, dirty jailbird." His hand slid beneath my shirt, settling on my warm skin. I bit my lip to keep from sighing.

"Get a room," everyone groaned.

"Sure, hold the fuck up while we ask for an adjoining suite. Maybe something with a view." He bit my ear softly, just enough to tug the lobe down, and lowered his voice so only I heard him. "When we get out of here I'm getting this hair messy and sprawled over my pillow."

Then his free hand tangled in my hair and he tugged my head back, not painfully, just enough to emphasize his point, before his lips found my neck again. I released a jagged breath.

Flip went back to shooting the shit with everyone, still massaging my scalp, his other hand tracing lines just beneath my belly button. I didn't even know what they were talking about. I couldn't think straight. Vision blurry.

An officer arrived at the iron gate, looking down at us with a curled lip and glare. I think he said something, but I was lost in a world of Flip.

His hot hands.

His hotter words.

"Tweetie," Flip said. I found his warm dark gaze, and he grinned slow and lazy and satisfied. He grasped my chin, gently. "When you look at me like that I have half a mind to stay in jail."

"Jesus, *fuck*," Romeo said, popping our steamy bubble. "Just keep it in your pants for five minutes, yeah? Normally I'd be all about this, really encouraging you to just stick it in her—" I hid my embarrassment in Flip's shoulder, just before Romeo was abruptly cut off.

The sound of rattling iron let me know Romeo had once again been shoved, into the bars this time. That's when I pulled my head from Flip's shoulder to see the iron gate was open and all the gods stood on the outside. When had the gate opened?

I don't know how we got released so quickly. We were barely in jail before bail was posted and as far as I knew, none of us had enough money for *one*, let alone all five. The officer couldn't have looked less pleased to pull us out.

"Someone has friends in high places," he muttered bitterly. Romeo shimmied against his chest and tipped an imaginary hat at him. We all shoved him out before we got rearrested.

Just outside the building, we stopped short. A man in a well-fitted suit and a woman in a pale blue dress blocked the steps. The woman argued with the man, but when they spotted us, they stopped. She grabbed the man's arm as he came to us, and he shook her off.

"Dad," King said and my breath pulled. The similarities were impossible to miss now—his dad's silvery blue eyes, his mother's creamy, mocha skin. "Here to get us rearrested?"

I wondered if his parents had been the ones to post bail. If they were the *high places* the officer had been referring to. Maybe they felt bad. Then his mother spoke, and I knew I couldn't be more wrong.

"If I have to set that place on fire I will, Kingston. I will light the match—" She broke off, pain strangling her vocal cords, and turned to her husband. "He was barely in there for an hour." The words were muffled against his shoulder.

Awkwardly, we kept walking past his crying mother.

"Come home." His father's eyes were pleading, piercing, pained. We stopped, then one by one we all fell back, leaving only King.

"Nate," King's dad yelled. "Stop. Please." Flip froze and instinctively I gripped his hand harder. I didn't want him to go back, not after we'd finally gotten together.

But how selfish was that?

I loosened my hold.

"It's okay to want to go home," I whispered. "It's okay." A moment passed like forever. I knew he missed them. I saw it in his eyes, even now.

But then he squeezed my hand. "I am home."

No one went with King's parents. King spoke with them for over an hour, and by the end, they looked slightly mollified, but I could tell by the look in their eyes it wasn't over. Maybe some of what drove them was because they didn't understand us, but mostly it was pain. Loss. They'd never give up. Not until they had King again. Maybe not even until they got Flip too. Whatever King had said to them, whatever he'd done to save Patchwork, was just a Band-Aid on a bullet wound.

When we arrived at Patchwork, at first it looked the same. Same graffiti quilt, same ornate shingles and lacy molding, but as we got closer, it became visible: so many threads they created a feathery, silky curtain from the strings hanging off the porch.

Jewel-toned and strung at different heights, one thousand origami cranes. Well, not one *thousand* but as many as could be hung in the short time. Pants, Bacon, and Sparky were still in the middle of hanging them, and when Pants saw us, he fell off a ladder.

I'd actually forgotten I'd asked them to do me this favor. There was so much craziness after the competition, what with being *arrested*.

Flip froze, and suddenly I was unbearably nervous. Nerves hummed electric beneath my skin. I looked from the cranes to him, back and forth. Our audience waited. The longer Flip went without a word, the worse my nerves tangled.

This was silly.

I shouldn't have done this. He was going to think I was such a fool.

The silence stretched.

"I just..." I spoke softly. "I wanted to help your wish come true." I wanted to show him I would do anything.

Flip was so, so quiet, his face an unreadable mask.

"This was stupid. I'm sorry." I headed to the porch to, I

don't know, tear them down so we could forget this ever happened, but Flip gripped my wrist, spun me to him. I landed against his chest, breath leaving me in a rush.

"I couldn't get a thousand—" Before I could finish, his lips were on mine, palms anchoring my cheeks.

A searing kiss.

My hands around his neck, then sliding down the thick, corded muscle, over his Adam's apple. Gripping his shirt. On my tiptoes, biting, sucking, swallowing. Another throat clear, but this time I didn't care we had an audience.

Intent rushed through me with every swipe of the tongue.

When Flip pulled back, he was fuzzy and hazy, his taste still on my lips, my hands still grasping the collar of his shirt. He searched me, thumb gently brushing my jaw, waiting until everything came back into focus.

When he spoke, his voice was low. "It's time to put the awe back in your eyes."

FLIP

The guys followed us to my bedroom, whooping and hollering like it was some medieval bedding ceremony. I slammed the door and heard their muffled laughter disappear down the stairs.

"Assholes," I said under breath. When I turned around, Tweetie was watching me. In a baggy graphic tee, too-big jeans, and a beanie covering her curls, this was how I wanted her, how I always wanted her. Small, pouty lips and a button nose. Her wild, intense curls like the look in her eyes. Pocket-sized body that fit me perfectly, hidden under layers and layers of clothes, only for me to see. Unwrapping her would be like opening a present.

Tweetie watched me with an inscrutable look in her bright eyes. I only had a second to wonder over it, then she was sprinting at me. She jumped and I caught her, back slamming against the door.

"Hi," I said on a laugh. Then her mouth was on mine, hot and hurried, small hands in my hair, messing up my hat, tearing it sideways.

Fuck.

Whatever got into Tweetie, let it never leave, please.

I took charge of the kiss, slowing down the tempo, exploring her mouth with deliberate strokes. She broke on a sharp, musical sigh that went straight to me. I tightened my grip beneath her thighs, hoisting her up so I could go for her throat, her collarbone, beneath her jaw.

"I..." Nerves caught her voice, a swallow bobbing. I sucked that too. "I missed you. I love you so much, Flip. You were always my dream. My god. I never want to be apart again." The confession wrapped around my heart like silk, all at once tightening and comforting.

"I don't know," I said, pushing her shirt aside some to kiss her shoulder. "Maybe we should screw up our lives more often if it means you'll attack me like this."

"Shut up," she said, but smiled, a grin that showed the small, almost unnoticeable chip in her incisor from the accident. I pressed my lips to hers again, swiping my tongue across the fracture.

When I pulled back, her hands tightened around my neck, smile soft on her face.

"I'm not stopping this time," I warned. "Even if the entire fucking house is outside, or if the police station kicks down our door, I'm not stopping." Her breathing quickened, chest pressing against my own. "I've waited long enough for you. So tell me now, Tweetie. Tell me now if you want to stop."

A breath passed like an eternity.

"Promise?" Her blue eyes gleamed. *Fuck. I'm done for.* I carried her to my bed. Her grip loosened on my neck as I lowered her. I caught it with one hand.

"Keep your hands on me."

Her mouth parted, eyelids dropping. Holding my weight above her, I took a minute to look at her, a minute to realize this was happening, it was real. Tweetie was in my bed, her wild curls were on my pillow, and in a moment I would tangle them.

"Do you want to go to the floor?" Nerves fluttered her voice. "I'm fine with the floor. Or couch. Or really anything—"

"Shh." I pressed a kiss to her lips. "As long as you're here, I'm fine." Lips still connected, her eyes grew, then narrowed.

"You *were* there last night," she said through our kiss.

I lifted up, giving her a lopsided grin and room to breathe. "Busted."

I pushed back her hair, needing to touch her as I waited for her reaction. I'd snuck into her room without permission, while she was upset with me, no less.

After the knocks were replaced with pained whimpers, I'd gone insane listening. I'd had to do something.

"Thank you," she whispered. My chest clenched, hand frozen in her curly tangles. Our eyes locked, the air stilled.

I slid my hand deeper into her curls, grip strong and sure.

"Give me everything," I said, voice hoarse. "All of it.

The blushes and wide eyes, your whimpers and cries. You've been fighting the world since you were a child, but now trust me enough to stop fighting." I slid a hand up her thigh, pushing her legs apart. "Give in to me."

"I don't know what I'm doing," she whispered. "At all."

A small smile. "I'll teach you." I brought my hand from her hair to her face, ran my knuckles along her neck, stopping at her pulse, feeling the violent thrum. "Teach you how to love me." Up and down her neck I slid my knuckles, watching the simple touch part her lips and turn her eyes hazy like a sunset.

"Teach you I love you. Every day. For however long you'll have me, Tweetie."

She tugged on my neck, pulling me on top of her.

TWEETIE

Ragged breathing was the only sound. Flip was in briefs, legs on either side of my thighs. I was only in my thin, cotton underwear. His dark eyes traveled my body in starvation.

I was worried.

Beneath his thighs of steel, abs hewn from marble, and a jaw so sharp it could cut glass, I felt unworthy. He was a god, and what was I in comparison? But then his eyes found mine and he spoke.

"Fuck me," he said, voice strangled. "Look at you. You're going to kill me." Warmth flooded me in a blush I could feel. Big, strong hands searched every inch of me, sure in their work. Places I never would have considered Flip would want to touch, he was determined to explore.

My ankle. Beneath my knee. My hip bone. The sides of my waist.

"I'm going to keep you like this forever," he groaned. "Open. Naked. Under me where you belong." Then his lips were on my stomach. Between my thighs. Everywhere. And I was lost to them.

Bite.

Gasp.

"That sound," he groaned. "Make it again." To make sure I did it, he softly clamped his teeth on my thigh, before swiping his tongue across to heal me. I threw my head back and bit my shoulder to keep from crying out.

Flip slid up my body and caught my chin. He was silent, staring at me with heavy, loaded eyes. A rocky breath, then his stare flicked to the mark on my shoulder.

"I can't decide which is sexier. You biting your shoulder, or hearing you cry." His thumb grazed my lower lip, and the air thickened.

I darted my tongue out, licking his thumb.

His lids dropped, ravenous. "Fuck." He pushed his thumb into my mouth and I traced my tongue along it. Seeing how hard his muscled chest pushed with his breaths and the way his eight-pack tightened against his tattoo was such a turn-on. He was as close to the edge as I was.

I squeezed my thighs, needing some kind of release.

He felt the movement and released a low noise, deep in his throat.

I pressed my fingers to his tattoo—our tattoo. I memorized the ridges and grooves of his thumb while I gently touched his inked-over muscles. It felt monumental: this tattoo, us, the moment.

And then everything stilled.

Flip dragged his thumb from my lips, palms grasped my face, eyes glowing—*burning*. I nipped at his palm. I was done. I couldn't take the waiting.

Then his mouth found mine. Swallowed and sucked like he was starving. He didn't let me control a single moment. It was fast and hot and heated, I had to catch breaths as if caught in waves. His kiss promised everything.

"I love you," he said as he sucked my lower lip. Then he paused, lips still pressed to mine. "You are my everything. I will try so fucking hard to give you everything." Then he attacked my mouth again, not giving me a chance to respond. So I told him in my kiss.

You're my *everything and that's all I need.*

I put two thumbs into his briefs and tugged them down, past a perfectly taut butt.

He had me out of my underwear just as quickly.

And then he was there, between my thighs. So hot and hard and there was nothing between us. No one to come to the door, no secrets to stop us.

"Are you ready?" His words were so rough and warbled, they were hardly discernible. He was barely holding himself together. Yet still so sweet and gentle and tender, like always.

I wrapped my legs around him, telling him *yes* in a kiss.

We didn't stay in bed long before the need to get out and shred hit us both, but I could still feel him, was still sore from him. It wasn't anything like I'd felt before, like when I had a bad slam; this was new, the *best* sore. Every movement brought back memories of Flip.

We'd lain in bed after and I'd been worried he'd be uncomfortable. Flip wrapped himself around me, nose to my hair, whispering so many sweet and tender things the worry melted away as I nearly melted into him. Now Flip stretched his arms high into the pink sunset, revealing the sharply cut muscles of his Adonis belt, and my eyes dropped, mouth going dry. I could see it through his jeans, see *him*. I should've been writing sonnets to *that*. I squeezed my thighs, remembering him inside me.

"Promise to tell me if it hurts."

"I'm okay. I'm...perfect."

"You okay?"

I gasped, pulled from the memory and into the present, into Flip's arched brow. I'd been staring at his jeans for a minute, and he looked at me with a mixture of confusion and humor.

I rubbed my neck. "Huh?"

"What are you thinking?" His voice was low; dark, arrogant humor matched the crook hooking his cheek.

"I..." My brain stuttered, violent heat racking my body. He let out a low, laughing rumble like he knew *exactly* what I was thinking and it went straight to my gut.

Flip dropped his board and stalked to me, a simultaneous predatory and worshipping look in his eyes. I knew that look. He'd spent *hours* on me with that same look, held my gaze through everything, dark, glowing, and focused, determined to put the awe back in my eyes, as he'd said. And I'd begged him for hours, not quite certain what I needed but certain I'd needed *something*.

"I was just thinking about skateboarding..." I lied as he arrived at my feet, still so nervous and awkward, even after we'd shared everything.

His hands came to my neck, thumbs grazing my cheek,

a soft smile on his face now. "Hey beautiful." He pressed a soft, closed-mouth kiss to my lips. "Have you named it yet?" He knew I was lying, and he was giving me an out.

Now I didn't want one.

I couldn't think, drunk on the warmth spreading out from the single spot where his lips had been connected to mine.

He laughed, low and arrogant. "Your trick." His hands traveled from my neck, down to my shoulders, rubbing my biceps.

"I...I think I'm going to call it a kickflip."

He stopped. "I can't tell if that's good or bad." He'd kick-started everything. My love for skateboarding. My career. My heart.

It was definitely good.

I shrugged coyly.

He gave me a look like he knew I was keeping something, but let it go. With another short kiss, he dropped me and grabbed his board.

We skated for hours together, until the sun was rising warm and fuzzy orange against the trees. Then he hopped off his board, kicking it to the other side with one foot. His eyes landed on me, the same predatory look, slightly subdued, a bit mischievous.

Nerves crawled up my spine. "What?"

Without words, Flip hopped on mine with me, pushed my hair back, caressing my face. I don't know if I'd ever get used to this. Someone who looked at me the way he did. Who held me the way he did. With such utter devotion.

Flip kissed me deeply as my board rolled unevenly with our weight. He kissed the way he'd moved inside me: slow and tender, using my sighs as our tempo. And like in bed, he loved to drive me wild. Push me to the edge. Use his tongue to tease, his bites to test my limits. Until I curled and melted into him and begged for more. Only when my nails did more damage than his teeth did he give me what I wanted.

I couldn't breathe. Beyond begging, grasping and dragging along the muscles coiled beneath his warm skin.

And then it happened.

Miraculous.

An explosion.

His name on my tongue, in the air, in breaths and bursts. A prayer against his skin. Our eyes locked, a kiss so deep I was certain it touched my soul. Satisfaction glittered when he pulled back. He touched the corner of my eye, voice like crushed velvet.

"There it is."

Suddenly we crashed, so wrapped up in one another the board hit the curved wall of the ramp. We fell in a mess of laughter and limbs.

"First rule," he said with a smile.

I hopped off his chest, giving him my hand. "But do you know the second rule?" I asked.

Flip arched a brow, shaking his head while taking my hand.

I tugged him up and said, "I'll catch you."

THE END

EPILOGUE

PIP

A string of lanterns and fairy lights lit up the fog, and the curiously beautiful patchwork graffiti stood stark against the overcast sky.

The house I told myself I'd never seek out.

Home of Kingston Ayers, once the baddest, most popular, most *arrogant* boy in school.

I was the bookworm, the fool, the *freak*, who'd given my first kiss to him, only to have him turn around and use it as a tool to torment me.

Kingston Ayers, a boy now known as *King*. Corrupt to some, but a Rebel God to others.

If I had anywhere else to go for help, you'd bet I'd be there in an instant. Instead I'm running right into the arms of the Corrupt of Heaven Falls, praying for help from a man who'd only ever used my tears as hydration.

I took a deep breath and knocked.

The same, small pretty blonde who'd tried to talk to me

when Bizzy and I made the mistake of visiting King answered.

"Hey!" She perked up. "I know you. You're King's—" She was cut off, shoved back behind a massive body. *Kingston.* My entire body resonated and vibrated with his presence. The boy who'd stolen my heart and never gave it back.

"I told you never to come here." He couldn't have been colder. No emotion. Just like when he asked me for help. Showed up after *years* of no communication. No response to my letters. Nothing. Needed me because the place he'd run away to, run from *me* to, was under siege.

Never mind our families had been at war since that fateful night ten years ago, he needed my help to save his new family. He called again just a few weeks ago, to get them all out of jail. At first, I'd been so angry I could barely think. But now I saw the opportunity.

Once upon a time I'd been the goth and he'd been the golden boy. Now I'd shed my combat boots for Chanel flats and Kingston was no longer coveted, he was Corrupt, but I knew better than to think I had the upper hand. Fate had simply granted me this one fleeting moment.

I owe you, he'd said. Maybe Kingston thought little Pip wouldn't actually collect.

I gripped my arms, nails digging into my soft pink jacket, eyes on the floor.

I swallowed, and looked up, eyes locking with Kingston. "Kingston." It fell from my lips, needy and hot in a traitorous breath.

Kingston everyone mouthed, eyes wide.

"What?" The blonde, curly haired one asked. "What's going on?"

All four of his friends sat up straight, eyeing me curiously.

I was shaking—shivering, practically. I knew fear bled from my eyes and the quiver in my voice was high, a violin string plucked.

Which must have made my next words all the more confusing.

"I'm here to collect your debt."

ALSO BY MARY CATHERINE GEBHARD

Patchwork House

Skater Boy (Patchwork House #1)

Patchwork House #2 Summer 2019

Patchwork House #3 Fall 2019

Patchwork House #4 Winter 2019

www.PatchworkHouseSeries.com

The Hate Story Duet

Beast: A Hate Story, The Beginning

Beauty: A Hate Story, The End

Owned Series

You Own Me (Owned #1)

Let Me Go (Owned #2)

Tied (Owned #2.5) FREE!!

Come To Me (Owned #3)

Standalones

Elastic Heart

ACKNOWLEDGMENTS

I don't know about you, but acknowledgments are my favorite part of a book. I love seeing who supports the author behind the scenes. So, these are my supporters.

My alphas and betas, Sonal, Kris, Amanda, Phala, Nikki, and Julia. They're the rockstars who read my crazy ramblings and saw it for what it could be

My reader group, GetHard. They put up with all my inappropriate memes and waited more than a year for my next book. It's such a wonderful, inclusive place, and Sonal and Sasha do such a wonderful job admin-ing.

My street team is new, but I couldn't be happier for the girls inside it. They blow me away with their support.

Nancy Smay came to my rescue when I had to reschedule my editing at the last minute and did such a great job.

Becca with Edits in Blue gave me valuable content editing insights. She also happens to be a pretty amazing human who helps me put out all my fires.

Ellie with My Brother's Editor did my first round of proofing and I will always recommend her. Not only is she great but she's a genuinely good person who loves this community.

Caitlin with C. Marie did my second round of proofing. She's always fantastic and I can't not have her on a project.

Karen is quickly becoming my girl Friday. I've lost track of how many times my husband has said, "I get it, you like Karen."

Hang Le did *such* an amazing job on this cover. It's honestly everything I wanted. It was a hard road to get my vision out, but she was nothing but amazing and professional.

Bloggers and bookstagrammers are consistently a huge help, and this release was no exception. I'm so grateful to everyone who signed up to promote me.

The authors in this community. It's obvious that so many authors just want everyone to succeed, and that's so amazing.

My family, who I can share a book cover or a blurb with, and they'll freak out and get excited with me. Or maybe leak the cover two months before the reveal, simply because they're just so excited...

Rachel and Collin, who took me into their home in Korea and gave me so much inspiration for so many things, who took care of me when I was sick and partied with me and gave me the cutest, nicest nickname ever and the inspiration for Tweetie.

My friends, who love me and help me and laugh with me, friends who are very different, but that makes it so much better.

My husband, the love of my life, and the man who supports all my endeavors. Who doesn't groan (anymore) when I jump up in the middle of a conversation to write down something that inspires me.

And to everyone and in between...I love you!

Now this is a little different but, I want you to write your name in, whether it's in ink in your paperback or a highlight on an ebook...

_____

Because thank YOU for helping me on this journey and continuing to support me.

Made in the USA
Columbia, SC
05 March 2020